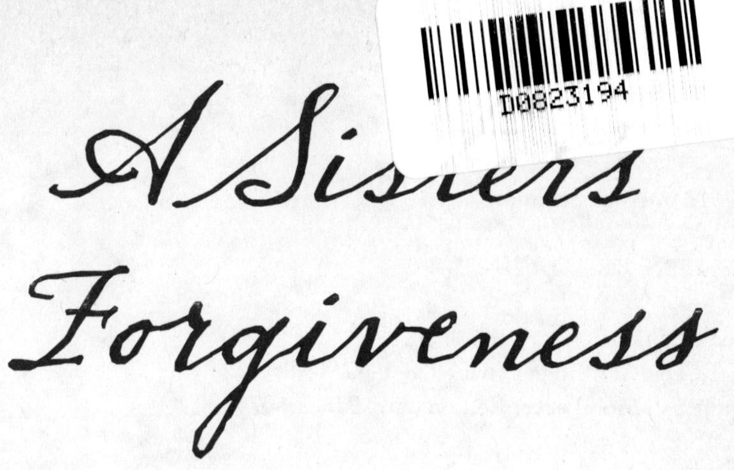

The
Women of Pinecraft

ANNA
SCHMIDT

Print ISBN 978-1-61626-235-8

eBook Editions:
Adobe Digital Edition (.epub) 978-1-60742-850-3
Kindle and MobiPocket Edition (.prc) 978-1-60742-851-0

For more information about Anna Schmidt, please access the author's website at the following Internet address: www.booksbyanna.com

Cover design: Kirk DouPonce, DogEared Design

Published by Barbour Publishing, Inc., P.O. Box 719, Uhrichsville, OH 44683, www.barbourbooks.com

Our mission is to publish and distribute inspirational products offering exceptional value and biblical encouragement to the masses.

Printed in the United States of America.

Dedication/Acknowledgments

For my wonderful new friends in Sarasota:
You know who you are,
and you know that I could not have done this without you.

Contrary to the Hollywood image, writers rarely work alone. Stories evolve, and for fiction to come alive there must be a foundation in fact. As the saying goes, it takes a village. Here are the generous and supportive and inspiring "villagers" who walked with me every step of the way as this story unfolded:

My agent, Natasha Kern—every story that sees the light of publishing begins with her. She keeps me moving forward by her belief in me and her sometimes very necessary cheerleading to keep me going.

Editor Rebecca Germany gave me the wings to try something I had never tried before, and I will always be grateful to her for that generous gift. I am also indebted to Traci DePree, who in editing the manuscript found ways—large and small—to make it better.

My writing critique group—Donna, Katie, Karen, and Kathleen—read first (and second and possibly third) drafts and were honest enough to say what they thought and suggest solutions to the problems they uncovered. And when they saw the result, they made me smile all over with their enthusiasm for the story.

Members of the Florida Mennonite community located in the unincorporated community of Pinecraft in the heart of Sarasota continue to offer their support and wise counsel. Rosanna and Tanya read the pages and corrected me when I went astray from what people of their Mennonite faith would say and do. Doris and Grace shared breakfasts and lunches with me where we talked about the story and how best to bring it to life.

And for this story, I was so very blessed that the guy who cuts my hair knew an attorney who knew others in the justice system of Sarasota who each generously gave of their time, expertise, experience, and support for the project. They have all requested anonymity, but there are no words adequate enough to thank them.

Prologue

Tessa

Trapped.

Her mind reeled with the possible solutions. She could remain where she was until someone came along, but she was in a lot of pain. And maybe like the guy who fell into the canyon and had to cut off his own arm, she would be better off getting out of this mess herself.

Vaguely she remembered hearing a lot of shouting—both before and after the fact. After all, by the time the shouting started, there was pretty much nothing it could change about the reality that the car was going to hit her.

No, that wasn't exactly true. On this day after their annual family picnic, on her first day of high school, she'd come out of the house to wait for her cousin Sadie. Down the block a car had turned the corner going fast. Too fast. It hit a patch of water and started to skid, and then it righted itself, although it was still on the wrong side of the street. Then her dad came outside fooling with the umbrella, and she'd started toward him, assuming the erratic driver would continue on down the street. She was smiling because her dad never could figure out how to open an automatic umbrella.

But then he had shouted at her and pushed her away. She'd

first thought he was just irritated about the umbrella and getting wet, but then she realized that the crazy driver had turned into their driveway.

The car had suddenly fishtailed—an image that oddly worked under the circumstances—the car as big as a whale flipping its back end to find balance in the pouring rain. And in an instant, Tessa saw the reason for the erratic driving. Sadie was at the wheel, but her hands were in the air, and Tessa thought she could hear her cousin screaming along with her dad.

"The brake," she mentally shouted now, but words failed her as she saw the car coming at her. It struck her, lifted her, and then dropped her hard to the ground.

For reasons she didn't understand, she had put out her hands as if to stop the car. Foolish, pointless gesture. She heard her dad yell her name, and that was when everything went silent—and dark—and she felt herself sinking, fighting to stay afloat but being dragged under.

It was only yesterday they had all gathered for the family picnic. . . .

. . .the day had been sunny and beautiful

. . .but in the night had come the rain

. . .and it was still raining so hard

. . .and Sadie was screaming

. . .and her dad was yelling at someone to call 911

. . .and the bulk of the car was there, silenced at last, but the heat from its engine warmed her

. . .and she could feel her father's strong arms cradling her and hear his voice intermittently soothing her and urging her to stay with him

. . .and then her mother was there, too

. . .and a lot of other people—people she didn't know

. . .and everyone was so very upset

. . .and she wished she had her journal and Grandpa's pen so she could write to them—especially her mom and dad—and tell them it would be all right.

Part One

"Blessed are those who mourn,
for they shall be comforted."
MATTHEW 5:4

Chapter 1

Emma

Emma Keller had lived in Pinecraft, Florida, her whole life. And from the time that she entered her first year of school, her large extended family had gathered at the beach to bid farewell to the summer and gear up for the busy school year and tourist season that lay ahead. It was in many ways her favorite time of the year. Now, as mothers themselves, she and her younger sister, Jeannie, had assumed responsibility for organizing the day. There was just one problem—Jeannie was nowhere to be found.

Typical, Emma thought, but she was smiling. Her younger sister was such a treasure in the lives she touched, and Emma was certain that wherever Jeannie was, she was making someone's day a bit brighter.

"Mom will be late," Jeannie's fifteen-year-old daughter, Tessa, announced as she helped Emma lay out the food for the noon meal. Around them a dozen other cousins, aunts, and uncles were all pitching in to cover the tables, tend the smaller children, and start fires for grilling the chicken and hamburgers. Emma took a mental roll call and realized that her daughter, Sadie, was also nowhere to be found.

"And have you seen Sadie this morning?" she asked her niece.

Tessa hesitated. "She went somewhere with Mom."

"Wearing her clothes or yours?"

Tessa grinned. "Hers." It was no secret that Sadie often longed for the more liberal traditions of the Mennonite faith practiced by her cousin's family. To that end, she had been caught more than once borrowing Tessa's clothes. The girls were a year apart in age but close in size. And it only made matters worse that Jeannie condoned this behavior.

"Give Sadie a break, Emma," Jeannie would say. "She's got to try her wings a little, test herself. Have a little faith in the way you and Lars have raised her. She'll be fine."

For generations, Emma and the rest of her family had dressed in the traditional garb of their conservative faith. The females wore small-print dresses with long or three-quarter sleeves and a skirt that reached at least midcalf. For males, it was a collarless shirt and black trousers held up by suspenders, sometimes with a jacket or vest.

As a girl, Jeannie had dressed as plain as Emma. Then she married Geoff Messner, a high school coach from Sarasota. When Geoff agreed to convert, the couple had joined a more liberal branch of the faith. Now Jeannie dressed in the same clothes worn by any respectable non-Mennonite woman seen shopping on Main Street. And Jeannie did love to shop. Just last spring she had given Sadie a denim jacket with colorful stitching that she'd only worn maybe half a dozen times. It had quickly become Sadie's favorite item, and she rejoiced in any day or evening cool enough to wear it. Emma would not be surprised to see her daughter wearing it to the picnic despite predicted temperatures in the mideighties.

Emma and Tessa worked in tandem organizing the food into categories—salads, casseroles, meat dishes, and desserts—and Emma couldn't help but reflect on the differences between her daughter and Jeannie's. Tessa was quiet, reserved, and—in Emma's son, Matt's, words—a brainiac. A sweet girl and an honor student with a maturity that made others—including sixteen-year-old Sadie—turn to her for advice. It was impossible not to marvel at Tessa's genuine selflessness and attention to others. She had inherited that from Jeannie, of course, but on a whole different level.

"Here they come," Tessa said, nodding toward her mother and Sadie as the two of them crossed the park, arm in arm, whispering to each other like schoolgirls. "Looks like they have a secret," she added without an ounce of envy. "Did you bring the pies, Mom?" she called, and Emma knew by the way Jeannie clapped a hand over her mouth that she had completely forgotten her one job—to pick up the pies their eighty-two-year-old grandmother had baked.

"I'll go get them," Emma said.

"On your bike? No, you stay," Jeannie said. "Geoff can go." She waved to her husband and headed across the park to where he was helping the other men rearrange heavy wooden picnic tables.

"Geoff's busy," Emma said as Jeannie came closer.

"Em, it will be hours before we serve the pies, so stop being such a worrywart and let me handle this, okay?"

"Okay." It was true. Emma was given to worrying. Once when she had been especially concerned about Sadie's admiration for a group of teens that she had met at a non-Mennonite gathering, she had turned to Jeannie in frustration. "Don't you ever worry about Tessa? I mean, right now she's okay, but as she gets older and has more contact with outsiders. . .?" she'd asked.

"You worry enough for both of us," Jeannie had assured her, and then she had tweaked Emma's cheek. "Thanks for that," she'd added with a grin.

But Emma was all too aware that life could be hard, especially for children growing up in a society that was estranged from the outside world. And especially when they lived in a community on the very outskirts of that world, crossing its boundaries many times a day as they went about their business. She and Lars had decided to allow both Sadie and her fourteen-year-old brother, Matt, to attend the nearby Christian Academy for their high school years as a way of exposing them to the ways of others without losing the focus on their faith in the process. But she still worried. How would her children fare as adults? Would they be content to follow the stricter faith that she and Lars had raised them in, or would they—like Jeannie—want more freedom, more assimilation with the outside world?

"Hi, Mama," Sadie said, giving Emma a sidelong glance meant to gauge just how much trouble she might be in for being so late.

Where were you? were the words that sprang to Emma's lips, but she swallowed them, heeding her husband's advice to temper her first impulse in favor of a more diplomatic approach. "Oh Sadie, there you are. I was looking for you," she said as if she'd hardly noticed her daughter's tardiness. "Could you please slice those loaves of bread and set them in baskets—one on each table?"

Sadie blew out a soft sigh of relief and sat down on one of the benches to slice the bread. "Sorry I was late," she murmured.

Emma understood that Sadie wanted her to ask what had kept her—clearly her daughter was anxious to tell her something. She was fairly glowing with the excitement of whatever adventure she had shared with her aunt. But then Sadie could just as easily take affront to Emma's inquiry and refuse to tell her what was going on. Patience was the answer, as it so often was when raising teenagers, or so Emma had discovered. "You're here now," she said and tucked a wisp of Sadie's long hair back into place. "When you've finished slicing the bread, go find your brother and make sure he's set up the play area for the little ones; then you can take charge of watching them."

There was no doubt in Emma's mind that her son, Matthew, had already completed the list of tasks she'd given him. He—like his cousin Tessa—was very dependable when it came to such things. In some ways, Matt at fourteen was the more mature of her two children. It was Sadie she worried about despite Lars's assurances that both their children would turn out just fine.

"Can't Tessa do that?" Sadie begged. "She's so much better with the kiddies than I am."

"The children love you and you know it. You'll make a wonderful teacher one day, Sadie."

Sadie's face twisted into an expression of pain. "What if I don't want to be a teacher, Mama?"

"I thought—"

"What if I want to do something else—something more. . . exciting."

"Such as?" This sudden change in her daughter's outlook for the future gave Emma pause. From the time she was four, Sadie had talked of nothing else but someday being a teacher. "A nurse?"

Sadie's frown tightened. "There's more to life than teaching school or being a nurse or housewife," she protested.

"All noble callings," Emma reminded her.

"Sure, and for some people—like Tessa, for example—probably the very best thing. But for somebody like me. . ."

"You're sixteen, Sadie. You've got time."

"I want to go places, Mama," she replied as she filled baskets with bread and covered them with dish towels. "There's so much beyond Pinecraft."

Emma looked at her daughter. To Sadie the world outside the boundaries of their lifestyle was exciting and mysterious. To Emma it was frightening, a place where innocence could be crushed in a heartbeat. And yet she understood that to try to dissuade Sadie from her dreams would only make her cling to them more vehemently. "You've got time," she repeated. "Now please go check on your brother." Clearly weighing the pros and cons of the mundane task of slicing bread in favor of something that at least gave her the freedom to move around the park, Sadie took off at a run. As Emma watched her go, she couldn't help thinking that Sadie would make a wonderful teacher—and someday a wonderful mother, for she had inherited the best traits of Emma and her sister along with her father's wry sense of humor and easygoing manner. Lars was right. She was young. In a couple of years, she would sort everything out.

"What's up?" her husband asked, coming alongside her and nodding toward Sadie. "Why were she and Jeannie late?" His tone held no censure, just simple curiosity.

"Not sure yet, but the two of them have been up to something."

Lars shook his head and chuckled. "I assume we'll be the last to know."

"As usual," Emma said. She smiled up at the man she had

known since she was a young girl. The tall, thin boy who had lived across the road from her parents—an Amish boy then. His grandparents on his mother's side had been Swedish, and he had inherited the white-blond hair of that side of the family. But his eyes were the deep blue of the sea. Emma had fallen for him the minute she saw him.

He was the eldest of eight brothers and sisters, all of them gathering now in the park, surrounded by spouses and children of their own. When she and Lars were teenagers themselves, she had assumed that he would be drawn to the livelier—and prettier—Jeannie, but it was Emma whom he had courted, announcing to her his intention to marry her as soon as they were of age.

And in spite of her delight that he had chosen her over her sister, she had fired back that she would never marry an Amish man—especially one of Swedish heritage. She had told him that such a combination did not bode well for his ability to be flexible and open-minded like her father and brothers were. The very next Sunday he had started attending services at the conservative Mennonite church her family attended, and he converted just before their wedding.

"Our girl is coming into her *Rumspringa*," he said now of Sadie.

"That business of running-around time is from your ways," Emma reminded him. The Amish tradition was to permit children in their teens to have a time when it was considered all right to explore the more liberal ways of the outside world. The idea was that this would help them understand the serious commitment they were making when they decided to be baptized and become full members of the faith.

Lars shrugged. "Still, whether you believe in Rumspringa or not, she's got all the signs—restless, curious about the outside ways. It won't do to try to stop her exploring, Emmie."

"*Ja.* I know. It's just. . ."

"The kids will be fine," he assured her, smoothing the lines of her forehead with his thumb. "Both of them—look who they got for a mother." He waved to someone across the park. "Your folks are here—looks like your mama brought enough food to feed the whole group single-handedly."

"She always worries there won't be enough," Emma said, shaking her head as the two of them headed for the parking lot to help her parents unload the car.

"*Die Mutter und die Tochtor*," Lars said with a chuckle.

Like mother, like daughter. Emma only wished that the same could be said of Sadie and her.

Chapter 2

Jeannie

The sun was setting by the time most of the extended family and their guests headed back to their homes scattered across the area. Some went by bicycle—the elders and single cousins—while those with children crowded into older model cars and drove away, leaving a trail of fine sandy dust in their wake.

Jeannie watched as her husband, Geoff, helped Lars and Matt reposition the picnic tables and fold the cloths covering them for Emma to wash. Tessa and Sadie were given the job of policing the area for any trash that might have been left, while Emma and Jeannie packed up the last of the food.

"All right," Emma said, drawing Jeannie's attention away from Geoff, "where did you and Sadie go this morning?"

Jeannie had been having second thoughts about her impulsive act all day. What had she been thinking to go behind her sister's back that way?

"Sadie didn't tell you?" she hedged.

"Don't dodge the question. You know she didn't, or I would have said something and she wouldn't be finding ways to avoid her father and me. So just tell me." Emma's eyes widened. "Did you buy her that skirt she's been admiring in that shop on Main Street?"

"It's her news. Just keep an open mind, okay?" Jeannie turned away without waiting for Emma to agree. She called out to the others, "Hey, everybody, sun's setting."

It was a tradition the two young families had adopted years earlier when they had become the unofficial organizers of the annual picnic. They were always the last to leave, staying to watch the sun slip beyond the horizon, marking the end of summer and the beginning of the school year for the children and in many ways a change of seasons for the adults as well.

In the coming week, Matt would start his last year at the small Mennonite school that all three children had attended for the first eight years of their educations. Tessa would start her first year of high school at the Christian high school where Sadie would be a sophomore, and where Geoff would take on the role of assistant principal in addition to his responsibilities as athletic director and coach. He was nervous about that, although he had applied for the position, citing their need for the extra income. He had also joked that maybe they ought to think about going back to the old, simpler—meaning less expensive—lifestyle that Emma and Lars followed.

Jeannie had tried not to take offense at that. After all, she and Geoff had agreed that she would be a stay-at-home mom when Tessa was born, participating in volunteer activities when there was time while focusing primarily on being a homemaker and parent. But over the years, they had gotten caught up in "stuff," as Geoff called it whenever he looked over the monthly bills.

Jeannie held her tongue, although she wanted to remind him that hosting the entire football team for meals several times a season did not exactly come cheap. And he was the one who had insisted they buy a four-bedroom house when it was just the three of them—and they knew it always would be.

She watched as Emma waited for Lars and their children and then saw her sister's family join hands as together they walked out to the beach. Although she would never admit it—not even to Emma—the truth was that Jeannie had always seen the ritual of the sunset as a bittersweet moment—sweet in the way that she and Geoff were so blessed with family and friends, bitter in the passing of time—Tessa growing up and moving closer to the day when she would head off to pursue interests of her own. The day when it would just be Geoff and Jeannie alone in that big empty house. She shuddered at the thought.

Tessa came alongside her, taking her hand as they headed down the narrow sandy path. Geoff was already on the beach, and when they stopped beside him, he wrapped his arms around Tessa's shoulders as he rested his chin on top of her head. Lars had his arm around Emma's waist and his free hand on Sadie's shoulder while Emma pulled Matt to her. Jeannie tried not to think about the fact that only she stood alone—unconnected to anyone by touch.

The two families waited in respectful silence as the orb of sun sank lower and lower, streaking the sky around it in vermilion and orange. And just as the sun disappeared, they all closed their eyes and silently prayed. It was part of the tradition, and usually it was a moment that brought Jeannie comfort, a sense of peace.

Not this time, she thought. She was too consumed with guilt over her impulsive act of earlier that day. Perhaps if she talked to Sadie. Perhaps she should forewarn Emma. *Perhaps I should have minded my own business.*

After the moment of silent prayer, they stayed awhile longer, reluctant to let the day go. Sadie, Matt, and Tessa strolled along the low tide line looking for sand dollars that might have washed ashore, while their parents scanned the horizon for any sign of dolphins. As dusk settled over the beach, they all walked in silence back toward the parking lot.

"Okay, Sadie-girl," Lars said. "Time's up. What's the big news?"

Jeannie saw Sadie glance at Tessa, who nodded encouragingly. Clearly she had already shared her news with her cousin. Of course she would. Despite the year difference in their ages, Sadie often turned to Tessa for support. But then Sadie looked pleadingly at Jeannie. "You tell them," she said.

"It's your news," Jeannie reminded her.

"Well," Sadie said, drawing out the word as she studied the ground, "how about I drive us home?"

"Oh Sadie, stop stalling and just. . ." Emma began; then she stopped and looked from her sister to her daughter and back again. "*Nein.* You didn't," she said softly.

"Ja," Jeannie admitted and knew from the way Geoff shoved his hands into his pockets and kicked at a stone in the parking lot that she had been right to regret her actions.

"Did what?" Matt demanded.

"I got my learner's permit today," Sadie told him. "Auntie Jeannie took me." She faced her parents with a hint of defiance. "I'm of age, and you said that I could get it this year. Dad even signed the form and got it notarized so it would be ready once you agreed, and. . ."

Jeannie found it hard to meet Emma's gaze. Her sister was speechless. For much of the summer, Sadie had begged her parents to let her get the permit, but Emma had put her off. She had never actually refused her, but she had found excuses for postponing the inevitable. Jeannie had pleaded Sadie's case to no avail.

"I thought maybe if," Jeannie said softly as she edged closer to Emma. "I mean, I know how hard this is for you and. . ."

You didn't think at all, she could almost hear Emma wanting to yell, but Emma would never start an argument and spoil the day for everyone. Instead her sister cleared her throat and turned her attention to Sadie.

"There will be ground rules," she began.

Sadie grabbed her hand and held on. "I know, Mama, and you don't have to worry a bit. I'll do anything—extra chores—anything."

Jeannie saw Emma glance over her daughter's head at Lars, seeking his counsel on what to do, begging him with her eyes to say something. He nodded and began listing the terms.

"If ever I see or hear from others that you were not wearing your seat belt. . . ," he said, leaving the possible punishment to Sadie's imagination. "And there is absolutely no using a cell phone for any reason when the car is in motion."

"Okay, Dad. I get it."

"I'm not finished. One scratch on person or vehicle, and if ever you get behind the wheel without either your mother or me. . ."

"Or Aunt Jeannie or Uncle Geoff?" Sadie interrupted hopefully.

Geoff held up his hands in the sign of calling time out in a basketball game. "Leave me out of this," he said laughing, but he was looking at Jeannie, his eyes questioning why she would do such a thing.

"You can leave me out of this, too," Matt declared, standing a little closer to his uncle, coach, and mentor.

"You're fourteen," Sadie reminded him. "Not an issue." She turned back to her parents. "So no driving without an adult in the car. . . ."

"A licensed and responsible driver," her father corrected.

Emma closed her eyes for a long moment. "All right, it's done, but you heard what your father said. One infraction, and you forfeit your permit and we do not have this discussion again until you are eighteen years old, understood?"

Sadie nodded solemnly then burst into a grin and hugged Tessa. "Oh, we are going to have so much fun," she squealed. Then catching the mood of the adults surrounding her, she hastened to add, "I mean, once I learn to drive properly. Just think, Tessa, I can pick you up for school, and we can—"

"Time enough for you to daydream later," Lars said gently. "It's getting dark, and the no-see-ums are out in force tonight. Let's get home before they eat us alive."

"Have their own picnic," Matt chortled, nudging his uncle with his elbow as Geoff put his arm around Matt's shoulders.

The two families gathered up the last of their belongings and walked across the park to their cars, the men in the lead with Matt, the two girls, their heads bent close whispering excitedly, and Emma with Jeannie.

"I know I overstepped," Jeannie said. "I just thought—I guess I didn't think. It's just that Sadie is like my own daughter just as Tessa is like yours, and. . ."

"Sadie is not Tessa," Emma replied, her voice tight.

"Meaning she's not my daughter?" Jeannie said defensively.

"Meaning she's not the *same as* your daughter." Even in the dark, Jeannie knew that Emma was struggling to remain calm.

"In spite of the fact that she's younger, in many ways Tessa shows more maturity and responsibility than Sadie did at her age—than Sadie does now. Sadie is like you, Jeannie—she lives in the moment, and sometimes that's a wonderful trait. You, for example, have moved mountains with that attitude."

"And the problem is?"

"Sadie is not only not your daughter—she is also not you. Don't get me wrong. I love that she has your free spirit and ability to reach out to others. In time I hope all of that will be tempered with a certain wisdom that comes with experience and age, but right now. . ."

"Okay, I see your point," Jeannie said as the full tsunami of guilt at her impulsive act washed over her, spoiling the day. "Geoff is always saying that I need to think things out more carefully." Jeannie glanced over to where her husband was talking to Lars. She tried to gauge Geoff's mood, but he had his back to her. "I seem to disappoint him a lot these days."

"How are things?" Emma asked, following her gaze. Emma's tone had gone from tight to sympathetic in a heartbeat. "I mean with you and Geoff."

Emma was the only person Jeannie had talked to about the recent problems in her marriage. For the last several months, she and Geoff had struggled to find their way. He had spent long hours at the academy, and she had gotten more involved in her volunteer work. Emma had noticed—and asked.

"We're. . . Things are a little. . . It's better," she said, but her response sounded unconvincing even to her.

"But?"

Jeannie forced a smile and waved off the question. "It's all the pressure he's under—the new job as vice principal, the start of a new football season. You know how intense he can be when it comes to his work."

But Jeannie understood that her husband was something of a mystery to her family. He had not been raised plain, and while on the surface Geoff was a gregarious and outgoing man, there were times when he could be withdrawn and come across as aloof, even cold. "We just need time," she whispered, wondering who she was trying to convince—Emma or herself.

Emma's strong arms came around her, drawing her close. "You've had a rough road to travel lately. I'm sorry I haven't been there more for you."

"Are you kidding? You're the one constant I know will always be there for me—supporting me—and hopefully forgiving me?"

Emma laughed and released her. "Don't pull that baby sister act on me. You messed up, and you know it."

"Yeah. I did."

"Are you ladies coming?" Geoff called from the parking lot. He was standing near a lamppost, and Jeannie saw that he was smiling, but still a hint of impatience came through the smile.

"On our way," Jeannie called back as she linked arms with Emma. "So, we're okay?" she asked.

Emma pulled her a little closer. "We're fine," she assured her. "Just promise me that when Matt is old enough to drive, you'll. . ."

". . .tell you before I take him to get his learner's permit—got it." She patted Emma's hand. "Wasn't it a wonderful day?"

Emma hugged Jeannie, and in that hug was forgiveness. "It was a very special day—one we'll hold onto for a long time."

Jeannie giggled. "At least until this time next year—just wait and see what surprises I have planned for you then." She took off running, and Emma chased after her as they had so often done as teenagers. They were still laughing breathlessly when they reached the cars where Lars and Geoff and the children stood waiting.

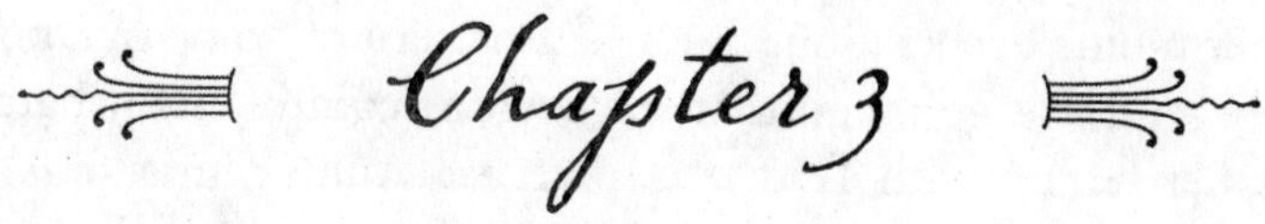

Chapter 3

Tessa

Being an only child had its advantages. It also had its pitfalls. Like when a kid's parents weren't getting along. Lately Tessa's mom and dad had seemed like they were heading down different paths. Her dad was all about his work and was worried about finances more than usual. Mom, on the other hand, seemed to go the other way. She was always inviting hordes of people to the house for suppers or cookouts and such, like she needed to fill the house with any warm body she could find.

While they didn't fight like some parents did—shouting and such—the way they had gotten so quiet around each other was even more disturbing.

While working on a report on the Clinton presidency, Tessa had come across a photograph of Chelsea Clinton walking between her parents when their marriage was pretty much in the tank. Chelsea was holding hands with her father on one side and her mother on the other as if she and she alone were the link keeping their family together.

Tessa was sure that things with her parents weren't anywhere near as bad as they had been with the Clintons, but still. . .

Of course, she wasn't really an only child in the usual sense. Her mom and Aunt Emma were so close that it really was like having two moms plus siblings in the form of her cousins, Sadie and Matt. The two families did practically everything together, and the three kids were back and forth between the two houses so much that they kept clothing and other personal items at each other's houses.

Of course now Aunt Emma was upset with Mom, with good reason as far as Tessa could see. What had given her mom the idea that taking Sadie for her learner's permit behind Aunt Emma's back was anything like a good surprise? Tessa saw it as evidence of her mom's desperation. She had a pattern of going overboard when stuff was going on that she couldn't control, like whatever was happening with Dad. And because Aunt Emma was her mom's best friend as well as older sister, Tessa had to believe that she would understand and eventually everything would be all right. Still, in her humble opinion, it had been a really bad move.

She sat in the backseat of the car, watching her parents for signs of healing. Surely the sunset on the beach, if not the tradition of the annual family gathering, had given them pause for thought. She waited, hoping the silence was a sign of calm rather than indifference. As usual her mom made the first move.

"Nice day," she murmured in a voice Tessa knew was for her dad's ears only. Once upon a time, he would have glanced over at her and grinned, maybe taken her hand in his, even kissed her knuckles. They had always been touchy-feely that way, to the point that sometimes Tessa felt as if they had forgotten she was even in the car. But not tonight.

Tonight he just kept driving.

Her mom turned in her seat, restrained by the seat belt from making full eye contact. But her smile was that fake one that she used when she was nervous. It dawned on Tessa that her mom was as mystified as she was by the chasm that stretched between the occupants of the front seat.

Okay, so she had to do something—anything to break the tension. What would Chelsea do? She tried to imagine what the former president's daughter would have said to her parents. Would she have chattered on about her life? Or would she. . .

Mom was talking—something about being ready for the first

day of school—a topic that Tessa understood was of far greater importance to her parents than it was to her. Even her dad. . .

That's it. I'm starting a new school. Dad's starting a new job there. . . . Instinctively she knew that Chelsea would focus on the obvious connection among the three of them—school.

And lo and behold, it worked—sorta, kinda—at least with her mom.

Chapter 4

Jeannie

Once again she had messed up. And although she truly believed that Emma had forgiven her, Geoff was a different matter. Leaving Jeannie out of the family circle while they all watched the sunset was about as clear a sign as he could have given her that things between them were not good. She didn't think for one second that it was intentional. Geoff was just terrible at hiding his true feelings. If he was upset, she knew it, and if he was upset with her, then he would usually take the easy way out and focus all of his attention on Tessa. The tension in the car was so thick it would take a chef's knife to cut through it.

Jeannie drew in a deep breath, squeezed her eyes shut, and sent up a silent prayer. "It was a nice day," she ventured as Geoff steered the car around the maze that was St. Armand's Circle until they reached the turnoff that would take them across the Ringling Bridge toward home.

He made a sound that could be interpreted either as agreement or indifference.

Silent treatment alert, Jeannie thought and turned in her seat to talk to Tessa. "Have you got everything you need for tomorrow, Tess?"

"Pretty sure I do—at least everything on the list the school put online."

"Excited?"

Tessa shrugged. "You know how it is, Mom. Starting a new school year is always a little exciting."

"Well, it's a blessing that you'll have Sadie there to show you the ropes."

Up to now, Tessa had attended the small Mennonite school that Jeannie and Emma had attended as kids. It was the one piece of her past that Jeannie had insisted on keeping after she and Geoff joined the more liberal branch of the faith. At the little Mennonite school, students of all ages worked at their own pace, moving from level to level as they completed the required work. Jeannie had such wonderful memories of her years there, and when she realized that Tessa was a shy, studious child, she had persuaded Geoff that attending her old school—at least until Tessa was ready for high school—would be an advantage.

"Dad?" Tessa leaned forward so that her face bridged the space between her parents.

"Hmmm?"

"If it's okay for the first day, I'd like to bike to school with Sadie."

Geoff chuckled, and Jeannie felt herself relaxing slightly. Leave it to Tessa to put him in a better frame of mind. "Not cool to arrive with the vice principal?"

Tessa giggled. "Not cool at all, but very cool to arrive with one of the popular kids."

"I'm crushed." He sighed dramatically, and Jeannie and Tessa both laughed.

Suddenly the tension that had held them all captive evaporated like the morning fog as Geoff pulled the car onto their driveway. Together they piled out and started unloading the picnic supplies and lawn chairs and other equipment they had hauled to the park. Tessa ran ahead of them to put away leftover food in the kitchen while Jeannie and Geoff took care of storing the lawn chairs in the garage.

"Looks like rain," Geoff said, checking the western sky that still held a hint of light.

"Smells like it, too," Jeannie agreed as she slipped her hand into his. "Maybe it will cool things off." She felt his fingers tighten on hers.

They stood together looking up through the giant fronds of a cluster of palm trees toward a starless sky. "Is Emma okay?"

Jeannie didn't need to ask what he meant. "She was upset—rightly so. Oh honey, I realize now that I shouldn't have agreed to take Sadie, but I was sure that Lars was trying to find a way to convince Emma. He'd already signed the paperwork. He didn't want to disappoint her, and neither did I." She shrugged. "It just seemed like. . ."

Geoff sighed and wrapped his arm around her, pulling her close and kissing her temple. "Honey, by now you know that how things may seem to you may not always be the way they are for others. I mean, Emma must have had her reasons for delaying this, and even if you don't agree. . ."

"Yeah, I know. It's just that sometimes Emma can be so strict—our folks were that way. You'd think that would make a difference—that she would understand that in this day and age Sadie needs. . ."

"Sadie's not your child, Jeannie. I know that you love her—we all do. What's not to love? She lights up a room, but it's up to Lars and Emma to decide such things. They're her parents."

"You're right." She hugged him, and then trying to cling to the lighter mood, she added, "You're always so wise. I'm sure that's why the school board named you vice principal."

Geoff groaned. "Don't remind me."

"You're going to be great. The kids already love you, and the teachers and staff have great respect for you. You can't lose." She smoothed back his hair and saw the shadow of doubt cross his features. Geoff had always been her rock. "Why do you think Tessa turned out to be such a great kid? It's because of the example you set for her."

"She also has you. . .and Emma."

"But you. . ."

His smile won out over the worried frown as he shrugged off

her compliment. "So, here you are sending the two of us off to conquer new challenges," he said.

"That's right, and frankly I think we'd all better get some sleep. Tomorrow is going to be a busy day." She stood on tiptoe to kiss him, and she couldn't help being a little disappointed when he released her after a quick peck on the lips.

"Coming?" he asked as he started for the house.

"In a minute." She watched him go inside, heard the television come on. Things were better, she thought. Just not what they had been. She felt the first drops of rain and lifted her face to them before going inside.

Tessa had already put everything away in the kitchen, and Jeannie could hear her daughter upstairs in her room. In spite of assuring them she already had what she needed for school on the drive home, Jeannie had no doubt that Tessa was double-checking her backpack. When she was satisfied, she would come downstairs, set the backpack on the straight wooden chair by the back door, and then come to the den that did double duty as Geoff's office and the family's television room to kiss them both good night.

Jeannie took out a gift-wrapped package she'd been saving for this occasion and set it on the chair. Then she went into the den and perched on the arm of Geoff's chair while they watched a sports report together.

As she had predicted, only moments passed before Tessa came downstairs. "What's this?" she asked, coming into the den and blocking the television as she held up the present.

"Well, look at that," Geoff said. "Somebody left me a present."

"Dad, it has my name on the card."

"No kidding. So, are you going to open it or just wave it around all night?"

Grinning, she carefully untied the wide satin ribbon then rolled it around her fingers and laid it aside. She then opened each taped section of the wrapping paper, pressing the paper flat as she laid it on Geoff's desk.

"At this rate, we won't need to set the alarm because you'll still be opening your present when it's time to get up," Jeannie teased.

"The ribbon and paper are part of the gift," Tessa reminded her. "You taught me that." She laid aside the top of the box and then spread the white tissue paper inside. "Oh my," she whispered as she lifted out a handmade journal and an old-fashioned fountain pen. "I love them."

"We thought maybe you might want to start a new journal," Geoff said, clearing his throat as if it had suddenly filled with emotion. "And the fountain pen was your grandfather's."

Geoff's father had owned a small newspaper back in Iowa where Geoff had grown up. After Tessa was born, her grandfather had written her a series of letters with this, his favorite pen. He'd sent a letter to her on every birthday until his death a year earlier, when the pen had been given to Geoff. "Now it's your turn to write," Geoff told her.

"But write what? I have nothing to say."

"How about letters to us?" Jeannie suggested.

"You're kind of right here, Mom."

"I know, but you could write letters to us that we could read later—like when you're off to college or on your wedding day or when you have your first child or. . ."

"Stop it, Mom," Tessa said laughing. "You're going to have me living my whole life before I'm out of high school."

Geoff was laughing as well. He looked at Jeannie the way he used to look at her when they were courting. His eyes twinkled with that same surprise and curiosity that fueled her interest in him from their first meeting. She looked from Geoff to Tessa and grinned. For the first time in weeks, she felt sure that everything was going to be all right for them.

Geoff held out his hand for Tessa's new journal and flipped through the pages. "That's a lot of blank pages," he said. "I figure you'll have it filled up by. . ."

". . .Tuesday," Jeannie said, knowing that when Tessa started any new project, she became single-minded about finishing it.

"I'm going to start tonight," Tessa said when Geoff handed back the book. She clutched it to her chest, her eyes sparkling. "Thank you so much—it's perfect." She started up the stairs then turned back. "And, Mom. No peeking."

"Me?" Jeannie asked, pointing to herself. "Why would that even cross your mind?"

Both Geoff and Tessa rolled their eyes.

"Promise?" Tessa said, and it was clear that she was asking for a serious commitment.

"Promise." Jeannie placed one hand over her heart.

Satisfied, Tessa blew them both a kiss and hurried off to her room.

Jeannie was watching her go when she felt Geoff's arms come around her, his lips close to her ear. "Thank you," he whispered.

"I would never have violated. . ."

"Not for the promise," he said, turning her so they were facing each other. "For raising such a wonderful kid."

Suddenly shy, Jeannie fingered his shirt collar. "I didn't do it alone."

"But you're the one who has given her confidence and your gift for taking care of others."

Jeannie's heart was so full that she circled her arms around his neck and laid her cheek against his chest. "You make me so very happy—you and Tessa are my whole world."

She felt the rumble of his chuckle deep from in his chest as his arms tightened around her. When he spoke, his voice was so soft that she had to stay very still to hear him. "We're going to be all right," he said, and she couldn't help but wonder if he had meant to speak the words aloud.

She looked up at him and stroked his cheek. "I love you, Geoff Messner."

He grinned. "That's Vice Principal Geoff Messner," he teased.

"No. That's Geoff Messner, the best husband and father God ever created."

He kissed her then, and as they walked upstairs together arm in arm, Jeannie silently prayed the prayer she had prayed every night and every morning of her life. *This is the day the Lord did make; let me be glad and rejoice in it.*

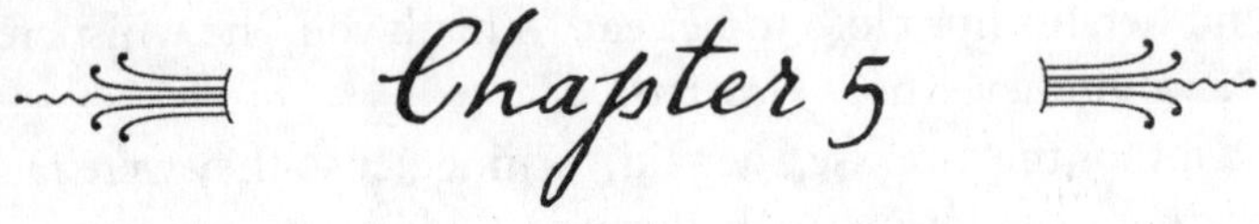

Chapter 5

Emma

After weeks of sunny days with cloudless blue skies, the day after the annual picnic dawned with an unexpected and relentless downpour. Emma was making breakfast for the family, although she was well aware that whatever she prepared would probably be eaten on the run. Sadie was already on the phone for the third time that morning, and Matt could be heard banging around in his room, searching no doubt for the supplies that he and Emma had shopped for a week earlier.

She smiled and shook her head. As organized as their parents were—everything in its place—neither child seemed to have inherited that particular trait. Emma could almost imagine the disaster area that Matt's room would be after he left for school. Sadie's room would be no less messy. But in her room, the bed would be covered with rejected items of clothing. For a girl who dressed plain, she could come up with an endless number of combinations of tops and bottoms.

"We can't ride our bikes in this," Sadie moaned. "Dan says he could come by here and pick me up, and then we'd go get Tessa." She delivered this news in a tone that Emma understood was a plea for permission as she covered the receiver with one hand and waited.

Emma exchanged a look with Lars, and he nodded.

"The streets will be slick," Lars told her. "Tell Dan to drive carefully."

Sadie grinned and murmured something into the phone; then she giggled as she hung up and took a long swallow of her orange juice.

Emma turned back to the stove. She had wanted Lars to say that he would drive the girls to school when he took Matt. Dan Kline was a nice boy. He was also a senior and president of the student council as well as the quarterback on Geoff's football team. Emma could see no explanation why he had fastened his attention on Sadie—a mere sophomore. He was older—and by definition more experienced when it came to dating. Of course, that was the real problem—Sadie was dating the boy. Not in groups, spending time with him and his friends or hers, but actual dates—long walks or bike rides and such. Surely Sadie was too young for anything so serious.

At least Lars had stood with her on that one. He had told Sadie that unless they were attending a school or community function with them or Dan's family, she and Dan were to limit their time together to twice a week—during the day.

"Oh Dad," Sadie moaned now as she took a bite of the donut that Emma had gotten up before dawn to make as a special treat for the first day of school, "Dan's eighteen. He knows how to drive in rain."

Lars put down his newspaper. "Ja, und it's because he's eighteen that I worry," he said quietly. "Young men of his age tend to think they are indestructible and that anyone with them is as well."

Emma hoped that maybe Sadie's comment had raised enough of a red flag that Lars would reconsider. In their home, as in most conservative Mennonite homes, the man was the head of the household, and wife and children alike looked to him to make these kinds of decisions. But he picked up his paper again. Sadie rolled her eyes and then turned her attention to Emma. "How do I look?"

"Sehr gut."

Sadie groaned and punched in a number on the phone that under most circumstances was kept in her father's workshop behind the house and used primarily for his business. It was a mark of the importance of this first day of school that Sadie was allowed to use the phone. "Hi, Auntie Jeannie, is Tessa ready?"

Sadie giggled at Jeannie's response. "What's she wearing?"

A beat and her expression turned pained. "Not the black ones. I love those boots."

Emma could hear Jeannie's laugh muted by the phone Sadie clutched to her ear.

"Okay, so tell her Dan is picking me up anytime now, and we'll be by for her in fifteen minutes." She sighed heavily. "I know. I know. Trust me, Dad has already made the point." She listened for a moment then blew her aunt an air kiss and hung up the phone.

Emma knew that she and Jeannie were in agreement when it came to Dan Kline. Although not of their faith, he came from a good family, and his parents were good Christian people. Dan regularly attended church and was an outstanding leader when it came to organizing other young people. But next year he would be off to college while Sadie had two more years of high school to finish. One of the things Emma and Jeannie had discussed more than once was that Sadie would be brokenhearted when Dan left and that they would need to help her mend.

"You mustn't get used to the idea of Dan picking you and Tessa up for school, Sadie." She stopped speaking and took a sip of coffee, hating the way she sounded so like their spinster neighbor, Olive Crowder.

"We won't," Sadie said as she gulped down the last of her orange juice. "But think of it, Mom. This is Tessa's first day at the academy, and think how the other kids will sit up and take notice when she walks into school with Dan."

Emma understood that at least on some level Sadie was sincerely doing this for her cousin. Like Jeannie, Sadie wanted Tessa's first day of high school to be special. It did not occur to either of them that Tessa really did not care about making a first impression socially. She had confided to Emma that she was far more concerned about whether she would be able to keep up academically with the other students.

A Sister's Forgiveness

Sadie looked out the window for the fourth time in ten minutes. Dan was running late, which wasn't unusual, but the last thing Emma wanted was for him to be rushing on a rainy day like this one. Just when Emma was about to suggest that maybe Lars should drive Sadie after all, a car horn beeped and Sadie grabbed her backpack. "That's Dan." Her voice trembled with excitement. She blew Emma and Lars a kiss as she flew out the door.

Emma watched from the kitchen window as Sadie scampered around the front of the car and climbed in. Dan had not gotten out to open the door for her; rather, he had leaned across the front seat and pushed it open. She heard Sadie laughing as the door slammed and Dan shifted into reverse, spinning shell gravel as he peeled out of their driveway.

"They'll be all right," Lars told her as he reached around her to put his cereal bowl in the sink.

"He's too old for her."

"Two years' difference," Lars reminded her. "We have four years between us."

"But that's different. We're adults. She's a child yet, and he's—"

"Sadie is a smart girl. This too shall pass," Lars said as he reached for his hat. "Matt? *Es ist spat,*" he called as he passed the hallway that led to the bedrooms. "I'll take Matt to school, and then I'll be in the shop if you need me." He kissed her forehead. "Stop worrying," he advised.

After everyone left, Emma finished washing the breakfast dishes and then poured herself a second cup of coffee. Lars was right. Sadie was very good at sizing up people. And Lars had made an excellent point. He'd just turned fifteen when his family moved in across the street from Emma's. She had been eleven. She certainly did not need to be reminded of a time when she'd developed a crush on a handsome popular older boy—a time when she would have done just about anything he asked of her if he would just walk her home from church.

"Have faith," she murmured as she sat down at the kitchen table and reached for the phone.

Chapter 6

Jeannie

The first day of a new school year was always chaotic around the Messner house. Who was she kidding? Most days were chaotic around their house. But on this day, Geoff was especially anxious. He would never admit it, but Jeannie was well aware that he had hardly slept the night before, and the tension she thought they'd finally laid to rest was back, stretched like a wire between them.

He was running late and that made him even edgier and more impatient. And as was so often the case, it was her fault. It wasn't the first time in their sixteen-year marriage that Jeannie had put something that Geoff or Tessa needed in a place where she was sure to find it and then had promptly forgotten where that was. Only Tessa remained calm in the face of her parents' panicked conversation.

"Look in the bathroom," Jeannie shouted as she searched through the kitchen drawer designated as the catch-all for the bits and pieces of life that had no real home.

"Why on earth would you put the keys to the gym storage shed in the bathroom?" Geoff shouted back.

"Just look, okay?" Jeannie continued rummaging and muttering to herself. "I'd never put anything so important in here, so where are they? Think!"

"Why hide the keys at all?" Tessa asked as she completed her assignment of going through Jeannie's purse.

"Because the shed is new this year, and your father didn't want to add the key to his key ring until he'd had a chance to make copies for the staff. I had the copies made yesterday and then put the original and the copies"—suddenly her face lit in a relieved smile—"in our storage shed. Got 'em," she shouted to Geoff as she grabbed the keys for the small shed behind their house where they kept the gardening tools and other outdoor equipment.

"I'll get them," Tessa said, taking the keys from her and shaking her head at this latest example of her mother's skewed logic. "You make Dad his bagel." She slid her arms into her father's rain slicker, pulled up the hood, and wrapped the sides around her as she dashed across the yard.

By the time the sliced bagel popped up from the toaster and Jeannie was spreading on peanut butter, Tessa was back. She placed the keys on the table next to her father's travel mug and hung the key to their shed back on its hook. Geoff rushed into the kitchen and pocketed the keys as he pulled out a kitchen chair and threw his tie over one shoulder to prevent spilling anything on it. He took a long swallow of his coffee. "You look nice, sweetie," he told Tessa. "Ready for your first day of big-kid school?"

Tessa shrugged. "It's the same as any other first day, Dad—just another step on the ladder."

But Jeannie did not miss the way Tessa nervously smoothed her shoulder-length straight hair, tucking it behind her ears and then immediately flipping it forward again. She placed the bagel in front of Geoff and then brushed Tessa's bangs back from her forehead. "Dad's right," she said. "You look great—no one will guess it's your first day. They'll probably think you're a new kid moved here from some exotic location."

"Sadie's coming with Dan to pick me up," Tessa told Geoff as she slipped the straps of her backpack over her shoulders. "Is that okay?"

"Sure, sweetie." Geoff liked Dan a lot. The boy was Dan's star quarterback, and Geoff had a lot of respect for his talent on and off the playing field. But he couldn't keep a hint of disappointment out of his voice. Jeannie knew that when he'd seen that it was raining, he'd been hoping Tessa would change her mind and ride with him. Tessa wrapped her arms around Geoff's shoulders and kissed his temple. "Ah Dad, if it rains again tomorrow, then I promise to ride with you and all the rainy days after that—it's just that on the very first day. . ."

"Got it," Geoff said with a grin. "Can't start out arriving with the vice principal."

"You're also the coach, and other kids might think that's pretty cool," Tessa teased back. "Maybe when you wear your coaching clothes instead of the button-down shirt and tie. . ."

"Okay, okay, you win. Go ahead and make your entrance with your cool cousin and the quarterback today, but I'm going to hold you to that rainy day promise."

Tessa laughed, and as always the sound of it filled Jeannie with utter joy. This beautiful, intelligent, and incredibly kind girl was their daughter—their only child—and as much as she enjoyed Emma's children and was flattered by how much Sadie shadowed her, Tessa was a gift beyond anything that she and Geoff could have imagined. They didn't even regret the fact that they had not been able to have more children. The house was so often filled with cousins and Geoff's students and Tessa's girlfriends, who loved gathering in Jeannie's large open kitchen while she made them pizzas and homemade cookies and other snacks, that on the rare occasions when it was just the three of them, it felt like such a blessing.

In fact, Jeannie often felt a little sorry for Emma. Whenever Sadie brought friends home, they always went off to Sadie's room. "Young people feel so comfortable in your house—with you," Emma had said more than once.

"I'm sure that it's just the difference in the girls' ages—at their age, one year can make a huge difference," Jeannie had assured her. "Sadie and her friends are just going through that parents-are-not-to-be-trusted phase." But based on the number of times she had heard Sadie bemoan her parents' conservative lifestyle and the number of sentences that began with "I just wish. . . ,"

Jeannie wasn't at all sure that this was just some teenage phase Sadie was working her way through. And the truth was that she couldn't begin to imagine that Tessa would ever deliberately close herself off from her parents.

"The three Messners," Tessa had announced one night, flourishing her arm like a sword. "One for all and all for one." And laughing, Geoff and Jeannie had raised their arms to meet hers.

"Have a wonderful first day," she said now as she hugged Tessa close. She released her, but her hands rested on Tessa's shoulders. "Our baby is growing up, Geoff."

"Mom, I'm not going off to Africa or anything," Tessa protested, but Jeannie noticed how her daughter hung on to her for just a moment longer than she normally did. "Love you both," she called as she hurried out the door.

The cordless phone that Tessa had left on the counter rang. Jeannie glanced at the caller ID information and picked it up on the second ring, even as she straightened Geoff's tie and accepted his kiss good-bye. In all their married lives, the sisters had not missed their morning call to start their day. She glanced at the clock and saw that it was later than she realized.

"Chaos central," she announced, shooing Geoff toward the door and mouthing, "Go. You'll be late."

She handed him an umbrella. "Give this to Tessa. I don't want her catching cold standing out there in the rain." She blew him another kiss then closed the back door after him as he wrestled the umbrella open. "Sorry about that," she said as she settled back in for the daily exchange of schedules with Emma. But before she could say anything more, she heard the squeal of car tires moving too fast and too close followed by Geoff's shout. There was an ominous thud and then silence. With Emma still talking in her ear, Jeannie walked to the open back door and stepped outside.

For an instant she was paralyzed. Surely this was a dream—this surreal scene with an unfamiliar car sideways in front of their closed garage door, the black umbrella Geoff had taken for Tessa open and rolling slowly across the driveway, and Geoff on the pavement cradling Tessa in his arms. She was vaguely aware of Dan Kline standing next to the car holding his side while Sadie sat on the wet ground on the driver's side as if she had simply slid from the car. She was crying hysterically, deep gulping sobs. The only other sound was the annoying beep signaling that the key was still in the ignition.

Jeannie could not seem to make her feet move. So many choices—Tessa, Sadie. . .

"Call 911," Geoff shouted.

Without a word to Emma, Jeannie hung up and dialed 911, all the while standing outside the back door, oblivious to the rain as she stared at her precious child. Tessa's backpack was still attached to her limp shoulders, and her hair fell in wet clumps over her pale face.

"What is your emergency?" the operator asked.

"My daughter," Jeannie began, but words as well as her voice failed her as she fell to her knees next to her husband and child.

A neighbor she hadn't been aware of had run across the yard and now took the phone. Briskly he handled the emergency operator's questions, glancing at Geoff for confirmation when the question was whether or not Tessa was conscious.

"No." He paused. "Breathing?"

Geoff nodded as tears rolled down his cheeks. "Tell them to hurry," he whispered.

"On their way," the neighbor assured him. "Yes operator, I'm still here. . .neighbor. . .looks like a car accident. . .I don't know. Two kids. One of them is a relative of the victim."

Victim. The word echoed so loudly in Jeannie's head that she was unaware that the neighbor had continued to talk, moving closer to the car as he did. She was vaguely aware that she was no longer hearing Sadie's hysterical rantings. She glanced over and saw her niece huddled against the side of the car. She was soaked to the skin, her arms locked around her knees, her eyes riveted on Tessa as she rocked back and forth, mumbling to herself.

Jeannie's mind raced with all the things she should be doing—calling Emma back and telling her to come, asking someone to check on Sadie and stay with her until Emma could arrive. But none of that came close to the urgency she felt to save her beloved child.

"There's no blood," she said softly. Geoff, taking it for a question, shook his head.

It was true. There were no outward signs of injury. No blood. No awkwardly twisted limbs. Tessa was just lying there, her eyes closed, her breathing shallow but steady, her face serene.

Jeannie scooted closer to him, and together they held Tessa between them until they heard the shriek of the siren coming down their street. Someone had picked up the umbrella and was shielding them with it.

"Hang on, sweetie," Geoff murmured. "Just hang on," he begged, his voice choked with sobs.

In what seemed like minutes and at the same time hours, the emergency team arrived and took charge, prying Tessa away from Geoff and Jeannie, turning them over to the waiting arms of concerned neighbors who now filled their driveway and front yard. Three EMTs surrounded Tessa, examining her and reporting their findings even as they started an IV and placed her carefully on a gurney. Through it all, the one thing that struck Jeannie was how very still and calm Tessa seemed.

So like her, she thought, for always in the midst of turmoil, Tessa was the serene one. And to Jeannie, her daughter's stillness seemed a good sign. She took hope from it. She was clutching Geoff's hand when he followed the gurney. She saw Emma running up the street, getting no farther than the front of the ambulance when Dan Kline intercepted her, waving his hands wildly.

Looking past the hysterical Dan, Jeannie could see Emma trying to make eye contact with her. Her expression was full of questions—questions to which Jeannie had no answers. All she knew was that her baby was lying on a gurney that three EMTs were shoving into the back of an ambulance, and Geoff was urging her to ride with Tessa.

"I'll be there," Geoff assured her and backed away so the doors could be shut. Just before they closed, she saw that a police car had also arrived and an officer was talking to one of the EMTs.

He nodded, glancing toward Dan's car and then back to the ambulance just as the doors slammed shut.

"Sadie," she shouted. "Check on Sadie."

"There's another unit on the scene, ma'am," the young man riding with her said.

She nodded and stared blankly around the cramped interior of the ambulance. It was odd how the wail of the siren seemed to come from somewhere far away now that they were inside the vehicle. Jeannie clung to Tessa's fingers, knowing she should be asking questions. The problem was that she didn't know what questions to ask. Besides, the EMT was busy working on Tessa and reporting his findings to the driver up front. She had to assume that he was talking to someone at the hospital, preparing them to care for Tessa the minute they arrived. The EMT in back didn't look old enough to be out of high school, but his actions were performed with a quickness and precision that gave Jeannie confidence in him.

"She'll be all right," she said softly, and when this brought no assurances from the young man, she repeated it as a question. "My daughter is going to be all right?"

"She's hanging on," he replied, and Jeannie wondered why she had added "for now."

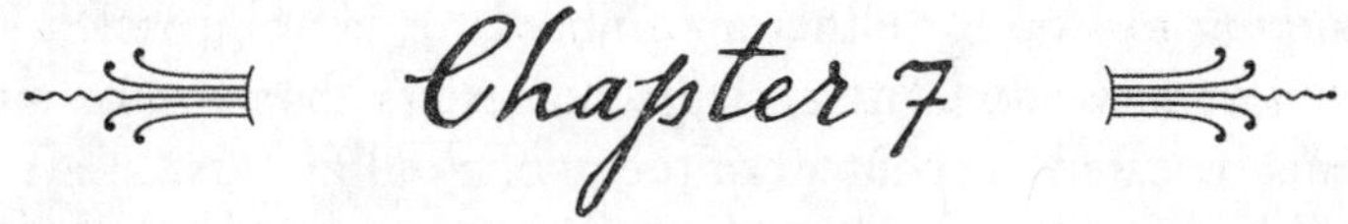

Chapter 7

Emma

At first Emma was merely irritated when Jeannie suddenly cut off their morning conversation in midsentence. Her sister was easily distracted and assumed everyone she left waiting would understand. There were times when Emma wanted to remind her that she couldn't just. . .

But the muted sounds that followed Jeannie's abrupt departure triggered an innate warning system, telling Emma that something was seriously wrong. She heard crying and shouting as Jeannie obviously carried the mobile phone closer to the crisis. Then she distinctly heard Geoff say, "Call 911," and the phone went dead.

"Lars!" she shouted out the open back door, thankful that at that exact moment her husband had pulled their car into the short driveway. "Lars, don't get out. Somebody's hurt at Jeannie's. Just wait while I call Hester to meet us there."

Hester Steiner was a registered nurse and—aside from Jeannie—Emma's best friend. The two of them had known each other since elementary school, and Hester was also close to Jeannie and her family. Emma dialed Hester's number, her fingers suddenly clumsy on the phone's keypad.

"Well, good morning," Hester said brightly.

"Hester, can you come to Jeannie's right away? Someone's

been hurt or fallen ill."

"What happened?" In a heartbeat, Hester's voice went from chatty to professional.

"I don't know. Jeannie and I were talking, and all of a sudden she stopped talking and there was a lot of shouting and crying in the background, and then I heard Geoff tell her to call 911."

"On my way. Shall I swing by?"

"No, Lars and I are leaving now. We'll meet you there."

She hung up the phone and ran out to the car without bothering to stop for either an umbrella or her rain jacket. On the short drive to Jeannie's large home less than a mile away, Emma repeated the content of the phone call to Lars.

"Maybe it's a neighbor," Lars said as he patted her knee to still it from shaking. "We don't know that it's one of them."

"Sadie had just left with Dan Kline to pick up Tessa," Emma murmured, "and Matt. . ."

"Is already at his school. I just took him there myself, remember?"

"Right," Emma said. "I imagine that Geoff was on his way when. . ." She could not complete that sentence. What had her brother-in-law seen? Who was in need of emergency medical help? How bad was it? "Maybe it's a fire and everyone got out safely," she said, suddenly preferring that scenario to imagining one that involved people being hurt. "Geoff would tell Jeannie to call 911 for a fire."

"A couple more blocks," Lars assured her as he turned onto Jeannie's street.

Emma leaned forward, willing the car to cover the distance, straining to see—what? Smoke? Flames shooting from a rooftop? Would the pouring rain have already doused a fire? But the fact was that everything looked deceptively ordinary except that there were people gathered in Jeannie's front yard. Emma recognized neighbors that she and Lars had met before. Dan's car was pulled into the driveway, although the driver's side door was standing open. Someone was on the ground next to the car, but because the car was sitting diagonally across the driveway with its front tires resting on the lawn, she couldn't see if it was Tessa or Sadie or someone else. An ambulance blocked the entrance to the driveway.

She broadened her view to encompass the entire yard and entrance to the house. Sadie's bike was leaning against a cluster of palm trees. Sadie had left it there the day before—the day of the picnic—the day she had ridden it over there so that she and Jeannie could go get her learner's permit.

Dan was standing at the foot of the driveway looking lost and scared. He was holding his side, and he had a cut on his cheek. The side door that led from the kitchen out to the driveway was open. Up near the garage door someone was holding a large black umbrella over a group of people kneeling next to someone else on the ground. Suddenly she was certain that one of the two people she couldn't see had to be Sadie. Lars pulled to the curb, and Emma was out of the car before he could come to a full stop.

Sadie? Not Sadie. Please, dear God, not my daughter.

"Where's Sadie?" She shouted to no one and everyone. She was fighting her way through what suddenly seemed like throngs of people but was really only one man on his cell phone pacing back and forth as he talked and a woman peering anxiously down the street toward an oncoming car, waving to the driver as he made the turn onto their street. Emma registered that this was a police car, lights flashing, siren wailing. The car stopped behind the ambulance.

Instinctively, Emma made a wide berth past the back of Dan's car, noticing again that the driver's side door was open and that the quiet chirping of the warning to remove the keys was muffled by the unfurled airbag. And then she saw her daughter, soaked to the skin but alive. Sadie was huddled on the ground, pressed against the side of the car, her arms clasped tight around her knees and her head bowed low as she rocked back and forth. Just when Emma started toward her, the EMTs shouted for people to clear the way as they raised the gurney from ground level onto its rollers so they could get the lifeless form on it to the waiting ambulance. Emma glanced at the gurney and froze.

Tessa.

Everything that happened from the instant that Emma

spotted Sadie seemed to happen in a blur. The team of emergency technical people sped past with Geoff and Jeannie running to keep up. Jeannie looked at her with eyes that seemed like those of a blind person—wide but unseeing—and Emma was momentarily torn between the call to tend to Sadie and the need to comfort her sister. Each of them needed her. Each of them was in such pain—maybe not physically but surely spiritually. She closed her eyes, praying for guidance, and that was when she heard the scream of more sirens arriving. She opened her eyes to find Dan Kline blocking her way.

"Oh Mrs. Keller, I shouldn't have—I mean, we didn't mean to. . ." His eyes were wide with fear, his blond hair plastered against his head. The boy was over six feet tall, but he was crying like a kid half his size, and he was dangerously close to a complete breakdown.

"Dan, calm down. Has someone called your parents?"

"I don't know. I just. . .it was the rain and the streets and the. . ."

"Are you hurt?" She gently touched his cheek where the rain had thinned the blood. But she saw that it was no more than a scratch.

"No, ma'am. I don't know. . .maybe a little. My side hurts."

Then blessedly, Lars came loping toward them, kneeling next to Sadie, who remained completely incoherent in her babblings. She refused to look up when Lars called her name. "She doesn't recognize me," he whispered, his voice choked with panic.

Emma started to turn back to Sadie, but Dan grasped her arm. His eyes were unfocused and wild, and his grip tightened when she tried to move.

"Daniel," she said firmly, and she was relieved when it had the desired effect of making him pay attention. "A second ambulance has just arrived. I need for you to go to them and tell them that Sadie is hurt then get yourself checked over and have them call your parents. Can you do that?"

"Yes, ma'am, but. . ."

"No time for explanations now, Dan. Do as I ask."

She waited until the boy turned away, biting her lip to keep from shouting after him, "Stop. I need to know now. What happened here? What did you do?" Just then she spotted Hester crossing the street, pausing to speak with one of the medics. At the same time, Geoff was helping Jeannie into the back of the first ambulance.

"Go," she heard one of the EMTs yell as he slammed the double doors and raced around to climb into the passenger side of the ambulance. The shriek of the siren drowned out everything else.

"Hester, over here," Emma shouted above the growing noise as people filled the street and yard. In spite of the fact that one of the newly arrived EMTs was attending to Sadie, Emma wanted her friend to reassure them that their child was going to be all right.

"I'm a registered nurse," Hester explained. The young woman nodded and accepted Hester's presence without question. The two of them knelt to either side of Sadie while Lars and Emma stood by and waited.

After what seemed an eternity, Hester looked up at Emma and shook her head. But Emma didn't know how to interpret that. Was Hester telling her that Sadie was not hurt? That she was hurt and it was bad?

"She's most likely in shock," Hester said, standing up so she could talk to both Lars and Emma. "There don't seem to be any other injuries—a couple of bruises and a pretty nasty cut on her lip. She probably bit it on impact. It's pretty deep. She'll need stitches."

The paramedic helped Sadie to her feet. She continued mumbling to herself. "I thought—we were just fooling around—Dan was laughing at me. I glanced away for just a second. . .not even a second. . ." Finally, Sadie looked directly at her parents for the first time, her eyes luminous with disbelief. Then she collapsed against Emma's shoulder, and her words were obliterated by her sobs.

Emma held Sadie and tried to comfort her as she tried to make some sense of what had happened. As if studying a jigsaw puzzle—its pieces scattered across the dining room table, Emma slowly began picking up one piece and then the next as she put together a plausible picture. She replayed every detail of what she'd seen when she and Lars arrived. She remembered first being confused by the odd angle of the car. Sadie had been crouched by the driver's side of the car. Dan stumbling around on the other side—the passenger side.

As the sound of the siren faded, she looked down the street and caught sight of the ambulance carrying her sister and niece as it turned a corner. She closed her eyes, envisioning Jeannie inside that ambulance with Tessa.

The sisters had not exchanged a word, and yet Emma knew everything that Jeannie must have been feeling in that moment. She had seen in her sister's blank stare mirroring the utter disbelief, that her daughter—her only child—could be the person lying on that gurney. Emma tightened her hold on Sadie and rocked her as she had when she was a baby.

"Shhh," she whispered. "One step at a time. Tessa needs all our strength right now, Sadie. She needs our prayers." She stroked Sadie's hair. "Come on now. You've lost your prayer covering, and if ever there was a time. . ."

"It's in the car. In my backpack," Sadie said setting off a fresh wave of tears. "I took it off. I. . .and now God has. . ."

"Shush," Emma said, pulling Sadie closer. "You know better. We'll find your covering, and then we'll all go to the hospital."

"I'll get it for you," Lars said, clearly relieved to have something concrete that he could do.

He went to Dan's car—the passenger side. One of the police officers was standing by the car, and when Lars reached in to take the prayer covering and the backpack, the officer stopped him. The two men had a brief conversation, and finally the officer allowed Lars to take the prayer covering, but he followed him back to where Emma waited with Sadie.

"Evidence," Lars said when Emma raised her eyebrows in silent question. "The car needs to be examined. And Sadie will need to answer some questions."

Of course. It was an accident like any accident. There would be questions. Sadie would be questioned. And Dan. Emma's heart went into overdrive as her instincts to protect her child from any further agony on this morning came to the fore. "She needs medical attention," she told the officer.

Hester was sitting on the curb next to Dan. "They both do," she added with a nod toward Dan.

"We'll see that they get it," the officer assured her. "For now. . ."

Emma took a step that positioned her between the officer and Sadie.

Lars touched her arm. "Emma, their ways may not—"

Without a word, Emma turned and led Sadie toward the second ambulance. She was speaking with the paramedic when the officer caught up with them. But before he could reach them, Geoff grabbed the man's arm.

"I have to get to the hospital, and your partner says I can't take my car because we can't move this one until—"

"You can ride with me," Lars said, indicating his car across the street. "Emma will go with Sadie. The paramedic says that she's going to need stitches and to be completely checked over by a doctor," he continued, addressing the police officer.

The officer glanced toward the second ambulance. Dan was being helped into the passenger seat. "Okay, your daughter can ride along in that ambulance—in the back. My partner will ride with them."

"I want to—" Emma began.

"Ma'am, you and your husband can follow in your car, but your daughter and her boyfriend. . ."

"Let's go," Lars said, taking Emma's arm and guiding her across the street before she could say anything that might further antagonize the police officer. Geoff was already in the car, his head resting against the window as he stared into space.

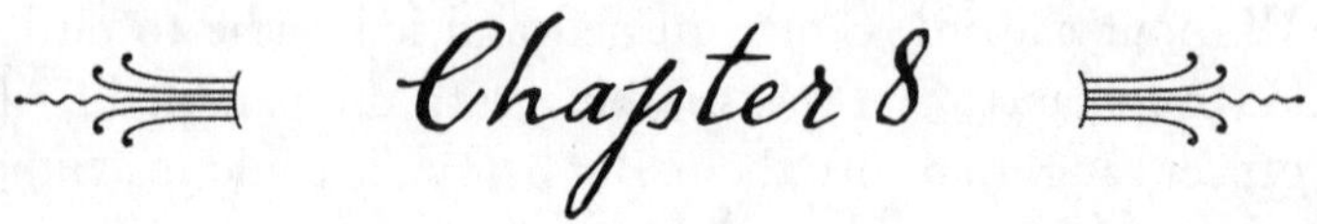

Chapter 8

Jeannie

At the emergency room, a team of medical personnel came running toward the ambulance as soon as it pulled into the circular drive. In a flurry of activity, the EMTs delivered information about Tessa's status at the same time they lowered the gurney to the ground and started wheeling her inside. Just as they got past the automated doors, someone gently pulled Jeannie aside.

"Ma'am, please step over here," the gray-haired woman said. "We need you to give us some information so the doctors can treat your daughter."

"No." Jeannie dug in her heels.

The woman looked a little shocked. Had no one ever dared to refuse the protocol before? Jeannie couldn't imagine that. "My husband will be here shortly, and then one of us will be glad to give you any information you need. If the doctors need her medical history, then they need me to be nearby."

Logic had never been Jeannie's strong suit, but she felt certain that she was making a good case now. "So either you come with me to wherever they have taken my daughter and ask your questions, or it will just have to wait." Jeannie patted the woman's hand, removing it from her arm and heading down the hall and through the double doors where they had taken Tessa.

Moving quickly she checked every cubicle and room in the emergency ward until she saw a cluster of men and women in white coats and green scrubs at the far end of the U-shaped area. She heard footsteps behind her as she started running toward the doctors.

"Jeannie," Geoff called, catching up to her. "Where is she?"

"Back here, I think." She'd never been so glad to see Geoff in her life. He grabbed hold of her hand, and together they hurried toward the curtained area where someone had set Tessa's backpack on a chair.

"We're her parents," Geoff announced unnecessarily as they pushed their way into the midst of the medical team surrounding Tessa. She was lying on her back, her hair fanned out behind her, her clothing open, exposing her thin upper body. Jeannie felt Geoff's grip tighten. "Can we cover her? She gets cold so easily," he said.

One of the white coats glanced at a woman in scrubs who nodded and turned to Geoff and Jeannie, taking their elbows as she gently ushered them into the area just outside the sliding glass doors of the cubicle. "The doctors need to put in a tube to help her breathe," she said. "We're doing everything we can. Just please wait right here and let the doctors do their job. You're just a few feet away from her. She knows you're here."

Geoff and Jeannie nodded in unison, and the nurse went back inside the cubicle and pulled a curtain closed behind her. Geoff wrapped his arms around Jeannie, and she rested her cheek against his chest, feeling the strong pounding of his heart against her face. Somehow that gave her strength.

"She'll be all right," she murmured. "Tessa is a fighter—quiet, yes, but you always said you'd rather have a strong silent player on your team than one who—" She was babbling, and Geoff quieted her by stroking her hair and tightening his hold on her. The question uppermost in her mind—the question of what happened—could wait. For now all that mattered was that Tessa was getting the medical help that would bring her back to them. Jeannie closed her eyes and silently prayed for her daughter's full recovery as she forced herself to ignore the mental pictures of her beautiful daughter forever crippled or living in a coma or somehow less than her smart self. The idea that Tessa might die was not allowed.

"Mr. and Mrs. Messner?"

They looked up at a short, stocky man with Albert Einstein hair and wire-rimmed glasses. "I am Dr. Morris. Your daughter is bleeding internally. We need to perform surgery immediately. Will you give consent?"

The nurse who had ushered them from the room stood behind the doctor holding a clipboard with some papers. Geoff ripped it from her hand and glanced at it, searching for the blank space to write his name. "Here?"

"And on the next page as well," the nurse said.

Geoff scrawled his name in both spaces and handed the clipboard back to the nurse. "Can we see her before you take her to surgery?"

Dr. Morris pulled back the curtain and with a single glance cleared the small room of medical personnel. "Make it quick. We need to go now," he said, and Geoff nodded.

"Thank you," Jeannie said, her voice choked with fresh tears.

She and Geoff approached the gurney that held their daughter as they had once approached her crib when she was a baby, hesitant and with a certain sense of disbelief. Then it had been because they had been blessed with this beautiful new life and given responsibility for watching over her. Now their disbelief grew out of a surreal sense that everything that had happened to their little family in the last hour had been some kind of horrible nightmare.

"Hey, sweetie," Geoff crooned, taking Tessa's small hand in his large one. Tessa's fingers twitched, and Geoff glanced at Jeannie, his eyes filled with fresh hope.

Jeannie moved to the other side of the gurney and took Tessa's other hand. "We're right here, Tess. Dad and me—right here." Her voice broke, and silent tears dropped onto the sheet the nurse had covered Tessa with. Jeannie found herself fascinated by the polka dot pattern her tears were creating there. She had never felt more helpless in her life.

"You need to fight, Tessa," Geoff said. "That's the way you help the doc get you back to us. You hear me?"

He was using the voice he used in a game when he wanted to inspire his players to keep playing hard against an opponent that was much bigger and stronger than they were. Jeannie felt an inexplicable annoyance. This was their daughter, not his basketball or football team. The doctor cleared his throat, and Jeannie was aware that he had pulled open the curtain and was waiting to take Tessa away.

"How long?" she asked, her voice husky. "The surgery?"

Dr. Morris moved a step into the space. "Difficult to say," he told her. "A couple of hours at least. I'll send someone to give you updates if it goes past that, okay?"

Jeannie felt as if she was bargaining for time on Tessa's behalf—two hours to bring their beautiful laughing child back to them? Or was he talking about two hours just to get her to the point where she could begin the long weeks and maybe months of recovery? Or after two hours would. . . ? She would not allow herself to think beyond those two alternatives. "Two hours," she whispered as she bent to kiss Tessa's cheek and smooth her silken hair away from her face. She tucked a strand behind her daughter's ear as Tessa had done herself that very morning—this very morning—for the large clock on the wall outside the cubicle showed the time as just a minute past nine o'clock.

She stepped away to let the aides unlock the gurney wheels and start down the corridor, but Geoff held on, walking briskly and then trotting to keep pace until they reached an elevator. The nurse gently pulled him away. A second elevator opened, and an aide exited with a young man in a wheelchair followed by an older couple. Dan Kline and his parents. *If Dan is hurt, then what about Sadie?* Jeannie wondered. The Kline family disappeared behind a curtain.

Down the corridor, the light above the elevator carrying Tessa was clicking off floors: 2-3-4. . . . Jeannie stood frozen in the now barren cubicle, her hand outstretched as if to rescue her child from a fall. Then she saw Geoff still facing the elevator. His broad shoulders slumped, and then began to shake uncontrollably.

Relieved to have something to do, Jeannie picked up Tessa's backpack and went to comfort her husband.

"Come on," she said as she saw an aide waiting patiently by another bank of elevators and understood that the young woman was there for them.

"I'll take you to the surgical family waiting room," the aide said as she held the doors of the elevator open.

"There's a chapel just across the hall here," she continued as they exited the elevator after the short, silent ride. She indicated the chapel as if she were leading some kind of tour while Geoff and Jeannie made their way blindly down the corridor after her. "And a café just around that corner and down the hall."

A café? Seriously? How about just a plain old, ordinary hospital coffee shop?

Jeannie couldn't even remember what floor they had come to, but the aide seemed well practiced in her mission, and Jeannie could not help but give herself over to the young woman for the time being.

"There's free coffee and tea in the waiting room," the aide said, continuing her tour. "And vending machines down the hall that way. Oh, and there's also this private room you can use." She opened a wooden door. "It's a good place to sit down with the doctor once the surgery is over." She waited for some response and got none. "The waiting room is just around the corner."

"Bathrooms?" Jeannie asked as they turned a corner.

"Right here and also—"

Jeannie let go of Geoff's hand and practically ran for the door. She locked herself inside the small room with its porcelain sink and single toilet and a mirror that Jeannie found herself staring into as she wrapped her arms tightly around herself.

Who is that? The face staring back at her was nearly unrecognizable—a parody of the woman she had been just hours earlier. The mouth was twisted into a kind of silent scream, and the eyes—always so lively and filled with plans for the day—were lifeless.

Her entire body began to shake and heave as if she were caught in the riptide of a turbulent sea. Wave after wave of sheer terror crashed over her until she thought she could not breathe, and yet she was aware that the tiny bathroom echoed with the sounds of her sobbing. Guttural growling sounds interspersed with the kind of high keening such as she had sometimes heard emanating from women in Middle Eastern countries mourning the loss of a loved one. All the while her eyes remained dry. And in her mind she repeated, *Please, please, please*, as she continued to lock eyes with the stranger in the mirror.

The faith of her childhood had taught Jeannie to turn to God—even for small things, and this surely wasn't small. Surely a loving God would understand her cry for help now. She was a mother, and her only child was even now surrounded by strangers—strangers holding scalpels and attaching machines to keep her breathing.

Please.

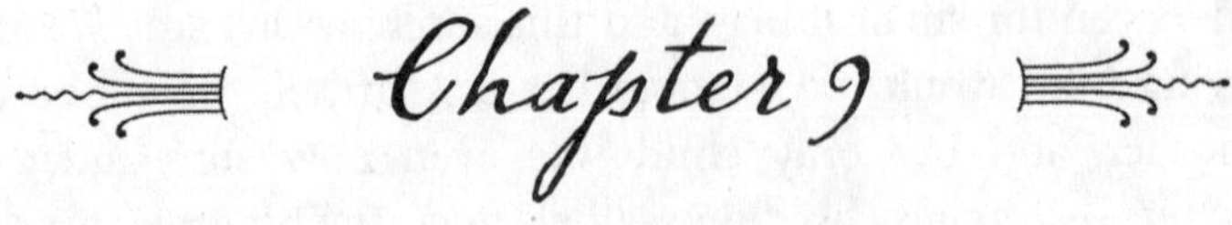

Chapter 9

Lars

As Lars and Emma had driven Geoff to the hospital, Lars had resisted the urge to squeeze his brother-in-law's shoulder once he and Emma were in the car. Everything about Geoff's posture showed that he wanted—needed—to be alone, but Lars couldn't resist offering some encouragement. "Tessa will be all right," he said as he kept both hands on the wheel and focused on the road.

To his surprise, Geoff nodded. "There wasn't a scratch on her—no blood at all," he murmured. "I think she hit her head. Just dazed maybe."

"We'll all pray that you're right," Emma said. No one spoke again until they reached the hospital. Lars drove all the way hunched forward, squinting at the road the way he always did, as if operating a motorized vehicle were still foreign to him.

They arrived just behind the second ambulance that carried Dan and Sadie. Geoff leaped from the car and ran into the hospital.

"Where is she?" he demanded of the desk clerk as soon as they were inside the emergency reception area. "My daughter—Tessa Messner—fifteen—just brought in. . . ."

The gray-haired woman glanced toward the double doors

and then back at Geoff. "Your wife is with her. I need to get some information."

Geoff tossed his wallet to Emma. "Take care of this," he said and headed through the doors.

Emma looked from Lars to the paramedic wheeling Sadie through the doors. She was holding an ice pack to her lip. Not ten seconds later, Dan Kline was escorted into the small reception area. His parents arrived a moment later, and Dan's father brushed past Emma, demanding to see the person in charge immediately.

"Dad," Dan moaned, but his mother took his protest for a cry of pain and began to cry as well.

"You need to wait your turn, sir," the receptionist said even as she indicated that Emma should take a seat at her window. "And you are?" the exasperated clerk asked Emma.

"Tessa Messner's aunt and godmother." Emma rifled through Geoff's wallet to produce insurance cards and other identification. "My daughter, Sadie, is—"

"One patient at a time," the woman said. She made copies of Geoff's cards and passed them back to Emma. She typed in bits of information on her computer and finally turned to Emma. "Now, what happened?" she asked, nodding toward Sadie.

Although Lars understood that the receptionist was looking only for information about Sadie's condition and not seeking details of the accident, he also understood that this was a question they were all going to face time and again in the days to come. His wife gave the only answer she knew to be absolutely true.

"I don't know."

The clerk exchanged a look with the police officer who was right behind Dan, and then said something to someone behind her. A man in scrubs came to the door and called Sadie's name.

"Can we go back there with her?" Emma asked. "And can we see our niece—Tessa Messner?"

The man in scrubs deferred to the desk clerk who picked up the phone and repeated the question. "Yes, godmother, I think. Amish, right?" She glanced at Emma.

"Mennonite," Lars corrected automatically, although he could not think how their religious affiliation could possibly matter.

The clerk nodded and then hung up the phone. "Your niece is being taken to surgery. Let's get your daughter treated and then see where things stand." Once again she glanced at the officer. "Next," she called, and Dan's father stepped past Emma and Lars to lean against the desk, his face only inches from the receptionist's.

"Do you know who I am?"

"That's what I'm here to find out," the clerk replied wearily.

"Excuse me," Emma said. "My sister—Tessa's mother. . . ?"

"Will be in the surgical waiting room," the clerk assured her, and Lars did not miss the way the woman looked at her with an expression of abject pity when just ten minutes earlier she had been annoyed with the entire family.

The man in scrubs stepped forward and grasped the handles of Sadie's wheelchair. "This way, folks," he said. The police officer followed close on his heels as he wheeled Sadie into an area with a bed and one straight chair and then pulled a curtain to give her privacy. "The doctor will be right in," he said and disappeared.

"Ma'am," the officer said, indicating that Emma should take the lone chair.

"Danke."

Sadie was staring blankly at the floor. Lars stood next to her, his hand on her shoulder. Sadie showed no reaction, no expression at all.

"Sadie?" Emma said.

Nothing.

Lars exchanged a look with Emma and then glanced at the officer. The man was standing outside the cubicle, his back to them, his hands clasped behind his back.

"She's so still," Emma mouthed.

"Der Arzt. . . ," Lars began, and at that moment a nurse came in, slid the sliding door closed, and softly asked Sadie for her name and birth date, checking to be sure the information matched what was typed on the paper bracelet the receptionist had given Emma to wrap around Sadie's thin wrist. The questions were simple enough. Name. Date of birth. But Sadie remained mute and staring at the floor. Lars answered for her until the nurse came to

the tough question, "Can you tell me what happened?"

Sadie looked up for the first time. "We hit Tessa," she whispered, and then she started to shake, her entire body convulsing.

"Are you cold?" Emma asked, edging closer to where the nurse was bent over Sadie.

Sadie said nothing.

The nurse wrapped a blanket around her shoulders, and finally the shaking subsided. "Sadie," she said, her voice now gentle and kind, "we need to check you over for any injuries you may have sustained beyond the cut on your lip. Are you in pain? Can you tell me where it hurts?"

Sadie sat stone still for a second and then pointed to her chest.

"Did you hit your chest on something?"

Sadie shook her head vigorously. "I hurt in my heart. We hit Tessa," she repeated, staring at the nurse as if the woman wasn't very bright. Then she turned to Emma. "We hit Tessa," she repeated and then seemed to fold in on herself as she clutched her arms tightly around her body and once again started to rock back and forth.

"Okay, okay," Lars said, patting Sadie's hand. "That's enough. We need the doctor in here."

The nurse looked over her shoulder at him. "I really need to—"

"Der Arzt," Lars demanded. "Doctor now."

The nurse looked from Lars to Emma.

"Bitte?" Emma pleaded.

With a nod, the nurse put away the blood pressure cuff she had started to attach to Sadie's thin arm and left the room.

Sadie continued her rocking.

"Sadie, let's keep the ice on your lip," Emma said, kneeling next to her and pressing the ice pack against her face. From the corridor outside the exam room, Lars could hear the booming voice of Dan's father. He also heard a calmer male voice say something about running some tests as he assured Mr. Kline that as soon as they knew what they were dealing with, Dan would receive the treatment he needed.

The calmer voice came closer, ticking off instructions to some unseen person as he moved. There was a brief exchange with the police officer, and then a tall young man in his midthirties entered the cubicle. He focused all of his attention on Sadie. Lars liked him immediately.

"Hello, Sadie. I'm Dr. Booker. I need to take a look at you and ask you some questions. Would that be all right?"

Sadie kept rocking.

"Help me get her onto the bed," he said softly, addressing Lars for the first time.

Without a word, Lars scooped Sadie into his arms and set her gently on the narrow hospital bed. She instantly rolled to one side, facing away from them, and curled herself into the fetal position. Dr. Booker was undeterred. He pulled on a pair of latex gloves as he walked to the other side of the bed and bent to examine her lip. "That's going to need some stitches. I could use my special pink thread if you like. My niece likes pink." He continued to probe and examine. "How about you, Sadie? What's your favorite color? I'm partial to blue myself—or green. My mom said that's because I'm the outdoors type. I like nature—water, trees. . . ."

Gradually Lars saw Sadie's arms and legs start to relax.

The nurse had come back to assist Dr. Booker, and the two of them worked in a reassuring rhythm, checking Sadie for any signs of further injury. Apparently satisfied that her split lip was the worst of it, he quietly explained each step of the process for closing the wound. "Okay, Sadie, this is some stuff to freeze the surface so you won't feel anything. I'm thinking no more than half a dozen will do the job, but if you like, I can make tinier stitches and give you more."

Nothing.

Dr. Booker glanced at Emma and Lars, seeming to notice their plain dress for the first time. "I'll bet your mom is pretty good with a needle and thread—maybe I should let her make these stitches."

Sadie stared wide-eyed and unblinking at the ceiling.

As the doctor went about his work, his tone changed slightly and Lars understood that he was addressing them. "I'm going to suggest that Sadie be admitted at least overnight. Right now she's showing all the classic signs of shock, but I'd like to make certain there's nothing else going on."

"The officer. . . ," Lars began, lowering his voice and glancing toward the corridor where the officer had positioned himself just outside Dan's cubicle.

Dr. Booker clipped the thread with a small pair of scissors and then pulled off his gloves. "I doubt it will happen, but don't be surprised if they decide to assign someone to her while she's here." He gave a nod toward the hallway where the policeman was talking quietly to one of the nurses.

"I can stay," Emma volunteered.

"He means the police," Lars explained, and Dr. Booker nodded.

"I'd like to get some X-rays—not that I suspect anything. But since she's not really responding to touch or perhaps pain, we want to be sure. And we should consider a psych consultation."

Lars nodded. "We will wait here," he said.

"Actually, we'll probably take her right to a regular room once we get those pictures taken."

The nurse stepped forward. "It could be some time before we can get her to and from the X-ray department and have a bed for her. I understand that it was your niece who was also in the accident?"

"She's in surgery," Emma said. "My sister's child. . ." Her voice trailed off.

Dr. Booker and the nurse exchanged a look. "Why don't I have someone show you to the surgical waiting room? You can wait there, and we'll come get you as soon as Sadie is settled."

"I can't go with Sadie?"

"You could, but I thought you might want to use this time to check on your niece?"

Lars had never seen Emma look so torn.

"Jeannie will be needing you." He spoke to her in their Dutch-German dialect. "Sadie is in good hands for now."

"Ja," Emma replied, but her eyes were on Sadie.

"All right," Lars said, reverting to English to include Dr.

Booker and the nurse in the agreement. "We will wait."

Obviously relieved, the medical duo left the cubicle, the nurse assuring them that someone would be along soon to transport Sadie to radiology.

As soon as they were gone, Emma got up and went to Sadie's bedside, covering her tenderly with the white hospital blanket and leaning in to kiss her forehead and examine her stitches.

"Are they even?" Lars asked. And for the first time since they had left their house, he saw a shadow of a smile play across Emma's beautiful face.

"Perfect," she replied.

As his wife gently fingered Sadie's hair away from her face and the swollen blue area around her mouth that the doctor had repaired, Lars couldn't help but pray that everything that had been ripped open in those few seconds earlier that morning would be so easily restored.

Chapter 10

Emma

This way," an aide said, motioning for Lars and Emma to join her at the elevator after Sadie had been taken for X-rays. They pressed into the elevator that was already crowded with people in medical garb. Everyone stood facing forward toward the doors, and no one spoke as the elevator stopped at each floor.

A local, Jeannie would have called it with a sigh of impatience. Both Jeannie and Sadie had little time for dawdling. Their days were filled to the minute, and they were always anxious to be on to the next item on their agenda. Tessa, on the other hand, took time to savor life, appreciating the simple details of her daily routine.

Lars stood next to Emma. He kept a strong hold on her, and yet she felt a wave of fear grip her to the point that she thought her knees might actually buckle. She placed her hand in the crook of Lars's elbow and held on.

The elevator doors slid open, and the aide led the way around the corner and into the waiting room. Emma was surprised to see that they were the only ones there. Jeannie and Geoff had not yet arrived, and there were no other families keeping vigil for a loved one in surgery. Lars surveyed the room and chose a cluster of chairs close to the windows. "Over here," he said, and Emma followed him and began dragging additional chairs to the area.

"What are you doing?" Lars asked.

"We need more chairs. Jeannie and Geoff will need a place to wait, and Hester will surely be here, and once the news spreads. . ."

Lars placed his hand on her arm. "We can add more chairs as needed," he told her. "*Sich hinsetzen* and gather yourself. Jeannie is going to need all your strength."

There was a rustle of movement outside the waiting room entrance, and Emma saw Hester and her husband, John, enter the room. The sight of her good friend was such a relief that Emma went to her and for the first time since arriving at Jeannie's house, squeezed out a few of the tears that she had carefully repressed. Lars was right. Her daughter and sister would look to her for strength and reassurance.

Hester hugged her tight for a long moment. "I'm right here," she murmured. "Hang in there, and we'll all get through this together, okay?"

Emma nodded and gave herself over to that moment of comfort in her friend's embrace—a moment she somehow knew she would need to come back to many times in the days to come. For if they had taken Tessa to surgery, then that had to mean that it was going to take time for her to heal. "Thanks for everything you did for Sadie and for being here," she murmured, and Hester released her. It occurred to Emma that Hester had not once asked her what had happened. She loved her friend all the more for that.

While John talked to Lars, Emma told Hester about Sadie. "There's a policeman waiting to question her as soon as they finish taking X-rays and get her settled into a room," she whispered.

"It's protocol," Hester said with a dismissive wave of her hand. "There's a coffee machine," she added, nodding toward the refreshment area on the other side of the room. "There's bound to be hot water. I could make you a cup of tea."

Tea—green tea, Emma thought, remembering that just a few weeks earlier Sadie had announced that she was on a strict diet to eat healthier. "Green tea," she had told Emma. "It contains antioxidants that are very good for the immune system."

"Iced or hot?" Emma had asked her, and Sadie had been stumped.

"I'm not sure it matters," she had said uncertainly, but then she'd grinned. "But from now on, it's milk or green tea or water. No soda. No coffee. And no juice drinks. Those are so incredibly loaded with sugar." She'd made a face as if disgusted that the beverages that had been her choice for most of her sixteen years had suddenly left a terrible taste in her mouth.

Emma gave Hester a weary smile then shook her head. "Perhaps later," she said. "Thank you." She fixed her gaze on the doorway. "What am I going to say to Jeannie?" she asked.

Hester hesitated and then sat in the chair next to Emma and took her hand. "Jeannie and Geoff will need a little time, Emma. Right now all they can think about is Tessa."

Emma heard the rustle of someone approaching and glanced back toward the door. Geoff was standing in the doorway, looking as if he might shatter into a thousand pieces at any second.

She started toward him, feeling as if the distance between them was far greater than just the width of a small waiting room. And just when she was within two steps of her brother-in-law, Geoff walked past her as if she were an apparition. He went to the far end of the room, where he turned a chair to face the window and literally collapsed into it.

The aide who had accompanied him stood in the doorway, as if unsure of what her next move should be.

"My sister? Mrs. Messner?" Emma asked.

The young woman pointed to a closed door marked with the skirted silhouette used to indicate female. "Shall I check on her?"

"No thank you. The family is here now. We'll be all right." She looked back and saw Hester and John standing next to the chair where Geoff sat slumped forward, his large hands dangling helplessly between his knees.

"We were just fooling around."

That was what Sadie had said, and suddenly Emma understood that they all had to accept the reality that whatever had happened to Tessa, Sadie had played a major part in it.

Out in the hallway, Emma tapped lightly on the restroom

door. From inside she could hear sounds that were heartbreaking and terrifying at the same time. Those sounds were so foreign to her, and yet there was no question that they were coming from her sister—the carefree woman who could bring a smile to anyone's lips.

"Jeannie? It's Emma. Open the door."

The silence that replaced the sobs was almost more distressing than hearing Jeannie wailing. Emma tried the knob and found the door locked.

"Jeannie?"

After what seemed forever but was in fact only seconds, Emma heard the click of the lock. She pushed in on the door at the same time that Jeannie pulled, and the door flew back, banging against the wall as Jeannie stumbled forward and into Emma's arms.

Emma lost her battle to choke back the tears. She let them flow freely now. And the sisters stood locked in each other's arms—one of them dressed plain with her prayer covering knocked sideways by her sister's embrace, the other dressed in jeans and a T-shirt three sizes too large for her, her flaming red curls flattened into clumps against her cheeks by the rain and her tears.

"What happened?" Jeannie sobbed. "I don't understand."

Oh, the questions they must face in the days to come. Even if Tessa made a full recovery, Emma knew that once the relief passed, there were bound to be questions. The truth was that she was beginning to have a pretty good idea about what had happened.

The position of the driver's seat had told its own story—too close for the long legs of Dan Kline. It had been the passenger seat that had been pushed back to its full depth—and reclined. Sadie would never recline a seat. Sadie had once told Lars that she thought that was so dumb. Why wouldn't people want to see where they were going?

Had their impetuous, adventurous daughter persuaded Dan Kline to let her drive them to school? Or was it Dan who had suggested the switch in drivers? The roads were wet and slick with the heavy rain—a rain that followed weeks of drought. Surely the boy would have taken that into consideration. Surely he would have reminded Sadie that he was only eighteen and that Florida law required a driver on a learning permit to be accompanied by another driver over the age of twenty-one. He was a responsible kid—most of the time.

Oh, there was going to be blame enough to go around for all of them, Emma thought. But they would weather that and whatever else came their way as they always had—as a family of strong faith.

"Come on, Jeannie," Emma said as she guided her sister across the tiled hall and into the carpeted waiting room. "Geoff needs you."

Chapter 11

Sadie

Sadie, my name is Lieutenant Benson. I need to ask you some questions about what happened earlier today."

Sadie kept her gaze fixed on the wall opposite her. She was in a hospital room. She could tell by the whiteboard on the wall that announced: "Your nurse is Marcie."

She had little memory of how she'd gotten here. Her dad was standing by the window while her mom fussed over her, adjusting her pillow and rearranging the covers. They were nervous.

"I'm with the Sarasota police," the man in uniform continued.

"Dad and I will be right here, Sadie," her mom murmured. "There's no reason to be afraid, okay?"

Until that moment, Sadie hadn't really felt much of anything, but now as details of the morning came back to her, she felt heat rush to her face, and her stomach lurched. The clock read 10:25. At night? No. Morning. She could hear the rain beating against the window the way it had been scratching at the car windows when she was driving. She glanced toward the light and saw that it was still daylight outside.

Lieutenant Benson pulled a straight-backed chair closer to the bed and sat down. "Before I begin, there are some things I need to be sure you understand."

Sadie found that the man's voice was not unkind—not bossy like she might have expected. Or angry with her. She had really steeled herself for everyone to be so very angry. It was confusing that her parents weren't upset with her for driving with Dan when they'd been so very clear about the rules.

"You have the right to remain silent. If you give up that right, anything you say can be used against you in a court of law."

Her mom gasped and looked at her dad, but the officer continued, "Tell me what you think that means."

"It means that you—" Emma began speaking to Sadie.

"I need your daughter to tell me, ma'am."

Sadie swallowed, but there was no saliva in her mouth. "It means that I don't have to talk or answer your questions if I don't want to," Sadie said. Her voice sounded like one of those automated message voices. "I don't want to." She did not blink or break her focus on the whiteboard: *Your nurse is Marcie.*

Lieutenant Benson cleared his throat. "Got that. You have the right to have an attorney present now and during any future questioning and—"

"It is not our way," Lars interrupted, but Lieutenant Benson ignored him.

"If you cannot afford an attorney, then one will be appointed for you." He waited for Sadie to respond.

"We're not poor," her mother said. "Just plain. My husband makes a good—"

Sadie saw her father's hand move, and her mother stopped speaking in midsentence.

Lieutenant Benson spoke to her. "Sadie, do you understand that you can have an attorney—a lawyer—if you want one?"

"We don't know any lawyers," Sadie said. She pushed herself a little higher onto the pillows and locked eyes with the lieutenant. "I understand my rights—you just Mirandized me, right? Well, I don't want to answer any questions, and we don't do lawyers." She glanced at her mom. "My stomach hurts."

"Okay. Well, that's your choice," Benson said as he put away the notepad and pencil he'd taken from his shirt pocket. He looked up at her father. "My advice, sir, is that you consider hiring a lawyer to represent your daughter."

Sadie sighed and focused once again on the whiteboard.

Her parents followed the officer into the hall, and she heard him talking to them. ". . .right now culpable negligence but. . ."

Sadie's eyes darted toward the door, and for the first time it dawned on her that she was possibly going to be arrested and charged. She listened harder.

"Dan Kline," she heard her father say.

"He's been ticketed for allowing your daughter to operate his car."

"So you're telling us that Sadie might be arrested while Daniel. . ."

Sadie felt a wave of panic. She didn't want to cause trouble for Dan. He had a full college scholarship. If he was arrested, that could ruin his whole future. She pushed back the covers ready to go to Lieutenant Benson and tell him everything.

"Dan Kline wasn't driving the car, sir," Lieutenant Benson said. "There are witnesses that saw your daughter at the wheel."

Sadie tried to swallow around the lump that suddenly seemed to fill her throat. Uncle Geoff had seen her. So had Tessa. "I was the one," she whispered as once again she saw Tessa's face in the instant before she was struck, her eyes wide and questioning as the car careened toward her. *I was the one*, repeated in Sadie's brain as she climbed back into bed and pulled the covers around her, covering her ears to block out everything that had happened. But even there she heard the drumbeat of the words. *I was the one.*

Seemingly out of nowhere, her mother's arms came around her, holding her, protecting her. "Shhh," she whispered. "Everything will work out."

"Dr. Booker has admitted your daughter for observation," she heard Lieutenant Benson tell her father. "But once she is discharged. . ."

Sadie's choking sobs blocked out the rest of his words.

"And then?" she heard her father ask moments later as her sobs tapered to a whimper. His voice was shaking in a way that Sadie had never heard before.

"She'll be taken downtown for booking. Again, sir, right now the case against her is borderline."

All of the air seemed to go out of her mother as if someone had pierced her with a needle, and Sadie realized that she had been listening to what the officer was saying as well. "No," she whispered and held Sadie tighter.

"Mr. Keller, take my advice and do your daughter a favor. Hire a lawyer," Lieutenant Benson repeated.

"That is not our way," Sadie heard her father reply, and then she heard the quiet click of the door as her father came back inside the room and closed the door, leaving Lieutenant Benson out in the corridor.

She pulled away from her mother and found her voice. "Am I being arrested?"

"No," her father assured her through gritted teeth. Then very softly, he murmured, "Maybe."

"It's what they have to do, apparently, when there's been a serious accident," her mom explained.

"But Tessa's going to be all right?"

"She's in surgery," her mother said. "The doctors are. . ."

There was a tap at the door, and Sadie's dad opened it to Hester Steiner. Her mom's friend looked really awful, as if she had just heard the most horrible news ever.

"Hester? Are you. . . What is it?" her mom asked in a voice that sounded like she couldn't find the breath she needed.

Hester glanced at Sadie and tried a smile that didn't come close to working. She motioned for Sadie's parents to follow her into the hall.

"We'll be right outside the door," her mom said as she gently shut the door.

Sadie strained to hear what Hester was telling her parents. ". . .did everything they could but. . ."

Then she heard her mom moan, "Tessa? Please, God, no."

And in that moment, she knew. Tessa was dead.

And it was her fault.

Part Two

The beginning of strife is like
letting out water. . .
PROVERBS 17:14

Chapter 12

Jeannie

Jeannie glanced around the kitchen. She was home, but how was that possible? She had no clear memory of how she'd gotten here. And how could this possibly be the same day? The same house? The same kitchen with its breakfast clutter untouched? And robbed now of the promise of Tessa ever coming through that door again, how could this place ever hope to lay claim to being a home?

Jeannie sat on the edge of the kitchen chair and waited for someone to tell her what to do next. Emma or Geoff, one of them would tell her how she was supposed to go on with her life without her beloved child—her only child—her Tessa.

She thought about Geoff's face when they had heard the news. She had turned to him after Dr. Morris quietly reported that Tessa had died of massive internal injuries. She instinctively knew that Geoff's expression of utter despair had mirrored what he was seeing in her eyes. In that instant, they had both gone from being the parents of a loving, bright, kindhearted, and generous child to being childless. There was a name for children who lost their parents. They were orphans. But for parents who lost their child? There was nothing. No longer a parent, what was she?

As if observing the activity around her from another universe,

Jeannie was vaguely aware of Geoff now in the next room. He was talking to someone on the telephone. She caught snatches of his side of the conversation and understood that he was talking to their pastor. Across the kitchen from where Jeannie sat staring at nothing, Emma was making tea. It was what Emma did whenever something went wrong in Jeannie's life. She came to her house, made tea, and listened while Jeannie poured out all of her frustrations.

How petty those discussions seemed now. Jeannie complaining about Geoff's job and how much time he spent doing it. About how now with extra duties as vice principal he would be home even less, and when he was there, more than likely he would be working. She had even moaned over Tessa and how she spent all of her time studying, and why couldn't she be more social like Sadie?

Sadie.

Suddenly she recalled seeing her niece sitting on the pavement next to the car, her arms wrapped around her knees, her head bowed. She remembered Emma kneeling next to Sadie. What she didn't remember was asking after her niece.

"How's Sadie?"

Emma glanced up, clearly surprised that these were her first words since coming home. "They're keeping her overnight for observation," Emma said. "The doctor ordered something to help calm her and make her sleep."

Jeannie stared at Emma again, trying to make sense of her surroundings. It came back to her that Hester had driven Geoff and her home, where they had been given over to the gentle care of Geoff's mom and her own stalwart parents who were now out on the lanai making phone calls of their own. Meanwhile Hester had returned to the hospital while Lars picked up Matt from school. "Why are you here? You should be with Sadie."

"Lars is there, Jeannie, and Sadie was already sleeping when I left. He was going to sit with Matt and help him understand everything. I'm here with you—where I want to be."

Jeannie went back to staring, this time at the dishes still on the table. Tessa's empty juice glass. The napkin—cloth, she had insisted on for the environment's sake—folded neatly to one side of a plate coated with dried egg yolk and the strawberry jam that she and Emma had made together earlier that year. In fact, they had put up enough jars that they were still being sold at the farmers' market to raise funds for the fruit co-op. Her utensils perfectly aligned on the plate. On the chair near the door sat her backpack exactly as her backpacks had sat every school day morning since Tessa's first day of kindergarten. Jeannie had clutched it to her chest all the way home from the hospital and then placed it there herself.

The very idea that either of them would ever again be able to function normally seemed ludicrous. How could anyone ask Geoff to go back to a job where he was working with children every day—where it would be impossible not to remember that this was the year Tessa was supposed to be there with him?

What was she thinking? This wasn't real. It couldn't be. Surely any minute Tessa would come down the stairs, pick up the backpack by its double straps, and sling it over one shoulder. Just a day earlier she had practiced carrying it that way, noting that kids in high school who wore their backpacks properly were considered dorky, according to Sadie.

Surely Geoff would complete his call and then shout up the stairs for Tessa to hurry or they would be late. Surely none of what had happened over the last few hours was real. Surely she was ill—delusional with fever.

Emma set a steaming mug in front of her and then ran the flat of her hand over Jeannie's back. But she said nothing, just stood there for a long moment as they both listened to Geoff's side of the phone conversation.

"Yes."

"No."

"I don't think that's necessary."

Jeannie realized that he was no longer speaking with their pastor. Every inflection told her that he was talking to a stranger, and the long pauses between his short replies made her curious. She picked up her mug of tea and walked into the den, where just the night before they had gathered as a family while Tessa opened her gift. Behind her she heard Emma start to clear away the breakfast dishes. She heard water running in the sink—Emma never used the dishwasher. She heard the back door open and close. Heard Emma greet someone in the low somber tones that she instinctively knew would become the norm for all conversations in this place over the coming days. And she ignored it all as she moved woodenly toward the den, where her husband was on the phone with a stranger that he really didn't want to be speaking with.

He stood at the window, his broad shoulders blocking the view of the lemon-lime tree that he had planted on Tessa's first birthday. He seemed older somehow, although his sable-colored hair was as thick as ever, and his stance was the same as when he stood on the sidelines of a game coaching his team.

"I'll check with my wife," he said now and turned around, startled to see her there in the doorway but recovering instantly as he slid one hand over the receiver. "Monday afternoon?" he asked.

"For?"

His face crumpled into a series of pockets and wrinkles as if someone had grabbed it like a piece of clean paper and wadded it into a ball and then released it. "The funeral," he croaked.

Jeannie felt the way people did when they dreamed of falling and then woke with a start, as two strong hands clasped her shoulders and pulled her upright and Emma relieved her of the mug of tea now spilling its contents onto the carpet.

"You need to sit down, Jeannie," their good friend Zeke Shepherd said in that calm no-worries voice that was his trademark. He helped her to a chair and then held out his hand for the phone that Geoff was still clutching. "And you need to let somebody else do that."

Geoff willingly handed over the phone and then sat on the hard straight-backed desk chair while Zeke took charge. That in itself had to be an aberration. Zeke was not a take-charge kind of guy. He was a combat veteran who had chosen a life on the streets, the type of person who made his way through life in a live-and-let-live manner. Rules were for people who had no idea of who they were or why they had been put on this earth.

Jeannie was pretty sure that Geoff—like her—had not even realized Zeke was there. But then that was Zeke—he came and went on his own schedule and in his own way.

"Zeke Shepherd here, friend of the family," he said and then listened. "Yeah, well, we'll get back to you on that. Otherwise, have you got what you need to. . .to go get her?"

He listened again.

"Got it," he said and clicked off the phone as he set it on Geoff's desk.

Jeannie looked at the clock that sat on the bookcase. Two thirty. There were hours she couldn't account for—time that had passed in a blur after the doctor left the waiting room. Any minute surely Tessa would walk through the door and calmly report that her first day of high school had been "fine." Her teachers were "fine." Her class schedule was "fine." Her new classmates were "fine."

Jeannie continued staring at the clock for a long moment. It was real, she thought, and nothing Emma or Geoff or anyone else could say would change that. The word *funeral* had been applied to their Tessa. She was to be mourned and buried within a matter of days. That was the way of things. How many times had she been at the homes of neighbors and family for this very purpose? How many times had she been the one uttering the meaningless words meant to bring solace and comfort?

She stood up and walked back toward the kitchen where she picked up Tessa's backpack.

"Jeannie?" Emma's call seemed to come from far away as Jeannie slowly climbed the stairs. The backpack was heavy. How many times had she fussed at Tessa about not overloading the bag? How many times had Tessa rolled her eyes and moaned, "Mom!" How much would she give to have that very conversation right this minute?

She stopped on the landing and stared at the backpack for a long moment, knowing that she wasn't yet ready to go through it. That would be like admitting. . . She retraced her steps and positioned Tessa's backpack on the chair where it belonged.

"Jeannie?" Emma reached out to touch her arm, but Jeannie ignored her, and this time she went all the way up the stairs without hesitating. She walked into her daughter's room and stood there taking in her surroundings. The room was pristine—bed made, everything in its place, clothes hung, drawers and closet door shut. And yet the aura that was Tessa was everywhere. It came from the way she had folded her nightgown and tucked it under her pillow—a bit of the lacy hem peeking out. It was in the very scent of a bowl of fresh fruit that Tessa kept on her desk. It was in the flattened cushion in the small rocking chair where Tessa liked to sit every morning and every evening to read her Bible.

Jeannie stood there taking it all in. Then she closed the door and locked it before crossing the room and sitting down in the rocker to stare out the window at what had to have been what Tessa had seen on her last morning on this earth.

Chapter 13

Geoff

Time had no meaning.

Outside the sun had come out and the skies had cleared, but the sun was low in the sky, and this day that had begun in a deluge of anticipation and excitement would soon be gone.

In the hours that had passed since Zeke handled the call with the funeral director, the house had slowly filled with people—family, friends, neighbors, kids Tessa often invited over, kids Tessa knew from church, kids from Geoff's athletic teams, teachers and other staff that he worked with, people Jeannie worked with in her various volunteer projects. A steady stream of people coming up the front walk, the women carrying some covered dish or basket, the men and young people parking their cars or bicycles wherever they could find a space.

Dan's car was gone now, but no one parked on the driveway as if worried that the space might be needed by someone older or frailer. Or maybe it was just that that space was tainted now—forever stained with Tessa's unshed blood.

Geoff stayed where he had gone when Hester and John had driven them home from the hospital, in the den. It was the room where he had always felt closest to Tessa. It was where she came to study while he graded papers or worked on reports. It was the room where the two of them watched and analyzed college games on the small television in the corner. He would sit in the cracked leather club chair, and Tessa would sit cross-legged on the floor. Jeannie would make them a huge bowl of popcorn then tell them not to ruin their appetites as she headed off to attend to one of what Tessa referred to as her mom's do-gooder projects.

He sat in the chair now, picking absently at the cracked leather as if picking at a scab. He allowed the flow of people to move around him, hearing the hushed tones the women spoke in as they took over the kitchen and set out or stored the food offerings. Once in a while one of the men would enter the den, clear his throat, and offer some condolence. Geoff was amazed at how easily he had fallen into the routine of standing to accept the handshake—or sometimes the hug—before murmuring, "Thank you" when the person stopped speaking and then adding, "I just need some time," releasing the person to go back into the large great room where most people had gathered. He never actually heard the words people spoke to him, but he saw from their faces that it was some form of how sorry they were.

He felt irritation at that. Sorry for what? For him? He didn't want their pity. For the fact that they had not been able to stop this horror from happening? Like he was?

Guilt welled up in him like wet cement, oozing into every crevice of his being. He had been right there when the car raced toward his child. Why hadn't he done something?

"Geoff?"

His sister-in-law set a plate of finger food on the side table next to his chair. "You should eat something," she said. "You haven't eaten since breakfast—"

"Where's Jeannie?" he asked, ignoring the food.

"Still upstairs," Emma replied. "I tried to talk to her. Maybe if you went to her?"

Emma was right. Jeannie needed him—they needed each other. This was their child taken from them too soon. Their home forever stripped of her presence. Their lives forever changed.

"Can you do something about maybe getting folks to move along and give us some time?" he asked.

As if time would help—as if they could somehow get over this.

"Sure." Emma handed him the plate of food. "Try to get her to eat a little something," she said as together they walked into the hall and he started up the stairs.

He was aware that the house packed with people had suddenly gone silent. Only after he had reached the landing at the top of the stairs did conversation resume. He walked woodenly past the bedroom he and Jeannie shared. The bed had not been made. It was something—like the breakfast dishes—that Jeannie would have done once she had seen Tessa and him off to school.

He passed the guest room—the room that Tessa often referred to as her mother's office since it was more often a catchall for whatever project Jeannie was involved in than it was a haven for guests.

The bathroom was still in the disarray he'd left it in that morning after cutting himself shaving and then later scouring the cabinets and drawers for the missing shed keys.

The door at the end of the hall was closed, and hanging from a hook was a cloth angel holding a hand-lettered sign that read: THIS ROOM PROTECTED BY ANGELS.

Not really, Geoff thought as he tried the knob. It was locked.

"Jeannie? It's just me." He didn't recognize his own voice. It was so weak. He waited, and then when no sound came from the other side, he cleared his throat and rattled the knob. "Come on, babe. Let me in."

He detected a faint rustling sound as if Jeannie might have been curled up in Tessa's bed. Maybe she had cried herself to sleep. Maybe he should leave well enough alone.

The latch clicked, and he waited, but she did not open the door, so he did and was speechless at the scene. Spread across every possible surface were Tessa's clothes, arranged in outfits, he realized, complete with matching shoes and accessories. They hung on hangers from the curtain rods, on the back of the closet door, and on dresser drawer knobs. There were three outfits laid out on the daybed—like two-dimensional bodies, the tops propped against the back of the bed with the skirt or jeans spread over the quilt and matching shoes set precisely below each outfit on the floor.

"What are you doing, honey?" Geoff asked, fearful that while he was sitting downstairs his wife had quietly gone mad above him.

"We have to decide what she'll wear," Jeannie replied, and he saw that she was dry-eyed and studying each option in the same way she and Tessa had studied the choices of what would be best for Tessa's first day as an upperclassman just twenty-four hours earlier.

"Her favorite outfit is what she wore this morning, of course. Needed to look her best but also be comfortable, but the EMTs had to cut that." She made a face. "This one comes pretty close," she mused, fingering a stretchy lime-green top that looked as if it might fit a doll but certainly not a real person.

She stood transfixed in front of the outfit lying in the center of the bed. "The boots are a nice touch," she murmured as she sat down and picked up a tall tan suede boot. She seemed to lose her train of thought for a moment. Geoff sat next to her and put his arm around her. "The boots," she continued, "she bought with Sadie at the thrift shop." She shook her head. "They were to share them, with Sadie only wearing them when she visited. Tessa made me promise not to breathe a word of it to Emma."

Geoff took the boot from her and set it with its mate on the floor.

"That's why they're here in Tessa's closet," Jeannie continued. "So Emma wouldn't know. . .like the way I took Sadie for her learner's permit. . .so Emma wouldn't know until it was too late. . . ."

Geoff felt tears the size of raindrops fall onto the back of his hand, and he gathered his wife in his arms as she broke down completely. Her soft red hair, like expensive silk, brushed his face, and the scent of her almost blocked out the unique fresh laundry scent of Tessa's clothes surrounding them.

Still holding Jeannie, he leaned back against the pile of pillows at one end of the bed and looked around his daughter's room. He had rarely seen it from this angle. Oh, maybe a couple of times when he had sat with her when she was a little girl and told her bedtime stories or read her one of her favorite books. But now it came to him that this was what his daughter saw every morning when she woke up. She had opened her eyes to this room that very morning and thought. . .what?

He pulled Jeannie closer as he fought back his own tears.

"Geoff, what are we going to do?"

"We're going to go on." What he didn't say was that he had no idea how they would manage that.

Dusk had come by that time, and now Tessa's clothing was cast in shadows, shadows that were somehow comforting.

"Emma sent me up with a plate of food," Geoff said. "I left it on the hall table."

"We should probably go downstairs," Jeannie ventured, and her tone told Geoff that she hoped he would not agree.

"Folks will understand," he said. "Let's just stay here a little longer."

She curled into him, seeking his warmth, his strength, his assurance that somehow they would find a way to get through the next days and weeks. The problem was that Geoff was wishing he had a safe harbor to pull into as well.

"We have to make the arrangements," she whispered after several long moments in which they were both aware of people leaving, car doors closing. Engines started and conversation grew muffled among those left downstairs. "There are people—out of town—that we need to call. . ."

"Emma can make those calls."

Jeannie sat up suddenly, and in the waning light he saw that her eyes had gone wide with shock. "She's still here? She should be with Sadie."

The rage that swept over him in that split second made it hard to breathe. "Lars is there," he managed.

"She must be. . ." She pushed herself off the bed. "Emma said they kept Sadie for observation. Did they tell her? About Tessa?"

He realized for the first time that Jeannie didn't know what he knew—that it had been Sadie behind the wheel when the car struck Tessa. Now was not the time to tell her, he decided. She'd been through enough—too much—already.

"I'm not sure what Sadie's been told, but that's up to Emma and Lars. They'll do what they think best, Jeannie."

Jeannie flicked on a lamp, and Geoff blinked in the sudden brightness. She studied the various outfits for a moment and then took one down from the curtain rod. "This one," she muttered to herself and headed for the door.

"Where are you going?" Geoff asked.

"Sadie needs her mother. And we need to get Tessa's clothes to. . .to. . ." She stopped moving and stared into space, practically catatonic in the doorway. She shook her head, squared her shoulders, and forced herself forward. "To the funeral home," she said, grinding out each word as she walked woodenly down the hall and paused only a fraction of a second before descending the stairs.

Geoff could not help but admire her. Jeannie had always been a just-do-it kind of woman. It was one of the things that had attracted him to her from their first meeting. She was not big on protocol or rules, but with her sunny disposition and features that made her look younger than her thirty-some years, she won hearts and minds without even realizing what she was accomplishing.

"The president should send Mom to the Middle East," Tessa had said one time. "She'd get them all talking to each other in no time."

Geoff took one last look around his daughter's room, taking the time to study the items on her dresser, the stuffed animals that shared shelf space with her books, and the fashion show of outfits that Jeannie had staged. Then he turned off the lamp and left the room, closing the door behind him. When he reached the top of the stairs, he saw his best friend, Zeke, standing at the front door, holding the shoes Jeannie had selected.

Did Tessa even need shoes?

"Jeannie wants to take these clothes over to the funeral home," Zeke said when Geoff reached the bottom step. "I told her I would do it—or maybe Emma could or Hester—but. . ."

"We'll do it tomorrow. Right now I just want to make sure Jeannie eats something and gets some rest." He saw in his friend's eyes that they both knew that the chances of such a thing were slim to none. Zeke handed him the shoes.

"Maybe a doctor could give her something to help her sleep?"

"We'll get through it one hour at a time," Geoff said, not for one second believing they would ever survive this. "Thanks for being here—for both of us."

"No. . ." Zeke shook his head vigorously, and Geoff knew that he had caught himself about to deliver his signature, "No worries, man."

"See you tomorrow," Geoff said, opening the front screen door for Zeke. Emma had done what he'd asked of her—most of the visitors had already left. The street was deserted now as the darkness of night settled over the neighborhood. Zeke headed for the bright orange van he used to deliver produce to markets for the co-op.

Up and down the block, the houses were lit, the golden lamplight spilling out the windows and across the lawns. Those people were counting their blessings, Geoff thought. Those people with children were thanking God that this horrible day had not happened to them. They were holding those children a little tighter tonight. He felt his chest clench as if someone had attached a vise and tightened it until he was having trouble breathing.

For one moment, he thought he might be having a heart attack. For one moment, the idea that he might die along with his only child brought him a measure of comfort. But then he heard Jeannie and Emma coming toward the porch and he remembered that he was the man in this family. He had lost a child, but he still had a wife and others who would look to him for the strength they would all need to get through this. His mom, Jeannie's parents, not to mention his siblings, in-laws, Tessa's cousins, and so many others.

And as he turned to Emma, intending to thank her for all that she had done for them that day, all he could think about was that she still had two children, one of them responsible for the accident that had robbed him of his daughter.

"Where's Matt?" he asked.

"When. . .after. . ." Emma took a breath and cleared her throat before continuing, "Lars picked Matt up from school so he would hear the news from us. Then they went to be with Sadie at the hospital. We thought it best if they had a little time. . . ."

"Yeah. It's good to have time, Emma," Geoff said as he brushed past her on his way back inside.

Chapter 14

Emma

Emma hugged Jeannie and waited until her sister had followed Geoff back inside the house before retrieving Sadie's bicycle. When Hester had driven Emma to Jeannie's house earlier, she had seen Sadie's bicycle still leaning against a cluster of palm trees in the front yard. There was something so poignant about seeing that bicycle where it was so often left whenever Sadie visited the house. It seemed like everything must be all right after all. That the girls were upstairs in Tessa's room, giggling over some silliness or the confidences the two of them so often shared.

"I could load it in the trunk," Hester had offered, following her gaze as she stood at the end of the driveway.

"No, leave it. I'll need a way to get back to the hospital later."

"You'll be okay?"

"I'll stay busy," she promised.

"Be strong," Hester had whispered as the two friends embraced.

On her way into the house, Emma had avoided looking at the closed garage door. It was a relief to see that Dan's car was no longer on the property. In fact, there was no sign of the accident at all.

She had wondered if Dan Kline was being kept overnight for observation like Sadie was. She'd also wondered if the full weight of what Sadie had done—or let her feelings for Dan Kline allow her to do—had hit home yet. What did a sixteen-year-old think in times like these? Was Sadie reliving the accident? What had she seen as she frantically tried to stop the car? Had it even registered in her brain that Tessa was gone forever?

"I've got this," Lars had said as if reading her hesitation to tend to her sister when her child also needed her. "Jeannie's going to need you there to help Geoff and her deal with all the well-meaning people who will be coming to their house once the news gets out."

"Hester could. . ."

"She needs you, Emma."

So before going inside to make the tea that would be the start of comforting her sister, Emma had wheeled Sadie's bike across the driveway and around to the side of the house where it would be out of sight when Jeannie and Geoff got back.

Now, hours later, she pedaled along the usually busy but at this time of night practically deserted main thoroughfare that bisected Pinecraft. With nothing to distract her, she allowed the full horror of the day to wash over her. She saw what they would face separately and alone in the days to come. Geoff's parting remark about time had stalked her every block of the way. Sadie had been reckless in that carefree way that made her so much like Jeannie. It wasn't the first time, but this time everything was different. How would Geoff and Jeannie ever be able to forgive her? How would Sadie ever forgive herself? As Sadie's parents, how should she and Lars react—should they punish her? Surely realizing that her foolish act had caused an accident that had ultimately ended with her beloved cousin dead was punishment enough for anyone.

And Matt? What about Matt?

He was so very attached to Geoff. Lars was not athletic, and having been raised Amish, he had not learned the contact sports like basketball and football that Matt found fascinating. But Geoff had taken Matt under his wing the minute he recognized a gift in their son despite his small stature. Geoff had patiently worked with Matt after school and on weekends. He even allowed Matt to be on the sidelines during the games that Geoff coached. And she couldn't begin to count the times that she had seen her son and her brother-in-law exchange a high five while seated in front of the small television in Geoff's den watching a game together.

Tessa had usually been there as well, Emma thought now. Matt had grudgingly admired his cousin's grasp of the finer points of the various sports.

"She's not bad for a girl," he had muttered.

Emma waited for the light and then pedaled across the nearly deserted highway to the hospital. She parked the bike near the valet parking station and ran inside. The lights had been dimmed in the lobby area—past visiting hours, Emma realized. She followed the maze of corridors to the bank of elevators that would take her to Sadie's floor, and as soon as she arrived, she saw a uniformed woman chatting with staff at the nurse's station. With relief she realized that the uniform was different from the one worn by Lieutenant Benson. The patches on the woman's shirt identified her as part of the hospital's security staff.

She hurried past, wanting nothing more than to have some time with Lars and the children without the presence of others. She felt such a need to gather them into her arms and hold on for a very long time. She wanted to lie next to Lars and pretend this day had never happened. She wanted to feel his strength and know as she had known from the day she met him that everything would be all right, that he would make it all right.

But she shook off such feelings as she passed the small waiting area and saw that it was filled with neighbors and fellow members of their congregation. The first person to come forward was Olive Crowder. Olive was not a hugger, but as she came to meet Emma, she stretched out her arms, and Emma gladly accepted the rare invitation to walk into their circle.

"How's Sadie?" she asked.

"Sleeping," Olive told her. "Lars got both of the children to lie down, and when I checked on them a few minutes ago, they were both sleeping."

"Das ist gut," Emma murmured. "Und Lars?"

Olive glanced back at Lars, who was surrounded by a cluster of men, including Hester's father, Arlen Detlef, who was also their senior pastor. The men were all frowning as if someone had raised a weighty question that needed special consideration. Arlen was stroking his thick white beard.

As she worked her way through the crowded room to Lars, Emma paused to accept the condolences of the other women and thank them for coming. They had brought food—a beautiful cake, a fruit pie, and at least three perfectly formed loaves of bread. The thought of eating anything made her physically ill, so she turned her gaze back to Lars.

"Guten abend," she murmured as she squeezed past several of the men to take her place beside her husband. She was unsure of her role here. Was she expected to play hostess and offer food as she had at Jeannie's house? A foreign house to these people, in that it was not plain in its furnishings, and its other occupants were anything but plain in their dress.

Except Tessa.

It was true that Tessa had not exactly dressed in the conservative small green, blue, or gray prints that Emma had Sadie wear, and she certainly did not use a prayer covering of any sort. Her fiery red hair—so like her mother's in color—was worn straight down, not pulled up in a bun. But even in her modern dress, she had preferred quieter styles than Jeannie did.

Emma suddenly thought of the outfit that Jeannie had brought downstairs to take to the funeral home and knew that it would not have been Tessa's choice at all. Perhaps she should call Jeannie. No, she would go over there in the morning. By then Jeannie likely would have recognized on her own that Tessa would want to be dressed in something quieter.

". . .officer said there would be a full investigation," Lars was saying.

To her. He was telling her something important, and she was thinking about clothing.

"I don't understand the need," she said. "We know what happened. It was a horrible accident, and one child is dead while the other. . ."

"Still, the authorities have questions," Arlen said. Emma realized that some of the people in this very room had already been questioned.

"But they are not our authorities," Lars reminded him. "We are not of their ways." He looked from the minister to Emma. "There will be questions, yes, but nothing so formal as an investigation. It was, as Emma has said, a terrible, terrible accident."

As he spoke, Emma understood that he was looking for assurances. But the other men said nothing.

"Lars," Pastor Detlef said after an uncomfortable silence had fallen over the gathering, "the circumstances here are. . .unusual. The General Assembly has long held that one of ours charged with a violation of the law and summoned to appear in court may indeed make use of the services of an attorney."

"But. . ." Lars started to protest, but Arlen held up one hand and continued. "However, the person accused must not permit the attorney to try to build a case based on denial of what the accused knows to be true."

A hush fell over the room. Several people bowed their heads. Everyone knew what the pastor was telling them. "The attorney's role is only that of establishing the truth, pleading for clemency in the case of guilt, and arguing the supremacy of God's higher law over that of the court."

Emma turned to Lars. "Is Sadie going to jail?"

"Lieutenant Benson intends to take Sadie into custody as soon as the doctor discharges her, Emma. You heard him say that. We have to think about how we can best protect her."

"There is basis in scripture to argue for alternative solutions." Arlen turned the pages of his worn Bible until he found the passage he needed. "Right here in the book of Luke," he said, adjusting his glasses. "As you go with your accuser before the magistrate, make an effort to settle with him on the way, lest he drag you to the judge, and the judge hand you over to the officer, and the officer put you in prison." He closed the Bible and faced Lars. "You must decide the path you will take. Meanwhile we will all pray for your Sadie."

The others nodded.

As the full impact of what lay ahead for Sadie hit her, Emma staggered and reached for Lars's arm to steady herself.

"Emmie"—Lars led her to one of a half dozen identical chairs—"you're exhausted."

"You both are," Olive said. "We'll be going now," she added in that no-nonsense tone she had that made people do her bidding. Everyone moved slowly toward the door, assuring each other as they left that Emma was indeed all right, that it had been a terrible day for the entire family, and that once they had some rest. . .

The voices trailed off as they moved down the hall. Emma couldn't help but wonder, *Once we've had some rest, then what?*

"Emma, can I get you something before I go?" Olive asked.

"I'm fine," Emma assured the older woman. "I'm just suddenly so very tired, and tomorrow. . ."

And the day after that and the week after that. . .

"Get some rest even if you can't sleep," Olive advised. "I'll stop by Jeannie's first thing tomorrow. And you know that Zeke Shepherd will be there for Geoff. You and Lars just take care of Sadie and Matt and yourselves—you've all suffered a terrible loss today."

Emma sat in the chair while Lars thanked Olive and Pastor Detlef and the others for coming. After what seemed a long time, he came back into the small room, and then he just stood there until Emma realized by the heaving of his chest that he was crying. She went to him. No words were necessary as they wrapped their arms around each other and hung on.

"Let's go check on the children," Emma said. She took Lars's hand and led him down the corridor. The security guard glanced at them but continued her conversation with the nurses.

"Mama?" Sadie was standing in the doorway to her room. Emma held out her arms, and Sadie ran to the safety of her mother's embrace. She was wearing a hospital gown and robe that were far too big for her, and Emma could not help thinking about the clothes she'd worn earlier that morning. Clothes so carefully selected from the limited range of choices that any conservative Mennonite teen might have.

"You're so lucky," Sadie had moaned to Tessa two days earlier. "You can wear anything you like."

"And you are so lucky that you're the kind of person that others want to be friends with no matter how you look," Tessa had replied without a touch of jealousy or malice. It was a truth they all recognized, for Sadie drew people to her like hummingbirds to sugar water.

"You'll have lots of friends, too," Sadie had told Tessa. "You'll see. Smart is the in thing these days, and nobody is smarter than my genius cousin."

Emma recalled how later, over glasses of iced tea, she and Jeannie had relived that conversation. "They're like we were at their age," Jeannie had said and then had gone on as only Jeannie could to lay out her plan for the girls' future.

Now Sadie seemed incredibly small and fragile as she pressed close to her parents. How on earth were they going to see her through everything she had yet to face—the funeral, facing Jeannie and Geoff, the full pain of the realization that Tessa was gone? Emma refused even to think about her daughter being arrested.

"Can we all sleep here tonight?" Sadie asked, her voice muffled in the cloth of Emma's dress.

"Oh honey, I'm not sure. . ."

"Matt's already sleeping. The nurse gave him a blanket and everything."

"There's nothing to be scared of," Lars told her, stroking her hair.

"We're not scared," Sadie replied. "Well, maybe we are, but don't we all just need to be close right now?"

Emma and Lars looked at each other. "Yes, that's exactly what we need," Lars said. "I'll just let the nursing staff know that we'll all be here for the night."

"I'll go with you," Sadie said, following her dad down the hall to the nurse's station.

On the one hand, Emma was thrilled to see her daughter acting more like her usual self. On the other, Dr. Booker had already warned them that he had little case for keeping Sadie in the hospital longer than overnight. And if he failed to keep her longer, she would be discharged and immediately taken into custody.

Emma walked into the semidarkness of Sadie's hospital room. It was small but private, and that was something to be glad about. As Sadie had told them, Matt was curled up on a reclining chair, the hospital blanket cast off to one side. Even as a baby he had always curled in protectively as if there were some need to fend off danger. His expression now was not what she would describe as peaceful. His brow was furrowed and his mouth was drawn into a thin straight line.

She knelt next to him and touched his shoulder. "Matt?"

He rolled to his back and blinked up at her. "Mom?"

"Right here," she said. "You okay?"

He pushed himself to a sitting position and rubbed his eyes with his knuckles. "It's true?" His features lit by the hall light begged her to tell him it had all been a mistake.

"Ja," she said.

"But. . ." The logic he was so fond of employing failed him, and his mouth worked though no sound came out of it.

Emma sat on the arm of the chair and put her arm around his thin shoulders. "But there's nothing to be afraid of, Matt. It will take time to get through the sadness and the terrible, terrible loss. You will always miss Tessa, but. . ."

"Is it true that Sadie killed her?"

For an instant, Emma stopped breathing. "Where did you hear such a thing?" she gasped.

"That's what Sadie told me. She said it was all her fault that Tessa died—that she killed her."

"Tessa's death was an accident, Matt. Do you hear me? A horrible accident."

Matt's head bobbed in the affirmative, and Emma realized that she had grasped his shoulders and shaken him. She hugged him to her. "Sorry," she murmured against his hair tousled by sleep. "So sorry. We need to talk about this together—all of us as a family. There's a lot we're going to have to work our way through, okay?" Emma's assurances that they would get through this somehow rang hollow even as she thought the words.

"Yes ma'am." Matt pulled the blanket a little closer, and Emma instinctively gave him some time to collect himself.

"Mom?" He did not look at her, just sat fingering the blanket. "I never really thought about somebody dying so young before—I never really thought it could happen to one of us."

"Me neither," she admitted.

Chapter 15

Lars

How was a man supposed to protect his family? How could he turn back the clock to a time when his wife and daughter and son were happy and safe? When their house rang with laughter and was filled with extended family and friends sharing plans and dreams for the future?

Lars drew the blade of a handsaw across a thick board and began the rhythmic back-and-forth strokes that would change that board into something else—in this case something he sorely wished he were not called upon to craft. He was building a coffin. Tessa's coffin. The large board would be changed by the cutting and sanding and finishing, much the way his family had been changed by the event that led to Tessa's death.

It was Saturday, a day that Lars normally reserved for doing his paperwork and making trips to the lumberyard with Matt to choose the wood he would need for the coming week. But today was different. Today was the day that he would pour everything God had given him in the way of carpentry skill into making a coffin for Tessa.

Although Emma had awakened earlier with the same outward calm with which she had greeted every day of their lives together, she was not the same—none of them were. The morning before, she had tended to the housekeeping chores in Sadie's hospital room, folding up the bedding the nurses had brought for them so the whole family could stay the night and wetting paper towels from the bathroom to wipe down all the surfaces in the room the same way she wiped the countertops and kitchen table and stove every morning at home.

The nursing and hospital housekeeping staff had tried to stop her, but Emma had continued her cleaning alongside them, using the time to get to know each one of them a little better. It occurred to Lars that she was nurturing those strangers the same way she nurtured their neighbors and friends. And when one large maintenance worker had pulled his wallet from his hip pocket and proudly showed Emma photographs of his grandchildren, Lars had thought that there might actually be a chance that Emma would see them all through this the same way she had shepherded their family and Jeannie's through countless other lesser catastrophes in the past.

And yet there was something different about her. Something in her eyes. The kind of furtive wariness of an animal that fears it is about to be trapped. Before, her eyes had always been alive with curiosity in spite of her inclination toward worrying. Now they were clouded by dread and doubt.

Before. . .

All of time now seemed to be divided into before and since—before the accident, since Tessa's death. No one spoke the actual words. Such sentences usually broke off abruptly, but the meaning was clear. Before the accident, his daughter had been a lively, outgoing girl who was enormously popular with her friends and classmates and much beloved by their large extended family. Before the accident, his son's world had revolved around sports—games played, games watched, games analyzed at length usually with his uncle Geoff. Before the accident, there had not seemed to be enough hours in the day to do all that they needed or wanted to accomplish.

But since. . .

The accident had happened on Thursday—odd to begin a school year at the end of a week, but Geoff had explained that the school board had decided that the first three days of the week needed to be given to faculty and staff to do all the things necessary to assure a smooth start for the students. So Emma and Jeannie had set the family picnic for Wednesday afternoon, and on a rainy Thursday morning, their children had headed off to school.

Only one of them—Matt—had made it there.

By that evening, Tessa was dead and Sadie was confined to the hospital. On Friday Lars and Emma had split their time between the hospital and Jeannie and Geoff's home, and they had been thankful when Dr. Booker had announced his intention to keep Sadie in the hospital for the weekend. But he had been overruled by hospital protocol, and late on Friday Sadie had been discharged, taken downtown to be charged and then taken—without them being allowed to go with her—to spend her first night in the juvenile detention center in Bradenton.

In this new and unfamiliar and frankly frightening realm of living, Sadie would be allowed limited visits and phone privileges. She would attend classes during the day and have chores to complete, just as she did at home. She would dress in the faded blue jumpsuit mandated by the county. She would not be allowed to wear the traditional prayer covering or keep her Bible close at hand. On Wednesday of the coming week, she was to appear in court for her arraignment, where she would plead guilty or not.

"Guilty of what?" Emma had protested. "It was an accident."

How can today be only Saturday? Lars wondered as he continued to plane the wood that would form the curved lid to Tessa's coffin. The funeral was scheduled for Monday afternoon. Would the judge hear their pleas and allow Sadie to be there? Lars was not so sure. He was not certain of anything when it came to the ways of the outside world, a world that now held the fate of his beloved daughter in its grasp.

Matt's response to everything happening around him was to become more talkative, filling any lengthy silence with reports on how things were going with the current football season—at his school, in the college ranks, and with the professionals. He continued to pepper his delivery of this information with such things as "Uncle Geoff thinks that. . ." or "Uncle Geoff told me. . ." And he needed only the slightest encouragement to keep talking, a nod of Lars's head or a murmured but distracted "Really?" from Emma.

"I think when I get out of school I want to be a coach," he had announced as the three of them shared their first meal since Sadie's arrest.

"What sport?" Lars had asked, grateful for any distraction.

Matt had shrugged. "All of them."

Lars had looked across the table at Emma and seen the fleeting lift of the corners of her mouth. And that almost-smile had been a lifeline for him. They would get through this somehow, and one day they would be able to do all the things they had done before—smile, laugh, plan a future.

The cut piece of lumber clattered to the concrete floor of the workshop, and Lars put down his saw and blew the excess sawdust off the edge of the board, examining it closely for any possible flaws. He was sanding the board when he heard Emma's bike tires crunch the crushed shell driveway.

By the time he got to the screen door of his shop, she was already on her way into the house. With Sadie confined and their ability to see her limited, Emma filled her hours helping Jeannie prepare for the funeral. Normally this was Emma's day to help out at the thrift shop, and she would come straight to his workshop full of news she'd heard from customers and other volunteers.

But since the accident, their family was the news. He watched as Emma went inside and returned a moment later with a broom and dustpan. "Emma?"

She paused but did not turn.

"Come on out here and give me a hand with this," he said, holding the screen door open.

"I've got housework, Lars," she replied.

"And plenty of time to attend to that." For some reason he felt compelled to break the cycle of her need to be constantly busy—cleaning, cooking, doing laundry. "You can't keep going on like this, Emma." He knew by the way her shoulders tensed that she understood what he was saying.

She swept a small pile of dead leaves into the dustpan and set it with the broom on the back stoop as she started toward him. "Why?" she asked when she was almost there. "Why can't I do what I want? Why do I ever have to do anything again?"

Amazingly her response gave Lars a flicker of hope. She sounded like Sadie, who had always leaned toward the dramatic. "You don't have to do anything," he said handing her a wood block wrapped in sandpaper and indicated the edge that needed work. "We have a choice, Emmie. We can shut out everything and everyone and hide behind chores. Or we can find some way to move forward. Shutting all this out may seem the easier path, but it seems to me that as time goes by, it might be a decision we'd regret."

By the way she ran the sandpaper over the rough edge of the board, he could tell that she was listening, hesitating now and then as she considered his words.

"It's so very hard."

"Ja. Life's like that."

He set up a second board to cut, and the conversation between them was drowned out by the whoosh of the saw moving back and forth.

After they worked in silence for a while, Lars saw her pause and study the rough penciled drawing he'd made, noting the dimensions for the piece. She watched as he cut another board, and then she said, "I know you've made coffins for others in the community, Lars, but what is it like making a coffin for Tessa?"

The directness of the question startled him, and he had to wonder what other unspoken thoughts she might be entertaining. "I don't know. I never really thought about it. Don't misunderstand—I am taking special care—all of the special care that Tessa deserves."

Emma nodded. "She would have liked that. She always thought your furniture pieces were the finest." She actually smiled. "There was this one day when the girls and Jeannie and I were at Yoder's and these women were in the next booth. They were snowbirds, we guessed, from the way they talked and were dressed and all. Anyway, they were going on and on about how they'd always heard that Amish furniture was the best made anywhere."

She was sanding the edge of the board now with smooth regular strokes, as if for a moment everything was as it had been before and she was just relating this incident. Her voice was livelier than Lars had heard it since that moment at the hospital before they'd gotten the news—that moment when there had still been hope.

". . .and Tessa just turned around and said, 'Well, my uncle was raised Amish, and he makes the most beautiful furniture you've ever seen. You should give him a call—his name is Lars Keller.' And remember? They did. That one woman came here with her husband and ordered that dining room set from you."

Lars nodded and kept working, afraid to break the special moment of memory.

"Tessa said she might just have to ask you for a commission."

"What did you say?"

"Nothing, but your daughter told her good luck with that. She said that everybody knew that you're cheap."

"Thrifty," Lars corrected with a smile.

It was so wonderfully normal—this conversation with his wife. This time together in his workshop. This banter. But as quickly as it came, it was gone. Emma sat staring at the sanding block she held in one hand for a long moment. Then she placed the block on Lars's workbench and stood up.

"The kitchen floor needs washing," she said.

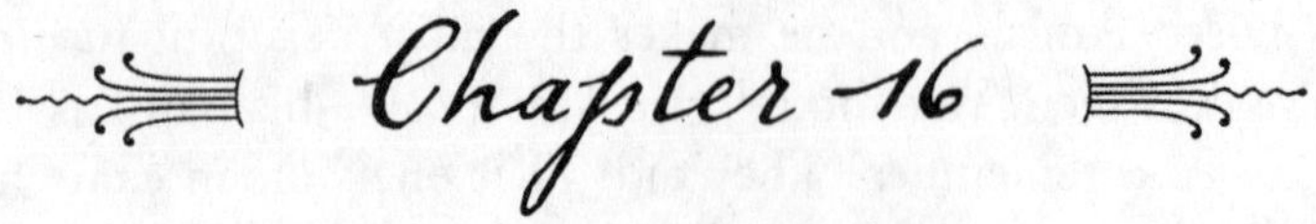

Chapter 16

Sadie

Sadie had never been more terrified in her life. The whole day had been a nightmare from which she couldn't wake up, and now it was night and she was in jail—or detention as she'd been corrected by the ginormous, uniformed African-American woman driving the van as she was transported from the police station to the center. "No, miss. That place we just left? That was jail. This is different."

How? she wondered. *Worse? It couldn't be worse, could it?*

The rain had stopped. In fact, it was a beautiful, clear day—a Friday. She should be out on her bike with Tessa sharing stories of what had happened in school. Instead, she had spent the day in her hospital room, and then the social worker lady had come to tell them that she was being discharged. Right behind her had stood Lieutenant Benson.

The ride to the juvenile detention center took forever and at the same time was over way too soon. Sadie glanced at the other girl in the van. She looked a lot younger than Sadie, and she sat curled up as if trying to make herself disappear. When they were first escorted to the van in shackles and handcuffs, Sadie had tried to give the girl an encouraging smile, but the girl had refused to make any eye contact. Sadie had made the same attempt at eye contact with the guard sitting with them with no better results. Finally, she had given up and stared out the window for the remainder of the trip.

Tessa was dead. Dan had disappeared into thin air. No word. No visit. Nothing. And when she'd asked about him, all her mother would tell her was that Dan had been treated for minor injuries and released. "He's with his family," she'd said as if that should end the discussion. And then Sadie had been arrested.

The world had gone insane.

The van driver turned into a driveway between a couple of one-story concrete buildings then waited for another uniformed person to open the gate that led into a wire enclosure before driving in. The uniforms—as she had decided to call them since there seemed to be so many of them and distinguishing one from another took more effort than she could muster—exchanged brief banter while the gate was closed again. Only then were she and the other girl allowed to leave the van.

Sadie was exhausted. Like a sleepwalker, she followed instructions. Whatever the uniforms told her to do, she did without protest.

Once inside the building, she was told to remove all her clothes. She did not protest, nor did she make any comment when a female uniform searched her from head to toe, including looking inside her mouth and examining her even "down there." She was directed into a shower. She was then given a whole new set of clothing—a faded blue jumpsuit, underwear, socks.

Once she was dressed, she was taken to a room where another uniform asked her more questions—not about Tessa or the accident, but things like whether she wanted to harm herself.

"Well, duh," she wanted to say. *"My best friend is gone forever, and it's my fault. What do you think?"* But she said nothing.

"You can call your parents now," another uniform told her.

How could she? How could she ever explain? All the time they'd been with her since the accident, not once had her parents asked her what had happened. But the question had been there in their eyes. She was well aware that her day of reckoning had only been postponed.

She said nothing.

"You know, a kid like you from good people like your folks seem to be. . . All I'm saying is that's not always what we see here. They're probably waiting to hear from you," the uniform said, holding the phone out to her.

Sadie focused on her hands. From somewhere outside the small room, she heard doors slamming.

"Call your folks," the woman urged again.

Sadie took the portable phone from her and punched in the numbers. It rang once and started to ring a second time, and then she heard her father's voice. It was supper time, and he hadn't turned off the phone. That alone gave Sadie a feeling of relief—that whatever happened, her dad would take care of her.

"Hello?"

She collapsed into tears, and the phone slipped from her fingers and clattered to the concrete floor.

Vaguely she was aware that the uniform had rescued it and was talking to her dad. "Yes sir. Well, understandably she's a little. . .she's upset, but she's here and getting settled in. Tomorrow. Thirty minutes. Yes sir. Good night."

Sadie continued to cry. Then she began to shake.

"Your folks will be here to visit tomorrow. How about something to eat?"

Her mother would have wrapped her arms around Sadie and held her until the shaking stopped. The uniform offered food as if the two of them were out shopping or something and the idea of eating had just occurred to her.

Sadie shook her head vehemently. She wanted to go home. She wanted to turn back the clock. She wanted this to be over. "So tired," she managed through sobs and hiccups. That had to be the understatement of the year. The truth was that she was exhausted on every level—physically, mentally, and especially spiritually.

They moved through another series of locked doors into a larger room furnished with molded plastic chairs that looked really uncomfortable. At the opposite end of the room were a series of tables with attached stools similar to the tables in the cafeteria at the academy. Near the door they'd come through was a kind of podium-style desk. Sadie glanced up and saw cameras attached to the ceiling and a series of identical doors around the perimeter of the large room.

The uniform unlocked one of the doors and held it open. Inside Sadie saw two concrete risers the size of her twin bed at home and a metal toilet attached to the wall just inside the door. There was also a small window high on the wall opposite the door. It was still light outside. She glanced at a wall clock imprisoned in a metal cage. Seemed like everyone and everything was in jail around this place.

"Not tonight," another uniform told the woman with Sadie. "She's on watch status until mental health can evaluate her."

The uniform led her back out into the larger room where someone had placed a mattress on the floor. The guard handed her a pillow and thin blanket. "You'll sleep out here tonight."

Did they think she was dangerous? That she might try to escape? What? The one thing that was crystal clear was that her jailers were not inclined to provide her with information beyond the basic. *"Sit here." "Wear these clothes." "Sleep there."*

She took the bedding and curled up on the mattress. The two uniforms talked in low tones that Sadie was too exhausted to interpret, and then one left while the other took up her position at the podium desk. "Just so you know," she said, "I'll be right here all night, and about every thirty minutes I'll be checking on you. Got that?"

Sadie rolled onto her side and pulled the blanket up so that it covered her face. From somewhere outside, she heard a train whistle and thought it must be the most forlorn sound she had ever heard. But she was so wrong

It wasn't the train whistle that made her long for her own bed. It was the slamming of all those doors as they'd led her through this place, especially the one heavy door just outside the room where she lay on a mattress that was nothing like her bed at home, under a blanket that had been through too many washings.

Chapter 17

Lars

In spite of the advice of Arlen Detlef and other leaders of the congregation that he hire a lawyer to defend Sadie, Lars was uncomfortable with the whole idea. But on Monday morning, Lars awakened well before dawn.

Emma was sleeping for once, and he was thankful for that. With the accident, preparing for the funeral, and now with Sadie being held in detention, neither of them had gotten much rest these last several days. He realized that for the foreseeable future, every new day was likely to arrive with a fresh set of challenges to be faced. The night before, he and Emma had come as close to a shouting match as they had ever come in all the years of their marriage.

Oh, they had disagreed in the past—even argued. But they had never lost their tempers with each other to the degree that they had flung angry words around like fists. They had never looked at each other with such repressed fury—such doubt. That had been the most painful blow of all. The way that Emma had looked at him, her mouth working but no words coming out, her eyes wide with distrust. "I'm going to bed," she had finally managed and had gone down the hall to the room they had shared for nearly twenty years, to the bed that she had declared on their wedding night should never be sullied by anger or ill will between them. Clearly time could change everything.

They had argued over the hiring of a lawyer. Emma wanted one, and Lars was not yet ready to give in to the ways of the outside system.

Why couldn't they talk to the judge? he had asked. They could go there with Arlen and others from the church and community and plead Sadie's case themselves. If the judge would only talk to Sadie, he would see for himself how filled she was with remorse and regret for her reckless act. And if he had children of his own, Lars continued, surely the judge would be sympathetic to the pain that Tessa's death had brought to both sides of the family.

"Besides," he'd reminded Emma, "Lieutenant Benson said the case was borderline, remember?"

"Well, Lieutenant Benson apparently has no say in that," Emma had replied. "You heard him, Lars—the state gets to decide these things."

"It is not our way to—" he had begun, but Emma had interrupted, her fists clenched at her sides, her voice tight, strangled with emotion.

"They don't care about our ways, Lars. They will do things *their* way. Sadie has violated *their* law. She is in their hands even as we speak. The news reports quote the attorney for the state as saying that too many teens are dying because other teens are not paying attention when they drive. He wants to make an example of our Sadie."

"Sadie is in God's hands," Lars had replied, and when Emma had rolled her eyes, looking more like Sadie than usual, he had felt his stomach lurch.

"And did you never hear that God helps those who help themselves?" She had practically spat the words at him, and there had been a terrible silence between them following that. Then Emma had touched his arm. "Lars, Arlen has given you the church's permission to hire a lawyer to defend our child. What more do you need?"

"Our ways do not allow for such—"

"Your ways? You mean Amish?" She looked down at her

hands and made an effort to relax them. She drew in a deep breath. "We are Mennonite, Lars. The children have been raised in that way, not your way."

"I realize that, but. . ."

"This is about what is best for Sadie—for our child—our Mennonite child. Pastor Detlef has given us the way we need to move forward. Will you do it for Sadie?"

As was so often the case for Lars, the world was moving far too fast for him to clearly comprehend what God's plan for him and his family might be. He hesitated, wanting so much to reassure Emma, to do what was best for his daughter, to salvage what he could from this horror for their family.

"I will pray on it," he had murmured.

And that was the moment when she had given him that look and announced that she was going to bed. Lars had watched her go. Torn between going after her and knowing that he had nothing more to offer her, he'd waited until the door at the end of the hall had quietly closed, and then he'd taken his Bible from its place on the bookcase by his chair and started to open it to the place where he had last left off reading.

But the book had slipped from his grasp, and rather than allow the precious volume to hit the floor, Lars had grabbed for it and found his thumb resting on the second chapter of Paul's letter to the Philippians. He started to read but stopped when he had reached only the second verse—the verse that read: "Fulfil ye my joy, that ye be likeminded, having the same love, being of one accord, of one mind."

He had looked up, removing his glasses as he stared down the dark hallway to the bedroom where a slim shaft of light peeked out from the bottom of the closed door. Emma was sure that hiring a lawyer was the right thing. She had all the proof she needed. Lars was certain of nothing, and yet the scripture counseled them to be of one mind—surely it was God's intent that they follow the will of the mind that had already resolved the question—in this case Emma's mind.

He had closed the Bible and placed it back on the shelf before turning out the lamp by his chair and then walking through the darkness toward that light. When he'd opened the door, Emma was in her nightgown and sitting on the side of the bed brushing out her hair. Hair that fell in rich auburn waves well past her waist. Hair that only he as her husband saw this way—wild and free.

He'd held out his arms to her, and she'd come to him. "I'm sorry," she'd whispered.

"I'll see to the lawyer first thing tomorrow," he had told her at the same moment.

And now morning had come—or nearly so.

Lars got up, dressed, and made his breakfast. He left coffee for Emma and set places for her and for Matt at the kitchen table. He wrote Emma a note and then he walked to town, leaving the car for Emma, and waited outside a storefront office door that read: Joseph P. Cotter, Attorney at Law, Specializing in Criminal Defense.

He had ample time to consider the small brick building that looked as if by mistake someone had plunked it down not twenty yards from the front lawn of the far more impressive courthouse. The building seemed solid enough and at the same time a little vulnerable. For reasons he couldn't understand, Lars found an element of comfort in that. He tried to imagine what Joseph Cotter himself might be like and envisioned a man, tall and slightly stooped by age, with white hair and alert blue eyes. Dressed in a suit that had cost far too much, he would wear a starched white shirt and a blue silk tie that matched his kind eyes.

"Excuse me," a male voice said, interrupting Lars's daydream. He turned and came face-to-face with a man of about thirty, dressed in a rumpled shirt and tan cotton slacks, with sandy hair that was thick and unruly. He had an apologetic smile, not at all in keeping with the mischievous dimple that punctured his left cheek, and his eyes were the color of coffee with cream. They looked sad and weary as if they had witnessed far too much pain and suffering.

Lars moved aside and watched as the young man produced a set of keys and began unlocking the door.

"Do you work here?" Lars asked. It was, of course, obvious that he did, no doubt a clerk or assistant to Attorney Cotter.

The younger man pointed toward the stenciled lettering on the window and grinned. "Yep. That's me all right." He chuckled and pushed the door open and flipped a switch. A ceiling fan started to slowly revolve. "Would you like to wait inside here? It's going to be a scorcher. I'd say the humidity reading is already somewhere around drenching."

He didn't wait for an answer but entered the office and kept talking. "I have one of those fancy new coffeemakers that makes a cup in a matter of seconds. Gift from the parents when I set up my practice."

He talked too fast and seemed to be in constant motion. He turned on the coffeemaker, opened an overstuffed briefcase, and removed a laptop computer, turned it on, and then set about rinsing out one of several mismatched coffee mugs, all the while continuing to talk about his family. Lars was drawn into the small, cluttered office in spite of his intention, now that he had actually seen Joseph Cotter, to look for Sadie's representation elsewhere.

"Just to make it official, I'm Joe Cotter." He extended his right hand.

"Lars Keller," Lars said, accepting the handshake.

"Mennonite, right?" Cotter was opening and closing a series of small drawers under the counter where the coffeemaker sat. "Thought I had some creamer here somewhere," he muttered. "Or Amish?"

"Both," Lars found himself admitting. "Born Amish. Married and converted to Mennonite." He could not think what it was about this vibrant young man that had him revealing personal details of his life, but he did not stop there. "My daughter, Sadie—perhaps you have heard of her case? She was arrested last week, and on Wednesday. . ."

He saw that he had Cotter's full attention now. "Auto accident last Thursday where another girl died?" He handed Lars a mug of steaming black coffee and then exchanged the small serving container for a fresh one before pushing a lighted button.

"You know the case, then?" Lars felt the easing of the tight lump that he'd carried in the center of his chest from the moment that he and Emma had first arrived at the scene of the accident.

Cotter picked up his coffee and took a sip. "In many ways, Sarasota is a small town, Mr. Keller, and a case like this? Well, it's unusual to say the least."

"My daughter needs a lawyer, Mr. Cotter."

"It's Joe or Joseph, okay? And there are far more experienced defense attorneys, sir."

Lars appreciated the young man's honesty, but he realized that Cotter had not said there were better lawyers—only more experienced ones. "I came here and waited for you."

Cotter grinned as he sipped his coffee again. "Well, I did set up shop in the very shadow of the courthouse, so I guess that old real estate adage is correct."

Lars had no idea what the young man was talking about.

"You know, the bit about location, location, location?"

"I have not heard this saying."

"So, let me be serious here. I could give you the names of some other lawyers to call," Cotter offered. "Of course, they tend to have full caseloads."

Lars considered the unorganized piles of paper and file folders that covered the desk where Joseph had placed his computer. He thought about the young man's age and warning that there were more experienced lawyers, but overriding all of that was a gut feeling that this was the man God wanted him to hire. This was the man who would ultimately bring Sadie home to them.

"So if I wait to see one of those more experienced lawyers, Joseph, I could be waiting far past the nine o'clock hour on Wednesday when my daughter will appear before the judge?"

Joseph shrugged.

"I don't know why you got to your office so early this morning, Joseph Cotter, but you did, and perhaps that is God's way of telling me that if you are willing to take Sadie's case, then I should hire you to represent her."

"Okay, let's get to work," Cotter said, lifting his coffee mug in a kind of toast. He set the mug down, hefted a pile of books from a straight-backed aluminum chair, and indicated that Lars should sit. Meanwhile he sat on the opposite side of the large wooden desk and rolled the black upholstered chair closer as he tapped the mouse on his computer, drained the last of his coffee, and glanced at the clock while he waited for the computer to warm up. "Wednesday at nine?"

"Ja. And our niece's funeral is this afternoon at three, and I was wondering—"

Joseph studied him for a long moment, his youthful features contracting as if he were uncertain of how best to convey all that he was feeling. "You want your daughter to be there. Let me talk to the powers that be and see what I can do, okay?" He picked up a pen and pulled a yellow notepad closer. "Okay, Mr. Keller, tell me what happened. Start from first thing the morning of the accident, and give me every detail."

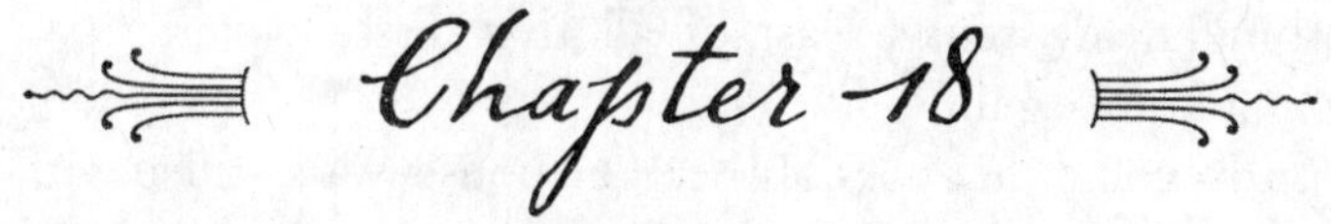

Chapter 18

Jeannie

She made her way moment by exhausting moment through the days and nights that marked the time from the moment the doctor had given them the news to the funeral that loomed over every minute of their lives. She observed the comings and goings of others as if she were watching a play or television show. She felt no connection to the activity that took place around her other than as a disinterested spectator. People gathered in her house, talking always in hushed tones but always turning the conversation to her well-being the minute she entered the room. Emma ran between the hospital, where Sadie had been kept overnight, and Jeannie's house, making sure everything was being taken care of. Geoff was gone for long hours at a time, and when he returned, his answer to her inquiry of where he had been was always the same.

"There are things that need to be done, Jeannie."

Lars had made the coffin in the shop where he normally crafted pieces of fine furniture. The workshop sat just outside the kitchen door of Emma's house. Tessa had loved to go there, loved the smell of the sawdust. Loved the fact that it was her uncle who created furniture designed specifically for the homes of the tourists who poured into Pinecraft during the winter months.

Jeannie had insisted on going to the funeral home with Geoff to see for herself that the staff there had dressed Tessa in the clothes Emma had convinced Jeannie to substitute for those she had originally chosen. She had stared down at her daughter, lying in the smooth pine box.

. . .laid Him in a manger. . . Random thoughts and bits of scripture memorized in childhood, apropos to nothing, flitted across Jeannie's mind from time to time. It was as if she were sleepwalking, her dreams surrounding her in no particular order. Nothing made sense, least of all that Tessa would never be coming home again.

How could that possibly be? The house was so filled with her essence. Her toothbrush lay on the side of the bathroom sink. In spite of the fact that Jeannie's parents and Geoff's mother took turns coming every day performing the usual household chores—making beds, dealing with the endless parade of food people brought, doing dishes, and so on—Jeannie insisted on doing some chores simply to keep herself occupied. In the kitchen she poured Geoff's coffee into the mug Tessa had decorated for him with the words WORLD'S GREATEST DAD, and then she reconsidered and poured the coffee into one of the regular cups from their set of dishes. She washed out the mug that Tessa had painted and placed it in the very back of the cabinet. But later that morning when she went to get something from Geoff's desk, the mug was there, half filled with coffee gone cold.

So many little reminders of her.

Outside were the orchids that Tessa had carefully planted in the trees. On the back screened porch were the shoes she wore to the bay to search for shells, and on the round glass table was the large Florida conch shell she had found only two weeks earlier. She'd spent hours soaking it in bleach and scraping off barnacles, then soaking it again to coax out the true sunset-orange color of the shell. She had been thrilled to find one so large and without flaws, especially one that held no living animal. Tessa would never take a live shell, and she had no problem reprimanding anyone who did.

Every room of the house that Jeannie and Geoff had bought

the year before she was born shouted Tessa's name. How odd was that given that Tessa herself had been such a calm and quiet child? A girl who much preferred the background, who liked observing others rather than being observed. Jeannie was the outgoing one. Jeannie and Sadie. . .

Sadie.

On the morning of the funeral, she overheard her mother and mother-in-law talking. Apparently Sadie had stayed only one night and most of the following day in the hospital, but late on Friday she'd been discharged and taken downtown to the Juvenile Assessment Center after she'd been arrested and charged. From there she had gone directly to a detention center. Surely, Jeannie thought, she had heard that wrong.

"Sadie's in jail?" she asked her mother.

"Oh honey, Emma didn't want to worry you with this."

"Is she or not?" Jeannie asked, her voice shaking.

"Yes," Geoff's mother said. "She's been charged with one count of vehicular homicide and one count of culpable negligence."

Jeannie's head started to spin. "But why?"

Geoff's mother looked at her as if she had just uttered a swear word. Her mother put her arm around her. "It's their way," she said softly. "When an accident like this one ends with someone dying, the authorities have to investigate, and in this case. . ."

"But Sadie? I could understand Dan being arrested, but—"

"Sadie was driving," Geoff's mother said as if stating a fact that everyone already knew.

"No. She couldn't have been." Jeannie turned to her mother-in-law. "Sadie only has a learner's permit, and Dan is only eighteen. Sadie knows full well that—"

"She was behind the wheel, Jeannie," her mother-in-law told her, her voice gentler now, as if realizing that she was breaking more bad news. "I thought you knew. I thought Geoff told you."

Jeannie shook her head. "I need to. . ." she mumbled without finishing the statement as she stumbled from the room and out onto the lanai.

Sadie was under arrest, charged with the ominous-sounding vehicular homicide. Her mother-in-law followed her. "You may as well know the whole story," she said.

"Yes, please," Jeannie agreed and nodded to her mother who had come to her rescue. "It's all right. I need to hear this," she said.

"According to reports in the paper and on television, the attorney for the state hopes to use the case to send a message about the rising fatality count among teenage drivers and their passengers," her mother-in-law said. "On Wednesday morning, Sadie will go before the judge for the first time. Until then she is being held in the juvenile detention center in Bradenton."

Jeannie could not begin to imagine how scared Sadie must be nor how worried Emma and Lars were. "But. . ."

Her mother-in-law patted her arm. "It will all work out, Jeannie. You needn't worry about it, especially not now. The courts will find the right way to handle this matter."

But Emma and Lars did not believe in the courts of the outside world. They did not vote or take part in the systems that governed the world they considered separate from their conservative faith. And yet she had nothing to offer them. It was everything she could do just to get out of bed in the mornings once she realized anew that this was day two—or three or five in this case—since Tessa had died.

"You should get dressed, Jeannie," her mother said. "We need to leave for the church in an hour."

So on that Monday afternoon—a day that by two o'clock had already seemed twice as long as any normal day—she and Geoff arrived at their church to receive mourners before the service. There was Sadie. She was dressed in a gray cotton skirt and a shapeless black sweater. She looked gaunt and hollow-eyed as she stood to one side of the room reserved for family to receive mourners before the service. Standing with her was a uniformed woman and, of course, Emma. Lars was there as well, standing with Matt, who looked lost in his too-big suit jacket bought larger so that it might last more than one season.

"He's growing so fast," Emma had sighed when the sisters had gone shopping for the suit at the Pinecraft thrift store.

Jeannie fastened her attention on Sadie—examining the

rush of feelings that swept through her upon seeing her niece for the first time since that horrible day. Her lively and vivacious niece, who could work a room full of people like any politician, now stood pressed against the wall, her shoulders hunched, her head bowed. In spite of her family around her, she looked so very alone. She looked the way Jeannie felt—as if the world had gone mad and she didn't know how to cope with that. Instinctively Jeannie's heart went out to her. She started toward her, but at that very moment, Geoff appeared at Jeannie's side and restrained her with a gentle touch. He took hold of her hand. "Honey, it's time."

Time. There was no time. Time had run out—for Tessa and now for Jeannie to cling to the hope that there had been some cruel mistake. The events of the last five days raced through her mind in fast-forward: breakfast. . .missing keys. . .the search. . .keys found. . .Tessa out the door with a blown kiss to meet Sadie. . .Jeannie more nervous about this first day of high school than her daughter was. . .Geoff out the door with a similar blown kiss and an umbrella for Tessa. . .Emma on the phone. . .a shout. . .the scream of car brakes. . .a dull thud. . .silence. . .

It occurred to Jeannie now that she had observed everything that happened after that in silence as if she were underwater. There were noises around her but none of them clear. Ambulance sirens, strangers huddled around Tessa, the ride to the hospital, the ER, the race to surgery, the interminable wait. . .

And here's where her recall of that day went from fast-forward to slow motion. Jeannie would never forget the way the doctor walked toward her. She relived every detail of his appearance in that moment. His surgical mask pulled down around his neck, his surgical cap and scrubs sweat-stained, his eyes refusing to meet hers or Geoff's, his long strides covering the distance. And the worst part was that she had known the minute he came through the door what he had come to tell them.

Leaning heavily now on Geoff as he led her into the sanctuary, she started to shake as she relived that moment that had changed their lives forever. Geoff wrapped one arm around her shoulders and pulled her close. So close that she could feel his warmth seeping into her suddenly cold limbs. His lips were so close to her temple that she could actually feel his breath.

She glanced up at him and saw that his jaw was set in that forward thrust that was so familiar to her. His eyes were blazing with the glitter of tears held at bay for far too long now. She grasped his free hand, offering him her warmth and strength in return. He looked down at her, and just as they took their seats in the front pew, his lower lip began to quiver.

The service seemed to go on for an eternity, but Jeannie did not want it to end, knowing what was yet to come. She tried to focus on the words of the minister—words about how death was no more than a passage to the other side, to heaven where Tessa, who had just a year earlier been baptized into the faith and accepted Christ as her Savior, would spend eternity. Words about how those present had best prepare themselves for the day when they would be called. Words about God's plan and how this was just a piece of that grander plan.

This? Jeannie felt like shouting. *This is my child, my only child, my baby, snatched from us before we had a chance to truly know her, before she had a chance to realize all that she could become, before. . .*

She knit her fingers together and then felt every fiber of her being tighten in unspoken protest to the outrage that her daughter was lying there before them in a wooden box. Try as she might, she could not open her heart to the idea that taking her child was something God needed to do for the greater good. She closed her eyes against the bile of anger that threatened to overcome her.

And then behind her, a throng of people rose as one and sang the words that had been a comfort to her all of her life.

Amazing grace, how sweet the sound
That saved a wretch like me.
I once was lost but now am found
Was blind but now I see.

Only Jeannie didn't see. She didn't understand this at all.

She looked sideways at Geoff. His lips were now so tightly pressed together that they had all but disappeared. His cheeks burned a bright red. He was sitting tall and straight, and his gaze was fixed on the wooden coffin that Lars had built especially for Tessa.

For Tessa. A box for Tessa.

Suddenly she imagined the coffin being placed in the ground, covered over with dirt, planted with grass and flowers. Tessa was in that box.

No. That was only the shell of her child. Tessa was in heaven. Tessa was with God. Tessa was not in pain or afraid or sick or frail. Tessa was safe and could never, ever be harmed again.

Jeannie clenched her fists and fought off the wave of nausea that threatened to send her stumbling up the aisle of the church to find a restroom.

The singing went on and on.

Please let this end, she prayed. But she knew in her heart that it was not going to end for them anytime soon. This was only the beginning. Tessa was gone. Sadie was under arrest. She heard a little cry of despair and realized it had come from her.

She felt Emma place a comforting hand on her shoulder. Emma and her family were seated in the pew immediately behind Geoff and Jeannie. Jeannie wondered why they weren't there beside them in the front pew. Tessa had been like another daughter to Emma, as Sadie was to Jeannie. But the grandparents were sitting with them in that front pew—three gray-haired people who had adored this child as Jeannie had. Her parents next to her and Geoff's mother next to him.

She glanced at Geoff. He returned her look with unseeing eyes then turned back to stare at the coffin. He would keep his vigil over Tessa until they lowered her into the ground. The night before, Jeannie had wakened to find Geoff gone. A note on the kitchen table read, *Someone should be with her.*

The words had hit her as an accusation. And as she had failed to keep her daughter safe, she had failed to be there to comfort her husband as he sat alone with their child—their only child.

Chapter 19

Geoff

At the cemetery, Geoff found himself fixated on Sadie. She looked different—more like Emma. Odd, when she had always reminded everyone so much of Jeannie. Tessa was the one who favored Emma. That was Tessa's role—not Sadie's. The thought irritated him, as did the way Sadie was dressed.

She wore the traditional garb of a conservative Mennonite—her skirt down to her ankles, her sleeves to her wrists, her hair wound into a tight, smooth bun under her prayer covering. Sadie had never worn the traditional white prayer cap before that Geoff could recall. She always opted for the black lace doilylike covering because it was less obvious, especially against her dark hair.

He shifted slightly, determined to see Sadie's shoes. Shoes were Sadie's passion—as they were Jeannie's. How many times had they laughed about Sadie in her somber Mennonite garb parading around in Jeannie's high heels? But not today. Today she wore plain black shoes.

Geoff looked at his niece again. From head to toe she was the picture of a devout conservative Mennonite. Was this contrition? Atonement? A ploy to fool others into having sympathy for her? Had Emma and Lars insisted? Or maybe the lawyer they'd hired? And to what end?

Sadie reverting to the traditions of her conservative faith would not bring Tessa back—would not undo what Sadie in her reckless, carefree way had caused. Suddenly Geoff saw the future clearly. He and Jeannie alone—their beloved child ripped from them without any chance to know her potential, to give to the world the gifts she had given them from the day she was born. And Emma and Lars shepherding Sadie through this, sharing the pain and agony of whatever sentence the court might impose, until one day they could wake up and think of Tessa only in passing while they went on with their lives.

He saw his nephew Matt watching him, his puppy-dog eyes large and soulful. Matt had always turned to Geoff whenever life became too much of a challenge. The boy loved his parents but he had built a bond with Geoff that went beyond games won and lost. More than once Geoff had taken Matt's side when Emma worried that playing team sports was too much of a physical danger for the boy. More than once he had listened as the boy agonized over his slim build and small size. "You'll grow," Geoff had assured him. "Just take a look at your mom and dad—both tall and athletic in build. Genes don't lie."

"And then there's Auntie Jeannie," Matt had said with a roll of his eyes. "What if I got those genes?"

It was true. Jeannie was petite and small-boned, almost fragile-looking. It was another of the things that had attracted Geoff to her when they first met. She looked like a porcelain doll with her fair complexion and unreal crown of curly red hair. But he had soon learned that she was anything but petite in personality and anything but fragile in the way she took on the challenges that came her way.

Until now. . .

He had never seen Jeannie so lost. For the last five days while they waited for family and friends from out of town to gather, while they endured day after day of people occupying their house and filling it with their whispered conversations and too much food, she had wandered through her days in a kind of stupor, her facial expression either one of permanent disbelief or unrelenting grief. In spite of the fact that his mom and hers showed up every morning ready to take over the day's mundane chores, Jeannie went through the motions of her routine at home—making beds, preparing meals from the endless parade of covered dishes. She'd even done the laundry. He had found her slumped to the floor of their room next to the bed, her fingers clutching a red sweater of Tessa's that had gotten mixed in with the whites and turned everything pink. He'd known she wasn't crying over the stained laundry, but it had shocked him when she had looked up at him, tears running down both cheeks, as she held up the sweater and said, "It shrunk. It's ruined, and it's her favorite."

Now, after a ride that he could barely remember from the church to the cemetery, he instinctively reached for Jeannie's hand. They were standing next to their child's open grave and waiting for the inevitable conclusion to the service, and for the first time he realized that it was raining, a light misting rain—gentle like Tessa. The sun was out, and somewhere he knew there would be a rainbow. Someone was shielding them with a large black umbrella, and all around them people had opened umbrellas of their own or taken cover under the umbrella-like foliage of an oversized saw palmetto tree.

He had a memory of the umbrella he'd been trying to open to shelter Tessa that morning. He saw her face, her smile, her eyes so alive and mischievous. Inside it felt as if his heart were cracking open.

Their minister had finally come to the end of his part of the service. The casket was lowered into the muddy hole, rivulets of water staining the wood. Tessa's classmates and friends from church filed slowly past the open hole. Several of them carried flowers that they tossed into the grave. Then Zeke, who had been one of the pallbearers, took Geoff's arm and led him to the mound of dirt next to the grave.

He handed Geoff a long-handled shovel. Geoff knew what he was supposed to do. He was supposed to place the first shovelful into the hole—the first step toward filling it—a step that the others would take as part of the ritual before the cemetery staff completed the work. He looked up and saw Sadie, her face buried in her father's shoulder, her thin body shaking.

Geoff fought against the temptation to go to her, drag her over to the grave, place the shovel in her hands, and insist that she—not he—be the first to bury Tessa. He wanted her to see what she had caused.

"You can do it," Zeke said softly, and for one incredible moment, Geoff thought that his friend might be giving him permission to play out his fantasy. But then he glanced around, saw all the expectant faces—some of them perhaps wondering if he would fail in this last duty to his child as he had failed to protect her that day when he stood by and watched helplessly as the car rammed into her and crushed her internally without so much as a scratch on her.

He thrust the tip of the shovel into the pile of damp earth and pushed it to its full depth with one foot. Then he swung around and dropped the load into the hole, closing his ears and mind to the plop of packed clods of gritty dirt onto the wooden box.

Zeke reached for the shovel, but Geoff held on. He loaded it a second time and then a third and then twice more before Zeke wrestled it from him and passed it to Lars. Then Zeke wrapped his arms around Geoff and held him upright as the two of them staggered back to where Jeannie was waiting.

She held her arms out to him, and he realized that he was sobbing uncontrollably—the first time he had cried since that terrible moment when the doctor had walked into the waiting room and the truth of what he was about to tell them had struck them all like a punch to the stomach.

"Somebody is going to pay for this," he gasped as Jeannie and Zeke walked him back to the chairs under the tent provided for the grieving family.

"Shhh," Jeannie whispered, and he could not help wondering if she meant to soothe him or to protect her sister and niece from overhearing.

Chapter 20

Emma

Emma was beginning to accept the fact that Jeannie was avoiding her. Over all of the time that had led up to the funeral, the sisters had been in the same place—the hospital, Jeannie's house, the church, the cemetery. They had often sat or stood within inches of each other. And yet there had been an emotional distance between them brought on by Emma's worry over Sadie and no doubt Jeannie's own dilemma of whether she should pity Sadie or blame her.

So as the days after the funeral passed with no call or contact, she tried on one level to understand her sister's reluctance to spend time with her. But on another it made no sense. The two of them had always been each other's rock when it came to getting through tough times. They were certainly no strangers to tragedy.

Their eldest brother had drowned when the girls were only six and eight. Their mother had battled cancer, and while she had won that fight in the end, for years it had fallen to the sisters to care for their father and siblings while their mother went through operations and rounds of chemotherapy that left her weak and unable to manage the routine of a large family. Through it all, Emma and Jeannie had turned to each other, sharing in the chores even as they shared their grief and worry.

So how was this different? They were both hurting. She thought of how terrified they had been at the arraignment when Joseph Cotter had told them that the state's attorney had actually considered moving the case to adult court. Under other circumstances, Jeannie would understand how frightened Emma had been. She would listen and console and reassure. That was what the two of them had always done for each other.

But as the days following the funeral passed without any contact with Jeannie, Emma began to worry. She moved through the regimen of household chores, getting back to the volunteer work that came as regular as the turning of the calendar—and through it all she sorted through the possibilities. How to make things right again? She came up empty every time.

With the funeral behind them and the counsel of Pastor Detlef as well as Jeannie's minister to try and return to some semblance of a normal routine, Emma had made the first move. She had decided to call Jeannie as she had always done first thing every morning. But she had gotten no answer. Seriously worried, she had ridden the family's three-wheel bike to Jeannie's house and found Geoff painting the garage door. He was dressed in a shirt and tie, and she assumed he was on his way to work. It seemed odd that he had stopped to paint the garage door, but then Emma had come to understand all too well that a person had to find his own way through the pain of grief.

"Is Jeannie inside?"

Geoff's hand had paused midstroke, but he had not turned to look at her. "Go home, Emma. She needs some time—we both do." He started painting again, drawing wide strokes across the surface of the garage door.

"But it's just me. I mean, I know there have been a lot of people. . ."

"Go home and leave us in peace," Geoff said, and although she could not see his face, the tightness of his voice told her that the words had been uttered through clenched teeth.

Emma stared at the kitchen window, trying to decide what to do. If their situations were reversed and Lars told Jeannie to leave, her sister would ignore him and march herself right up to the house. But Emma wasn't Jeannie, and as much as she wanted to go to her sister, she could not help but respect Geoff's pain. She understood how difficult it must be for him especially to distinguish between Emma, the sister of his wife, and Emma, the mother of the girl who had caused the death of his only child.

She got back on the tricycle. "Tell Jeannie that I'll keep calling, and when she's. . ."

Geoff laid the paintbrush carefully on the open can of paint and walked into the house, closing the door behind him with a finality that made Emma's heart thunder with fear for what the future might hold for all of them.

She turned the tricycle around and started slowly back toward Pinecraft, hoping with every push of the pedals that she would hear footsteps running behind her and that Jeannie would call out to her.

"I should have just gone inside," she had told Lars. "Jeannie would have. You know she would."

"Perhaps," Lars said. "Perhaps Geoff is speaking for her. Give her a few days at least, Emmie. This is uncharted territory—for all of us."

Emma had to agree. "Is Matt coming straight home?" Ever since Sadie's arrest, Emma had noticed a need to have her son close, to know that he was in his room or out in the workshop—not out in the world where he might get into a situation he couldn't handle—as Sadie had.

"He said he was going over to the academy to watch football practice." Lars cleaned some wood stain off his fingers. "Geoff's gone back to work then?"

Emma shrugged. "Looked that way. He was dressed for it."

"It might be the best thing for him. Get his mind onto other things at least for part of the day."

"And Jeannie? She'll be totally alone."

Lars frowned.

"What is it?"

"Look, I know how worried you are about Jeannie and Geoff, but, Em, our focus has to be on Sadie—on how we're going to help her find her way through this."

Emma felt a wave of irritation. Didn't Lars think she was as worried about Sadie as she was about Jeannie? Didn't he know that she lay awake at night trying not to imagine how confused and frightened their daughter must be—alone in a strange place with girls who, by some reports, were capable of violent attacks for no reason?

Everything was spinning out of control, and she felt so helpless. Her role had always been the strong one—the one everyone could turn to in times of crisis. Well, she was failing miserably now.

"I'm doing my best," she whispered, ignoring that Lars had reached out to her as she walked quickly back to the house.

Supper that night was a strained affair. Only Matt behaved as if nothing were amiss.

"How did the team look?" Lars asked after a prolonged silence had engulfed the family.

Matt shrugged. "With Dan Kline not playing, they've got problems."

"Don't talk with your mouth full," Emma snapped irritably, annoyed that Dan's name should ever be heard again under their roof. She glanced at Lars, who was looking at her with concern.

No, I am not all right, she wanted to say in response to his unasked question. *I have this horrible feeling that somehow we are waiting for another shoe to fall.*

"Excuse me," Emma murmured instead as she stood up and fled down the hall to the bedroom.

It took Lars less than a minute to follow her. He closed the door and sat down on the side of their bed next to where she had curled onto her side facing the wall. "I don't know what to do," she said. "I don't know how to help—either of them—Jeannie or Sadie." She gulped back the lump that seemed to have permanently taken up residence in her throat. "I have prayed and prayed for guidance, but I am so lost, Lars, and my greatest fear is that we are all lost."

She felt the mattress give as he lay down next to her, spooning himself to her back and wrapping his arms around her. He started to say something and then swallowed back the words. This was his way. He would not speak until he was certain that what he had to offer would make a difference.

"I spoke with Joseph today," he said after a moment. "I wanted to have a better understanding of what may come of this."

"And?" Every muscle in Emma's body went still and stiff.

"There's a strong likelihood that she will receive detention."

"She's in detention now," Emma argued.

"We're talking months—perhaps even a year or more," Lars said after a long silence in which she knew he was struggling to find the words that would cause her the least pain.

She pulled free of his grasp and turned to face him. "No. It was an accident. She didn't mean. . ."

"There are laws. . ."

"Their laws, not ours. Their justice, not ours."

"You've said it yourself, Em. We live in their world at times like these. And we need to prepare Sadie for what she may have to endure."

"Maybe we should consider some of those counseling services the intake worker from the probation department suggested."

Lars shook his head. "Joseph advises against that at least for now. Accepting such services could be viewed as an admission of guilt."

They stared at each other. *She is guilty*, Emma almost said. But they had already had that conversation. When Lars had hired Joseph, he insisted that Sadie must tell the truth about what had happened. "That is our way," he'd told the young lawyer.

"That is my way as well," Joseph had assured Lars, "and I would not expect her to do otherwise. But telling the truth about what happened that morning and pleading guilty to vehicular homicide are two entirely different matters. I'm asking you to trust me."

"Joseph believes that he can get the charge reduced to just 'culpable negligence,' " Lars told Emma.

"I don't understand these terms. Sadie certainly didn't mean to. . ."

"According to Joseph, the prosecution doesn't have to show intent—that she meant to do harm—just that she was driving in such a way that harm could be the result."

Emma's head was spinning with all this legal jargon. "Then explain to me why Dan. . . I mean, what about him and his responsibility in this?"

"We must let his parents deal with that. We will pray for him, of course, but Sadie—"

"Is a child. Surely that will count for a great deal."

Lars frowned, and she knew that she had not heard the worst of it. "What else?" she demanded, half sitting up.

He swallowed once, twice, and then simply stared at her as if trying to decide something.

"Tell me," she growled.

"If I understood what Joseph was saying, if the court agrees with the state, there is a good possibility that she could be sent somewhere across the state."

After her arraignment, Sadie had been taken back to the detention center in nearby Bradenton. She was to be held there while the lawyers built their cases—one for her and one against. Joseph had told them they'd be back in court in just three weeks. He'd made it sound like nothing, but three weeks without their Sadie at home and without the ability to see or talk with her whenever they chose seemed an eternity.

It was a short drive for them to visit her, but the visits were already so limited. Only on certain days and for certain times. If they moved her somewhere far away. . .

Emma began to shake, spasms that jerked her whole body and flung her head from side to side as the lump that had been in her throat ballooned in her chest. Lars pushed himself to a sitting position against the head of the bed and pulled her against him. "We will get through this, Emma," he promised, but the way his voice shook, she understood that he was no surer of such a thing than she was.

And lying there against him, she closed her eyes and gave herself up to the only One who could save their daughter. She prayed to God that somehow He would save Sadie, and them.

Chapter 21

Jeannie

Three weeks after Tessa's death, Jeannie left her house and started her morning run. The bay near the botanical gardens had become Jeannie's refuge. For reasons she didn't quite understand, it was the place where she felt closest to Tessa, so she marked the passing of the days and weeks since her death by going there. Each morning she crawled out of bed before dawn, pulled on sweats, and jogged the five miles from their home near Pinecraft, down Bahia Vista across Highway 41 to Orange Avenue and then around the corner to the place where the road curved near the botanical gardens and the exposed mud flats of the bay stretched out before her.

Depending on the timing of the tides, she could walk on the hard-packed sand all the way out to the point where the mussel beds had formed without ever stepping in water higher than her ankles. Even when the tides weren't with her, she would roll up her sweatpants, anchoring them above her knees. The clusters of shells were razor sharp, but the old pair of running shoes protected her feet as she picked her way carefully over the clumps. This was where Tessa had found her prized Florida conch shell—the one that sat in the center of the glass-topped table that dominated the screened porch at the back of their house. The lanai was where the three of them had so often gathered for supper on balmy nights. The place where she and Emma and Sadie and Tessa had played board games on hot summer afternoons once they had finished their chores and errands and volunteer work.

Jeannie walked on tiptoe across the flats, changing course when her foot sank suddenly into a pocket of soft, mushy sand. Houseboats and sailing boats with their dinghies attached bobbed in the bay, their rigging clanking softly against the metal mast poles like wind chimes. A blue heron scolded her for invading its territory and then lost interest as it speared a small fish and swallowed it down.

Breakfast, Jeannie thought. She had forgotten to set the timer for the coffee. Geoff would be annoyed. But then he often seemed either annoyed with or indifferent to her these days. At a time when the two of them should have drawn closer, they were drifting further and further apart.

Once Geoff started back to work, his entire morning routine had changed. No longer did he come to the table for his usual bagel, fruit, and coffee. Instead, he filled a stainless steel travel mug with black coffee and headed out.

Unable to face eating alone in that big, empty house, Jeannie had begun her routine of running every morning. But she had continued to set the timer for Geoff's coffee. He counted on that coffee being there.

"Too bad, so sad," Jeannie remembered Sadie commenting once.

Sadie.

Her beloved niece was being held in juvenile detention, awaiting the hearing—or adjudication, as the newspaper had reported—of her case. According to a voice message that Geoff's sister had left for Jeannie, she'd been fingerprinted and photographed like "any common criminal." Geoff's sister had reported this in a tone that indicated that the news should come as some sort of solace to Jeannie and Geoff. "Maybe there will be some justice for Tessa after all," she had concluded.

But that kind of justice—that eye-for-an-eye vengeance—was not what Jeannie had been raised to believe in. In the faith of generations of her family, finding true justice was about finding the path to forgiveness. And yet she and Geoff had lost their only child. No one involved had meant for that to happen, yet it had, and try as she might, Jeannie could not yet find it in her heart to forgive an act of such pure irresponsibility and selfishness. And neither could Geoff.

From the moment they left the cemetery, she had watched him close himself off more and more. At the house, filled with mourners wanting only to offer support and comfort, Geoff had said something about needing some time and disappeared. People had come and gone all through the long afternoon and well into the evening, but Geoff had stayed away. Jeannie had assured everyone that he would be back any moment, but hours had passed without a sign of him.

It was Zeke who had gone in search of him and finally located him, sitting alone in the bleachers of the athletic field at the school. Using the battered pay phone mounted on the back of the shuttered concession stand, Zeke had called the house to assure Jeannie that Geoff was unharmed.

"He needs some time is all."

The idea of needing time had become the anthem of the entire horrible and unthinkable event. What good was time going to do? Time certainly would not bring Tessa back. Time stretched out in front of them like a life sentence—life without parole. Life without Tessa.

And yet Jeannie was as guilty of using the excuse as anyone. She had heard Geoff send Emma away a few days after the funeral, telling her that Jeannie needed some time. She had avoided answering the door after Geoff returned to work, knowing it was some kind neighbor or fellow church member come to drop off a potted plant or covered dish. She had willingly allowed Geoff to steer her away from Sadie at the funeral, and later as she watched the uniformed guard escort Sadie from the cemetery, she had told herself that right now she needed to focus on Geoff—his needs, his pain.

They needed time.

But time was not working in their favor. The more time that passed, the wider the gap seemed to grow between Geoff and her. Each night he isolated himself in his den, citing the need to catch up on administrative reports or reviewing game tapes of the next football opponent and then coming to bed well after midnight. Even in the days between the funeral and his return to work, he had filled the hours with chores—repairing a shelf in the laundry room, resurfacing the driveway, trimming the shrubs that divided their house from the neighbor's.

They had taken to having their dinner—a meal that Jeannie created from the overflowing larder of food left by others—in front of the television. It had started a few nights after the funeral—after others had stopped filling the house with their whispers and covered dishes. Geoff had been watching the news, and Jeannie had called out that dinner was ready.

"I'll take mine in here," Geoff had called back. "There's a story coming up that I want to see."

Jeannie had prepared him a plate and then one for herself, and they had sat staring wordlessly at the television as they ate.

Now it had been nearly a month since they had sat down for a meal together at their kitchen table. Just yesterday she had put the placemats and cloth napkins in the laundry, and once they were dry, she had put them away in a drawer instead of back on the table. Every action or inaction like that one felt like one step closer to giving up on ever being able to make a life together without Tessa.

"Hey there, pretty lady," a voice called, and Jeannie turned to see Zeke coming toward her in a barnacle-covered dingy powered by a trolling motor. "I brought you something."

He cut the motor and beached the boat, then climbed out and dragged it onto higher ground. He wore ragged jeans rolled to midcalf, a faded T-shirt, and an old baseball cap. He was barefoot and had tied his long black hair back into a ponytail. He greeted her with the kind of sad, how-you-holding-up? smile that Jeannie had come to expect whenever she ran into anyone she knew these days.

"Close your eyes," he said, "and hold out your hands."

It was such an incredibly normal request that Jeannie allowed herself to let go of all the *should's* and *ought to's* of how she was supposed to be feeling and did as he asked.

He laid something in her hands. Small and slender, hard but also, she realized, a little fragile.

"Angel wings," he said softly as she opened her eyes and saw a petite matched pair of pure white ruffled seashells that carried the name so fitting to them.

"Oh Zeke, they're smaller than any I've ever seen and so perfect. Where did you find them?"

He shrugged. "Coming down the creek. They were covered over pretty good, but there's no mistaking that pure white color."

Jeannie ran her finger over the ridges of the shells. Surely this was a sign, a prayer answered. It was unusual enough to find a half of the bivalve. To find a matched pair was rare indeed. "Thank you, Zeke."

"No wor. . ." Zeke's tanned face turned a deeper shade of burnished red. "Sorry," he mumbled.

"No worries," she said. "It's okay, Zeke. I know what you mean."

Most of the time a gesture like this would bring tears to her eyes, but what she felt now was something different. The gift had given her a feeling that had been absent for days now. The perfection of the matched shells gave her a glimmer of hope.

"Would you like to go for a cup of coffee?" she asked Zeke and realized it was the first effort she had made since the funeral to reach out to someone other than Geoff.

Zeke studied her sweats and frowned. "You didn't bring any money, did you?"

He was right, and it was her turn to blush. "You could come to the house. The pot's all set. I just need to turn it on."

Zeke grinned. "You wouldn't have any of those cinnamon rolls you make, would you?"

"Not that I made, but certainly plenty made by some of the best cooks in Pinecraft."

"Emma?"

With one word he had changed the lighter mood he was working so hard to establish. But then that was Zeke's way. Just when she thought she had him figured out, he would surprise her by changing course.

"How is she?" Jeannie asked, knowing that Zeke wouldn't judge her for not knowing the answer herself.

"Sadie's in detention. They dodged a bullet when the state's attorney decided against taking the case into adult court, but the kid's still locked up."

He took Jeannie's elbow as she climbed into the dingy, then pushed the small craft into deeper water before getting in and pulling the cord to start the motor.

"And Dan Kline?"

Zeke shrugged. "His parents know people—you know how that works. He got ticketed and his license was suspended. Then he was sent home, but then I imagine Geoff already told you that."

"Not really," she murmured, thinking about how little she and Geoff shared.

Zeke frowned but made no comment. "You should call Emma."

"I know." But she couldn't bring herself to promise that she would. Besides, there were circumstances beyond what Zeke or others might think that kept her from reconnecting with her sister. As Geoff had reminded her on more than one occasion, things had changed. She still woke up every morning thinking that if she hadn't taken Sadie for her learner's permit, none of this would have happened. Then just as quickly she would repress that thought, unwilling to pile guilt on top of the already staggering load of her grief.

Emma had left numerous phone messages—none of which Jeannie had responded to, all of which she had saved. One morning her sister had even taped a note to their back door. Jeannie had found it when she came back from her run. "I'm here," it had read. "Call when you can."

Jeannie cradled the angel wings in one palm, fingering them as Zeke navigated around the sandbars of the bay. It was an unusual day for September—cooler and less humid. A perfect day for a boat ride. Jeannie was so very tired of the pain and the sadness and the pressing stone of loss she carried with her every minute of every hour. She leaned back and closed her eyes as

Zeke guided the boat up the channel to the creek that wound its way to Pinecraft.

"So, about Emma—you'll call her?" Zeke pressed.

"Can we just talk about something else—just for now?"

"Why talk at all?"

Jeannie gave him a half smile. "Sometimes it helps to remind myself that the rest of the world has moved on even though our world. . ."

"Oh, you want normal, do you? Right. Well, the fruit co-op is booming. Hard to keep up with everything, and here we are on the brink of a new growing season. First calls are starting to come in from folks wanting to schedule the volunteers to come pick fruit from their yards."

It had been a little over a year since Hester and others had organized volunteers from the Mennonite community to offer a service of collecting fruit from the yards of private citizens requesting the service. The fruit was then delivered to a packing house on the property that Zeke's brother, Malcolm, had purchased and set up as a foundation for the project. There Zeke and others from the community who were homeless or preferred a more unorthodox lifestyle came to sort and box the fruit and deliver it to the various food pantries in the area.

The project mirrored the work of similar co-ops operating as far west as California and as nearby as Tampa. But the Pinecraft co-op also offered Emma's strawberry jam as well as homemade orange marmalade and pies for sale at local farmers' markets. "Like I said, it's starting to get busy, and we could use some help. Might be good for you to come on back, as well. I mean, now that Geoff's gone back to work and all."

Jeannie and Emma and their daughters had volunteered regularly at the co-op from the day it first opened. Sadie had been a wonder at getting local publicity for the project, and Jeannie's phone had rung constantly with homeowners wanting to schedule a pickup of fruit from their yards. Tessa had been responsible for setting up a schedule that kept everything running smoothly.

Lars used to call them "the Fruit Loops" with that dry sense of humor that was his trademark. How Geoff had laughed at that. He and Matt had picked up on the tag and even made up a song about it.

They had laughed together so often through the years. Jeannie could not imagine laughing over such silliness ever again.

"I'll tie up at the park, and we can walk from there to your house, okay?"

"Sure." Leaving the boat at the park meant walking through Pinecraft to reach her house, which could mean crossing paths with Emma. Jeannie mentally ran through her sister's routine. It was Thursday. On Thursday she joined other women for the weekly cleaning of the church.

"Emma's in court today," Zeke said, reading her mind. "No worries."

But Jeannie did not miss the hint of sarcasm with which he delivered his trademark phrase, and for the rest of the trip, he said nothing more.

Chapter 22

Emma

On the day that Sadie's hearing was to begin—and possibly end—Lars and Emma arrived at the courthouse early. They parked in back and then walked past Joseph Cotter's small office, peering in the window to see if the young lawyer was inside.

"He's probably already left for court," Lars said.

Inside the courthouse lobby, they endured the curious glances of the uniformed staff as they went through the security checkpoint and then took the stairs to the third floor as instructed.

"This way," Lars said, pausing a minute to check room numbers. The corridor was carpeted and there were chairs and benches outside the closed doors that lined the wall opposite a wall of windows. "This one," he said, stopping at one of the doors and then trying the knob. It was not the courtroom where the arraignment had taken place. That courtroom was two doors down the hall. *So many courtrooms*, Emma found herself thinking, and she couldn't help but think that if the system needed more than one courtroom to handle all of the problems coming before the judges, then perhaps the world had far bigger problems than she'd ever imagined.

The door was locked. Through narrow glass windows to either side, Emma could see that the room was identical to the one they had been in three weeks earlier. Chairs like those she and Lars had sat in when Sadie was arraigned were lined up to either side of a center aisle and were separated from the area where the court's business would take place by a low polished wooden wall.

"We're too early," she said and took a seat on one of the benches positioned so that she could continue to monitor the activity in the courtroom. She tried to imagine Sadie riding in the locked van from the detention center in Bradenton. Would she be with other teens or alone? Emma hoped that she was alone, although what did it matter?

"It's not so bad," Sadie had told them every time they visited her. "They keep us busy from the time we get up until we go to bed, so the time passes."

"How's school?" Lars asked her every time, his repetition of the same question only emphasizing the fact that there were topics they would not raise and there was little else to talk about.

Sadie had smiled wistfully. "It reminds me of the Mennonite school. Every girl has her own work to do. You know there are all ages in here. The youngest is only ten," she whispered.

Ten years old, Emma thought as she watched Lars pace down to the elevator where he stood reading some sign. *What could a ten-year-old possibly do that would result in her being locked up?*

A woman dressed in tan slacks, a white shirt, and a brown leather jacket took a seat on the next bench over. Emma glanced at her, but the woman paid no mind. A few minutes later, an older African-American woman came down the hall from the direction of the elevator and joined the first woman.

"I can't have her moving back home," the older woman said. The first woman nodded. "I have the other children I have to consider. Last time she was sent home she got so mad she threw the television across the room. Smashed it to smithereens."

The other woman made a noise of sympathetic understanding, and Emma shuddered. Was this girl being held in the same place Sadie was? She prayed not and then prayed for forgiveness for eavesdropping, but as Lars continued pacing the corridor, she found herself leaning closer to listen to the two women.

"She lied to my face," the younger woman said. "We have the whole thing on video. She knew we did, and yet when I asked her if she hit that girl, she said no."

The woman that Emma had decided was the mother of the girl in question sighed wearily. "She does that all the time—lives in a world of her own, that one. Her mother was the same."

So, she's the grandmother, Emma thought. *So young.*

There was a moment's pause, and then the woman in the leather jacket said, "So you're on board with our sending her away?"

The grandmother nodded. "I don't see any other solution. You've tried everything possible—counseling, medication. None of it works. Maybe if she realizes she's not getting out for a good long time, she'll change."

Emma was incensed. How could any mother—or grandmother for that matter—just give up on a child the way this woman seemed to be doing?

"She's a very angry girl," the younger woman agreed.

Then help her, Emma wanted to tell them. *Hold her. Pray with her. Anything but give up.*

"She doesn't believe for a minute that she's going away," the grandmother said.

Why should she? It's unimaginable that a child. . .

Lars had stopped pacing and had come to sit beside her. He was looking at her with a worried frown. "Emmie? Are you all right?"

"Yes," she lied and immediately sent up a silent prayer for God to forgive her. "No. What if they send Sadie so far away that. . . ?" she whispered.

"One step at a time," Lars said, his voice tight. "You know what Joseph told us. Today the state will present its case, and then Joseph will tell Sadie's side of things. Remember, he said that it's unlikely the judge will decide today."

"And she'll have to go back to that place?"

"Joseph is going to try to argue for her to be released to us. He seems to think that he has a pretty good chance of getting that."

There was a rustling of clothing on the bench next to them as the two women got up and entered the now-open courtroom. Lars and Emma followed them, taking seats in the front row behind what they had learned at the arraignment was the defense table. The other two women sat across the aisle from them, and gradually the chairs behind them filled in with people who had business with the court.

In front of the low banister that separated them from the officials who would soon fill that area, Emma saw the state's attorney talking to his assistant. His last name was Johnson, she recalled. When it was time to begin, the judge would enter the courtroom from a side door behind the high counter where he sat. For now, in addition to Mr. Johnson, she counted the bailiff, the clerk responsible for recording the proceedings, and a couple of uniformed people she had seen when Sadie was arraigned. There was no jury for a juvenile case and no sign of the young man Lars had hired to defend Sadie.

"Joseph is late," Emma whispered then turned when she heard the door to the hallway open and close. A man and a woman entered the courtroom. They glanced briefly at Emma and Lars and then took a seat across the aisle and behind them.

"Dan's parents," Emma murmured, nudging Lars. "Why would they be here?"

Lars shook his head. "Don't know, but here comes Joseph."

The young attorney, looking not quite put together, entered the courtroom from a side door and nodded at them as he placed his brief case on the defense table and then turned to greet the state's attorney.

Emma laced her fingers tightly together as she watched the two men converse. They were both smiling at first, but then she saw how Joseph started to frown and shake his head. The state's attorney moved a step closer to Joseph to make his point. Both men seemed agitated—that could not be good for Sadie.

"Lars," she whispered and almost added, "do something." But what could he do? They had already tried everything they could think of. At Sadie's arraignment, Pastor Detlef and other leaders of the church had sat with them, and Joseph had assured them that the judge had taken note of this.

Even so, she had never felt so powerless. Her unrelenting prayers for God to show Sadie mercy seemed to fall on deaf ears, and yet she knew that there was some plan in all of this. Tessa's death, Sadie's arrest, the destruction of two families that had been so close. What could possibly be accomplished by such tragedies? And why one piled on top of another this way?

Just last night she and Lars had tried to answer Matt's questions—impossible questions about why God would test them this way. At least that was the explanation that Emma had come up with for herself. This was all a test—like Job's faith being tested over and over again. "This is our Job moment," she had told Matt.

Matt had given her a look of pity and frustration. "I have homework," he'd said quietly and gone to his room.

Earlier that morning, he had come to the breakfast table, gobbled down his food without a word, and then headed out the door.

"Do you want me to tell Sadie anything for you?" Emma had asked.

Matt had hesitated but not turned around. "Tell her that. . . ," he began, but then he shook his head and left, closing the back door softly behind him.

Emma had gone after him, but by the time she reached the door, he had already mounted his bike and taken off for school. "Matt," she had called.

"I'll be late," he shouted back as he turned a corner and rode out of sight.

She shook off the memory as a side door opened and a female guard escorted Sadie into the courtroom. She wore the faded blue jumpsuit and shackles on her ankles. Her hair was down and fell across her face as the guard led her to the defense table.

Sadie nervously tucked her hair behind her ear, and Emma sucked in a breath when she saw that Sadie's cheek was bruised and she had a fresh cut over one eye. It took a moment for Emma to realize that Lars had gotten up out of his seat and moved to the railing. The bailiff started toward him just as Sadie said, "I'm okay, Dad. It's okay."

"Sir, please take your seat, or I'll have to ask you to leave," the bailiff instructed.

"Give us a minute," Joseph said. The bailiff nodded. Joseph opened the swinging gate and took Lars's arm as he escorted him back to his seat. The attorney sat in a chair next to Emma. "They tried calling you, and when they didn't reach you, they called me. Sadie was attacked late yesterday at the center. She was treated in the infirmary. The girl responsible will be removed to another facility."

"We need to take her home," Emma pleaded. "Please, help us."

"I'm working on it. Just promise me that you'll stay calm, okay?" His eyes were on Lars.

"What kind of place is that?" he asked through clenched teeth. "I thought it was a place where children would be safe."

Joseph looked down. "It's a juvenile detention center, Mr. Keller. That means that there are going to be kids there who have problems. Some of them unfortunately believe that the only way to protect themselves is to lash out."

"What happened?" Emma asked.

"I'm not clear on all the details, but the girls were at dinner, and Sadie had bowed her head to pray. For some reason that set another girl off. She grabbed Sadie by her hair, and when she did, I assume Sadie resisted." He shrugged as if Emma should be able to figure out the rest for herself.

"Sadie would not have resisted," Emma told him. "It is not our way. She would have given that girl anything she wanted."

Joseph looked skeptical. "Perhaps you underestimate. . ."

Emma bit her lip. "I know my daughter. Will the other girl be punished?"

"I guarantee it," Joseph replied, and Emma realized that he thought that this was exactly what she wanted to hear.

"Without discussion? Without a chance to explain herself, to apologize?"

"Apparently the whole thing was caught on video camera," Joseph explained. "She hit Sadie in the face and then pinned her down and punched her repeatedly. She'll be here later today and probably be sent to a more secure facility. She definitely won't be back where Sadie is."

Emma wondered if Joseph truly believed that somehow this news would comfort her. He was talking about another child in trouble. Surely there was a better way other than that of moving the girl from one locked facility to another. She glanced across the aisle at the two women she had overheard talking outside the courtroom and locked eyes with the woman she was certain was this girl's grandmother. The two of them exchanged a look that spoke volumes before the other woman looked away.

"What happens now?" Lars was asking Joseph. "I mean, now that the judge knows that Sadie is not safe there."

Emma saw the way that Joseph studied his scuffed loafers for a minute before answering, and she knew that he had no good news to offer them. Their nightmare was going to continue, and their only recourse was prayer.

"Go do your best," she said softly as she touched the sleeve of Joseph's suit jacket.

The bailiff tapped Joseph on the shoulder at the same moment and nodded toward the judge's bench.

"The judge is coming in," Joseph told them. "You'll be all right?" Again he focused on Lars.

Lars took Emma's arm as the two of them sat down and the bailiff called out, "All rise." The judge entered the room and took his place in the high-backed chair that seemed to Emma suddenly to resemble a throne.

The judge studied some papers that the bailiff handed him and then looked at the state's attorney and nodded. It struck Emma that he had not once so much as glanced at Sadie—had not seen her bruised face, had not noticed the way she sat with her hands folded and her head bowed. *Look at her*, Emma silently pleaded as she stared at the judge.

She was a good girl who had made a horrible error in judgment. There was no need to sentence her—she had already been sentenced by her actions. Every day for the rest of her life she would have to live with what she had caused. Wasn't that enough? For this judge, this court? Wasn't that enough for God?

Emma made a strangled sound as she tried to breathe around

the fear that gripped her. The judge glanced her way and frowned, and Lars coughed loudly as he pulled out his handkerchief to blow his nose, drawing the judge's attention to himself. The judge paused for just a moment as he glanced from Lars and Emma to Sadie and back again. A hint of surprise crossed his features as he returned his gaze to Emma, taking in her plain dress and prayer covering. Then he turned to Mr. Johnson and instructed him to present the case for the state.

Unexpectedly, Emma felt a fleeting shadow that she named hope. The man had seen them—had really looked at them and Sadie for the first time. Surely that was a sign—the first positive sign since that terrible rainy morning. Emma closed her eyes and sent up a silent prayer of thanks.

Chapter 23

Matthew

The world had gone crazy as far as Matt was concerned. How was it possible that his life had gone from boring and normal to crazy upside down? Stuff had been coming at him like the rocks hurled at him by a bully when he rode through his neighborhood after taking a shortcut on the way home one day.

Tessa was dead—as in *d-e-a-d*. Grasping that alone was beyond huge.

Then add in the fact that his sister was in jail—had been fingerprinted and everything, according to what a kid at school had told him. He'd actually gone to the main downtown post office one day and studied the wanted posters for any sign of Sadie's face. One of the kids who had once been his friend had insisted he'd seen her mug shot there.

Add to that the fact that his parents barely talked anymore, at least not to him. They talked to each other, usually in whispers that stopped the minute he came into the room. Then they would give him these fake smiles that didn't really reach their eyes, and his dad would ruffle his hair, and one of them would ask some dumb question like how football practice or school had gone that day.

They didn't care about football—his dad didn't even approve of contact sports. And neither one of them knew the first thing about how the game was played or about the plays that his uncle Geoff was truly brilliant at crafting to beat the opposing team.

Uncle Geoff.

Matt rested his chin on his palm and stared out the window of the small schoolhouse. What had he done to make Uncle Geoff so mad? For the umpteenth time, he went over every move he'd made since the funeral. He'd at least been able to pinpoint the timeline to that being when his uncle had started to ignore him or turn away and pretend to be busy with his players or something else whenever Matt was around.

Before then they'd had a routine. After school, Matt rode his bike to the academy where he would stand on the sidelines while Geoff ran the team through their after-school practice. When that ended, the two of them would run laps around the quarter-mile track that surrounded the football field. On Saturdays, Matt always went over to his uncle's house for lunch and to watch college games on TV—either football or basketball, depending on the season. Tessa often joined them, but Sadie never did.

Matt didn't mind having Tessa there. Every once in a while, she would make a comment about a player or play that actually made sense. Sadie, on the other hand, would have wanted to chatter all the way through the game about the uniforms, the school colors, the fact that getting grass stains out of football uniforms had to be a real chore.

He missed Tessa.

He even missed Sadie. The house was too quiet without her. Meals were eaten in silence until he decided to start filling the silence with babble about sports. Never mind that any information that Matt had about how a college team or professional team was doing came from his reading the sports section of the Sarasota *Herald Tribune* instead of from conversations with his uncle.

Every day on his way home from school, Matt would ride his bike past a coffee shop where he knew he would find a used copy of the sports section. He would fold the paper and put it in his backpack and spend the time between finishing his after-school chores and supper reading up on the various teams. It amazed him that his folks never seemed to catch on that he was suddenly able to spout off statistics he'd never shared before. Clearly they either weren't listening or they weren't nearly as smart as he had always thought they were.

But, on the other hand, these were tough times for their family, and maybe his going on and on about sports was the one thing that he could do to help bring things back to normal again. Of course, that wasn't likely to happen as long as Sadie was in jail. What if the judge sent her away for real? Right now she was in a place called a juvenile detention center in a town just a few miles away. His folks were allowed to visit her for half an hour at a time four days a week, and Sadie got one fifteen-minute phone call a week.

But he wasn't allowed to go along for the visits. He was just a kid. It did help some when he'd heard his mom say that she didn't like to think of either one of her children being in "a place like that," and if he never had to see it, all the better. But he wanted to see it. He wanted to see Sadie. He wanted to ask her what it was like in there. And more to the point—now that his uncle Geoff wasn't talking to him—he needed Sadie. She had always been the backup to Uncle Geoff—the one Matt could go to with his questions and problems when his uncle wasn't available. She'd never laughed at him or made him feel dumb. In spite of the way she always seemed to be thinking about herself, Sadie was a good listener. He missed that.

But he was still mad at her. At school everybody—even the teachers—were talking about what Sadie had done. His friends had suddenly decided that they had other things to do whenever he asked about going somewhere with them or having them come to his house. She'd ruined everything for everybody.

Then there was Tessa. It was like after she was buried nobody wanted to talk about her. Were they supposed to pretend she never existed, or what? Is that the way grown-ups handled death? He tried to remember the times somebody old—like his grandparents' age—had died. It seemed to him that people couldn't stop talking about the dead person, telling stories about funny things that person had done or said.

Tessa had made them laugh plenty of times.

"Matt!"

Matt blinked and looked up at his teacher. Miss Kurtz did not look happy, but then she rarely did. "Ma'am?"

"I asked if you had completed your English assignment."

Matt tried to cover his paper—the one he hadn't yet started much less finished. "Almost," he hedged.

Miss Kurtz held out her hand. "Time's up."

Reluctantly, Matt handed her the paper. She scanned it and frowned. "You only answered the first three questions, Matthew," she said, and he didn't think it was his imagination that her voice had gotten softer. "What's going on?"

He shrugged.

"Matthew, please step out into the hallway with me for a minute." The suppressed giggles of a couple of his fellow students followed him to the door. "That'll do, class," Miss Kurtz scolded as she followed him into the hallway.

Matt waited, his mind racing with the excuses he might offer for his poor performance lately.

His teacher sighed. "What's going on? Talk to me, Matt."

"Ma'am?"

Another heavy sigh. "Don't play dumb, Matt Keller. You are an excellent student, as your sister was before you. But these last several days. . ."

"My cousin was killed, and my sister killed her," he reminded her and was as surprised as she obviously was by the sarcasm that colored every word.

"Manners, young man," she scolded, but he could tell that her heart wasn't in it. She was looking at him strangely. "Is there something you need to talk about, Matt?"

"No, ma'am. Sorry, ma'am. Can I go now?"

She opened the door to the classroom and waited for him to return to his desk, but her question stayed with him.

Yeah. I need to talk about why God would let Tessa die and in such a terrible way, and why He would make it so that it's my sister who killed her, and why my mom keeps talking about how this is our "Job time," and why when I need to talk to him more than ever, my uncle Geoff looks at me like I'm somebody he'd like to never see again.

Chapter 24

Sadie

In the surreal state that she had dwelled in ever since the accident, Sadie tried hard to focus on what her lawyer was telling her.

He was semi-cute for someone over thirty. Not as good-looking as Dan by any stretch of the imagination. He was of average height and slim, whereas Dan was tall and muscular. And the lawyer's hair was wavy and light brown while Dan's was the color of sunflower petals.

She had seen Dan's parents glaring at her when she turned around as her dad had practically jumped the barricade. The guard that had ridden with her to court had told her that they had been unable to reach her parents to let them know she'd spent the night in the infirmary.

"They turn the phone off for the day when we have supper," she'd explained.

"We left a message."

"They wouldn't hear it until they turned the phone on this morning, which they probably haven't done because Dad isn't going to work today since he's coming to court."

"You don't have a cell phone?" The woman had seemed stunned at the very idea of being so out of touch.

Sadie had actually laughed. "It's not our way." She quoted

the line her parents had given her and Matt time and again. But laughing made her jaw ache where the other girl had hit her, and she quickly sobered. "You'd be surprised at all the things that are not our way," she added.

Like courtrooms and detention centers and lawyers. For the hundredth time she wondered how Joseph Cotter had managed to persuade her parents that her only chance was a plea of not guilty when she couldn't be guiltier. It was not their way to lie—even about something so horrid.

"All rise," the bailiff announced.

Sadie felt her hands begin to shake, and she clasped them behind her back as she got to her feet and waited for the judge—a small dark-haired man with black-rimmed reading glasses perched on the end of his nose—to take his seat. The high-backed chair seemed way too large for him in exactly the same way that Matt's Sunday clothes seemed too large for him.

In unison everyone else took their seats, and a hush fell over the room. It was a little like being in church the way everybody did stuff at the exact same moment. The bailiff handed the judge some papers, and they exchanged a brief but unintelligible conversation. Then the judge glanced up. He looked first at Sadie, studying her face for a moment, and then she realized that he was looking at her parents behind her. His dark, thin eyebrows lifted slightly, and he cleared his throat and turned his attention to the state's attorney.

"I assume you have an opening statement, Mr. Johnson?"

The prosecutor was on his feet at once, striding to the podium reserved for his side while Joseph Cotter remained seated next to her.

Sadie tried hard to focus on what Mr. Johnson was saying, but her mind wandered. She wondered why Dan's parents were here. She wondered where Dan was and if he was mad at her. She had tried using one of her phone privileges at the detention center to call him, but his cell had been disconnected. And when she tried calling his house, his mother had told her in no uncertain terms that Dan was not available and she should not call their number again.

It had been worse the time she had tried calling Aunt Jeannie. Uncle Geoff had answered the phone, and hearing his voice—so sad and devoid of his usual good humor—she had burst into tears. There had been a long pause on the other end of the line and then a soft click as her uncle hung up on her. She had tried to call a few other times in the three weeks she had spent at the detention center awaiting her hearing, but neither Jeannie nor Geoff had ever picked up, and when the phone had gone to voice mail, Sadie had found that she had no words. On those occasions, she had been the one to hang up, and finally she had stopped calling.

". . .show that she exceeded the speed limit and drove erratically in conditions that were dangerous for her, her passenger, and anyone she might encounter. Further. . ."

Johnson was talking about her. He was making her sound like an irresponsible monster, like someone who had intentionally set out to hurt Tessa. That wasn't the way it was at all. She had tried to be so careful about staying under the speed limit. Then Dan had said that she needed to speed up, and she had remembered that on the way to the picnic when Jeannie let her drive, her aunt had told her that it was sometimes as dangerous to go too slow as it was to drive too fast. "You'll soon get the rhythm of it," Jeannie had told her.

Sadie felt her lawyer staring at her and realized that she was close to smiling at the thought of time spent with her aunt. She was drumming her fingers on the arm of her chair. Joseph nodded toward her fingers and frowned. Sadie folded her hands together to hold them still and tried to concentrate on what the state's attorney was saying.

"Call your first witness," the judge said. He shuffled the papers on his high desk and then looked up as the bailiff escorted Mr. Diehn, Tessa's neighbor, to the stand.

"Please state your occupation and home address, sir," the attorney instructed.

Mr. Diehn—who was a little hard of hearing—did so in the loud voice that was his normal conversational tone.

"And tell us what you were doing just before seven thirty on the morning of August 28th."

"I was leaving for work. It was raining, and I had just pulled out onto the street and driven to the corner."

"What were the road conditions?"

"Well, it hadn't rained for several weeks—most of the summer we were in a drought, don't you know. The rain was coming down in sheets, don't you know, and the roads were covered over in places. And slick," he added as an afterthought.

"Did you see this car that morning?" Mr. Johnson held up a photograph of Dan's car and went through the routine of entering it into evidence. Sadie half expected Joseph to object, but he didn't, just made scribbled notes on his yellow legal pad in a script that was so tiny Sadie couldn't begin to read it.

"Sure did. That car almost ran smack into me. If I hadn't—"

"Who was driving the car?"

"Well now, like I said, there was a torrential rain coming down, and windows were fogged with the humidity and all, so I can't be all that sure." He turned to the judge. "I had the air conditioning turned up, helps make the defrost cycle work better, don't you know."

Joseph was on his feet immediately. "Objection. Calls for legal conclusion."

"Sustained," the judge murmured.

Mr. Johnson started to ask his next question, but Mr. Diehn turned back to him and interrupted. "I do know that there were two people in that car, and I do know that it was going a little too fast for the conditions." He seemed satisfied with his answer, punctuating it with a sharp nod of his head.

Joseph stood up a second time. "Objection."

"Sustained," the judge repeated before Joseph could even say why he'd objected.

Mr. Johnson returned to the prosecutor's table and sat down. Joseph stood up and smiled at Mr. Diehn. "Good morning, sir. Just a few more minutes of your time. Did your car skid or slide on the morning in question?"

"No sir. I'm a cautious driver. My wife says sometimes I'm too cautious."

"Did the car you saw like the one in the photograph slide or skid?"

Mr. Diehn frowned. "Not that I noticed—just came at me a little close, you know? A little too close."

"Then how did you determine that the rain had made the roads slippery?"

"Common sense. No rain for weeks is bound to result in a buildup of oil and other stuff from cars running over the same road time after time. Bound to be."

"And you say your windows were steamed up with humidity, and the pouring rain made for poor visibility?"

"That's right. Those youngsters could barely see their hand in front of them much less—"

"And what about you, Mr. Diehn? I know you said you had your air conditioning and the defroster running, but were the windows on your car steamed over, and did the pouring rain in even a small way hamper your ability to see clearly?"

Mr. Diehn glanced past Joseph at Mr. Johnson, who did not look back at him. "I reckon you've got a point there," he admitted.

"So just to be clear, you saw a car that resembled the one the state's attorney showed you in the photograph turn the corner where you were waiting—"

"At an unsafe speed," Mr. Diehn interrupted.

Joseph smiled. "Ah yes. Thank you for reminding me. And how were you able to determine the speed of this other car?"

Mr. Diehn actually grinned. "Instinct and over forty years of driving, son."

"And did this car hit your vehicle?"

"Came pretty close."

"But no actual contact—no damage? You didn't have to veer out of its way?"

"No. I gave the driver a blast of my horn, and that probably was the reason why that car—" He pointed toward the photo lying on the prosecutor's desk.

"Thank you, sir. No further questions."

Mr. Johnson called his next witness, another neighbor that lived next door to Tessa. She and her husband had heard the crash and come running outside. Her husband had been the one relaying information to the 911 operator. But as far as Sadie could tell, Joseph was able to make it clear that neither this woman nor her husband had seen the actual accident or events that may have led up to it.

There were three other neighbors and one other driver whom Sadie must have passed while making the trip to Tessa's house, but none of them really added much to the state's case. Then a forensics expert as well as the surgeon who had operated on Tessa were called to testify.

Each of them laid out the massive injuries that had led to Tessa's death—a broken collar bone, broken ribs, a torn spleen, injury to her lungs, injury to her liver, brain injuries, and internal bleeding.

One thing that Sadie had noticed was that unlike the dramatic court scenes on television, here the lawyers and judge spoke to each other in normal tones. They didn't seem to worry about whether those in the chairs behind the little wooden fence could hear. Sadie herself had to sit forward and really listen hard to follow what was happening. The list of Tessa's injuries was delivered in a dry, no-nonsense manner that irritated her.

This was Tessa they were talking about. Tessa who had sustained these horrific assaults to her body. Had she felt pain? Had she known she was dying? Had she forgiven Sadie before she died?

She was starting to feel nauseous as the list of injuries was repeated. Every time the doctor named one of the things that had contributed to Tessa's death, it felt as if he were hurling stones at Sadie. Her mind raced with images of her cousin's lifeless body. She tried to concentrate on something else and block out the drone of the testimony. What she wouldn't give for a bowl of her mom's chicken noodle soup. That would settle her stomach.

The doctor finally left the stand, and Sadie took a deep breath, forcing herself to relax. Surely that had been the worst of it. Now the prosecuting attorney would stop and her attorney would begin to make the case for her.

"The state calls Daniel Kline," Mr. Johnson said in a voice that sounded as if he were making a comment on the weather rather than calling Dan to the stand.

Sadie resisted the urge to smooth her hair and bite her lips to give them some color. Dan was here. He would tell them what had happened, how it was an accident, how all she was guilty of was driving with him instead of a real adult.

He looked wonderful. He was dressed in his best Sunday clothes—crisp pressed khaki slacks, a light blue shirt, a chocolate brown tie, and a navy sports jacket. Sadie was embarrassed for him to see her looking so awful. But she needn't have worried. He walked straight to the front of the courtroom without so much as a glance her way and took the oath to tell the truth, the whole truth, and nothing but, and then sat down.

Mr. Johnson stood so that he was between Sadie and Dan as he asked Dan to state his name, age, and occupation for the record. He asked him if the car in the photo was his. He asked if he had operated that car on the day in question. He asked if anyone else had driven that car that morning.

"Yes sir. Sadie Keller."

Johnson stepped aside and pointed to Sadie. "The defendant?"

"Yes sir."

"You knew that she was underage?"

"She has—had—her learner's permit."

"But you at age eighteen did not fill the state's requirement that an adult twenty-one or older be in the vehicle?"

"No sir."

"Was anyone else in the vehicle?"

"No sir."

"Tell the court how it happened that the defendant was illegally driving your vehicle on the morning of August 28th."

Sadie gave Dan an encouraging nod. Tell them. Help this nightmare end. She was certain that this was the moment when Dan was going to make it all right for her. He would tell the court how she had hesitated, how he had insisted, how much he regretted—

"She was all excited about getting her learner's," Dan began, and Sadie fought a smile, knowing that her lawyer wouldn't like it.

"It was only like a mile from her house to her cousin's house," Dan continued, but his expression was all wrong—tight-lipped as if he were fighting to keep his emotions in check. "I didn't see the harm, and she can be pretty persuasive." He slumped forward and bowed his head. "I didn't see the harm," he repeated, and his voice broke as he looked down at his hands.

"Who was at the wheel of your vehicle when it went out of control, striking fifteen-year-old Tessa Messner with such force that she later died on the operating table?"

"Sadie Keller," Dan mumbled. He turned to look at the judge. "I wish I could have done something to make it right, but I was too late."

"No further questions."

Sadie had moved to the edge of her chair, and she was grasping the table. Joseph leaned close and whispered, "Stay calm." Then he stood up and moved toward Dan.

"So just to be sure we're clear here, it is your sworn testimony that my client asked to drive your car from her home to her cousin's house?"

Dan shrugged.

"Words, Mr. Kline," the judge instructed.

Dan sat a little taller and looked directly at Joseph. "That's what I just said." He sounded angry.

"And you gave in to her request because"—Joseph consulted his legal pad then turned back to Dan—"and I quote, 'She can be pretty persuasive'?"

Sadie saw Dan's cheeks flush. "Well, she can."

"What year in school are you, Daniel?"

"I just started my senior year."

"And my client?"

"Sophomore."

"Am I right in stating that you made a plea bargain with the state's attorney's office?"

Dan looked at Mr. Johnson. "Yes sir."

"What were the terms of that plea bargain?"

"I pled guilty to the charge of culpable negligence."

"In exchange for?" Joseph prompted.

Dan hesitated the way he did when he wasn't sure of the right answer. Sadie's heart went out to him. He looked as scared as she felt.

"Mr. Kline?"

"I agreed to testify here today."

"Against my client?"

"To tell what happened."

"And once again, just so we are very clear, you are telling this court—under oath—that it was Sadie Keller's idea to—"

"Objection. Asked and answered," Mr. Johnson said.

"No further questions," Joseph said and sat down.

Sadie couldn't believe it. Dan had lied. More to the point, he had lied after swearing to tell the truth. What kind of Christian was that? Why would he possibly. . .

"The state calls Geoffory Messner to the stand."

Uncle Geoff? Couldn't be. Why would he testify for the prosecution?

Sadie heard a gasp behind her and turned to find her mother half out of her chair and her father standing. The judge was banging his gavel, and the bailiff was taking hold of her father's arm, and other people—like Dan's parents—were also standing. Everyone was talking and shouting, and it was all because of her, because of what she had done. She turned in a slow circle, seeing everyone yelling, but suddenly Sadie could bear it no more. She shut her eyes and opened her mouth to release the screams she'd been swallowing back now for days.

Chapter 25

Jeannie

News traveled fast in a close-knit community like Pinecraft and even though Jeannie and Geoff technically lived in Sarasota, Jeannie heard about Geoff's appearance at Sadie's hearing within half an hour of the event itself.

Although Zeke had stayed for a cup of coffee, Jeannie could see that his heart hadn't been in the visit. Clearly torn between his loyalty to Geoff and Jeannie and his concern for Emma and her family, he'd left as soon as possible. But he'd again challenged Jeannie to get back into the community, and so she'd decided that a good first step would be to resume her habit of shopping at the fresh market in Pinecraft. There were still plenty of casseroles and breads and cakes and pies in her freezer and refrigerator, but she was hungry for the lighter fare of fresh fruit and a green salad.

The news of Geoff being in court had come to her in whispered conversations that abruptly stopped as she moved around the store, nodding to those she knew and receiving in return a quick glance before the person gave her a nod or smile and then pretended interest in the produce. These were Emma's friends and neighbors, and although Jeannie had grown up in this community and among these very people, and even though she was used to people's sympathetic glances by now, the demeanor of the patrons in the fresh market was different. They looked at her with eyes that questioned even as they covered their mouths with their cupped hands and murmured to their companions.

Jeannie's guilt over avoiding Emma almost overwhelmed her, and she was on the verge of making some excuse about why she had not been in touch with her sister when Olive Crowder stepped up next to her and made a show of studying the bananas.

"Hello, Olive," Jeannie said as she selected a large bunch of the fruit and placed it in her basket. "The bananas look especially nice today." She'd almost said that they were Tessa's favorite, but she'd caught herself, swallowing back the now familiar bile of grief that seemed to rise in her throat every time she thought of her daughter. "Geoff loves to slice them over his cereal at breakfast," she forced herself to say instead.

Her mention of Geoff seemed to give Olive the opening she'd been hoping for. "Ja, I'm sure he does." The older woman pursed her lips as if she'd just bitten into an especially tart lemon. "I'll come straight to the point, Jeannine." Olive had always called Jeannie by her full given name. "Everyone appreciates the pain and suffering that you and your husband must endure, but testifying against your own sister's child, your own niece?" She clucked her tongue. "You were raised to walk on the path of forgiveness and reconciliation, Jeannine. What is to be gained if they send that child to prison? It will not bring your Tessa back, and what else might you lose in the bargain?"

"I wouldn't. . .I couldn't," Jeannie protested. The very idea that anyone who knew her might think her capable of such an act was unimaginable. She realized that she had made no effort to keep her voice to a murmur, and the other women apparently saw that as their invitation to join the conversation.

"Maybe she wouldn't, but when it comes to her husband. . .," she heard one of the women mutter.

"What about my husband?"

Olive studied her for a moment then held up her hand to forestall any further comment from the others. She took hold of Jeannie's elbow and guided her outside. "Please don't try to pretend that you are unaware that Geoffory was in court today to testify against Sadie—to testify for the prosecution," she told her.

They had to be joking.

Geoff?

He had struggled with his emotions to be sure. He had been depressed, morose, and yes, angry. And it was true that since the funeral, conversation between them had been limited to information about where one of them might be going, or whether he needed anything from the store, or a reminder that he would be late because he had a faculty meeting. But this? Sadie was family. He could never. . .

"Sometimes it's hard for one raised outside," Olive said as if Jeannie had spoken the rush of thoughts aloud. Olive's voice was unusually soft, appeasing. "Even after conversion there can be ties to the old ways."

"What old ways, Olive?" Jeannie felt irritated that the woman would say anything against Geoff. He was a pillar of the church, a respected educator and coach. Everyone in Pinecraft—be they old- or new-order Mennonite—admired him.

Olive pursed her lips. "An eye for an eye is not our way, Jeannine. That's all I'm saying here."

"And it's not Geoff's way either. He is not a vengeful man."

"He's a former outsider who has lost his only child to a senseless accident," Olive reminded her. "In his upbringing, forgiveness and reconciliation would have been mixed with Old Testament justice. His parents made it clear at the funeral that they blamed Sadie. Why, they barely acknowledged that child. I suppose others might understand, but. . ."

Jeannie turned back to the gathering inside the store. The customers and clerks were all listening to what Olive was telling her and watching her with such pity. Well, she didn't want or need their pity, and she would stand by her husband. If Geoff had gone to court that day, then he had his reasons. She walked back inside and replaced every item from her basket in its rightful place, and then she left.

But she could not shake the words Olive had spoken. She had said that Geoff had gone to testify—against Sadie. *There had to be some other explanation*, she thought as she walked home.

The prosecutor must have required Geoff to appear in court, and Geoff hadn't told her because he hadn't wanted to worry her. That had to be it. Geoff would never. . .

But later that night as they sat in separate chairs in front of the television eating their supper off of paper plates, Jeannie decided to break the silence between them by telling him about the encounter at the fresh market.

"Can you imagine?" she said as she warmed to her story, throwing in details about who was there and how each reacted and what Olive Crowder said and did. And all the while she waited for him to laugh it off or wave his hand dismissively as he gave her a simple explanation of just how the rumor must have gotten started.

But Geoff said nothing. He just chewed his food and stared at the television.

"It's ridiculous, of course," she said, finally running out of steam in her attempt to present the situation as one worthy of their disdain. She took her plate and his and headed for the kitchen. "I think there's some of that baked peach pie left," she called over her shoulder, aware that her hands were shaking as she walked the short distance from the study to the sink. "Geoff? Do you want peach pie?" She heard the annoyance and fear in her voice.

"I was there, but I didn't testify."

He was standing in the doorway, the television flickering behind him.

Jeannie set the plates on the counter and took a step toward him. "Why were you there at all? I mean, we could have gone together. Emma would have appreciated that—and Lars—and Sadie."

Geoff's features contracted with pain. "I have asked you not to mention that girl's name, Jeannie. Can you do that much for me? For us?"

"That girl? She's part of this family, Geoff."

"She is as dead to me as Tessa is," he replied and turned on his heel and went back to the den. A moment later, Jeannie heard the television volume go louder and become a jumble of channel surfing as Geoff punched the remote repeatedly.

Ignoring the cleanup of their supper, Jeannie walked slowly

back to the den. "Please stop walking away from me," she said as she reached over his shoulder and removed the remote from his hand. She aimed the device at the television and clicked the power off. "Talk to me," she said calmly. "Tell me why you were at the courthouse at all." She knelt next to his chair and took his hands in hers. "Help me understand, Geoff."

"There's nothing to tell. I went there to testify, but when she saw me, she started to scream, and the judge ordered a recess until Monday. . ."

"Sadie started to scream?"

He did not argue with her use of her name this time. "Yeah." He actually shuddered at the memory. "It was like some wild animal howling in pain," he said.

Tears filled Jeannie's eyes. Would this never be over for them? Would the hurt just go on and on? "Emma?"

"She was there, and Lars. I thought he was going to punch me, but then I realized that he never would."

"What did they say? Emma and Lars?"

"Nothing. Emma ran off to a side door where the guard had taken her. . ."

"Taken Sadie?"

Geoff gave her an impatient look and nodded. "The bailiff let Lars and Emma go to be with her and then cleared the room."

"Who else was there?"

Geoff shrugged. "People I didn't know, probably for other cases. Dan's parents." He must have seen the next question coming. "Dan testified."

"So the judge ended it before you had to testify. Then it's over now." Jeannie knew that she was trying to reassure herself, knew that she wanted only to block out the realization that it wasn't over at all. She so badly needed for something about this whole nightmare to turn out to be all right, and if that was that Geoff had been stopped from testifying so that he could reconsider, then she would take that crumb and thank God for it. "I'll speak with Emma. I can simply explain that you've reconsidered, that you didn't realize what testifying could mean. She and Lars will understand that you—"

"I'm going to testify, Jeannie."

"But why?"

"How about asking the real question here, Jeannie? How about asking why not?" His voice was raspy, as if he didn't have the strength to argue but was determined to fight on. "Isn't that the question you should really be asking for Tessa's sake?"

Jeannie stared up at him, this stranger with her husband's face. She didn't understand this side of him, this rage that seemed to build a little every day. "Help me understand why you would do this," she pleaded.

"Because I saw what happened." He ground out each word as if afraid she would miss one. "I was outside there. Your beloved niece almost struck me. Do you understand that you could have lost both of us?"

"But it was an accident, Geoff. A horrible accident. Sadie never intended to hurt anyone."

Geoff looked at her as if she were as much a stranger to him as he had become in these last several days to her. "Do you hear yourself, Jeannie? It's Emma or Sadie you worry about—not Tessa and certainly not me." He stood up and stepped around her. "Well, here's the thing, Jeannie. I know you love your sister and her family, but I'm not wired that way. My only child is gone—forever. . ."

"Stop it," Jeannie hissed, getting to her feet to face him. "Stop talking like you're the only one who has suffered the loss of Tessa—she was my child—my only child, too."

"Then maybe you ought to start acting like it instead of looking for ways to defend her killer." He turned away, grabbed his baseball cap, jammed it on his head, and left the house.

Jeannie waited for the sound of the car starting but instead heard the steady pound of his feet as he ran down the driveway and on down the street. She knew where to find him. He would be at the track at the school, running off his anger and grief. It was hardly the first time their evening had ended this way—with him running off steam and Jeannie at home alone.

Like a robot, she went through the motions of putting the kitchen in order and setting the coffeemaker timer for the following morning. Then she remembered that tomorrow was Friday and a teacher's work day for Geoff. The weekend would start early.

Memories of the plans she and Emma would make to spend such days off with the girls—just the four of them—hit her like an unexpected wave at the seashore. This would be a long weekend, and weekends, she had discovered, were in many ways the worst. It was easier to get through the hours that Tessa would have been in school. But weekends were always a time when they did everything together. On Friday nights, they would all go to the football game and then out for pizza. On Saturdays she and Emma and Tessa and Sadie would spend the day together—working at the fruit co-op, shopping, or going to search for shells in the bay. And on Sunday after each family attended services at their separate churches, they would spend the rest of the day together, going on outings or just sharing an afternoon and evening of board games or shuffleboard followed by a potluck meal filled with chatter and laughter and togetherness.

As lights came on in houses up and down the block, she switched off the kitchen light and started upstairs, but then she turned and retraced her steps to the wall phone in the kitchen. She dialed the number for retrieving their voice mail.

"You have no new messages," the electronic voice reported. "You have eighteen saved messages."

Eighteen saved messages—all of them from Emma. None of them returned. She hadn't known what to say. Aware that Geoff needed time to forgive Sadie, she had kept her distance from Emma and Lars out of respect for Geoff. She had hoped that once the funeral was over and he had gone back to work, he would realize that Emma and Lars and Matt—and yes, Sadie—were family. But it was clear that he was going to need more time, and she would not abandon him when he was in such obvious pain.

Still she needed support as well, and in the absence of Geoff's ability to offer her that, she pressed the key to retrieve the first message and give herself the gift of the comfort and strength that she knew she could find in her sister's voice.

Chapter 26

Geoff

By the time Geoff reached the track, he was already soaked with sweat. He had run full out from the house to the athletic field where he had spent so many good times, celebrated so many victories with his teams, coached and cajoled and parented young boys into the fine young men they had become. This place was the setting for his success. The house he had run from had turned out to be the setting of his greatest failure.

His anger and guilt combined to push him forward in spite of the burning pain in his chest and the heaviness of his legs. He was out of shape. The extra duties as vice principal had cut into the time he usually took to work out at the end of every school day. Work out here with his players, or on off days, run with Matt, who was always hanging around waiting for practice to end and hoping for an invitation to join Geoff in laps around the track.

The kid was an excellent runner, and once he filled out a little, he'd make a good running back. Matt had an instinct for the game of football that was impossible to teach. He had a phenomenal grasp of the intricate plays that often had to be dumbed down for others.

But ever since the funeral, Geoff had avoided any contact with his nephew. After practice if he saw Matt hanging around, he headed back inside the school with his players without so much as a glance at Matt. It wasn't the kid's fault. Geoff knew that, and it certainly wasn't fair to him. But Matt reminded him of Lars and Emma, and that reminded him of Sadie, and that took his mind places that he really didn't want to go.

It was the same at home. It had gotten so that he had to bite his tongue sometimes to keep from reminding Jeannie that none of this would be happening to them if she had thought before she took Sadie for that learner's permit. But that was a line he would not cross. Jeannie would be devastated if she knew for one minute that he harbored this thought. At the same time, Geoff suspected that she already carried the weight of regretting that impulsive act with her every waking hour. Speaking the accusation aloud would take their marriage to a place so dark that they'd have no hope of ever recovering, and it scared him to think how close he'd come to shouting that very accusation at her earlier.

He took another lap and focused on his breathing, steady outbursts of air as he pushed his way around the track, quarter mile by quarter mile. He tried to empty his mind, to focus on nothing more than the uniformity of his stride, the form with which he ran. But each puff of his breath came out sounding like Jeannie's question: *"Why?"*

Because a child has died needlessly. . . .

Because our child was that child. . . .

Because justice demands that Tessa's death come with a cost for the one who caused it. . . .

Because Sadie has always been too free-spirited, too oblivious to consequences, too reckless in the way she treats others. . . .

Because testifying against Sadie gave him back a feeling that he had control over the situation, that he could do something to make things right.

Testifying was the only way he'd come up with to dampen his own overwhelming guilt—the guilt that he'd carried with him from the moment he'd realized that in trying to protect her he had actually sent Tessa to the exact spot where the car had hit her. Every time he relived the force of that blow, he forgot how to breathe.

Why couldn't Jeannie understand that?

Why did she always choose her sister and her sister's family over her own? How many times in all the years of their marriage had he heard her say, "but Emma needs" or "Emma doesn't understand" or "Emma says" or "Emma thinks"? How many times had they changed the plans he had made with others to include Emma and Lars and their kids? And worst of all, how many times had Jeannie turned to Emma for support or comfort or advice instead of to him?

He heard footfalls behind him. Jeannie was a good runner, and if she had decided to come after him, maybe she had begun to understand things from his point of view.

"Hey, man, hold up."

He stopped running and turned to see Zeke Shepherd bent nearly double, his hands on his knees as he tried to catch his breath. Geoff walked slowly back toward his friend.

"You okay?"

"No worries," Zeke gasped, but he took a minute longer to catch his breath.

"Did Jeannie send you?"

Zeke glanced up, and the way he cocked his head suggested that his friend had no idea what he was talking about. "Actually, I was going to camp out here tonight under the bleachers. Forecast said something about rain and. . ." He blinked up at Geoff. "Why would Jeannie send me to find you?" Zeke stood up straight, still massaging his side.

The streetlights outside the ball field were dim enough and distant enough to cast the field and track in shadows. "We had a fight."

Zeke released a long sigh. "Well, I can't say I didn't see that one coming. Okay, I lied. I heard about you being in court today, so I stopped by. Jeannie was on the phone and told me you'd gone for a run, but she didn't send me to get you."

"Probably calling Emma so the two of them could commiserate over what a terrible guy I am."

"Whoa. So it's a pity party we're having. Got it."

Geoff felt a twitch of a smile. Nobody but Zeke had ever

talked so straight to him—he wouldn't allow it from anybody else. But from the time Zeke and his family had moved in across the street from Geoff when both boys were ten years old, Zeke had shown Geoff that he was not especially impressed with Geoff's size or athletic ability.

"You wanna be my friend or not?" he'd asked bluntly one day after the two of them had gotten into a roll-around-in-the-dirt-without-landing-any-punches fight on the playground.

Geoff wasn't used to such a direct question. "I don't know," he'd hedged.

Zeke had gotten up, dusted himself off, and headed for home. "Take a day to think it over," he'd said. "I think it might work out, but it's your call."

The following morning, Geoff had fallen into step with Zeke on their way to school. Neither one of them had ever mentioned the fight again, and they had been fast friends from that day to this. Geoff doubted either of them could even remember what they had fought about. He knew he couldn't. Even a separation of years while Zeke was in the service in the Middle East and Geoff was in college had done nothing to loosen the bond formed in that silent no-need-for-words walk to school.

As they walked in step around the track now, Geoff looked down at Zeke, who was a good three inches shorter and twenty-five pounds lighter than he was. "You think I messed up." It was not a question.

"I think you're hurting just like Jeannie is and Emma is and Lars is and Matt is and, yes, just like Sadie is."

They walked the next half of the oval in silence. "I think I'm losing faith," Geoff murmured.

To his surprise, Zeke chuckled. "You can't lose what you've never really taken hold of, Geoff. You're neither fish nor fowl, as they say. You treated conversion like it was nothing more than moving from one house to another. I'm not saying you don't believe. I'm just raising the question of what it is you do believe."

"I used to believe in a loving God, but what kind of God takes an innocent child's life and leaves everybody that ever knew her or loved her reeling?"

Zeke shrugged. "Have you talked to Jeannie about this?"

"Her faith is unshakable."

"You're sure about that? Even now?"

He wasn't sure of anything when it came to his wife these days. They spent their time in different stratospheres even when they were in the same house—the same room. It was a relief for him to leave for school every morning as he suspected it was for her to see him go. Clearly she didn't want to be with him, because lately she was up and out running before he even crawled out of bed.

"Maybe I made a mistake that day that I turned Emma away. She means well, and she probably could be a comfort to Jeannie. It's for certain that I'm not filling that particular role. It's just that ever since the funeral, I find that I can't handle anyone from that family being around."

"Jeannie's a big girl. If she wants to see Emma, you aren't going to stop her. And the fact is, for everyone involved it's all still so fresh—like an open wound. You'll find your way back to each other in time, and my guess is that Emma and Lars understand."

"And then there's Matt," Geoff said. "How do I explain to him why I've turned away, why the very sight of him makes me remember every second of that morning even though he wasn't there, had no part in it at all?"

"That's a whole other ball game, my friend—no pun intended. Look, Matt comes about as close to hero-worshipping you as his upbringing will allow. But right now you need to focus on Jeannie. Mattie's got his folks. You and Jeannie just have each other." Zeke gave Geoff a not-so-subtle nudge with his elbow. "Come on, man. Go home to your wife."

"First tell me that you understand why I'm still going to testify."

"Make me understand," Zeke challenged.

Geoff ran a hand through his hair. "It's like I'm speaking for Tessa, telling what I saw, because Tess must have seen almost the same thing. Surely that's important—for someone to speak for Tessa?"

"When you put it that way, it makes some sense. You might

want to try that with Jeannie." He picked up the guitar he'd left leaning against one of the scoreboard uprights and slung it over his shoulder. "I got to get my beauty rest," he said with a grin. "Farmers' market on Saturday. Payday." Zeke had regularly played for the tourists crowding the closed-off street at the weekly farmers' market in downtown Sarasota, leaving his guitar case open to receive their tips. It was one of his main sources of income.

Geoff shook his friend's hand. "Thanks for hunting me down. Maybe Jeannie and I will come to the market this week. It would be a nice break for her—for both of us."

"Great idea. And may I suggest that you plan to support your local musician friend by bringing along some cash—as in large bills," Zeke shouted as he trotted off the field.

Feeling better, Geoff took one more lap around the track and then headed for home. Zeke was right. He hadn't explained things so that Jeannie would understand why he was doing what he was doing, why he needed to do things this way. Once he told her that it was for Tessa. . .

But somehow the words that had come so easily and concisely when he was talking to Zeke failed him entirely when he tried to explain his reasoning to Jeannie.

"For Tessa?" she asked incredulously. "You seriously think that our daughter, that sweet, caring child, would want anything to do with contributing to the problems that Sadie already has?"

"I think she can't be here to tell her side of things, and someone—I—can do that for her."

"Her side? What does that even mean?"

They were back to shouting at each other. He didn't want this. He had imagined that he would come back and explain and they would go upstairs to bed where for the first time since the funeral they would curl up together and hold each other through the night.

"Geoff, do you understand that Sadie could be sent away for a very long time?"

"What I can't understand, Jeannie, is why you seem determined to put Sadie's future ahead of your own daughter's complete lack of any future at all."

"I am doing the only thing I know to do. Tessa is gone, and I can't change that, but if we can save Sadie. . ."

Geoff couldn't believe he was hearing her right. "Where is your anger, Jeannie? Where is your fury that this girl you have spoiled rotten for most of her life has repaid you by thoughtlessly taking the life of your only child?"

"That's a solution? An eye for an eye?"

Geoff felt as if he might explode under the tension of his anger and his wife's total lack of understanding. "I'm going to bed," he said. "I told Zeke we'd come to the market this weekend."

"I can't."

"Why not?"

"It's visiting day at the detention center." She did not try to hide the defiant look she gave him.

"You're not going to see her!"

"I listened to Emma's messages while you were out. Almost daily reports about how Sadie was doing in that place. And in all of them the underlying message is that she needs the chance to tell us how sorry she is."

"My heart bleeds for her pain," Geoff said sarcastically.

"I'm going to give her that chance, Geoff. It would be good if you came with me so she can apologize to us both."

"And then what? We all join hands and sing 'Kumbaya' together?"

"Or we could do things your way and destroy another life or two in the bargain," she snapped.

Geoff felt his legs go weak with physical and emotional exhaustion. He sat down on the third step and put his face in his hands. "Jeannie, this is insanity. I'm asking you not to go."

"And I'm asking you not to testify." She edged past him on her way upstairs. "Stalemate," she said softly as she walked down the hall past their bedroom and into Tessa's room. A moment later he heard the door close.

He got up and retraced his steps down to the kitchen and den where he shut off the lights and turned the lock on the back door. Then he unlocked the door and stepped outside the way he had that rainy morning. He stared at the place where Tessa had been standing laughing at him as he wrestled with the umbrella. She had taken a step toward him, prepared to help. If he hadn't stopped her, she might have been safe—the car might have missed her as it did him.

At the end of the block, he heard a car backfire, and he remembered the sound of Dan's car coming up the street. It had caught the pool of water that covered half the street and sent it spraying into the air. He closed his eyes against the memory of the car coming at them, at him.

"Tessa, move!" he'd shouted as he tossed the umbrella aside ready to take the blow for her. She had leaped away, but the car had spun suddenly in the opposite direction entirely. The back end had caught his precious daughter and sent her sailing until she'd landed with a soft thud on the driveway.

Now he stared down at the spot and then up at a sky filled with stars. How could anyone who knew what had happened here ever believe again that God was in His heaven and all was right with the world?

Chapter 27

Jeannie

The door to the bedroom she and Geoff shared was closed when Jeannie came out of Tessa's room after a sleepless night spent crying as she went through her daughter's things for the hundredth time since the funeral. The one thing that she had not found was the journal that she and Geoff had given Tessa the night before the accident.

She thought if she could just find that journal and see what Tessa had written in it, she might be able to show it to Geoff. Perhaps Tessa's own words—whatever they might be—would convince him once and for all that vengeance was not justice. But the journal was nowhere to be found.

Usually Jeannie would have called Emma to come and help her in the hunt. But she would not ask Emma to come now. It would only upset Geoff further. She regretted their argument, and yet she would not back down on this one. If Geoff thought he was speaking for Tessa, then so was she. Tessa would be more concerned for Sadie than for herself. That was the way they had raised her, and that was why it was so hard to understand why Geoff could be so unforgiving when it came to Sadie.

The phone rang, and automatically she glanced at the display to check caller ID.

Hester Steiner's name popped up. Jeannie had promised Zeke that she would return to her volunteer work at the fruit co-op, and no doubt he had passed that message along to Hester. Well, why not? The work there would at least fill some of the hours that stretched before her endlessly each new day. She picked up the phone.

"Okay, okay, I'll be at the co-op on Monday," she said in what she hoped passed for her usual pre-accident teasing tone.

Hester chuckled. "That's good news, but actually I was just calling to see if you have time for coffee this morning. A friend from my college days is in town to start a new job, and I thought the two of you ought to meet."

Ought to meet was an odd way to put the invitation.

"Why?" Jeannie blurted before she could censor herself.

"Just say you'll come," Hester replied further, adding to Jeannie's suspicion. "How about that place on Main Street that you and Emma like?"

"Is Emma coming?"

"No. I wouldn't do that to either of you without first asking. How's half an hour?"

Jeannie checked the clock. It was still early. She certainly had little else to do. Why not enjoy a latte and meet Hester's friend? It would be good for her. "Okay. Sure. See you there."

As she hung up the phone, she heard the shower turn on in their bathroom. Knowing that Geoff was in the shower, Jeannie went back upstairs to their room and changed from the clothes she'd worn the day before into a pair of denim Capri pants and a green cotton blouse.

"I'm going," she called out, standing at the partially closed bathroom door. "Geoff?"

The water running was the only sound.

"Geoff? Did you hear me? I'm taking the car."

"I heard you."

She waited, but he said nothing more, and the water just kept running. "Okay. See you later," she said, fighting hard against the wave of irritation at his stubbornness. Or maybe she was the one who was unwilling to bend. He had brought on their argument of the night before, and it was up to him—

Reconciliation. Forgiveness. Wasn't that what she had said he needed to have for Sadie?

She retraced her steps.

"Geoff?"

No answer, but she had the sense that he was listening.

"I love you," she said and then softly closed the bathroom door all the way—just in case he didn't say anything back.

Jeannie was the first to arrive at the coffee shop. She chose a table outside, away from the street traffic and other customers. She pulled a third chair over from an adjoining table and sat down to watch for Hester and her friend. Moments later she saw Hester's car across the street, and then Hester and a petite woman of about Emma's age got out.

She was dressed plain and wore the simpler white kerchief prayer covering common among the younger conservative Mennonite women. Her caped dress was a light lavender, and the color worked well with her dark hair. Her skin was very pale and completely unblemished. Jeannie couldn't help but think that she would need to invest in some sunblock if she was going to move to Sarasota. Jeannie got up and waved to Hester.

"Over here," she called, and the two women hurried across the street, dodging traffic on their way.

"Jeannie Messner, meet another dear friend, Rachel Kaufmann," Hester said.

"Hester and I were college roommates," Rachel explained. "She used to rave about Pinecraft and everything it had to offer, so I finally decided to come down and see what all the fuss was about."

"You two get acquainted," Hester said. "I'll get the coffee."

"Tea for me," Rachel said.

"Got it. Two coffees and one tea."

Rachel and Jeannie took chairs opposite each other. Rachel leaned back and looked at her surroundings. "It's all so very. . .tropical," she said and then laughed. "Well, duh. But this is certainly what it feels like midsummer in Ohio where I come from." She fanned herself with her hand. "Are you from here originally, Jeannie?"

"Born and raised right in Pinecraft," Jeannie said. She could see Hester standing in line inside the small shop. "It's wonderful that you and Hester have stayed in touch over all this time."

"She's a terrific letter writer," Rachel replied. "Me? Not so much. But I'm good at calling, so between the two, we made it work." She leaned forward. "I met Hester's John. He's wonderful, isn't he? And they are so perfect together."

Jeannie found herself smiling as she recalled the rocky start that Hester and John had had. "Well, now they are. In the beginning. . ."

"Oh, I know. You should read the letters I was getting from Hester back then. But I knew the way it was 'John Steiner this' and 'John Steiner that'—I mean, after the first three dozen times his name came up in a matter of a couple of weeks—she was in love with the guy."

Jeannie laughed, and it felt odd—like something she used to do a lot in the past and then had given up on.

"Coffee for you. Tea for you, and coffee for me," Hester said as she arrived with three mugs of steaming liquid. She doled them out before taking the third chair.

"Hester tells me you just took a job here, Rachel," Jeannie said. "Do you have a family?"

"Yes. My husband was killed a year and a half ago. We have a son, Justin. He's twelve. When I was laid off from my job a few months ago, Hester suggested that I look for work here." She smiled at her friend. "I'm going to be working at the new hospital that just opened out on Cattlemen Road."

It seemed like it had been such a long time since Jeannie had allowed herself to think about the suffering of others. She felt ashamed and selfish. "I'm so very sorry for your loss."

Rachel gave her a grateful smile. "It's been a journey, but every day Justin and I realize that we are a little further along the path of healing. Of course, staying busy helps—work for me and school for Justin."

"Are you a nurse like Hester?"

"I have my degree in nursing but—perpetual student that I am—I went back to school and got my master's in psychology.

I'll be working as a chaplain and spiritual counselor."

Was this the real reason for Hester's call and sudden invitation to meet her friend? She shot Hester a look. "Subtle," she murmured as she took a sip of her coffee.

"Coincidence," Hester corrected, and suddenly the lighter getting-to-know-you environ shifted to one that was filled with questions and suspicion—at least on Jeannie's part.

"What's this really about?"

Hester sighed and set down her mug. "Rachel, tell Jeannie about the program that you and Justin took part in back in Ohio after James was killed." Hester focused all of her attention on Jeannie and added, "Just please keep an open mind, because the minute I heard about it, I wanted you to at least know that such an idea exists in other communities. Seems to me that it's something that could work here."

Jeannie relaxed a little. This was the Hester that everyone knew and admired. She was a woman always looking at her surroundings and thinking about ways to make things better. "Okay, I'm listening. What's the new program?"

"Actually, it isn't all that new," Rachel said. "At least not in some communities."

"It's called VORP," Hester interrupted.

"Which stands for. . .?"

"Victim Offender Reconciliation Program," Hester replied, her eyes locked on Jeannie's. "Rachel's husband was killed by a drunk driver."

"At first," Rachel said, picking up the story, "I didn't know what to do, how to react. I was so angry and devastated, and our son was really at a loss. He and his father did everything together."

"What happened?" Jeannie's mouth had suddenly gone dry.

"The driver was a young man, out of work, with two small children of his own. He'd hit rock bottom and started drinking early one afternoon and kept it up. Then he got into his truck, and on his way home, he crossed over the median and struck my husband's car."

When tears welled in Rachel's eyes, Jeannie reached over and squeezed her hand. "I know," she whispered. "I understand."

"Sorry," Rachel murmured. "Anyway, we were in the midst of the trial when I read something about VORP, and I thought maybe it could work. Maybe it would be a way for Justin—and me—to find some peace with this senseless loss."

"So, what did you do?"

"I contacted the organization, and they sent out a mediator to talk with me and with Justin. There were several steps along the way, but the upshot was that eventually we sat down with the young man. We met his wife and his children. It's a complex program, but in the end we came up with a contract—things that Justin and I asked the young man to do for us and himself and his family. He still went to jail, but he's following through on his end of things, and I think he's going to be all right."

He's going to be all right? What about you and your son? Jeannie wanted to ask.

And then as if reading Jeannie's mind, Rachel added, "And we're going to be all right as well. We're starting fresh—new job for me, new school for Justin." She looked away for a minute, gathering her memories. "Going through the program allowed us both to talk openly about how much we were hurting to the very person whose action had brought us that pain."

"Think about it, Jeannie," Hester said. "If we could get the justice system here in Sarasota to hear us out, it could be a way to help Sadie."

"Who's Sadie?" Rachel asked. Jeannie knew by her expression that she genuinely was unaware of the circumstances that had taken over her life and the lives of all of her family.

"Jeannie? Is it okay?" Hester asked, seeking permission to tell her friend what had happened. "I'm sorry. Sadie's name just popped out. Is it okay if. . ."

Jeannie shrugged and picked up their mugs. "Sure. Go ahead. I'll get refills for you."

"And you," Hester urged, "you'll come back and sit with us so we can talk, right?"

"I'll come back, but, Hester, I'm making no promises."

"None expected. Hearing us out is huge. I appreciate that. Thanks."

Inside the coffee shop, Jeannie took her time getting the refills. She did not want to be present for any part of the recounting of the accident that had taken Tessa's life and landed Sadie in jail. She could see Rachel and Hester through the window of the shop. Rachel was facing her, and Jeannie knew the exact moment that Hester must have given her the news.

She put her fist to her mouth and just sat there staring at Hester and shaking her head, as if by denying what she was hearing she might change the story. Jeannie recognized that reaction. It was a milder version of the one she had experienced when Dr. Morris told her that Tessa had died on the operating table.

Here was a woman who had experienced firsthand the kind of loss that Jeannie and Geoff had. Jeannie thought about how Geoff was so certain that if he could just testify, things would be better—at least for them. But what if what they both really needed was to speak out for themselves instead of against Sadie? She picked up the refilled mugs and returned to the table outside.

"So now that you know my story, can you honestly tell me that this VORP or any program like it can possibly make any difference at all?" Her words were laced with skepticism.

"It won't bring your daughter back, Jeannie. But I really do believe—in fact, I know from our experience—that if you and others who have been victimized by this horror are willing to try, it could be a new beginning."

"For Sadie?"

"For her," Rachel agreed, "and for you and your sister and your husband if they are willing to take part."

Jeannie released a bitter laugh and stood up, prepared to leave. "Wow, sounds wonderful. Where do I sign up?"

Hester frowned and glanced nervously at her friend, but Rachel just nodded. "I know it sounds like some kind of magic pill, but Jeannie, the program does work." She pulled Jeannie's chair a bit closer to her and patted the empty seat. "Will you let me explain?"

Jeannie hesitated for a moment then perched on the edge of the chair and waited for Rachel to regale her with stories of past successes—victims who had embraced their offenders and forgiven them wholeheartedly. But she was not at all prepared for Rachel's opening question.

"Jeannie, knowing that Tessa can't come back to you, what is the single most important and positive thing that you would want to come of the event that took your child's life?"

Images of Geoff, then Emma, then Sadie flitted across Jeannie's mind. Memories of Geoff and Matt tossing a football back and forth, of making marmalade with Emma and the girls in their large modern kitchen, of shopping with Sadie because both Emma and Tessa detested shopping. Memories of better times—times when they had laughed together and worked toward the same goals together and prayed together.

"Jeannie?" Hester said, covering Jeannie's hand with hers. "Are you all right?"

Jeannie realized that tears were sliding down her cheeks. She swiped them away with the back of her hand and looked at Rachel. "I want our lives back—the way things were before. I know it will be without Tessa, but surely for those of us left behind, we could find our way back to some semblance of the love and caring we shared before."

And having said it aloud, she realized that this was what she had been wrestling with through all the long days and nights since the accident. How could they be a family again?

"I know," Rachel said. "That's exactly what I wanted, for my son and me."

"Do you really think that you can help us?" Jeannie asked.

"I'll do my best," Rachel promised then hesitated a moment before adding, "Hester mentioned that you were thinking of visiting your niece. You might want to postpone that, Jeannie. My guess is that she won't be able to handle your visit—and more to the point, in my experience you're not quite ready for that meeting yet either."

Chapter 28

Emma

On Friday evening the family had just finished saying grace when someone knocked on the front door.

"I'll get it," Matt said and was up from the kitchen table and on his way to the front door before Lars or Emma could stop him. They heard the muffled exchange of male voices, and then Matt was back, followed by Joseph Cotter.

"I'm sorry to interrupt your supper," he said.

"Not at all. Join us," Lars invited at the same moment that Emma got up to set another place.

"We have plenty."

Joseph sat down in the fourth chair at the table—Sadie's chair. There was a heartbeat when Emma, Lars, and Matt all looked at each other, but they said nothing.

"I have sweet tea and lemonade," Emma offered.

"Lemonade is fine," Joseph replied as he waited for her to set his place and bring his beverage. When Emma sat down and Lars began passing him dishes of the shrimp, rice, vegetables, and rolls that Emma had prepared, Joseph filled his plate. Then he smiled. "It's been awhile since I enjoyed a true home-cooked meal," he said. "Thank you."

When the young attorney started eating without first saying

a silent prayer, Emma shot Matt a look that warned him not to make the comment that she could see coming. Matt rolled his eyes and went back to pushing food around his plate.

It occurred to Emma that lately their son had changed. For one thing, ever since he'd heard that Uncle Geoff had been in court to testify against Sadie, he had been quiet at mealtimes, no longer regaling them with sports facts. More often than not, he ate in silence and then excused himself, mumbling something about a quiz or homework. It was understandable, of course, given everything going on with Sadie and the break with Geoff and Jeannie. Still, she and Lars needed to remember that Matt needed them more than ever now. She resolved to speak to Lars about it later after Matt had gone to bed.

"Your friend Hester Steiner stopped by my office earlier today," Joseph said.

Lars looked at Emma but said nothing.

"She has this college friend—Rachel something-or-other. Anyway, her friend is a trained grief counselor, but more to the point, her husband was killed by a drunk driver a little over a year ago. I got to thinking that if you approved, it might be good to have her visit Sadie. After what happened in court yesterday, it's pretty clear that Sadie has reached her breaking point."

"Sadie wasn't a drunk driver, and besides, I don't understand why Hester would come to you before talking to us," Emma said.

Joseph ate another bite of his supper and took his time chewing and swallowing.

"Matt, if you're finished, you may be excused," Lars said.

Joseph cleared his throat. "Actually, you might want Matt to hear about this," he said quietly.

For the first time in days, Matt seemed interested in what was going on around him. He sat up a little straighter and focused his attention on Joseph.

"What is it that you've come to tell us, Joseph?" Lars asked. Emma felt the now-familiar tightening of her chest and throat.

"This friend of Mrs. Steiner's—Kaufmann—that's the name."

"She's Mennonite?"

Joseph nodded. "By her dress, I'd say she's conservative like you. She apparently has moved here from Ohio to take the chaplaincy at that new hospital just east of here."

"What's that?" Matt asked.

"Ministers at the hospital—trained people of various faiths who are there if needed for patients and their families," Lars explained. Then he turned his attention back to Joseph. "Go on."

"So, Ms. Kaufmann's husband died, leaving her to raise their son, Justin, on her own." Joseph glanced at Matt. "I think the boy is a year or so younger than you are."

"Why move here?" Matt asked.

"Good question. Apparently she lost her job a few months after her husband died, and Hester suggested she look for work here. But the key thing is that after her husband was killed, she took part in a program that's had some real success in cases like Sadie's."

Emma's heart beat faster. "She can help keep Sadie from going away?"

Joseph shook his head as he took a long drink of his lemonade. "She can't influence the court proceedings—at least not directly."

"So, what can she do?" Lars asked quietly, his disappointment obvious.

"Back in Ohio, she and her son took part in a program called VORP—Victim Offender Reconciliation Program." Joseph waited a beat to allow that to sink in then continued. "It's a program where the victim of a crime—or in many cases like yours, it would be victims—and the offender meet directly."

"How can there be more than one victim?" Matt asked. "Tessa was the only one who died."

Joseph looked at him for a long moment, and then he said, "You're a victim in this, Matt. So are Tessa's parents and your parents and grandparents and even Sadie."

Matt's face went nearly purple with anger as he shook his head. "Sadie's the one that caused this whole mess—she's the one that—"

"Matt," Emma scolded. Her son looked at her with such fury, such frustration that it took her breath away.

"I'd like to be excused," he mumbled already half out of his chair.

"Sich hinsetzen," Lars said quietly, pointing to Matt's chair. "We have a guest."

"But you said before. . . ," Matt protested, and then he slumped back into his chair and folded his arms across his chest, refusing to look at either parent.

"Go on, Joseph," Lars said.

Emma saw that Joseph was decidedly uncomfortable with the dynamics around the table. "Would you like more shrimp, Joseph? Or perhaps a slice of raisin pie?"

Joseph gave her a grateful and relieved smile. "It's been years since I tasted raisin pie," he admitted. "But let me help you clear."

"Matt will do that," Lars said.

Matt looked at his father and then got up and began clearing the dishes. "This is Sadie's job," Emma heard him mutter as he passed her with the stacked plates. She picked up the serving dishes and followed him to the sink.

"Matt? Has something happened at school that you haven't wanted to tell us?" She kept her voice low, mindful that Joseph was close by, although he and Lars were talking. But company or not, Matt was not himself.

Matt filled the sink with soapy water and laid the plates in it to soak. "I'm okay."

"Because I want you to understand that Dad and I realize that everything going on these last weeks has been hard on you as well as the rest of us. You can talk to us anytime about anything. It's just that right now Mr. Cotter is here, and he might be able to help your sister and—"

"And that's what matters right now," Matt said. "I get it, Mom." He shut off the water while she took down plates for the pie.

"Helping Sadie can help us all," Emma said quietly. Then when Matt made no comment, she handed him the clean plates. "Take these to the table, bitte. Coffee, Joseph?" she called out in what she had intended as a normal tone but realized was too shrill and tight with tension.

"No ma'am. The lemonade is fine," Joseph said.

At the table, Emma cut slices of the pie and passed the first slice to Joseph. He waited for everyone to be served and for her to be seated before taking a bite. He was a well-mannered young man even if he had started his meal without first thanking God.

"Wow," he said after tasting the pie. "That is seriously great pie."

In spite of her faith's caution when it came to accepting compliments, Emma fought back the first genuine smile she'd managed in days. "Danke, Joseph."

"I mean, help me out here, Matt. This whipped cream topping tastes more like. . . ." He frowned as he savored a bite of the topping.

"Marshmallows?" Matt said wearily. It was true that people unfamiliar with their whipped cream often described the flavor that way, but Emma did not like the way Matt was acting.

"That's it exactly," Joseph replied. He watched Matt for a minute, and Emma understood that the attorney had somehow realized that Matt was struggling to find his place in everything that had happened to their family. "Hey, Matt, Mrs. Steiner tells me that you're some kind of statistics genius."

Matt glanced up from eating his pie, his eyes interested but still wary. "She said that?"

"She did. When Rachel started rattling off the statistics about the VORP program's success rate, Hester said you were the one with a head for stats. Is that right?"

Matt shrugged. "Sports stats mostly."

"Stats are stats," Joseph observed and went on eating his pie. "Marshmallows," he repeated, nodding as he took another bite of the whipped cream.

Matt fought to hide his smile, clearly beginning to feel a connection to Joseph.

"I'm not a hundred percent clear on the details, but after Mrs. Kaufmann and her son participated in the program, she trained to become a mediator for other cases."

"She would be there if Sadie sat down with Jeannie and Geoff?" Lars asked, drawing the lawyer's attention back to the adults.

"Actually, that's only the first piece."

"What else?" Emma asked.

"The idea is to personalize the crime for the offender by showing them the human consequences of their actions."

"I think our Sadie is very aware of the human consequences of her action, Joseph. She grieves every hour for this terrible tragedy." Emma tried to keep her voice calm. The last thing she wanted to hear about was one more process that would only add to the suffering Sadie was already enduring.

"Well, the idea is to give the victims—those who often never have a chance to speak their piece in the criminal justice system—the opportunity to talk about their feelings directly to the offender."

"It is not our way to involve ourselves in such things, Joseph," Lars said, glancing at Emma. His tone reflected his doubt and discomfort. He had already gone well beyond what he believed to be the way to handle Sadie's troubles by agreeing to hire Joseph. Now this?

"And yet people of your faith are some of the strongest advocates for the program in communities where it has been used," Joseph said.

Emma saw Matt gauge the mood and decide that once again he needed to break the silence. "You said there were statistics?" Matt prompted, fully engaged now.

Joseph focused his attention back on Matt. "The program in one form or another dates back two decades, and there are now thousands of such programs operating around the world."

"Around the world—you mean in other countries," Emma said unable to disguise her skepticism.

"And here as well. There's more," Joseph said softly. Emma could see that her husband and son were being drawn into Joseph's presentation, but she wasn't interested in what others had done. She was only interested in how she could best protect her daughter. And she had her doubts that some stranger—whether or not she was an old college friend of Hester's—could ever hope to know Sadie or Jeannie or any of them well enough to make this work.

Joseph had continued to talk, and she forced her attention back to him.

". . .about two out of every three cases referred to the program result in a face-to-face mediation meeting."

Matt shook his head. "So they meet, and Sadie says how sorry she is, and Uncle Geoff and Aunt Jeannie get to say how sad they are. Then what?"

"Like I said—the meeting is only the first piece of it. The meat of the program is both sides sitting down together and drafting what's called a 'restitution agreement.'" He anticipated Lars's question. "The victims lay out terms by which the offender could make restitution for the crime. For example," he said, turning his attention back to Matt, "if Matt here had spray-painted my garage, I might make repainting the garage a condition of the agreement."

Matt's mouth fell open. "But Sadie. . ."

Emma was on her feet before her son could finish the sentence she saw coming. "How about another piece of pie, Joseph?"

Joseph hesitated then pushed his plate away and dabbed at his mouth with his napkin. "No thank you, and my apologies for monopolizing the conversation."

"Not at all," Emma said, relieved that he had given in to her need to change the subject.

"How often does it work?" Matt pressed. "How often does the offender actually repaint the garage or do what the victim wants?"

Joseph focused his attention on Emma, getting her permission to return to the discussion. When she nodded, he kept looking at her as he gave Matt his answer. "In over 90 percent of the cases, the offender completes the terms of the agreement—often within one year. Compare that to court-ordered restitution where there's only a 20 to 30 percent success rate."

"That's impressive," Lars said.

Emma sat down again and took a deep breath as they all turned their attention to her. "I realize that you have Sadie's best interests at heart, Joseph, and of course, Hester is a dear friend. She's also a close friend to Jeannie and Geoff."

Joseph nodded. "She told me that when the offender takes personal responsibility—instead of being ordered by a court to take responsibility—statistics show that everyone benefits."

"And in this case? Sadie cannot make this right," Emma quietly reminded him. Surely she did not need to state the obvious—that what Geoff and Jeannie understandably wanted was Tessa back in their lives.

"I asked the same question. Ms. Kaufmann made the point that the terms of any such agreement must fall within the realm of the possible. Restitution may be only symbolic. The key is to find ways to build a sense of justice between the victim and the offender. In her case, the young man is getting his high school diploma and attending weekly meetings of Alcoholics Anonymous, and he's written several articles on the dangers of drinking and driving that have been reprinted in a variety of newspapers."

A silence fell over the gathering. Emma looked at Lars while Matt looked from one parent to the other. "It could be over?" he asked Joseph finally.

Joseph cleared his throat. "Everyone needs to understand that this does not replace whatever the outcome of Sadie's adjudication may be. If the judge orders her to serve time, this won't change that."

"Then what good is it?" Matt asked.

"It gives you—all of you—a chance to practice what you have told me is 'your way.' It gives you the opportunity to forgive Sadie, and perhaps most of all, it will help Sadie to forgive herself. Of course, Sadie would have to—"

"No," Emma said. "I know you mean well, Joseph, and I can see where this sounds appealing, but having to face Geoff and Jeannie—" She could not find the words to describe the suffering that her child had already endured.

"Your sister knows about the program. She met with Ms. Kaufmann yesterday," Joseph said quietly.

"And Geoff?" Lars asked incredulous at this bit of news.

"I'm not sure whether he knows or not."

"I'll go tell him. He'll listen to me. I know just how to explain it," Matt said. He was up and out the door before anyone could react.

"Lars, stop him," Emma pleaded.

Lars nodded and headed out the back door. Emma could hear him calling for Matt to come back, and she could hear Matt's shouted reply. "It's okay, Dad. I know where Uncle Geoff will be."

Lars returned to the kitchen and shook his head. "I'll take the car and catch up to him," he said, picking up the keys.

"No, let me call Jeannie."

Lars looked at her with something that she could only identify as pity. "She won't answer," he reminded her.

"Why don't you and I go after the boy?" Joseph offered. "My car is blocking yours anyway. I could drive while you keep an eye out for Matt."

Lars nodded, and the two men headed out. "He'll be at the ball field," Emma called after them. "Geoff will have just finished football practice."

Lars waved from the open window of Joseph's car, and as Emma watched them go, she felt the need to do something—anything that might help her feel as if she was in control of something—so she picked up the phone and punched in her sister's number.

Chapter 29

Geoff

Practice had not gone well, and Geoff was glad there was no game scheduled for this week. After suspending Dan Kline for a month, Geoff had finally given in to pressure from other parents and alumni and let him come back. But the boy's head had been somewhere else, and he'd fumbled the ball so often that his teammates had begun to grumble. Geoff's work at school—especially his role as coach—was the one thing he counted on for a respite from the constant memory of Tessa's accident and the oppressive silence that had fallen over the house he shared with Jeannie from that day to this.

Shortly after Tessa's death, Jeannie had asked him about his feelings toward Dan. Of course, those had been the days when he and his wife were actually talking to each other. It was a fair question. It was also one that Geoff had not yet been ready to consider. The team needed Dan if they had any hope of repeating as conference champs this season. That might sound shallow to some, but Geoff could not ignore the power that such an accomplishment could have for the entire student body.

"Kline," he barked as he watched the players trudge toward the locker room, "what's your problem?" Stupid question. What did he think his quarterback's problem was?

Dan paused but did not turn around, while his teammates continued on their way. Even wearing shoulder pads, Dan walked like a young man defeated. Geoff had the urge to shake him, but he realized that his irritation with Dan was rooted in the fact that the boy had been in the car that day, had agreed to let Sadie get behind the wheel, had been texting his buddies instead of coaching her. Or at least that was the gossip he'd heard around school—gossip that stopped the minute he passed in the hallway or entered a room. The hours he spent at school had been filled with moments like that, but even so, it was better than the isolation and emptiness he felt at home.

For the last day or so though, it was obvious that Jeannie had something on her mind, something she was reluctant to talk about with him. Whatever it was, she'd been working overtime to soften him up. After several nights spent sleeping in Tessa's room or the guest room, she had come back to their bed the night before. And that very morning, instead of being up and out for her run before his alarm went off, she was in the kitchen cooking a regular breakfast for the two of them.

Knowing Jeannie, she had come up with some plan for putting the family back together again—reconciling with Emma and forgiving Sadie. As if he ever could agree to such a thing. If he never saw Sadie again. . .

"Coach?"

He'd completely forgotten that he'd called Dan back. His quarterback was facing him now, his helmet dangling from two fingers as he squinted at him in the setting sun. Apparently he'd muttered some excuse and was waiting for Geoff to accept it.

"Go on, hit the showers," Geoff growled, and Dan hesitated only half a second before trotting off the field. Geoff picked up the small whiteboard that he used to outline plays and acknowledged the wave of the manager across the field. The kid worked hard. He'd just finished putting away the equipment and locking the shed. As he headed for the locker room, he tossed Geoff the keys.

"See you, Coach."

"Good job."

The kid looked surprised but pleased and broke into a trot

as he left the now deserted field. Geoff realized that he couldn't remember the boy's name.

He took off his sweat-stained baseball cap and rubbed his forearm across his forehead. He was already drenched in sweat, so a long run before he showered seemed like a good idea. Besides, it would use up another hour before he had to go home. Before he had to face another evening of a house without Tessa. Another night of not knowing what to say to Jeannie. Another cluster of hours when he had to face his failure as a father and husband.

He put down his whiteboard and started to jog around the track. On the second lap, he heard footsteps behind him, gaining on him. He glanced over his shoulder and saw Matt dogging his steps with shorter but admirable strides for a kid his age. Geoff felt the predictable flicker of irritation that he'd experienced on seeing Matt ever since the funeral. He thought about picking up the pace. How far down had he fallen to run away from a kid?

Not just any kid.

Matt.

"Hey, Matt," Geoff called out as if he'd been expecting his nephew all along. "Just finished an extra practice and thought I'd get in a couple of laps, but it's getting pretty late."

"I've got something to tell you," Matt said as he came alongside Geoff.

The boy was barely breathing hard and certainly hadn't broken a sweat, although he'd been running full out to catch up. "Okay, walk with me." He headed across the playing field toward the school.

"It's about Sadie—well, all of us actually, but—"

"Not interested," Geoff growled. He forced himself to add, "Look, I admit I've been avoiding you lately, and I'm sorry about that. If you want to talk about school or sports or anything like that, I'm here for you, Matt. But your sister is off-limits."

Matt stopped walking. "But. . ."

Geoff wheeled around, his fists clenched at his sides. "Why can't you people get this? I don't—no, make that I *can't* bear to think about what Sadie did to us much less talk about it."

"But this is different."

"Give it up, Matt. You and your mom and your dad and everyone else needs to stop trying to convince me that I need to forgive and forget." He released a laugh that sounded more like a howl. "Do us both a favor and just go away, Matt."

Matt was looking at him with those puppy-dog eyes that so many times in the past had pleaded with him to help with some problem at home or school. Geoff sighed and softened his tone. "You're a good kid, but seeing you makes me think about your sister, and frankly I'm not a big enough man to be able to manage that—not yet. Maybe there will come a day, but this isn't it, so go home. If you care for me at all, don't be coming around here anymore."

He punched in the security code for the school's side door then rested his forehead against the doorjamb. "Look, this isn't about you, Matt. It's just that right now. . ." He shook his head and added, "Maybe in a year when you're enrolled here—maybe then. Okay?" But when he turned around, Matt was running full out again, this time in the opposite direction.

Feeling frustrated by the very idea that Matt would even attempt to bring up Sadie's name and also guilty for taking out his grief and anger on the boy, Geoff showered and changed, stuffing his dirty clothes inside a duffel before turning out the lights and heading home.

The kitchen light was on when he came up the driveway, and he could see Jeannie standing at the sink. She didn't even glance up when he drove the car into the garage. But her movements told him that it was because she was caught up in whatever she was doing rather than that she was deliberately ignoring him.

Inside the laundry room off the kitchen, he dumped his dirty clothes in the washer, added detergent, and turned on the machine. Through the open doorway, he could see that the table was set—for three. Seeing a place setting where Tessa normally sat took his breath away.

Half expecting to find Jeannie in a state of confusion and denial, he steadied himself and then cleared his throat before entering the kitchen. Jeannie was cutting vegetables for a salad at the kitchen sink. "Hey, babe, what's going on?"

"Oh, good, you're home," she said. "Do me a favor and turn

the oven down to three hundred, okay?"

Geoff did as she asked, all the while looking for signs that his wife had finally lost it and gone fully into the dream world of imagining that Tessa was still with them.

"I've invited a friend of Hester's to have supper with us," she said as she tossed the salad and then covered the large wooden bowl with plastic wrap and set it in the refrigerator. "Her name is Rachel Kaufmann. She and Hester were college roommates in nursing school. She's moving to Sarasota to take a position at the hospital. Oh Geoff, her husband was killed by a drunk driver a year or so ago. Now it's just her and her son, Justin."

"Aren't you three places short?" Geoff asked, feeling an odd sense of relief that Jeannie was fine after all. "John and Hester and the boy?"

"It was all so last-minute. John and Hester had a prior engagement, and Rachel had promised her son that he could spend the night with a friend he met at church. She was going to be alone, so I thought. . . You don't mind, do you?"

Geoff almost smiled. This was so typical of Jeannie. She would invite total strangers to join them for a meal, and then when it was a done deal, she would give him those huge green eyes of hers and say, "You don't mind, do you?"

He felt a tenderness toward her that had been sorely missing since the funeral. "And if I did?" He kept his voice light and teasing, like the old days. He tweaked her cheek and then cupped her face in his hands. "It'll do us both good," he said. "Get our minds on someone else."

Jeannie nodded, but Geoff did not miss the way she hesitated as if there was a little more to the story than she was telling him.

Paranoid. He shook off the feeling.

"What can I do to help?" he asked as he rinsed his hands under the kitchen faucet and dried them on a dish towel. Just then the doorbell rang, and Geoff glanced out the window and saw a bike parked on the driveway. "How about I get the door?"

By her dress and manner, Rachel Kaufmann was of the same branch of the Mennonite faith as Lars and Emma. It made sense, of course, since Hester and John were also conservative in their practice.

He forgot to smile as he opened the door and took in the pale blue dress, the white starched prayer covering, the tightly bound black hair. Seeing her made him think of Emma—and Matt.

"Hello," she said, her smile tentative in the face of his less-than-warm welcome. "I may have the wrong house. I was looking for the Messner home?"

"Rachel, come in," Jeannie called from the kitchen. "That's my husband, Geoff. Geoff, this is Rachel."

Geoff smiled and opened the door wider, inviting the woman inside. "It's nice to meet you," he said, offering her a handshake.

"Likewise. Hester tells me that you're both the athletic director and vice principal at a local high school," she said. "That's quite a lot on your plate."

"Plus he coaches football and basketball," Jeannie added, coming into the front hallway.

Jeannie was nervous. Geoff knew his wife. She had never met a person she didn't immediately bond with. No, if Jeannie had invited this woman to supper, she had already established a connection of some sort. He decided that her nerves came from being out of the habit of entertaining and making the small talk that came with the territory.

"Jeannie tells me that you've taken a job at the hospital. Are you a nurse?" he ventured.

Rachel laughed. "I was. But one day I realized that it was the emotional and spiritual wellness of people that intrigued me, so I went back to school and got my degree in psychology—counseling—"

"Oh my," Jeannie said as she made a dash for the kitchen. "I left the heat on under the rice, and it's boiling over."

Geoff felt his jaw tighten as Rachel followed Jeannie to the kitchen, offering to help. A shrink? Was this a setup? True, he and Jeannie had been anything but close lately. Even before Tessa died, they'd been having problems, but a counselor? They had their minister for that if they needed him.

Still, he wouldn't be rude. He was feeling guilty about the way he'd handled things with Matt. On the drive home, he'd thought about how he might make that right. After all, Matt was an innocent bystander in all of this. It was unfair—not to mention downright immature—to blame him or even connect him to what had happened. But he hadn't been able to bring himself to stop by Matt's house, and the chances of Lars allowing the phone on at this hour were slim. Tomorrow, Geoff had promised himself, he would get a message to Matt to come by practice after school.

Feeling a little less tense for having come up with a plan for reuniting with Matt, Geoff joined the women in the kitchen where Rachel was filling glasses with ice and water and Jeannie was dishing up their supper. After all, if this was Jeannie's attempt to get them both to counseling, all he had to do was politely say no.

"Looks great," Geoff said, relieving her of the platter stacked with pieces of baked chicken. He set it on the table then pulled out Tessa's chair for Rachel.

"Thank you," she murmured.

He waited for Jeannie to sit before taking his own place across from her. He held out his hands for them to take for the silent grace before the meal, and after a minute, he released Rachel's hand and gave Jeannie's an extra squeeze before offering Rachel the platter of chicken.

"Have you found a place to live yet, Rachel?"

"I have. Do you know Malcolm Shepherd? He and his wife, Sharon, have rented me their guesthouse. Justin and I can walk to everything—his school, the market, the post office, even to work if I want to, although that's a bit more of a hike."

"Malcolm's brother, Zeke, and Geoff are best friends," Jeannie said.

"So what will you be doing at the hospital?" Geoff asked.

"I'm to be a spiritual counselor for the children's wing. It's quite a facility they've built there." She cut a piece of her chicken. "Have you always lived in Sarasota, Geoff?"

"My family moved here when I was ten."

Jeannie laughed. "But he's still not considered a Floridian. People who were born and raised here can get pretty picky about that."

"Like your sister?" Geoff said, and then he forced a smile.

Jeannie hesitated, and he understood that she was trying to

determine if his mention of Emma was innocent or intentional. In order to break the uncomfortable silence that followed his comment, she answered Rachel's obvious question, "Emma has always teased Geoff about being a transplant from Iowa even though he barely remembers when his family lived there."

"So, Rachel, what exactly are the duties of a spiritual counselor?" Geoff asked, wanting to move the conversation away from Jeannie's sister and her family. To his relief, Rachel seemed happy to oblige. While they finished their supper, she regaled them with tales of how she had first learned of the job, and they laughed together about Hester's habit of assuming she could find a solution for just about any problem.

"So, how do you like Sarasota?" Geoff asked.

"It's so clean and quiet," she marveled.

"Just wait until the snowbirds arrive," Jeannie warned as she pushed back her chair and began stacking their plates. "It's such a lovely night, why don't we have dessert out on the lanai?"

"Let me help you clear," Rachel offered.

"No thanks. You and Geoff go sit and get better acquainted. Geoff, Rachel was a school nurse and guidance counselor before leaving Ohio." She handed Geoff a tray already stacked with coffee cups, flatware, and dessert plates for him to carry out for her.

"Really?" Geoff took his cue and escorted Rachel out to the lanai while Jeannie turned on the coffeemaker and prepared to slice what looked like his favorite peanut butter pie.

By the time Jeannie arrived, carrying the coffeepot in one hand and balancing the pie in the other, Geoff was beginning to relax. He liked Rachel. She had the kind of no nonsense manner that worked well in dealing with kids—especially teenagers. He couldn't help but think that the decision to cut her job for budget reasons was a great loss for the school where she'd worked before.

It occurred to him that Rachel might be a good person for Jeannie to confide in. Their other friends were too close to everyone involved, but here was someone who was not only trained in counseling, but had also suffered her own terrible and sudden loss. The fact that she was a lot further down the grief path than they were might help Jeannie through the worst of this.

Given the circumstances of her husband's death, Rachel might even understand why it was important for him to tell Tessa's side of things in court.

He leaned back in the rattan chair and accepted the large slice of pie that Jeannie handed him. "My favorite," he said, smiling up at her.

"Duh," she replied with a little laugh.

For one incredible moment, life was normal again. He and Jeannie were spending an evening with a new friend. And while Tessa would have shared the meal with them, by now she would have excused herself to go up to her room or out with her friends. Geoff could imagine that this was just another such evening, and he allowed himself the moment of fantasy.

Rachel and Jeannie were talking about the fruit co-op that Hester and John managed, when Rachel said, "It's so easy to underestimate the impact a program like that can have on the lives of people. It's like that with the VORP program."

Jeannie went suddenly very still and silent, her eyes flicking back and forth between Rachel and him, almost as if she were warning Rachel about something.

"What's a vorp?" he asked.

Rachel set down her pie plate and coffee cup and leaned forward, her eyes riveted on Geoff. "It stands for Victim Offender Reconciliation Program." She waited.

Jeannie took a sudden interest in watching a bird outside the screened lanai. Geoff felt his throat tighten.

He should have gone with his first impression: This was a setup.

He stood up.

"It was nice meeting you, Rachel. I hope you and my wife have a nice visit, but if you'll excuse me, I have some schoolwork that needs my attention." His voice sounded foreign to him—too tight and high.

"Geoff, hear her out, please," Jeannie pleaded.

But Geoff was already back inside the house and walking away from her—away from her plot to get him to forgive Sadie—as if he ever could. As if *she* ever should.

Chapter 30

Matthew

When Matt left the athletic field, he did not go home. He rode his bike up and down streets, turning corners without thought until he found himself in a strange neighborhood with no idea of how to get back to Pinecraft.

It was nearly dark. The houses he passed were small and crowded close to one another, and their yards were filled with stuff—old cars and rusted pieces of metal and tires. The fences—where there were fences—sagged, and a few of them had whole sections missing. The streets were narrow, barely wide enough for two cars to pass, especially in places where cars were parked along the road.

Every once in a while he would ride past a house and hear voices coming from the darkened porches or see the flare of a match followed by the scent of cigarette smoke. A couple of times he heard laughter coming from inside houses with the shades drawn but the windows open. Families gathered together the way his used to.

He kept turning down new blocks, trying to find his way back to a main street, and then he realized that he was riding in circles. A car came down the street fast, nearly hitting him. The driver blared his car horn and yelled something foul at Matt as he roared past.

As dark as it was, it had to be well past his curfew. He wondered if his parents would even notice that he hadn't shown up yet. These days they focused all their attention on Sadie or Sadie's lawyer or Sadie's case. His mom called his aunt Jeannie pretty much every day and left messages that Matt could tell were desperate attempts to break the silence between the two families. As far as he knew, Jeannie had yet to call back.

He'd been giving some serious thought to running away. There were a couple of good reasons why that was a good idea. One, maybe it would make his parents wake up and realize that life couldn't be all about Sadie all the time. And two—what exactly was there for him around here anymore? Uncle Geoff had made it clear that he blamed the whole family, including him, for Tessa's death, even though at the time of the accident he had been at school working on his math, totally unaware that Sadie had stupidly driven Dan's car and hit Tessa.

Of course, running away meant he would need some money. He could take some food with him and his bike, of course, but the food was bound to run out pretty fast. He'd been trying to think of some way he might be able to earn some cash and save it up until he had enough, like maybe twenty dollars.

Then Sadie's lawyer had told them about VORP, and Matt had gotten really excited. Here was something that might actually work, that might get his uncle Geoff to stop ignoring him and talk to him again and let him come back to practice and all. If that happened, he could probably stand the stuff at home. Uncle Geoff would understand. He would listen like he had before. Geoff was always teaching the team—and Matt—that no matter what, there was a way through the other team's line—a way to win. And this VORP thing sure sounded like it had potential.

But Matt had blown it. Why did he have to blurt out Sadie's name the very first thing?

He stopped to get his bearings then decided on a shortcut through a park where he heard voices and laughter. He saw a group of boys, their bikes carelessly abandoned on the ground as they gathered around a picnic table under a streetlamp.

"Three kings," one of the boys crowed triumphantly. "Read 'em and weep."

Matt edged closer. The boy picked up some coins from the table and turned to go. "My ma is gonna kill me," he told the others when they protested that he couldn't leave yet.

He went to pick up his bike when he saw Matt. "Hey, kid, wanna take my place in the game?"

Matt looked around and then realized that the boy was talking to him. "Me?"

"Yeah. Go on. Hey, guys! Fresh blood," he shouted as he pedaled off.

The other three boys turned around. They weren't much older than Matt was. In fact, one of them looked like he was at least a couple of years younger. Two of them were white, and the third boy was black.

"Wanna play or not?"

Matt realized that they didn't know that he was Mennonite. It didn't seem to dawn on them that he was wearing the plain clothes of his faith. For once in his life he could be just another boy. And if this was what boys outside of the faith did and they wanted him to play, then why not? He was already late, and he could probably get these boys to help him find his way home once the game was over.

"Sure." He dropped his bike alongside theirs and sat down in the empty spot the first boy had abandoned.

"Next hand," one of the boys muttered as he dropped two cards on the table and held out his hand to receive two fresh ones. The golden glow of the streetlamp cast just enough light over the table for them to see the cards.

The boy looked at his new hand and groaned. "I fold."

"Me too," the other white kid said.

"Ante up," the black kid said as he scooped up the pile of coins and placed a dime in the center of the table.

Matt stared at the coins as each boy put one in the pile. One of the older boys shuffled the cards. "You got to pay to play, kid," he said.

Matt started to get up. "I don't have any money with me," he told them, hoping they wouldn't get mad at him. "And I don't know how to play this game."

"No worries," one of the kids said with a grin. "I'll spot you."

No worries? Matt wondered if it was possible that they knew Zeke. The kid put another dime on the table and explained the game. It seemed simple enough. Every player got five cards to start. You tried to make the best hand you could, but you could also turn in cards you didn't need in hopes of getting ones that would give you a better hand.

The black kid explained what a good hand was. A pair, two pair, and so on. At school, Matt's best subject was math, and somehow this all seemed to make sense to him. He nodded and checked his cards.

"I'll take two," the boy next to the dealer said.

"Three."

"I'll keep what I have," Matt said, and three pairs of eyes glanced his way.

"Pass," the first boy said.

"I'll bet a nickel," the second boy said and tossed five pennies onto the pile of dimes.

"I'll see that," the third kid said, adding a nickel to the pile. "Up to you."

"I don't. . ."

The dealer slid a nickel his way. "At this point, you either fold—as I'm going to do—or you put the nickel in the pile."

"Then I owe you fifteen cents."

"Yep. If you want to raise the bet, then you'll owe me twenty cents. What's it going to be?"

Matt checked his cards. If he won, then he could pay the boy who'd loaned him the money and still have some left. He picked up the nickel and tossed it onto the pile, enjoying the clink it made as it hit the rest of the coins.

"Pair of sevens," one boy said displaying his cards.

"Beats me," the second boy said. "Let's see what you've got, kid."

Matt laid out his cards—three twos, an eight, and a six.

"And we have a winner," the boy who'd loaned him the money

said as he slid the money toward Matt, taking care to remove his fifteen cents. "Deal," he told the black kid.

"Ante," the black kid replied as he shuffled the cards.

They played several more hands until a car rolled slowly toward them. "Outta here," one of the boys muttered as he divided the money left on the table between them and gathered the cards. "Same time tomorrow?"

He was looking at Matt, but he didn't wait for an answer.

The car stopped, and Matt could hear the crackle of a two-way radio that indicated a police car. He glanced toward the car, and when he turned back, the other three boys and their bikes had disappeared. A police officer was walking toward him, shining his flashlight over the area.

"Hey, kid, it's pretty late to be out here in the park," he said.

"I took a wrong turn and got lost," Matt replied, shielding his eyes from the brightness of the beam.

"Won't your folks be worried?"

"Yes sir."

"Where do you live?"

Matt gave his address, and the police officer released a low whistle. "You did take a wrong turn, half a dozen of them. You're a couple of miles from there." He turned the flashlight toward Matt's bike. "That yours?"

"Yes sir."

"Well, let's load it in the back of the patrol car and call your folks. I expect they'll be pretty worried by now."

"They won't answer. The phone is for my Dad's work. They don't answer it after supper. If you just tell me the way back, I can get there."

"Amish, are you?"

"Mennonite."

The officer reached inside the patrol car and picked up the two-way radio. He turned away while he talked to someone on the other end.

"Okay, come on," he said, lifting Matt's bike into the trunk and then fastening the lid closed with a bungee cord. "We'll give you a lift."

Matt started to back away.

"You're not running away, are you?" the officer said, his tone laced with fresh suspicion. His partner started to get out of the car.

"No sir."

"Then get in the car," the partner said, opening the back door for him.

Matt did as he instructed. He stared out the window as the officer drove, trying his best to get his bearings. He had just made over a dollar playing a game, and he wanted to be sure he could find his way back to play again.

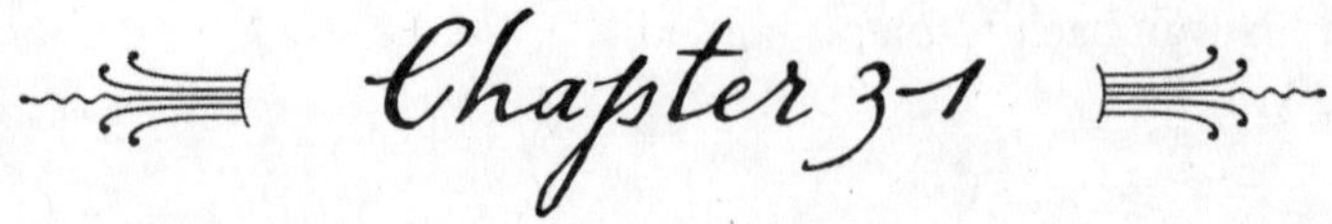

Chapter 31

Lars

When Lars and Joseph had followed Matt to the school, they'd seen Matt talking to Geoff. Since the two of them were walking across the field together and Geoff seemed to be listening, Lars had thought it best to give this possible break in the stalemate a chance. He'd told Joseph that everything seemed okay, and Joseph had driven him back home.

"Jeannie is probably serving them both huge bowls of ice cream right now," Emma said, clearly hoping that was the case. "I would call her, but she's not picking up."

"He'll be along soon," Lars assured her, but it was past eight o'clock, and he saw by Emma's anxious glances at the clock that she was as worried as he was. "You know, maybe I should drive over to Geoff and Jeannie's and pick Matt up. I mean, I don't like the idea of him riding his bike after dark."

"I'll go with you," Emma said.

"Nein, stay here in case he's on his way home and I miss him." He took his hat from the peg by the door and picked up the car keys.

He was outside with Emma standing in the doorway to see him off when the police cruiser pulled up in front of the house. Lars felt the breath rush out of his chest when he saw the official car and the officer getting out of the driver's side.

"Mr. Keller?" His partner had also gotten out and was opening the back door.

"Ja. . .yes?" Lars's heart was in his throat and beating hard as Matt got out. The boy did not look at either of his parents, just walked to the back of the cruiser to get the bike one officer was unloading.

"I've got it," Lars heard Matt say. "Thanks for the ride."

But the officer who'd been driving followed him up the driveway while his partner waited. He tipped his hat to Emma and then focused his attention on Lars. "Your son said he took a wrong turn. He was over in Payne Park."

Payne Park was the opposite direction from their house, Jeannie's house, or the school. Lars looked at Matt for an explanation. "What happened?"

"He. . ." Tears were rolling down Matt's cheeks.

Emma put her arm around their son. "Come inside," she said. "It's time for your shower." She ignored the officer as she ushered Matt past him and into the house.

"Is everything all right, Mr. Keller?" The officer was watching him closely. Then he blinked and looked even closer. "Keller? Any relation to. . ."

"She's my daughter. Our family has had some difficult days."

The policeman nodded. "Your son was awfully quiet on the ride home. I tried to draw him out—you know, in case somebody had. . .approached him. Sometimes a park, especially after dark. . ."

"I'll talk to him. We appreciate your bringing him home to us, officer. And now if there's nothing else?"

The policeman looked toward the lighted window of the kitchen and then back at Lars. "Glad to be of service." He walked back to his cruiser, shut the trunk, and got in. His partner got in on the passenger side, but they did not leave immediately. Instead Lars saw the two of them conferring, looking up toward the house as they talked.

Lars went inside and closed the door and shut off the porch light as well as the kitchen light. A minute later, he heard the police car pull away. They would file a report, and once again his family's name would be part of an official record.

Down the hall, he could hear water running. He followed the sound, and after confirming that Matt was in the shower, he went to find Emma. She was turning down the bed in Matt's room. "Did he say anything?"

She shook her head. "Not really. Whatever happened when he found Geoff, it didn't end up with them having ice cream together." She clutched Matt's pillow to her chest. "How could he have gone so far afield, Lars? Payne Park is all the way. . ."

"Downtown," Lars said. "I know." He sat on the side of the bed and bowed his head. He had never felt so lost, so incapable of doing the right thing for his family, for his children. God had blessed them with these bright and giving children to shepherd through this world, and after years of success, it seemed to him that he was suddenly at a loss about how to guide them. His daughter was in jail. His son had been brought home by the police.

"I suppose we should come up with some punishment," Emma was saying. "He could have called."

"He saw me turn the phone off after Joseph arrived for supper, remember? And we thought he was with Geoff."

"Ah," Emma sighed.

"The policeman recognized that we are—that Sadie is our daughter. I think he remains concerned that there may be more than one of our children in trouble."

Emma's eyes widened. "Surely not. Matt was lost—not causing trouble."

"These are different times for us, Emma," Lars said. "We have to face the fact that Sadie may have to go away for a time. We have to think about how all of this is affecting Matt."

Emma closed her eyes and sucked in a deep breath. "I am worried for him. Geneva Kurtz stopped me the other day. She says that Matt is not himself at school these days. She thinks perhaps the other children are keeping their distance from him. Why would they do that when he's in such pain, Lars?"

Lars had long ago given up believing that things wouldn't

change with each generation. Especially living here in Pinecraft on the very borders of a city like Sarasota where their children were so exposed to the ways of the outsiders. The life his children knew wasn't like the life he had known as a boy when he and his parents had lived on the farm up north. It wasn't even the way it had been for Emma and Jeannie growing up right here in Pinecraft.

More and more the ways of the outside world had made their mark, especially once the tourists had discovered the small community. Their fascination with the ways of the Amish and Mennonites was perhaps understandable, but Lars struggled with the lack of respect these outsiders showed for their customs. Sometimes it felt as if they were on display for the entertainment of others. But of far more concern was the attraction of their own young people to the dress and language and ways of these outsiders.

So many times he and Emma had had to quietly remind Sadie that such expressions as "so cool" or the sarcastic "Ya think?" weren't part of their way of speaking to others. Sadie's fascination with clothing had not come just from being around Jeannie or Tessa. More than once she had described to Emma some item of clothing she had observed on one of the tourists. It was always clear how much she had admired—even longed for—the garments. Lars had often heard Emma remind their daughter that to covet the goods of another was a sin. But Matt had always seemed indifferent to the ways of the outside world.

"Did his teacher say anything else?" he asked.

"His work is fine—when he does it—but more and more often she has to prod him to finish an assignment, and when she does, she told me that he has on occasion snapped at her. He always apologizes immediately," Emma assured Lars, "but still that's not like our son."

"No, that's not Matt at all."

Lars became aware that down the hall the water continued to run. He walked to the small bathroom the family shared and knocked at the door. "Waste not, son," he said, but he made a point of keeping his tone light, hoping that it would not be heard as a reprimand. Emma was right. Little attention had been paid to what Matt must be going through since the accident. It was past time for them to show their son that they were there as much for him as they were for his sister. "Finish up."

There was a beat, and then the water stopped and he heard a soft, "Yes sir."

When Matt came to his room dressed in his pajamas and carrying his clothes, Emma and Lars were sitting side by side on his bed. Emma immediately got to her feet and took the clothing from him, examining each item to see if it was clean enough for the boy to wear the following day before folding it over the single chair.

"So, you got lost," Lars said, patting the bed beside him. "It happens. What Mom and I don't understand is how you got so far from the school or Geoff and Jeannie's house."

Matt seemed to consider the merits of telling them what happened. Then he took a deep breath and poured out his story. "I was never at their house, Dad. I went to the ball field knowing Uncle Geoff had probably just finished practice, and I was right. He was taking laps around the track, so I caught up to him. I wanted to tell him about the program—about that VORP thing that Mr. Cotter was telling us about. I thought if I could show him a way that everything could be settled again, then maybe he wouldn't be so mad at me."

"He's not mad at you," Emma said. "Oh Matt, he's just so filled with sadness and grief. Sometimes in grown-ups that comes across as anger, but. . ."

Matt gave her a pitying look. "Mom, I know how it is, okay? Every time I've gone to watch practice since Tessa died, Uncle Geoff acts like he doesn't see me, and instead of taking a run with me once practice is over like we always did before, he just walks away."

"Mr. Cotter and I followed you to the ball field, son. It looked like you and your uncle were talking," Lars said.

Matt nodded. "Yeah. At first it was like maybe things would be okay. He didn't ignore me—he even waited for me to catch up to him. But I did it all wrong. I started out saying that this program was something that could help Sadie, and well, he's still really mad at her, and my bringing up her name seemed to make him even madder, and he. . ."

Matt drew in a shuddering breath and bit his lip. Lars realized that the boy was fighting back tears. It was obvious that the last thing he wanted to do was to cry twice in the same evening in front of his father. What kind of father had he been to this child that his own son was afraid to show his true feelings in front of him?

"Matt, it was wrong of Geoff to take out his feelings about losing Tessa on you. He's the adult here. He should have realized that you were only trying to help. You did a good thing in trying to offer an idea that could help."

"What happened after Geoff got mad at you?" Emma asked.

"I took off," Matt told them. "I just wanted to get away from there, so I started riding, thinking about what he'd said about not wanting to see me again for a long time, like probably not until I start school there next year." His voice trailed off. "Why did Sadie have to try and show off for Dan Kline? Now he doesn't even seem to care about her at all. It's because she was only thinking about Dan and how much she wanted him to like her. . . ."

Lars was so stunned at the bitterness he heard in the way Matt talked about his sister, the way he said Sadie's name as if it left a bad taste in his mouth, that he felt compelled to defend her. "Matt, Sadie is very sad and sorry for what happened that day. She knows how much hurt she has caused, and she will have to live with the consequences of her actions the rest of her life. Right now she needs—"

"Okay, I'm sorry." He turned to Emma to plead his case. "I just wanted so much for us to be a family again. I know Tessa's gone, but we're all still here. What about that?"

Lars could see that Emma had no answer to that, and truth be told, neither did he. He touched his son's bony shoulder and felt Matt tense.

"Say your prayers and then get some sleep, son. Tomorrow's another day." He moved aside so that Emma could hold back the covers while Matt crawled into bed and curled onto his side. After Emma had tucked him in, Lars sat on the side of the bed again. "Your mother and I have been blessed with you and your sister, Matt. This is a hard time for all of us, but if we place our trust in God's plan, we'll get through this together."

Matt looked at him with skepticism. "It's okay, Dad," he said wearily. "I understand how things are. I'll be fine. You and Mom just worry about Sadie."

"That's enough talk for tonight," Emma said as she switched off the small desk lamp, leaving the room in deep shadows cast by the single light from the front hall. "We can talk more tomorrow."

Recalling the conversation that Matt's teacher had had with Emma about his lack of attention and his growing hostility at school, Lars could only pray that it would also be a better day for their son.

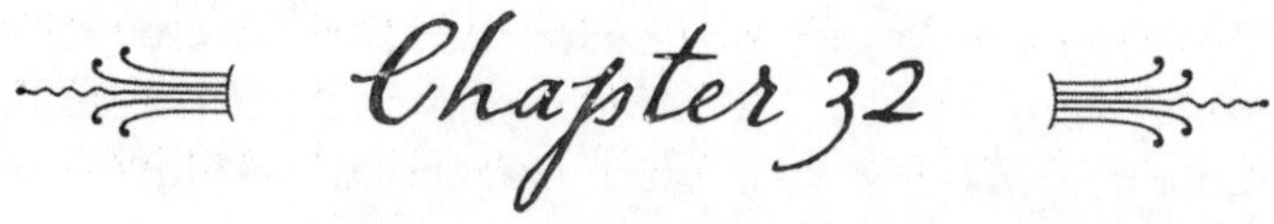

Chapter 32

Emma

Enough was enough. Something had to be done, and for once Emma was not going to be the one waiting for someone else to take action. After yet another night of lying awake while Lars pretended to sleep, Emma was up with the rising sun. She got dressed, left a note for Lars on the kitchen table, and headed for the bay. She was as certain as she had ever been of anything that Jeannie would be there.

Her sister was already at the far point of the mud flats where the mollusk beds jutted up from the clear, calm waters. Jeannie was picking her way over the sharp shells. She looked thinner and, even from a distance, she looked older—as if she had been beaten down by life. Or maybe Emma was simply projecting the way she felt on her sister.

The muck sucked at her shoes as she made her way out to the higher, drier sandbar. She passed several live tulip shells inching their way along and a huge lightning whelk with an interior that shone like pearls. She knew that Jeannie had passed them by as well. Neither of them would ever take a live shell no matter how large, rare, or beautiful it might be.

Jeannie remained oblivious to her presence, bent as she was over a cluster of mollusks as she peered closely at something hidden there.

"Is it a horse conch?" Emma called out, not wanting to startle her.

Jeannie turned slowly, shielded her eyes with one hand, and then nodded. "Ginormous, as the kids would say," she replied.

Emma smiled and felt a twinge of hope that just maybe they could find their way back to each other. "Alive?"

"Beautifully so."

"Did you see the whelk?"

Jeannie nodded and continued exploring the mollusk beds.

The sisters were shy with each other, skirting around each other like the egrets and little blue herons and other water birds around them. As was their usual practice, they came close to show the other a special find and then separated as they went in different directions, their heads bowed, their eyes searching the clear water for some new treasure.

It all reminded Emma of when they had been younger. They would have a falling out over something and promise never to speak to the other one again. Then it would dawn on them that they had just broken all ties with their best friend, and that would ignite the cautious but always predictable move toward making up. Sometimes it took only a matter of hours. Once or twice it had lasted overnight. This time it had gone on for weeks.

"I've missed you," Emma said as the sisters bent to admire a king's crown conch inching its way across the grassy bottom of the bay.

"Me, too," Jeannie admitted. "It's been. . .hard."

Jeannie had always been a master of understatement, and Emma almost chuckled, but this was not their usual disagreement. This time the stakes had been set far higher than either of them could ever have imagined possible.

"I can't possibly know what this has been like for you and Geoff," Emma said.

"But?" She sounded defensive.

"No 'buts,' Jeannie."

Her sister glanced at her skeptically then went back to shelling, moving away from her. Emma hoped that maybe she was thinking about how hard this had been on everyone—even those of them that had not directly suffered the death of a child. And she realized that this had been the most challenging part of the whole event—this kind of unspoken and unacknowledged but deeply felt contest about who among them was suffering most deeply.

Emma decided that if they were going to get anywhere, she had to risk saying aloud what everyone had avoided. "In one way, Jeannie, we've both lost our children. Tessa was not my daughter, but you know what she meant to us, how we loved her as one of our own."

Jeannie had stopped her cursory search for shells and was staring out across the bay to the islands beyond. She stood perfectly still, and Emma wondered if perhaps she hadn't heard her.

And then so quietly that Emma thought she might have imagined it, she heard Jeannie murmur, "How is Sadie?"

"She's pretty lost right now. It's hard to know what to say when we visit or how best to help her get through this. And, Jeannie, she must get through it. We all must. It can do no honor to Tessa's memory if we fail at that."

After a long moment, Jeannie turned around. She removed something from her pocket and held it out for Emma to see. "Zeke found these angel wings. Aren't they just perfect? So petite—like our Tessa was?"

Was it possible that with a simple exchange of observations about seashells the sisters had found their way to the open door that would allow them to talk after all this time? Emma kept walking to where her sister waited to show her the treasure of the sea. They stood side by side admiring the purity of the shell's white color and saying nothing for several long moments.

"Joseph Cotter stopped by last night," Emma said finally. "Lars and I think that the VORP idea is a good one."

Jeannie hesitated. "Geoff doesn't."

Emma let that pass. "What do you think?"

Jeannie breathed out a long-suffering sigh, and when she started to speak, it was as if a flood of all the things she'd been wanting to say for days came tumbling out.

"Oh Emma, what do I think? I think that I want this

nightmare to end. I think that I want my child back. I think that I want our life back. I think that I want to hear myself laughing again and singing again. I think that I want Geoff and me to start being in the same place at the same time with the same need to be with each other. I think that I want to utter a prayer that doesn't beg God to make this all go away but thanks Him for the blessings of our lives."

"Then let's figure out the best way to get there together, because that is exactly what I want as well."

The sisters slowly made their way back to the narrow beach entry to the bay. Along the way, Jeannie came across an empty moon shell and handed it to Emma, who accepted it for the gift and peace offering she knew it to be.

"I heard that the judge called for a continuance in court the other day," Jeannie said.

Emma nodded. "I think the combination of Dan Kline testifying for the state and then seeing Geoff about to get on the stand was too much for Sadie. She had a complete breakdown. The judge took pity on her and sent everyone home. We go back on Monday."

Emma wanted to ask if Geoff had changed his mind about testifying. She wondered if he could do such a thing, having already agreed to appear for the state. There was so much about the ways of these outside laws and courts that confused her. "It seems to me," she said as if she and Jeannie had been having a discussion about that very thing, "that everything to do with their laws and ways has to do with punishment and retribution."

"Maybe they've tried our way in the past," Jeannie suggested.

"It doesn't seem that way. On the other hand, Joseph tells us that the mediation program just might be a way that we could. . ."

"Save Sadie from having to go to jail?"

"She's in jail now," Emma reminded her sister.

They walked along in silence, a reminder that the chasm between them was not so easily bridged.

"Did you know that she was attacked?"

Jeannie stopped walking. "No. Was she badly hurt? What happened?"

Emma told her the story and about the conversation she had overheard in the hallway outside the courtroom. "I'm certain that she was that girl's grandmother. Can you imagine turning your back on a child? I mean, I don't have the right to judge them without a walk in their shoes, but still. . ."

"But you think that's what I've done? Turned my back on Sadie, who has always been like my own child."

"Oh Jeannie, I didn't mean—"

"I know what you meant," Jeannie said through clenched teeth, and Emma was stunned at her sister's bitterness.

They were walking past the gardens, taking a shortcut through the entrance to the parking lot and out to Orange Avenue as they often did in order to get away from the traffic on Mound Street.

"What time do you have to be back in court on Monday?" Jeannie asked after they had walked a couple of blocks in a tense silence. In the past, she had always been the one to find a way to break any tension between them, and Emma was grateful for her willingness to do it now.

"Nine o'clock."

They had walked past the neat lawns of the houses along Orange and crossed over the bridge on their way to Bahia Vista Street—the street that would take them eastward to Pinecraft. This was a walk they had taken together more times than either of them could count. It struck Emma that through the years they had talked about so many things while taking this same journey—boyfriends, parents, their husbands, their children.

"I'd like you to be there," Emma said softly. "In court with Lars and me. I'd like you to be there for Sadie, if you think you could manage."

Jeannie kept her eyes on her feet. "I don't know, Emma. Geoff will still testify, you understand."

Emma hesitated. "Well, maybe not then. I know how hard it's been for the two of you—I mean, even before you lost Tessa, there were. . ."

To her shock, Jeannie turned on her, her face aflame with rage. "You know nothing. For once in your life, Emma, stop assuming that you have the answers, because you don't. You didn't with Sadie, and you don't for me and Geoff." Tears welled in Jeannie's eyes. "You know something, Emma—here's how I'm going to fix this: I am going to stand by my husband before I lose him as well."

Emma was dumbfounded at the change in Jeannie. She barely recognized her anymore. "Jeannie, it's just that Geoff seems to want some kind of revenge. . ."

"Justice, Emma. He wants justice."

"Okay, but his kind of justice is not our way, not your way."

"Don't be so sure about that. Let God take your child—your only child—and we'll see how much forgiveness you can summon up."

"You blame Sadie like Geoff does," Emma whispered.

"Like you once said to me, Emma, there's enough blame to share all around. If you and Lars had put a stop to Sadie seeing Dan, much less getting into a car with him. . ."

Emma thought she might explode from the sudden thrust of pure anger that pierced her like a sword, releasing the venom of her temper. "Maybe if you'd thought for five seconds before going behind our backs—knowing that Lars and I were not ready for Sadie to drive. . ."

As soon as the words spewed forth, Emma covered her mouth with both hands to stop them. The sisters were facing each other on a public street, their anger crystal clear to anyone who happened to be passing. Fortunately, no one was.

"Oh Jeannie, I didn't mean. . ."

"Yes you did." Jeannie let her breath drain out slowly. "I can't do this, Emma. Maybe one day, but for now the only thing that I have left is my marriage. I don't expect you to understand that, but that's really not my problem."

Emma reached out for her, but Jeannie brushed her hands away and then held up both palms defensively. "Go away," she growled. "If you care at all for me, then go away and leave us in peace."

And not knowing what else to do, Emma let her walk away.

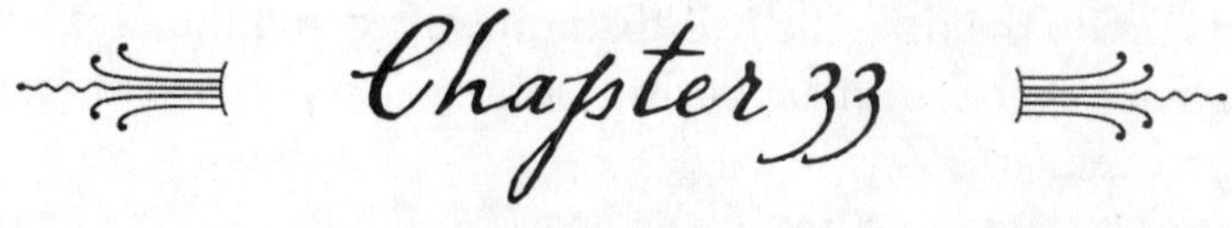

Chapter 33

Geoff

The second time Geoff was called to the stand, he was ready. He did not look either left or right as he walked to the front of the courtroom.

That morning Jeannie had announced her intention to be there with him. She was seated alone in the last row on the side behind the girl who had recklessly taken the life of their only child. On the other hand, he could not suppress his surprise that she was sitting alone—not with Emma and Lars, although there was certainly room in their row. Out of the corner of his eye, he saw that Jeannie was sitting up very straight with her head bowed and her hands folded in her lap as he passed by. Was she praying? For him? For them?

The night before, Geoff had slept in his office at school. After the whole VORP fiasco, things at home had gotten so bad that he had to get away—even if it was just for one night. So, knowing that Jeannie was probably out, he'd left her a voice mail saying he had a meeting that would keep him out late. She had not returned his call but when he'd gone into their voice mail later that night, the message was no longer there, so he knew she'd heard it.

And done nothing.

Well, what had he expected? That she would seek him out, come to the school looking for him? By what means? He had their only car, after all. He'd pulled a childish stunt intended solely to make her come around to his way of thinking. He wanted her to stop thinking so much about Sadie. He wanted her to forget about Rachel and her stupid VORP thing. He wanted his wife back on his side, fighting with him to find their way through this horror show. It wasn't her presence in the courtroom that was confusing; it was her choice to sit alone.

He took the oath the bailiff administered and then sat down in a hard wooden chair as Mr. Johnson, the state's attorney, approached.

Geoff stared straight at the lawyer as he gave his full name, residence, occupation, and relation to the defendant.

"I. . .she is my wife's niece."

"And yours as well by marriage?" Johnson asked.

"Yes," Geoff admitted, aware that Sadie had looked up at him.

"And what is your relationship to the victim, Tessa Messner?" Johnson had softened his tone.

"She's—was—my daughter."

"Sir, tell the court what you were doing on the morning of August 28th."

"Getting ready to go to work," Geoff replied.

Johnson gave him a look that encouraged him to go on.

"I was starting a new position at the school as vice principal, and I was running late." He didn't know what the man wanted him to say. Why didn't he just ask him yes and no questions?

"Go on."

Geoff closed his eyes, forcing himself to remember the day he wanted only to forget. "It was raining. I went outside. My wife had handed me an umbrella." He opened his eyes and glanced at Jeannie, who was watching him intently now.

"I don't. . . Why did I have the umbrella? I was going to drive to school." He realized that he was asking Jeannie.

Johnson glanced at Jeannie and then positioned himself to block Geoff's view of her. "Mr. Messner, you went outside, and then what happened?"

"I was trying to open the stupid umbrella, and Tessa was laughing at me."

"Your daughter was also outside?"

"Yes." He was irritated by the attorney's interruption. "Of course she was. She was waiting for her ride. It was raining. We were both going to be late." Then he remembered. "I was bringing the umbrella out for Tessa."

"Why didn't you drive her to school?"

"She wanted to ride with our niece and Dan Kline."

Johnson picked up the photograph of Dan's car. "This has been identified as Dan Kline's car. Was this the car your daughter was to ride to school in that morning?"

"Yes."

Johnson replaced the photograph on his table. "So, you were opening the umbrella to shelter Tessa from the rain while she waited. Then what?"

"Tessa was teasing me. I can never seem to get those automatic umbrellas to work. She came to help me, and that was when I saw Dan's car coming straight for us."

"And who was behind the wheel of that car, sir?"

"Her." He pointed at Sadie.

"Let the record show that the witness has identified the defendant, Sadie Keller." Next, Johnson held up a kind of floor plan that showed their house and the garage and the driveway and street. "Show us where you were standing," Johnson asked.

Geoff pointed, and Johnson drew a blue circle to indicate the spot. "And Tessa?"

Geoff pointed again. "But I pushed her back—I told her to get out of the way when I saw the car coming toward us." He tried to control the shudder that memory sent coursing through his body but failed.

"Now, Mr. Messner, I know this is difficult, and we're almost finished here, but please tell the court what you saw then."

Geoff closed his eyes again, squeezing them shut against the sight of his wife, his niece, his sister, and his brother-in-law, who in many ways had lost a child of their own that day. He thought about Matt and how when he'd gone to the kid's school to invite him to come back to football practice, Matt had looked away and muttered something about having something else he had to do.

"Mr. Messner?"

"Tessa stumbled away, and the car suddenly changed directions and went into a spin. The back end of it caught Tessa and flung her up and then down again, and then she was just lying there. . .not a mark on her."

"And once again, Mr. Messner, who was operating the vehicle that struck your child?"

"Objection," Sadie's lawyer said in a fairly normal tone. "Asked and answered."

"No further questions," Johnson murmured and sat down.

Sadie's lawyer took his time rising and approaching the stand. He smiled in a polite, friendly way that immediately put Geoff on alert. He sat up a little straighter.

"Sadie Keller is your niece, is that right?"

"By marriage, yes."

"Your wife and Sadie's mother are sisters, is that right?"

"Yes."

"How long have you known your niece?"

"All her life."

"So sixteen years. Your family and hers are close then?"

"We were until. . ."

"Would you say that Sadie is a girl who gets into trouble?"

"No."

"Is she a good student?"

"Yes."

"Were you ever concerned about her influence on Tessa?"

"No."

"Your daughter and Sadie were not only cousins, they were best friends—is that right?"

"Yes."

"In fact, you and your wife had agreed to Sadie's plan to have Tessa arrive for her first day at this new school with Dan Kline and Sadie because they were very popular with the other students, is that right?"

"Yes, but. . ."

"Dan Kline is the quarterback on the football team that you coach, is that right?"

Geoff's head was beginning to ache. The questions were delivered in a completely conversational way, but they were coming so fast. "That's right."

"Would it be fair to say that you've gotten to know Dan Kline fairly well in the four years he's played on your football and basketball teams?"

"Yes."

"Is Dan a good student?"

Geoff relaxed slightly. "Top of his class," he replied.

"Do you consider him to be a responsible young man?"

"Yes."

"And yet on the rainy morning of August 28th, he willingly allowed Sadie to drive his car from her house to yours, is that right?"

"Objection," Johnson snapped. "The witness has no way of knowing. . ."

"Withdrawn," Sadie's lawyer said, and Geoff thought that maybe it was finally over. But the rumpled young attorney only paused to glance at a note on his legal pad. "Mr. Messner, I'm going to ask you to think carefully now. When you saw the car come toward you and then swerve away, you've testified that your niece was behind the wheel."

"That's right."

"And did you see Dan Kline at that same moment?"

"Yes. He was in the passenger seat."

"Go on."

Geoff was confused. The barrage of questions answerable with a simple yes or no had changed.

"I don't understand."

"You've testified that Sadie was driving and that at the last second the car swerved, missing you and hitting your daughter. In that split second, what do you remember about Dan Kline's reaction to the situation?"

It was as if a veil had been lifted and Geoff saw clearly for the first time what had really happened that morning. "He grabbed the steering wheel and turned it hard to the right," Geoff said, his voice almost drowned out by the audible gasp that rippled through the courtroom.

Geoff sat frozen in the witness chair, his mind replaying the detail that had escaped him every time he had allowed himself to think about that morning. Dan had grabbed the wheel.

If he hadn't, would Tessa be alive today?

Chapter 34

Sadie

It felt odd seeing her uncle Geoff and aunt Jeannie in the courtroom—not exactly together, it appeared. Jeannie had come in and sat down alone in the last row, even though there were at least three empty chairs in the row where Sadie's parents were sitting. Then Geoff had come in when called to testify, but he'd barely looked at anyone other than the lawyers the whole time he was on the stand.

She hadn't been sure where Mr. Cotter was going with his questions, but when he'd asked her uncle about her—what kind of kid she was, Uncle Geoff had said she was a good person, a smart student, and Tessa's best friend. She wasn't sure why that gave her some hope, but it did. Surely the opinions of a man of her uncle's position in the community—a coach and vice principal—carried some weight, even if they were related.

"By marriage," she remembered Geoff saying at least twice. It was like he didn't want to admit to being family with her unless he absolutely had to. When she considered that, all hope flew out the window. Geoff was making it clear—under oath—that their relationship as uncle and niece was over.

But then out of the blue Mr. Cotter had asked him about Dan, and Sadie had gone on instant alert. Even though Dan had technically lied about her pleading with him to let her drive, Sadie had decided to forgive him. He'd been under a lot of stress, and maybe he hadn't thought he was lying at all.

Then Mr. Cotter had started to present her defense. He began by entering into evidence the depositions of a string of people who knew her well enough to talk about what a good student and all-around good person she was. Several of those very people were sitting behind her. Pastor Detlef had given her a kind smile as she entered the courtroom. Two of her teachers had also looked at her with sympathy. Sadie noticed that Mr. Johnson did not seem especially interested in what these folks might have said, and she began to have some hope that maybe he—like everyone else—just wanted to get this over with.

"The defense calls Sadie Keller," Mr. Cotter was saying, and Sadie realized that it was her turn to take the stand.

She stood up and went to the place where all the other witnesses had stood when they took the oath. But she couldn't take such an oath. It was against her religion to do so.

Mr. Cotter was explaining this to the judge, and then Mr. Johnson said that the state was all right with Sadie simply affirming her intention to tell the truth as their church traditions had taught them.

"All right," the judge said, turning to speak to Sadie directly. "You understand that you are agreeing to tell the truth here? That this court is relying on you to honor the teachings of your Mennonite faith and tell this court only the truth when you answer these questions?"

"Yes sir." Sadie's mouth had gone dry, and she cleared her throat. "I'll tell the truth," she assured the man in the black robe. "It would be a sin to tell a lie."

"Even if telling the truth may seem to get you into more trouble?"

Sadie swallowed. "I will not lie, sir."

The judge peered at her over the rims of his glasses. "And do you also understand that you do not have to testify at all, and that if you choose to remain silent, that cannot be used against you?"

"Yes, Your Honor. Mr. Cotter explained all of that to me."

"Very well. Get on with it, Counselor."

Joseph asked her to state her name, age, and address for the record. He asked her what school she attended. He asked her why Tessa was only that year starting to attend the academy. He asked her how she knew Dan Kline.

When Mr. Cotter had come to the detention center the day before, he had warned her that the easy questions would be the ones he asked first. The more difficult ones would come later. And then he had gone through the questions, making notes when she gave her answers and sometimes reminding her to answer each question in the simplest way possible without adding any further comment or observation.

When Mr. Cotter approached her, Sadie sat up straight and looked directly at the judge when she gave her answers, as Joseph had instructed. She was a good student normally, and she had caught on quickly to the rhythm of the give-and-take of the process of testifying.

"In your own words, Sadie, begin with the moment you got into the car with Dan Kline at your home, and take us through exactly what happened."

Mr. Cotter had prepared her for this. He had gone over and over the way she would tell what had happened. She wanted to be sure she got it right. She took in a deep breath as Mr. Cotter had instructed and slowly let it out. And then she began, talking only to the judge as Mr. Cotter had coached her. "He is the person trying the case, hearing the facts. In an adult case, there would be a jury and I would tell you to talk to them, but here it's the judge you need to convince." She closed her eyes for a moment, reliving for what seemed the thousandth time every tiny detail of that morning. And then she opened her eyes and told the judge everything she recalled about that day. And even though she was interrupted numerous times by Mr. Johnson's objections and Mr. Cotter's gentle questions, she pressed on. It all came back to her as vividly as if it were happening again, and although she tried to give the judge just the facts, in her mind she couldn't help but go all the way back to that day last spring when Dan Kline had first noticed her.

Dan Kline was undoubtedly the world's best-looking guy. A year earlier, Sadie would have done almost anything to catch his attention. He was tall—just under six feet—with broad shoulders and a slim muscular build. He moved with grace, and when he smiled, he had this dimple that made him appear boyish and almost shy. His eyes were an impossible shade of blue-green, and his blond hair had a way of falling over his forehead that just begged for a girl to brush it back with her fingers.

Sadie could still remember the exact moment when he had focused those eyes and that smile on her. It had been a rainy day much like this one, only it had been last April. Like some dork, she had actually looked behind her to see who the lucky recipient of his attention might be. He had chuckled—a sound that came from somewhere deep in his chest. "Yes, I'm talking to you, Sadie Keller."

He had known her name. She thought she must have misheard him, but he was calling her by name and telling her that he had heard that she was helping out at the fruit co-op that her mom's friend Hester Steiner had started. He wanted to do a term paper on the project, and maybe she could introduce him to some people there whom he could interview for his paper.

Sadie was sure that once she got him to the people he needed to meet, he would forget all about her. But how wrong she had been. Dan had continued to sit with her at lunch, and the day he got an A on his paper, he had caught up with her as she walked home from school and walked the rest of the way with her. That was the day she had introduced him to her father. That was the day that her father had pronounced him a "nice young man."

On the day of the accident, they were starting a new school year—his senior year. Sadie could not help but worry that as a senior he might want to rethink hanging out with a lowly sophomore. There were plenty of girls in his class who were pretty and smart and far more worldly than she was. She had to make sure that she looked her best and that she did nothing that would give him cause to view her as too young or immature for him.

"Do you want to drive?" Dan asked her as soon as they had turned the corner at the end of her street. He was looking at her with that little boy grin that always set her heart racing.

She giggled. When Dan had called her early that morning to suggest that he drive her to school, she had told him about getting her learner's permit. He knew the rules. He had to be teasing her.

"You know I can't. I just got my learner's. . ."

He cocked an eyebrow that turned his question into a dare. "I have a license."

"You have to be twenty-one in this state," she reminded him. "I mean, I have to drive with someone that old in the car."

"Now let's just think about this before you say no. It's what? Less than a mile to your cousin's place?" He pulled to the side of the street and let the engine idle. "Come on. What can happen?"

He was out of the car and coming around to her side before Sadie could protest.

"Come on already," he said, holding the door open for her, his shoulders hunched. "We're going to be late, not to mention that I'm getting soaked."

Her folks would have a cow if they found out. But this was Dan. The last thing she wanted was to start off the year with him thinking she was too chicken to try something just slightly forbidden—well, truly forbidden. But Dan did have a point—it was less than a mile with no really busy streets, and they would switch back once they got to Tessa's. Before they got to Tessa's.

She scrambled out and ran to the driver's side of the car.

"We have to stop and switch back when we get to Tessa's street," she said as she slid into the driver's seat. But then she ran her hands over the steering wheel and felt such a rush of power, of being grown-up. She couldn't help squealing.

"Okay, adjust the seat and the mirrors," Dan instructed as soon as she'd closed the door. "The flashers are on, so turn those off and put on your signal. Then slowly pull out as soon as you see an opportunity."

Sadie concentrated on following everything he said to the letter.

"Good," he said when she had pulled onto the street. He leaned his seat back and took out his cell phone.

"Who are you texting?" Sadie asked as his thumbs flew over the keypad.

"The guys."

The guys were Dan's teammates. Sadie forced herself to concentrate on the driving. There was a lot more traffic than she had expected, and it seemed like all the other vehicles on the road were racing past her at a fast rate of speed. A driver pulled around her, his horn blaring, and she clenched her teeth and tightened her grip on the steering wheel. The side mirrors and rear window were fogged up, so she was having trouble seeing other cars. She glanced at the console. "Where's the rear defroster?"

Dan punched a button. "Come on, Sadie, give it some gas, or we'll be getting to school sometime tomorrow." He continued texting without looking up.

Sadie gripped the steering wheel and pressed down on the accelerator. The car seemed to leap forward, and she immediately fumbled for the brake, sending the car into a slight skid. "What do I do?" she shouted.

"Just stay calm," Dan coached, but she noticed that his voice shook a little and he was sitting forward, the cell phone lying loose in his hand as he watched the road.

As she regained control of the car, she realized that he was laughing.

"It's not funny," she huffed as she bent forward over the steering wheel, as if that position would give her better vision. She looked over at him. "Stop laughing."

Now that she had managed to right the car and get back into the flow of traffic, he was back to texting and fighting a smile. Determined now to show him that she was not some kid, Sadie pressed down on the gas.

The speedometer hovered at just over thirty-five, but it felt as if they were doing at least sixty. It was exhilarating and terrifying but also fun. She hit a patch where the water had covered the road and was thrilled when a high wave shot up on Dan's side.

"Slow down for the turn," he said, and this time there was no humor in his tone. "That's her street ahead, right?"

Tessa's street was coming up fast—too fast—and Sadie

wrenched the steering wheel to the right and prayed that there wouldn't be a car coming out of the lane as she made the wide turn.

Her prayer went unheard. Once again she heard the blare of a car horn as Tessa's neighbor, Mr. Diehn, sped past. All she wanted now was to pull to the side and turn the driving over to Dan. She peered through the windshield, looking for a place where she could park so they could switch.

"Come on, Sadie, we're already running late, and with this rain, nobody's going to notice you driving. Just get to your cousin's," Dan said, his focus back on his texting. Then he started to snicker.

"What?" she asked, her patience with this whole business wearing thin. They were approaching Tessa's block, and the rain was pelting the car so hard that she had to shout to be heard.

Then Dan started to laugh out loud as his fingers flew over the keypad once again. He waited a beat and then laughed even harder. "Oh, that's rich," he muttered.

"What's so funny?" she demanded, only half aware that the more irritated she got the harder she pressed on the accelerator. They were almost at Tessa's driveway. "Are you making fun of me to your friends? Let me see," she said and made a grab for the cell phone with her right hand while turning onto the drive with her left.

"Keep both hands on the wheel," Dan shouted as the car started to skid.

Sadie wrenched the wheel to the left and looked out the window just in time to see that they were headed straight for her uncle Geoff, who had just come outside and was trying to open an umbrella. She slammed down hard on the brake and threw up her hands and screamed as Dan gave the steering wheel a hard wrench to the right.

Unimaginably she looked up, and there was Tessa, her eyes wide like the proverbial deer caught in headlights. Her cousin pressed herself against the garage door. Then there was a thud followed by a whoosh, and suddenly Sadie couldn't see anything but the white pillow of the airbag.

Sadie stopped talking, and Mr. Cotter stopped asking questions, and Mr. Johnson stopped leaping to his feet every twenty seconds with an objection. Everything went quiet—the way it had that morning. Sadie folded her hands, silently praying that her words had been enough to show everyone how truly sorry she was for what she had done. Her aunt was leaning forward as if to catch every word.

Sadie met Jeannie's tear-filled gaze, and for one unbelievable moment, she felt that after everything that had happened there might be a chance. Was there any hope that maybe someday her beloved aunt—Tessa's mom—would find it in her heart to forgive her?

Chapter 35

Emma

Joseph had gently guided Sadie through her testimony in spite of numerous interruptions and objections from the attorney for the prosecution. Step-by-step the story they had never heard—the story of what had actually happened that morning, leading up to and including the moment the car had hit Tessa—unfolded. Emma likened it to watching a ball of yarn slowly unwind as her knitting needles fashioned the thread of wool into socks for Lars or a sweater for Matt. As soon as Sadie repeated Geoff's revelation that at the last minute Dan had grabbed the steering wheel and wrenched it to the right to avoid hitting Geoff, Joseph Cotter thanked her and returned to his place at the table.

And just when Emma was breathing a sigh of pure relief that Sadie had weathered this ordeal without breaking down, Mr. Johnson stood up. "Just a few questions, Miss Keller," he said, looking at his legal pad instead of at Sadie.

Emma mentally went over everything Joseph had explained to them about procedure. The state's attorney would try to unravel the details of Sadie's testimony. "Not with malice," Joseph had assured them. "It's just that what he's been told by others—like Dan Kline—may not match exactly with what Sadie tells the court."

Like that it was Dan's idea for her to drive to Tessa's, Emma thought now. Sadie hadn't pleaded for him to let her drive. Just the opposite.

And yet in the end, she gave in and got behind the wheel.

Emma turned her mind back to what Joseph had told them would happen once the state's attorney completed his cross-examination, willing that part of the process to be over quickly. "If necessary," Joseph had told them, "I'll ask Sadie a few more questions, and then the defense—that's us—will rest."

"Then what?"

"Each lawyer will have the opportunity to make a closing statement, and then the judge will decide whether Sadie is guilty as charged. There are two charges against her, and she could be found not guilty of both, guilty of both, or guilty of one but not the other."

"What do you think he will decide?' Lars asked.

Joseph had looked away. "He's hard to read, and he's new in the system, so I'm not sure. Most judges develop a kind of pattern over time. If he decides against her on either count—or both—then there will be a disposition hearing."

"More time?" Emma moaned.

"Maybe not. It could happen right then, or the judge could schedule it for a later time."

"And Sadie would go back to the detention center?"

"That depends. The judge could choose to release her to home detention."

"He would do that?" Emma's heart had thudded with hope.

"He might—emphasis on *might*," Joseph warned.

With that in mind, Emma folded her hands and leaned forward, her focus on Mr. Johnson.

"Miss Keller, here's what this court needs to know."

Sadie met the lawyer's gaze without blinking.

"Did you or did you not of your own free will and in spite of knowing that it was against the law to do so, choose to get behind the wheel of Daniel Kline's car on the rainy morning of August 28th? And did you then drive eight tenths of a mile to your cousin's house, where you chose to take your attention away from your responsibility for the operation of that vehicle?"

Sadie blinked and glanced first at Joseph and then at the judge.

"Answer the question," the judge said.

"I don't understand—"

"I'll make it simple for you, Miss Keller," Mr. Johnson said. "Did you on the morning of August 28th choose to drive your boyfriend's car and do so in such a manner that you ended up killing your cousin, an innocent bystander?"

Joseph was on his feet immediately. "Objection," he sputtered.

"Withdrawn," Johnson said as he returned to his chair. "No further questions."

Sadie was excused. She hurried to take her place next to Joseph, leaning in to whisper something that Emma didn't hear. Joseph shook his head and squeezed her hand. Joseph stood up and walked to the small podium in front of the judge's high position to deliver his closing statement, but Emma could barely concentrate. Her fury at the way Mr. Johnson had asked Sadie about the accident threatened to overwhelm her. She folded her hands and bowed her head and prayed that God would forgive her for her anger and dislike of that man.

Then, after the state's attorney had made his plea for the judge to find the defendant guilty of the greater charge of vehicular homicide, the courtroom was silent for the second time that morning. The bailiff kept watch, and the clerk's fingers remained poised to record whatever came next. Lars reached over and interlocked his fingers with Emma's.

She knew that he was silently praying for the judge to find their daughter not guilty. The two of them fixed their gaze on the small dark-haired man in the voluminous black robe. He seemed oblivious to the presence of a courtroom filled with people as he studied a file on his desk. Emma realized that he was scanning the documents Joseph had handed him earlier—the depositions from Pastor Detlef and Sadie's teachers and neighbors.

Finally, he cleared his throat, and the bailiff told the defendant to rise. Joseph stood, taking Sadie's arm and coaching her to a standing position as well. The judge focused his attention on

Sadie, but Emma saw that he seemed to be thinking about all that he had heard as he stared at their daughter.

"Sadie Keller, you have been accused of causing the death of another human being through the reckless use of a motor vehicle. It is my decision that under the charge of vehicular homicide you are not guilty."

A collective rush of released breath whooshed through the room, and the judge held up his hand. "On the charge of culpable negligence, I find you guilty."

This time the reaction was an audible but hushed murmur. The judge waited for it to pass.

"I have been impressed by these depositions from others related to the stability of your family and community, and I have taken into consideration the duress that you have had to endure while being held in detention. Therefore, between today and the date set for the disposition hearing, I am releasing you to the custody of your parents."

Emma saw Sadie half turn and smile.

"This is not a get-out-of-jail-free card, young lady. It goes without saying, I should hope, that your learner's permit has been revoked and should be turned over to the clerk of the court as soon as you have retrieved your personal belongings." He leaned even farther forward, his dark eyes pinning Sadie. "I expect you to use the days between today and the disposition hearing to consider how your foolish desire to impress a young man ended in tragedy for a great many people you love."

Sadie nodded and murmured, "Yes sir. Thank you, sir."

Was it over? Emma wondered. But no, Sadie had been found both not guilty and guilty. Still, she was coming home—today. Emma squeezed Lars's hand and then turned to find her sister, wanting so much to share this moment with her, hoping that in spite of everything, Jeannie would share her joy that Sadie was coming home.

But Jeannie was no longer in the room.

It took time to sort out everything once the judge had made his ruling and set the date for the disposition hearing for three weeks later.

Three weeks until the next shoe would fall. Three weeks to have her daughter home and perhaps some semblance of normalcy to their lives, even if only for that brief time.

Emma tried to consider how best to handle this reprieve. It was important not to get their hopes too high. Joseph had explained that the charge of culpable negligence still carried the possibility of commitment plus payment of court costs. Further, it was going to be important that they not put too much emphasis on Sadie being home again. Although she suspected that Matt would see their relief and joy as further evidence that his sister meant more to them than he did, she couldn't help hoping that he would be happy for Sadie.

Lars was certain that Matt's recent habit of leaving the house as soon as possible after supper to meet some friends was nothing more than a combination of his age and the need to find some escape from what was going on around him. She and Lars assumed they would find him at the school playing basketball.

"He's trying to figure out how best to handle Geoff's rejection, and sports seems a healthy way to do that," Lars had told her. "I expect playing a game of pickup basketball—a sport that he knows his uncle Geoff respects—makes him feel a little closer to finding his way back into Geoff's good graces."

But Emma wasn't so sure that they had the entire story. One evening when she had attended a meeting at the church, she had driven past the school on her way home, thinking to offer Matt a ride since it looked like rain. The courts had been deserted, and when she got home, Matt wasn't there.

He'd shown up half an hour later, and when she told him she'd stopped by the school, his cheeks had gone beet-red and he'd looked away. "We were playing in the park," he mumbled.

Later she'd brought up the subject with Lars again.

"Emma, don't we have enough to worry about with Sadie's trial and all without you making up problems?"

She'd been stunned into silence. Lars had never spoken to her in that exasperated tone. He had always listened and comforted and even agreed to do something about whatever situation she was worried about at the moment.

Lars had immediately softened his tone. "Look, he's a good student, and he does his chores without you having to remind him. So if he's out playing basketball with some of Geoff's team, where's the harm?" He'd sighed heavily then. "Sometimes I wish that I could just go play a game of shuffleboard with the men."

"What's stopping you?" Emma had shot back, surprised at the vehemence in her voice. She knew full well why Lars no longer went to the shuffleboard courts. It was the same reason she had stopped working at the thrift shop and going to the fruit co-op unless she knew she would be working alone with Hester.

They didn't want to hear even a whisper of gossip about Sadie and her case, or how Geoff and Jeannie no longer had anything to do with Emma and Lars, or how they had been far too permissive with Sadie all along, and if they weren't careful, that boy of theirs. . .

Oh, she had heard it all. And she knew that Lars had as well.

"It's a pickup game of basketball, Emmie," Lars had said. "You remember how excited Matt was to even be included in their game. You must know how much it meant to him to have Geoff praise his talent on the court before. . ."

She remembered all too well. Geoff had assured them that Matt was "a good little shooter" and that one of these days he would "hold his own with the best of them."

"I know but. . ."

Lars had sighed. "Emma, I'm not sure how much more this family can take. Please just accept that Matt is doing the best he knows how, working his way through all of this—and so am I."

"Well, I'm sorry if my worrying about our son is a burden for you, Lars," she'd snapped.

"It's not my burden, Emma. It's yours, and I can't for the life of me figure out how to get you to set it aside so we can focus on what's really important around here."

"Which is?"

"Right now I'd have to say that keeping our daughter safely at home rather than back in some detention facility is a whole lot more important than whether our son is staying out playing basketball fifteen minutes longer than you think he should be."

It was the second time in just a matter of weeks that they had lost their tempers with each other. After years of marriage with little more than skirmishes, this felt like open warfare.

"I wasn't aware that you found my worrying such a problem," Emma chided, hating the way she sounded—like Sadie when she was at her worst.

Lars gently took hold of her shoulders. "Come on, Emmie. Let's not argue. We've been through so much together. We'll get through this as well."

She fingered the soft fabric of his shirt. "You're right. It's just. . .well, there has been so much attention focused on Sadie these last weeks, and—"

"Matt understands," Lars assured her.

She wished she could be as certain as he seemed to be. She looked up at him and wondered if in fact she had misread him. "You're as worried about Matt as I am," she said, stroking back his hair.

"Ja, but we must have faith, Emma—faith in how we have raised these children—Matt and Sadie."

He had a point. They were good children. Still, Sadie's situation had shaken Emma's faith in their ability to distinguish between right and wrong, especially when they felt backed into a corner. That was how Sadie must have felt that morning when Dan had practically dared her to get behind the wheel of his car. What kinds of pressures were being brought to bear on Matt? If she and Lars were having to deal with the gossip and speculation of others—no matter how well-meaning their friends and neighbors might be—then what was Matt having to endure at school? Children could be much crueler than adults. They often operated without the filter of commonly accepted standards of etiquette.

"Hey," Lars said as he pulled her closer, "Sadie's home, and for however long we have her, let's take this time to be a real family once again."

Emma nestled her cheek against his chest. "Yes," she said softly, but how could they be a real family again when a part of their larger family circle would still be missing?

Chapter 36

Sadie

She was home. For the first time in weeks, she stood before the small dresser mirror in her bedroom. The last time she'd stood in this spot had been that first day of school. August 28th. It was October now. Same year, and yet it seemed as if she had been away for a very long time.

She sat on the side of her bed and looked around at things that should give her a sense of relief and comfort. The stuffed manatee that her uncle Geoff had won for her at a church function. The shelf her dad had built to hold her collection of rag dolls made for her by her grandmother. The closet that held her clothes—skirts and tops in solid colors and small prints that looked foreign to her after weeks of wearing nothing but the required blue jumpsuit.

"Sadie?" Her mother pushed the door open with her toe and entered her small room. She was carrying a tray. "I brought you some tea and a slice of pie." She set the tray on Sadie's dresser, cleared now of the things she had left spread around that day when she was getting ready for school.

"Thanks." But she made no move to sit at her dresser and taste the tea or pie.

Her mother hovered near the door. "If you feel up to it later,

I could use some help in the kitchen. I'm making marmalade for the co-op."

Sadie glanced up. The marmalade for the co-op was usually made at the kitchen on the co-op's property—the big house where Hester and John Steiner lived. "Why here?"

Her mother looked confused and then understood her question. "I just thought—sometimes it's easier just to do it here where I have everything I need."

"We're not under house detention, Mom," Sadie said softly. "Just go on doing what you'd normally do."

"Matt's in school, and your father is out in his workshop, and I—well, like I said, even if you weren't here, I would probably just. . ." Her voice trailed off, and Sadie looked at her, really seeing her for the first time since she'd gotten home.

She had aged. Her skin was sallow. Her eyes darted around as if looking for something she needed to do. Her hands seemed to be in constant motion even though she was just sitting there on the bed with Sadie. She gave off a kind of nervous energy that didn't feel right.

"I'll come down now, Mama," Sadie said.

"No, have your tea." Her mother stood up and glanced around the room. "And rest," she added.

"Mom? I'm not sick. I don't need to rest or have tea brought to soothe my stomach or whatever."

To her shock, her mother's eyes welled with tears. "I know. . . I just. . . It's just so wonderful to have you home." She closed the door behind her, and a moment later Sadie heard the clatter of pans in the kitchen.

Sadie pushed herself off the bed and picked up the mug of tea. Her hand started to shake, and she couldn't seem to stop it, so she set the mug down again without drinking. She turned around and considered her room—the single bed, the dresser, a small desk and chair under the window that looked out onto the backyard and her father's workshop.

She went to the window and pressed close to the screen, breathing in the fresh air. It was one of the things she had missed most about being locked up—the inability to be outside whenever she chose. She saw her bike leaning against the side of the shed and remembered that the last time she'd seen it had been that morning. She'd left it at Tessa's the day of the picnic. When she'd turned too fast into Tessa's driveway, she'd caught sight of rain glistening off the bike's black bumper even as the car spun out of control.

How she wished that she had never gotten into Dan's car. How she wished that she had agreed to have her dad drive her and Tessa or drop her at Tessa's on his way to take Matt to his school so that she and Tessa could catch a ride with Uncle Geoff.

Tessa, she thought and closed her eyes against the memory that came every time she thought of her cousin and best friend. The memory of Tessa's face, her eyes wide with surprise, her hands out as if to somehow stop the car from hitting her as she scrambled directly into the path of the car's rear bumper.

She opened her eyes and wondered if she would ever again be able to think of Tessa as she'd been before that moment. Laughing shyly at Sadie's teasing, listening intently as Sadie poured out her dreams and disappointments to her, and most of all, loving Sadie like a sister—the way their moms loved each other—or had before that day.

She pressed the palms of her hands hard against the window sill. She had ruined everything for everyone. And she could not imagine how it would be possible to fix any part of it. She bowed her head.

Please help me, God. I don't know what to do, and I've hurt so many people. I don't care what happens to me, but please, please, please help them, especially my mom and Aunt Jeannie, find their way back to something that can make them happy again. Make them laugh again and love again. It was all my fault that Tessa died. Please, please, please don't make them suffer, too.

She saw Matt pedaling his bike up the street. It had been weeks since she'd seen him. As a juvenile himself, he had not been permitted to come for visits or to court. Sadie had been glad of that, not wanting to expose him to those places. She had tried to talk to him on the telephone, but their brief conversations had been pretty much one-sided.

"How's school?"

"Okay."

"Are you still going to Uncle Geoff's football practices?"

"Sometimes."

"How's the team?"

A grunt and then Matt would say something like, "Dad wants to talk to you," and pass the phone to him without so much as a "Good-bye" or "Hang in there."

Of course, in those early phone calls, she had really wanted him to tell her about Dan. How he was doing? Had his injuries from the accident healed? Had he asked about her?

That had been before she'd realized that it was not only Dan's parents who were preventing him from being in touch—it was Dan. He was certainly capable of reaching out to her if he wanted to. He couldn't visit her, but he could send a message through her parents. Maybe they were the ones preventing him from having any contact. Still, that day in court he hadn't even looked at her. And she could no longer deny that he had lied about how she'd come to be driving that day.

She fought against the anger that rose up in her like vomit every time she thought about what a fool she'd been. She'd known it was wrong to let him talk her into driving. It was raining, and he wasn't old enough. She should have said no. She shouldn't have worried about what he would think of her. What did that really matter anyway? He was going off to college in a few months and would forget all about her. That wasn't exactly news. In fact, she'd been thinking about that as she'd fallen asleep the night before the accident. She'd been awake a long time after the rest of the house was quiet, thinking how this was going to be her last year with Dan and how she wanted so much to make it the best year of her life.

Instead it had turned out to be the worst. She never could have imagined that she could mess things up so thoroughly for people she truly cared about and loved.

She waited for Matt to put his bike away and then head into the workshop. His after-school chores were to sweep up the shop and make sure the tools were put away properly. Sometimes he was allowed to work on a piece of furniture their father was making.

Sadie watched her brother trudge across the yard. He looked as if he were carrying the weight of the world on his shoulders, and it occurred to her that the trio of boys he usually rode home from school with had not been with him today. Then she realized that the one thing everyone she loved seemed to have in common with her was that they were moving through their day alone.

She thought about Uncle Geoff in court. After he testified, he'd walked out alone without so much as a glance at her or her parents—or Jeannie. Sadie had turned around in her chair to watch him, wanting to make eye contact to let him know that she wasn't mad about him testifying for the prosecution.

And then when she was testifying, her aunt Jeannie had been sitting apart from her parents—isolated in the back of the rows of chairs where spectators sat during court proceedings. She, too, had left alone. And now here was Matt, shuffling across the yard, his head bowed, his shoulders hunched as if walking against a stiff, cold wind.

If only she could have that one day back. . .

From the kitchen, she heard the sound of conversation. Drawn to anything that hinted at a break in the solitude that hung over their house, she opened the door to her bedroom and followed the sound.

A woman she didn't know was sitting at the kitchen table peeling oranges as she talked to Sadie's mom. She was dressed in the simple style that her family followed, and yet Sadie had never seen her before.

"Hello," she said as she entered the kitchen.

Her mom swung around and smiled. "Oh Sadie, did you get some rest?"

"I'm fine, Mom." Sadie focused her attention on the stranger. "I'm Sadie."

"It's good to meet you, Sadie. My name is Rachel Kaufmann."

"Rachel was Hester's roommate in college," Sadie's mom explained. She seemed nervous, and yet the woman—Rachel—seemed really nice. Quiet and watchful, but nice.

"Are you a nurse like Hester?"

"I was."

"Rachel and her son, Justin, have recently moved here. She's going to be working as a chaplain at the new hospital that just opened out on Cattleman Road," her mom said. But she said it in a way that sounded like she was afraid Hester's friend might say something that would upset Sadie.

"That's nice," Sadie replied. "Kind of like nursing, I guess, except in your case, you'll be working on healing the spirit not the body."

She saw a flicker of surprise cross Rachel's features as she smiled. "That's a wonderful way to look at it, Sadie. I hadn't thought of it quite that way. Thank you," she said as if Sadie had just given her a present.

Suddenly shy, Sadie looked away.

"What do you plan to do after you finish school?" Rachel asked.

She had to be kidding, right? Life as she had dreamed it was pretty much over for her, but she really didn't feel like explaining that to this stranger. She shrugged and turned to her mother. "I saw Matt come home. It's okay that I go out to the workshop, right?"

Her mother shook her head. "You know what Dad and I said. In the house unless you're going to school or church. It's for your own good. There have been some photographers and reporters asking questions in the neighborhood, and I don't want you to risk running into one of them. I'm sorry, honey. Let me call him and tell him to come in here."

"That's okay. He's got chores." She turned to head back toward her room. "Nice to meet you," she murmured as she passed Rachel.

To her surprise, Rachel put down the orange she was peeling and stood. She glanced at Sadie's mom, who was twisting a dish towel around her fingers, and nodded. "Sadie, do you have a few minutes? I'd like to talk to you about something."

Sadie's suspicion meter went all the way to panic. "Who are you really?" she whispered.

"I'm Rachel Kaufmann, a friend of Hester and John, and I'd like the chance to become your friend as well, Sadie. If you have some time now, I'd like to tell you about something that might help you to see some light at the end of this dark tunnel that I suspect you find yourself in these days."

All of this she delivered in a voice that was soothing and somehow comforting. But over the time that she'd spent in detention, Sadie had learned one thing for sure—never take anything at face value. The fact was that nobody could change what had happened or how that had permanently damaged everything that Sadie had taken for granted over her short life.

"Just hear her out," her mother was saying. She had put down the towel. Sadie heard the pleading in her voice.

"Sure," she said flippantly. "I've got nowhere to be."

"Sadie!" her mother said, but Rachel seemed unperturbed.

"How about we talk in your room, or would you be more comfortable—"

"My room works," Sadie said and started down the hall. It was true. Ever since she'd gotten home, she'd found that she was most comfortable in her room. Somehow she felt safe there. Outside her door were too many reminders of how much everything had changed. Inside she could still pretend that life was normal—whatever that was.

She stood by her dresser until Rachel sat down on the desk chair. "What I want to talk to you about, Sadie, is a program called VORP."

Sadie curled up on her bed and clutched the stuffed manatee to her chest. "That's a weird name," she noted.

Rachel smiled. "It is, isn't it? Especially for a program that's so intense." She rested her elbows on her knees and explained how the program worked. "It's not just a matter of saying you're sorry, Sadie," she said after going through the process.

"Yeah, well that's going to be a little hard anyway."

"How's that?"

Sadie stared at Rachel as if she had just arrived from another universe then very slowly she spelled it out for her. "In case you haven't heard, my victim is dead."

She announced this without so much as a hitch in her voice. Her tears were all spent. Crying was no longer an option. Tessa was dead, and it was her fault. Crying, as one of the uniforms had commented one night, was just an exercise in self-pity.

"You'd best spend your time figuring out how you're going to go on, girl," the female uniform had counseled. "You might be doing some time when this all shakes out, but that'll be short-term. You got to be thinking about the long term. How are you going to live the rest of your life? How is this thing going to make you better—stronger?"

Sadie had not answered her, seeing her lecture for the I'm-not-asking-you-for-an-answer speech that it was. But after that she had spent a lot of time thinking about what the uniform had told her. Every night she had prayed for guidance. But so far—nothing.

She looked at Rachel Kaufmann now and wondered if just maybe God had sent her a message in the form of this kind stranger. "What do I have to do?" she asked.

"In simplest terms, you have to find a way to forgive yourself."

Sadie laughed. If the woman was making a joke, she was making a really lousy one. "And just how do I go about doing that?"

"By first seeking the forgiveness of those you have hurt," Rachel said softly—"every one of them. And from what little I know of this, Sadie, it's a long list."

Part Three

. . .bearing with one another and. . .forgiving each other,
as the Lord has forgiven you.
COLOSSIANS 3:13

Chapter 37

Jeannie

The mail had begun to pile up on the table in the front hall. Every day Geoff collected it on his way in after school and dropped it there. Neither of them had done more than glance through the envelopes. In the first couple of weeks after Tessa's death, they had received dozens of cards and notes expressing the sympathy and shock of friends and extended family as the news traveled across the country.

At first they had opened those envelopes and read them silently. Jeannie would open the envelope, making some comment about how this person or that must have heard about Tessa. She would scan the verse printed on the card by the manufacturer and sometimes run her thumb over the embossed illustration. Then she would gird herself to read the handwritten message that always accompanied the commercial message.

"That's nice," she would murmur as she passed the card to Geoff and began the process all over again. At first Geoff read the cards as carefully as she did, but after the first three or four, he began taking the card from her, glancing at the illustration, and then without reading them, adding the card to the others they had already opened.

After the first dozen or so, they had stopped even opening

the envelopes. The messages brought them little comfort, just reminded them repeatedly of what they had lost, especially the personal notes sharing memories of Tessa. Jeannie knew that she should write back, thanking these dear, kind people for their expressions of sympathy, but she just couldn't bring herself to do it.

Bills that were mixed in with the cards were noted. "The electric bill came," she would say to Geoff as they sat in front of the television eating their supper.

"I saw it," he might reply.

But day after day, the stack of unopened mail continued to grow until one day after returning from her run, Jeannie was on her way through the front hall and brushed against the table, sending the whole pile scattering onto the tile floor.

"Okay, God," she muttered as she had so often done in the days before Tessa's death, "I'll do it now."

She sat cross-legged on the floor, the coolness of the tiles a relief after her run, and began sorting the mail into three piles—personal cards and notes, bills and other business, and throwaway mail.

The throwaway pile was the largest, the cards came in a distant second, and the bills a close third to the cards. *How long has Geoff let things slide?* she thought and felt the annoyance and irritation with him that had become far more common than the feelings of love and respect she'd always held for him before. It wasn't entirely his fault. She was the one who usually sorted through the daily mail and placed bills and such on his desk. Then he would attend to them at night when he did his schoolwork or worked on a new play for the team.

She began opening the bills. The more recent ones were within due dates, but their failure to pay the preceding month added late fees. Their credit card bill was over a month old and by now would carry a hefty finance charge on top of the balance. What on earth had she bought?

She ran down the list of charges, and in almost every case the charge brought a memory of Tessa. Tessa with her at the grocery store as she searched her purse for enough cash to pay and then pulled out her credit card. Tessa with her at the gas station, washing the windows while she pumped the gas, whatever conversation they had started in the car continuing. Tessa and Sadie and her at the discount store buying the supplies the girls would need for the start of the new school year.

Tessa. Tessa. Tessa.

She crumpled the bill then smoothed it and laid it with the other open bills before picking up the next envelope. The return address marked it as being from the billing department of the hospital. Jeannie breathed a sigh of relief. At least this one should be no more than a receipt showing that Geoff's school insurance had paid the charges. She decided that she would put that one on the bottom of the pile. It would be as much a relief for Geoff to see that at least one bill had been paid as it had been to her.

But as she scanned the page, shaking her head at the itemized list of charges, her heart beat a little faster and her brain shouted, *No!*

The number in the balance-owed column was five figures. Impossible. She had to be reading this wrong. She studied the information. Here was the line that showed the total of the entire itemized list. Below that was the line showing what Geoff's insurance company had paid. And below that was the ominous balance-owed line.

Stuck to the inside of the envelope was a yellow sticky note that suggested they contact the finance department to set up a payment schedule as soon as possible.

Jeannie fingered the stack of bills she'd already opened—with more to come—and mentally calculated the total. She included everything—the regular charge plus extra finance charges and late fees—and then she added the staggering sum to the bill from the hospital. For a moment she felt as if she couldn't breathe. How were they ever going to come up with so much money?

Geoff was already bringing in extra money from coaching just so they could meet their monthly bills and continue to live the way they did. On top of that, ever since the funeral, he had been so close to the edge. His anger and bitterness were eating him alive. This new burden would destroy him—destroy *them*. Somehow she had to find a solution to this. It was up to her. She got to her feet still clutching the stack of unpaid bills in one hand and the hospital bill in the other.

She placed the other bills on Geoff's desk, including the credit card bill that was sure to upset him all by itself. He would notice that the stack of mail was gone, and he would be furious if she tried to hide bills from him and the penalties continued to add up. But she took the hospital bill with her to the kitchen and picked up the phone. There was only one person she could trust to tell about this. Only one person who would know what to do.

Her fingers faltered over the keypad. She and that one person were once again not on speaking terms thanks to the way things had been left that day at the bay. Emma would know what to do, but Emma blamed Jeannie for the fact that Sadie had even thought about driving that morning. And because deep down Jeannie could not allow herself to admit that there was a grain of truth in her sister's accusation, she refused to turn to her.

She had to handle this alone. Find her way through one crisis in her life for once without leaning on Emma. She replaced the portable phone in its cradle then got down on her knees, resting her elbows on the hard wooden seat of a kitchen chair, and closed her eyes. "God, I need help. Please, show me what to do. You know that Geoff won't accept charity even if our church and the community are willing to. . ."

It was the way of their faith to see each other through hard times. If someone's house burned, it would be rebuilt—no charge. If someone lost a job and had bills to cover, the money would be raised. And Jeannie knew that it would be no different for them. But if she went to their pastor with the bill, Geoff would be upset. He was so very proud and so very stubborn.

The phone rang, and she shut her eyes tightly, ignoring the shrill sound. At that moment, a memory of Tessa suddenly came back to her as vividly as if it had happened yesterday instead of years earlier. Tessa had been only five, and the three of them had been at supper, their hands joined as Geoff led them in prayer. The phone had rung, and Tessa had half turned to jump down and get it.

"Not now," Geoff had said softly. "We're busy right now

talking to God, honey."

Tessa had considered that for a second, and finally the phone had stopped ringing. Then she had looked at Jeannie and said, "But, Mommy, what if that was God wanting to talk to us?"

Jeannie pushed herself to her feet and clicked the phone to see who had just called. "Rachel," she murmured. "Not exactly God."

To her surprise, she heard Geoff's car on the driveway. He was home early. Still holding the hospital bill, she went to the kitchen window. He was coming up the walk carrying his playbook and duffel bag. Then she remembered that he had a game tonight. Normally she went with him, sitting in the stands with Sadie and Tessa and Matt, but not lately.

"I'm going for a shower," he said, barely looking at her as they passed in the kitchen. After twenty minutes, she heard the water stop running, and a minute later she heard Geoff in their bedroom opening drawers as he dressed. Game night meant an early supper so he could be at the school early. She laid the hospital bill on the counter as she hurriedly searched the refrigerator for the makings of a cold supper. She cut up fresh fruit and put that out with potato chips and turkey and cheese sandwiches for him. She was just about to pour him a tall glass of lemonade when she remembered the bill.

She reached for it just as he came into the kitchen carrying the stack of bills she'd left on his desk. She hadn't heard him come downstairs, and his sudden presence startled her so much that she dropped the hospital bill and nearly dropped the pitcher of lemonade in the process.

"Easy there," he said as he bent to retrieve the bill. He glanced at the masthead as he pulled out his chair ready to sit down for his supper. "Another bill?"

Jeannie held her breath as he opened it. It seemed as if it took him a long time to read it—far longer than it had taken her to grasp the contents.

"It's high," she said. "I had no idea that—"

Geoff scraped back his chair and picked up the phone and punched in a number. "Roger? Yeah. Something's come up. Can you handle the team tonight? Okay. Yeah. Appreciate that."

He hung up and without a word headed for the door, taking the car keys as he went.

"Geoff?"

He stopped but did not turn around. "Do not try to stop me, Jeannie," he growled.

"Where are you—?"

"It's pretty clear to me that at least this is one bill we don't have to be responsible for. It clearly was sent to the wrong address," he said waving the bill in the air. "I'm going to make sure it gets delivered to the person responsible."

"Geoff, no. Please wait."

He kept walking and got in the car. "Jeannie, you have to face facts and choose already. Me or your sister and her family. You can no longer have it both ways. I'll be back later. In the meantime, you decide how it's going to be."

"Geoff, wait!" Jeannie shouted the words this time as he backed down the driveway and drove away fast. Don't you get it? I have chosen. I chose you.

Next door she saw a curtain move and knew that she had attracted the attention—and no doubt curiosity—of their next-door neighbor. She smiled and waved as she went back inside. To what purpose? Did she really hope the neighbor would simply think that Geoff had forgotten something? Not likely. It seemed to be well known up and down the street that the Messners were having marital problems.

Besides, she had more pressing matters that needed her attention. She ran inside, and for the second time that day, she picked up the telephone to call Emma. This time she was calling her sister to warn her.

Chapter 38

Lars

Lars was in his workshop when Emma came rushing in holding the phone. "Jeannie called. Geoff is on his way over here," she said breathlessly. She was still clutching the phone, and when the beeping told Lars she had forgotten to disconnect, he took it from her.

"All right." He lifted his white-blond eyebrows and waited for more information. Jeannie and Emma had not spoken for days, and the stress had begun to wear not only on Emma but on all of them. She walked through her days a lost soul, and he would have thought that a call from Jeannie would be something to lift her spirits.

"They got an enormous bill from the hospital today. Jeannie was going to try to tell him about it after tonight's game, but he found it, and now he's coming here."

"I don't understand."

"Jeannie thinks that he plans to present the bill to Sadie, Lars. To tell her that the charges are her responsibility. She's just come back to us. . ."

"Go back inside, Emma. I'll see to this." He had no idea what he would say. His brother-in-law was so different in both personality and temperament. The two men liked each other, but it had been clear for years that they walked along different paths when it came to what they believed and how best to put those beliefs into action.

Emma hesitated and then did as he asked. A few minutes later, Geoff's car pulled up in front of their house. He sat there a moment, staring straight ahead as if trying to remember why he'd come.

"Geoff?" Lars approached the car. "It's good to see you."

Geoff looked at him and blinked then got out of the car, pausing to pick up an envelope from the seat beside him. "I hear Sadie's home," he said ignoring Lars's greeting. It was apparent that he was struggling to keep his tone conversational, casual.

"Ja." Lars positioned himself between Geoff and the house. He didn't want to appear threatening, but at the same time, he had a duty to protect his family.

"I've got something for her," Geoff said, tapping the envelope against his thigh.

Lars held out his hand. "I can make sure she gets it. She's been spending most of her time in her room. The adjustment has been difficult."

"Really?" The word came as a sneer, but Geoff recovered. "No, I came to deliver this in person. I just need a minute of her time."

It was not in Lars's makeup to play games, and he was uncomfortable with this one. "We heard about the hospital bill, Geoff. Is that it?" He nodded toward the envelope.

Geoff's face went red with fury. "So, she made her choice," he muttered. "Did my wife call to warn you?" This time there was no attempt to disguise his contempt. Lars realized that it was directed not at him but at Jeannie.

"Come on, Geoff. What's to be gained by this? Sadie knows what she did. She's going to have to live with her guilt over Tessa's death for the rest of her days. Our hearts are with you and Jeannie, of course, but surely. . ."

To his surprise, Geoff laughed and looked up at the sky. "Let me get this straight, Lars. Your kid runs my kid over, and you want me to have compassion for her?"

Lars did not flinch. "That's exactly what I'm asking. For her and for Matt as well."

"Let's leave Matt out of this," Geoff said, looking away. "I've made an effort there, and your son. . ."

"We are family, Geoff, and we need to start acting like that again. Tessa's death has—"

"You and your family have no right to breathe my child's name," Geoff growled, his fist tightening around the envelope now, crumpling it.

"We have every right, Geoff, and you know it," Emma said coming forward to stand with Lars. "Tessa was like our own daughter. Sadie and Matt are as much your children as they are ours. If Sadie had been your daughter—if she and Tessa had both been your daughters—would you have turned your back on her? I don't think so. She's family, Geoff. Yours. Ours. It never mattered before, and it shouldn't now."

Emma moved a step closer to Geoff as she continued to talk without giving their brother-in-law a chance to reply. It worked. Slowly but surely, Lars saw Geoff's fingers relax slightly. "Won't you come inside, Geoff," Emma said, "so we can talk about this calmly? This bill has come as an added blow to you and Jeannie at a time when. . ."

It was as if she had reminded him why he'd come. He thrust the envelope toward her. "I want you to give this to Sadie. It's the least you can do for us—me. I want, need for her to see the dollars and cents cost of her actions, actions that cost a fortune and still ended up with Tessa dead." His eyes filled with tears. "Do it," he pleaded as he stumbled blindly back to his car.

"Geoff, I'll drive you," Lars said, following him.

"No," he shouted and slammed the car door behind him.

"Come on, Geoff," Lars pleaded, trying the door and finding it locked.

Geoff was pounding the steering wheel with his palms. After a moment, he stopped and his body sagged as if suddenly and finally all the fight had gone out of him. He opened the window a crack. "I'm okay, Lars," he said, sounding utterly defeated. "Could you just please go on inside and give me a minute?"

Lars did as he asked. Emma watched anxiously from the

kitchen window and reported that Geoff was just sitting there, his forehead resting on the steering wheel. "I'm calling Jeannie," she said. But just as she picked up the phone, Geoff started the car and drove away.

"Was that Uncle Geoff?" Sadie asked coming into the kitchen and glancing out the window.

Lars looked at Emma, and she nodded. "Ja," Lars said and pulled out one of the kitchen chairs. "He brought something that he wants you to see."

He saw that Emma was about to protest, but Geoff was right. There was no point in shielding Sadie from the aftershocks of her actions. "Sit down, Sadie," he said quietly even as he saw Emma signaling him not to do this.

Sadie did as he instructed and accepted the envelope her father handed her. She unfolded the bill and glanced over the figures. Lars knew the exact moment that she realized that the bill was for Tessa's care in the hospital. Her entire face seemed to simply melt. Her mouth sagged as her eyes became little slits, and her hands began to shake until finally he reached over and gently took the bill from her.

"There is a price to our actions, Sadie," he told her. "An emotional and physical cost and often a financial cost as well."

"What have I done?" she said, staring up at him. "Oh Daddy, what have I done? I've hurt so many people and now this. How will Uncle Geoff ever be able to pay such a large amount?"

"He'll have help," Emma told her as she pulled up a chair next to her and wrapped her arm around Sadie's shoulders. "That's what community is about."

"Sadie, this is the one thing we can fix," Lars said, "After everything you've been through—the accident, detention, the court proceedings—paying this bill is not your worry. It's not why I wanted you to see it."

"But, Dad, I have to find a way to help. Will the hospital give us time to pay it off? I could get a job after school and on weekends." Her face went suddenly blank. "Unless. . ."

"Unless?" Emma asked.

"What if the judge sends me away? How can I possibly

contribute anything if I'm locked up somewhere clear across the state?"

Emma and Lars looked at each other. "How about we call Rachel Kaufmann?" Lars suggested. "She might have some ideas."

"Yes, let's do that," Sadie said, getting up to get the phone.

"Sadie, wait, let's talk about this some more," Emma cautioned. "You've got so much on your shoulders right now. Maybe. . ."

"Mom, this is like the first clear sign that God is hearing my prayers to show me some way that I can make this better for those I love—for you and Dad and Aunt Jeannie and Uncle Geoff. This is a way that I can own up to the fact that it was my thoughtless behavior that brought all of this on our family. That it's time to stop feeling sorry for myself and really take a good hard look at how everyone around me is suffering."

"Oh Sadie, please don't take all of this on yourself," Emma pleaded. "There's blame enough to go around. We may not have been in the car, but your father and I could have stopped you from getting in Dan's car that morning. And what about Dan and his responsibility in all of this?"

"No. Rachel told me that how I decide to carry my guilt and remorse is what will matter when my turn comes to face God. Please let's just call and ask her what she thinks."

Lars had never been more impressed with his daughter. He, like others, had always thought of her as a girl more like Jeannie—full of laughter and lightheartedness—even giddiness. But the events of her life these last weeks had changed her, matured her. He felt hopeful again. Perhaps one day they might get past all of this—not forget Tessa, but heal the gaping wounds her death had brought.

"Sadie?" Lars touched her forearm to gain her attention. "Do you understand this program that Rachel has told you about? I mean, do you grasp the extent of it?"

Sadie nodded, but Lars was still not convinced.

"It's a two-way street—offenders and victims—both sides must be willing to participate, to honor the process. Even if you decide to make the effort required, it can't happen unless

Jeannie and Geoff agree."

"And you and Mom and Mattie and Gram and Gramps and probably others I haven't even imagined," Sadie said. "Yes. And I also understand that in spite of everything I may still have to. . .go away for a while."

Emma pressed her fist to her mouth then turned away, no doubt to hide her emotions from Sadie. Lars moved next to his wife and pulled her close. "All right, call Rachel, and then let's all sit down together and think this through." He held up the bill. "But, Sadie, you do understand that even if you worked all day every day for years to come, there is little chance you could ever. . ."

"But I could make a pledge—a promise that whatever I have, a part of it will go to some cause that best honors Tessa's memory."

"She would like that," Emma said, stroking Sadie's hair. "We could ask Jeannie what she thinks of that idea."

Sadie's hopeful smile lit her features. "You think then that Aunt Jeannie and Uncle Geoff will. . . ?"

"One step at a time," Lars told her. "Make your call and then go get your brother. It's time for our evening prayers."

Chapter 39

Matthew

Okay, so once again it was all about Sadie. Matt's parents hadn't even realized that he was right there, in his room with the door open, listening.

He got it that somehow there was this ginormous hospital bill—as Tessa might say. The doctors had charged all that money and still had not been able to save Tessa. What was that about? How could they charge for failing? When Matt failed to do his chores or complete his homework, there were consequences. What were the consequences for the doctors?

There weren't any, which was, Matt had decided, pretty much the way of things out there in the real world. The world outside Pinecraft where he would be living before too long. He carefully gathered up the coins he'd won playing poker with his new friends and put the money back in its safe place—the box that held his favorite T-shirt on the top shelf of his closet. Oh, his mom as well as Sadie knew that he kept that shirt in that box because it was so special to him. It was the T-shirt that Uncle Geoff had given him the night the team won the conference championship. But no one had ever touched the box. He was sure of that, because he had ways of marking it every time he took it down and put it back, and never had it been disturbed. So he felt it was the safest place to put his winnings.

Of course, in the last couple of games he hadn't won anything. In fact he'd lost. In the last game he'd lost everything he'd brought with him. He tried to limit himself, but the temptation to play one more hand had been too great, so he'd borrowed from the kid who had first loaned him money to get into the game and played on. But he'd lost, and when he'd said he would bring the money to the next game, the boy had said that he owed something he called "interest"—a percentage on top of the money owed as a kind of penalty. So now he owed that boy a whole dollar, and so far his winnings only totaled four dollars and fifty-three cents.

He'd set a goal for himself of twenty dollars, but in the past couple of days, he'd begun to rethink that sum. Ten should be enough, he'd decided.

"Matt?"

Sadie was standing in the doorway. Matt quickly shoved the box back from the edge of the shelf and turned around. "Yeah?"

"Evening prayers," she said.

"Coming." He glanced back at the box. He'd have to mark it later, because Sadie was still standing there.

"Mattie?"

He sighed. "Don't call me that, okay? I'm fourteen and that's a kid's name."

Sadie smiled and ducked her head to hide it, but Matt saw and it irritated him. "All right, Matt, I just wanted to say that I really appreciate everything you've done to help Mom and Dad while I've been. . .away."

"In jail," Matt corrected, tired of everybody trying to pretend that Sadie had just stepped out for a while. But the way her face twisted, he felt bad for having said it. "Sorry," he muttered.

"Anyway, I just wanted you to know that."

Matt picked at an imaginary piece of dirt on his shirt.

"Are you coming, then?" Sadie asked. "For evening prayers?"

Do I have a choice? It was something he'd heard one of the boys he played cards with say, and the others had seemed to like it. But it was not something he could say in this house. It would give him away. No Amish or Mennonite kid would ever be so sarcastic. But these days sometimes the ways of his new friends made a lot more sense than the ways of his family. Like this praying thing. God was not going to listen to the prayers of a nobody like him or, for that matter, to his Dad, who was a good man but not like important or anything.

"Matt, are you coming?" Sadie repeated when he made no move to follow her.

"Okay. Give me a minute, will you?"

Sadie hesitated, started to say something, but decided against it and left the room.

Matt centered the box on the shelf and then scooped up a handful of sand from the container where he kept the fossilized seashells he'd found and sprinkled a little around the perimeter. If anyone but him moved it, the sand would be disturbed and he would know. He had never considered what he would do if that happened, but soon it wouldn't matter, because he would be gone and so would the contents of the box.

In the living room, his parents were seated in their usual places. Sadie had taken a position on the floor next to their dad. Like everything else about his sister these days, that choice irritated him. So when his mom held out her hand to him, inviting him to sit next to her on the sofa, Matt accepted, curling into the curve of her arm as he had when he was just a little kid. It felt good—normal and safe.

His father opened his Bible and lifted out the purple ribbon bookmark. "Pray with me," he said, and the four of them bowed their heads. "May the words of my mouth and the meditations of our hearts be acceptable in Thy sight, oh Lord, our strength and our Redeemer. Amen."

The clock on the shelf near his father's chair ticked loudly in the silence that followed. A moment in which Matt knew he was supposed to offer a silent prayer of his own or simply reflect on his actions for the day just passed. But all he could think about was that the boys would have gathered already. That he owed money, and the kid had told him that the debt had to be paid in full with interest before the game started or he was adding another day's interest. They would be waiting for him—one of them impatient to have his money repaid.

He tried to focus on his father's voice, tried to figure out how long it would be before he could slip away.

"And commanded them that they should take nothing for their journey, save a staff only; no scrip, no bread, no money in their purse. . . ."

Matt sat up straighter. No money? Was it possible that he could do this—that he didn't need the money from the card game? He'd begun to feel really guilty about slipping away every night and trying to cover his tracks by saying he was meeting friends for a game, not exactly lying but certainly not telling his folks everything that was going on.

He still thought leaving was the best plan, but as his father continued to read from the Bible, a new plan began to form. The scripture talked about staying with strangers along the way, and he knew for a fact that in Pinecraft people opened their homes all the time to others just passing through—people they barely knew but took in because of their connection to someone who did know them.

What if he paid off the kid by giving him all of his winnings? That would be a way of seeking forgiveness for having fallen into card playing in the first place. If he no longer had any of the ill-gotten gains, as Olive Crowder sometimes called money like that, then surely that would take care of the guilt he'd been feeling.

His father closed the leather-covered Bible and set it on the table by his chair. Matt closed his eyes for the final prayer.

"Matt?"

He opened his eyes to find his dad looking at him. "Yes sir." He felt the flush of shame rush to his cheeks. Somehow his father had found out about his card playing and slipping out and his plan to run away. He was sure of it.

"You remember the program that Sadie's lawyer told us about?"

"Yes sir."

"Well, tomorrow, Mrs. Kaufmann—Rachel—is going to come here to talk to all of us about how we might put that program into action."

Matt looked at his mom. "Will Uncle Geoff and Aunt Jeannie be here?"

"Nein. Just us for now."

"Then what's the point?" He was so tired of having his hopes raised and then thrown back to the ground again.

"The point is that Rachel's program may be a way for your sister to. . ."

Matt stopped listening. It was about Sadie as always. They didn't care anything about fixing things between him and Uncle Geoff. It was pretty clear to him that even if she was sent off to a real jail, everything going on in this house would always be focused on her.

It was time to move on.

Chapter 40

Jeannie

Geoff was home again. Jeannie heard him moving around downstairs. She'd been so nervous after calling Emma and not hearing anything back from her that she'd busied herself once again searching Tessa's room for the lost journal. It comforted her to touch Tessa's things and be in her room, which still held the faint scent of her.

She waited for Geoff to settle somewhere so that she could gauge his mood. If he started fixing himself something to eat, then that would be a good sign. If he went into the den and switched on the television, that would not.

He did neither. Instead she heard him climbing the stairs. Each step he took seemed heavy with the misery that had taken over this once cheerful home they had shared with Tessa. She waited for him to come down the hall to where he could plainly see her standing in Tessa's room. But he didn't even look up as he reached the top of the stairs and turned the opposite way into their room. Curious, she followed him.

He was taking down a suitcase from the top shelf in their walk-in closet. The drawers to his dresser were partially opened. "What are you doing?"

He gave a look that implied Sadie's favorite word, *Duh*, and turned his attention back to his packing.

Speechless, Jeannie watched as he removed stacks of freshly folded T-shirts, underwear, and socks from the drawers and placed them in the suitcase. He couldn't be leaving her. Their faith had no room for divorce. No, there had to be some other explanation.

"Geoff? Talk to me. What happened when you went over to Emma's?"

He swung around and faced her for the first time since she'd entered the room. He laughed, but there was no amusement in the sound. "You mean Emma didn't call to give you a full report? Or more likely you called there and the two of you commiserated about poor, dear Sadie."

"Stop this and talk to me," Jeannie demanded, her voice tight with fury that he was being so rigid. But now his assumption that his way was the only way was wearing on her. How could he even think of deciding that they needed to go through this separately without discussing it? She might agree in the end, but she'd like the opportunity to be heard.

"Geoff, you know that all I want is the same thing you want—for us to find a way through this horror that we did not cause and cannot change." He looked so haggard and exhausted that her heart went out to him in spite of her anger. "Please, we have to get through this somehow. Wouldn't it be better if we did it together?"

"I can't, Jeannie." He sat down on the edge of the bed so hard that the suitcase and its contents tumbled onto the floor.

Jeannie remained by the doorway until she saw his broad muscular shoulders start to heave as he buried his face in his hands. In an instant, she was beside him, holding him as she had held Tessa whenever she was distraught over something. "We're going to get through this, Geoff," she said and realized that the words had become like some kind of Gregorian chant, she had repeated them so many times over these last terrible weeks.

He looked up but not at her. Tears were streaming down his cheeks. "I have to go. It's the only way I can see that either one of us is going to survive. I love you, Jeannie, but. . ."

She placed her finger against his lips, shushing him. "No 'buts'—not where loving each other is concerned."

But instead of holding out his arms to her as he had in the past whenever they had argued, he stood up and set the suitcase on the one chair in the room and began filling it with the clothing that had spilled onto the floor.

"I have to go," he said, and now with his back to her, he sounded so certain.

Jeannie rummaged through her brain, searching for the right words she could say to make him stay, but she found nothing. She shut her eyes and silently prayed for God to intervene, to make him see that this was not a solution. But nothing changed, and she had no words.

"I'll be downstairs," she said softly, hoping that maybe if she left him alone he would see the folly of this solution.

But a few minutes later, he came downstairs carrying the suitcase and a garment bag.

"Where will you stay?"

He shrugged. "I'll stay in my office tonight and then start looking for a room tomorrow." He set down his belongings. "About the bills. . ."

"They've waited this long," she said. "But Geoff, that's something to consider. I mean, paying for the house plus a place for you to live makes no sense. If you really think we need some time apart, then let me be the one to go."

"Go where, Jeannie? To Emma's?"

"I was thinking about my parents' house. They have a spare room," she said quietly.

"That's a good idea. But I'll be the one to go home to Mom. After all, this is my idea."

"You know, this place is big enough that. . ."

"This place is haunted," he said, his voice a raspy whisper. He picked up the suitcase and garment bag, filling his hands with things—instead of with her, Jeannie thought. "I'll call you tomorrow," he said. "We can work out some arrangement so that you'll have use of the car during the day while I'm at school."

"I have Tessa's bike," Jeannie reminded him.

They were talking to each other as if this were any normal day when they needed to work out transportation. Why was she being so nice to him? Why wasn't she ranting at him to come to his senses and see that she loved him and that without him she was completely lost? Why wasn't she begging him not to go?

Chapter 41

Emma

It was Olive Crowder who brought the news the following morning that Geoff had moved out of the house. "Now Jeannine is all alone in that big place," Olive said, clucking her tongue in disapproval. And when Emma said nothing, she added impatiently, "Well, Emma, what are you going to do about this matter?"

She had made herself at home, pulling out one of the kitchen chairs and plopping herself down while Emma prepared lunch for the meeting with Rachel Kaufmann.

"Jeannie is a grown woman, Olive. She has lost her only child. We need to respect the way that she and Geoff may choose to mourn that child whether or not we approve."

"Pshaw! Your sister needs you, Emma. She's not only lost her child. It would seem that she's lost her husband as well."

"Don't even speak of such a thing," Emma scolded. "Jeannie and Geoff may not be of our particular branch of the faith, but they are Mennonite, and if you are for one minute suggesting that they would even consider—" She could not even bring herself to utter the *D* word.

Olive did not lift so much as an eyebrow. "Geoffory converted," she reminded Emma.

"From Catholicism," Emma reminded her, "where I believe

they also believe in the vow of 'until death do us part.' "

"Don't lecture me, Emma." Olive took out an envelope and left it on the table. "I understand that there was quite a substantial hospital bill."

Emma eyed the envelope. "Geoff won't accept that," she said softly. "He thinks of it as charity."

"Well, of course, it's charity. Does he not know the meaning of the word?" Olive tapped the envelope. "I am leaving this in your care. I assume that at some point Jeannine and Geoffory will come to their senses and permit those of us who truly care about them to offer what help we can." She pushed away from the table. "I'm working at the thrift shop today. May I assume that you will not be joining us?"

"No. We have a guest coming for lunch." Emma hoped that would be enough information to satisfy Olive. She could not help but feel relieved when the older woman walked to the back door.

"Emma, you should call Jeannine," she said. "Today."

She did not wait for Emma's response. With a sigh, Emma picked up the envelope to put it away in a safe place. It was quite heavy and fat, and in spite of telling herself that whatever amount Olive had given was no business of hers, she gave in to the temptation to count the bills.

Inside the unsealed envelope was five thousand dollars in cash. Emma was so stunned that she counted the money four times before she hurried out to the workshop to tell Lars.

"Olive is a generous woman," was all that Lars said. He seemed distracted and barely glanced at the envelope.

"But where shall we keep it?" Emma asked.

"Keep it?" He blinked in the sun that was flecked with fine particles of sawdust. "The money was given to Jeannie and Geoff. They will have to decide where best to keep it, Emma."

"They won't take it—at least Geoff won't."

"Then give it to Jeannie." He turned back to his work, measuring a board twice before starting the cut.

"Olive says that Geoff has moved out of the house."

Lars paused in midstroke, but he did not look up. "Do you think that she and Geoff will ever forgive us, Emma?"

She knew what he meant. There was so very much to forgive—certainly they could have taken possession of Sadie's learner's permit until such time as they approved. And in spite of her youth, they had taught Sadie better than to give in to the temptation of impressing a young man when she knew her actions were wrong. And perhaps Emma's greatest failing was the one thing that she had finally confessed to Lars a few days earlier—that she had accused Jeannie of being the cause of all the trouble because she been the one to help Sadie get her permit in the first place.

"I don't know, but I need to do something about that. I'll be back in a bit," Emma said.

"Where are you going?"

"I'm going to take this to Jeannie—and I'm going to try to apologize."

"What about our lunch with Rachel?"

"Ask her to wait—better yet, have Sadie make lunch and get started. I'll join you if I can, but for now. . ."

She had mounted her bicycle and pedaled off before Lars could stop her or she could reconsider. If Jeannie had been guilty of overstepping when she'd taken Sadie for her permit, then how was that any worse than what Emma had been guilty of since their argument at the bay—keeping her distance, refusing to make the first move toward reconciliation?

She pedaled as fast as she could, and by the time she arrived at Jeannie's house, she was breathing hard and intent on her mission. She knocked on the kitchen door even as she peered in through the lace curtain that covered the side glass window. "Jeannie?"

Through the window she could see cardboard cartons, some of them taped shut, others spilling over with contents. The kitchen counters, normally cluttered with the small appliances that Jeannie favored—a coffeemaker, bread machine, blender, and such—were bare.

Unnerved, she tried the handle and found the door unlocked. "Jeannie?" she called out as she entered the kitchen and eased around the boxes on her way to the den where she could hear noise.

Jeannie was on a stepstool taking books down from the built-in shelves that lined two walls of the den. Already half the shelves were empty.

"Jeannie, what are you doing?"

Her sister did not look at her as she flipped through the top book on the stack she was holding. "Do you know how many of these we never got around to reading?" she asked. She was dressed in a plain brown cotton skirt that came to her ankles and a shapeless tan top. Her usual crown of flaming red curls had been tamed into a tight little bun under a white starched prayer covering. "Take these, will you?" she asked, handing Emma the stack before turning to gather more books.

"Are you moving?" Emma asked.

"I am cleansing," Jeannie corrected. "Simplifying. Getting back to basics—and my roots. I am starting over, Emma. It's really the only way I can see. That and surely all of this stuff will bring enough money so that we can at least make a dent in the bills we owe."

"You're going to sell these things?"

"Not just these. I already took a load of my clothes to that consignment shop on Bahia Vista. They only take clothing and maybe a few knickknacks, but there are shops around town that will take all sorts of things—books, cookware, dishes, even furniture." She came down from the step stool and deposited her armload of books into a box. "Of course it will take time, but it will be a start."

"What does Geoff say?"

"He doesn't know." She said this almost as if it had just occurred to her. "I think he might be pleased. He was always fussing about how much stuff we had."

"When did you decide. . . ?"

Her smile was like a beam of sunlight—brilliant and warm. "After Geoff left last night, I was determined to find the journal that we gave Tessa the night of the picnic, but then once I started, it felt as if she was here helping me, encouraging me. It was the most incredible feeling, Emma."

"Did you find the journal?"

"Not yet." Jeannie frowned. "I can't imagine where it might be. I've been through everything in her room several times."

"It's got to be here," Emma said.

Jeannie shrugged. "How about some iced tea?"

"That would be nice." She followed her sister into the kitchen and saw that when Jeannie opened the cabinet where before there had been at least three sets of glasses, there was now only one set of six glasses. While Jeannie took out the pitcher of tea from the refrigerator, Emma moved two boxes from kitchen chairs and sat down. She was still holding the envelope from Olive.

She waited until Jeannie sat down then slid the envelope across the table to her. "Olive stopped by. She asked me to bring you this."

Jeannie fingered the envelope with a half smile. "I'll put it with the rest," she said.

"The rest?"

"Never try to talk a bunch of Mennonites out of wanting to do their part. Charity or not, all morning the money has shown up in a variety of ways—slipped under the door, left in the mailbox, given to Mama." She shrugged.

"And how's Geoff taking that?"

Jeannie stared off into space. "I doubt he knows. Geoff is. . .a little lost right now, but in time. . ."

They each took a drink of their tea then drew patterns in the condensation on the sides of their glasses as they had done as kids.

"I came to ask you to forgive me," Emma said softly.

Jeannie looked up, startled, and then she started to laugh. "Forgive you? Oh Emma, that's too much. I'm the one. Why do you think I've been so all-consumed with this?" She waved her hand around the kitchen. "After Geoff walked out last night, the one person I wanted most to talk to was you, but I was so afraid that. . ."

"We're grown women, so why do we continue to dance around each other as we did when we were young girls?" Emma mused, taking Jeannie's hand between both of hers. "Wasting time when we of all people should realize how very precious every day, every hour, must be."

"I'm so very sorry, Em."

"Oh Jeannie, if you only knew how I have prayed for some way for us to find our way back to each other. I need you so much right now."

Jeannie seemed surprised. "You need me? But, Emmie, you're the strong one. I never was the one—"

Emma couldn't hold back her tears a minute longer. "I don't know how to talk about this with you." She lifted her shoulders and let them drop in utter defeat. "The truth is, I don't know what to say to anyone these days—Lars, Sadie, Matt—but especially to you, Jeannie."

Jeannie pulled her chair closer and placed the flat of her hand on Emma's back. "Talk to me."

"How can I? You have lost a child, your only child. While I still have both of mine—at least for the moment. Yes, it's true that Sadie may yet be sent away, and Matt. . ."

"What about Matt?"

Emma shook her head. "I don't know. Outwardly everything seems all right. I mean, it's understandable that he's a little lost right now with all the attention we're having to focus on Sadie. His grades are fine, but his teacher is worried about subtle changes in his attitude at school. And I have to say that my mother's instinct tells me there's something terribly wrong. I don't know how to talk to him about it, and every time I try, I just have this feeling that I'm only making things worse."

"What if I ask Geoff to talk to him? You know how he's always looked up to Geoff."

"Matt tried going to Geoff to tell him about Rachel Kaufmann's program, but Geoff sent him away. Matt was heartbroken, and yet I understand why Geoff acted as he did."

"Now you just stop that, Emma. We are family, and just because this horror has happened within our circle, that does not mean that we abandon each other." Jeannie got up and began to pace—a pattern Emma recognized as a sure sign that she was concocting some plan to solve everything. Under normal circumstances Emma might have been alarmed, but oddly the idea that Jeannie might come up with some solution—no matter how far-fetched—was comforting.

Suddenly Jeannie turned to her with a smile. "Got it," she said.

"I'm almost afraid to ask," Emma said, but she risked a smile as well.

"We need to prioritize—first we need to do whatever we can to help Sadie's cause with the judge. Surely if the judge heard about this victim offender reconciliation contract, he might go easier on her."

Emma glanced up to where there had once hung an elaborate kitchen clock, but it was gone. "Rachel's probably at the house now. We were going to have lunch and then talk about the program. We thought at least we could work out something with Sadie, even if you and Geoff—"

"Excellent way to start," Jeannie said as she carried their glasses to the sink and then picked up her house key. "Let's go."

"You would. . . ? I mean, I thought that because Geoff. . ."

Jeannie glanced around. "I really don't see Geoff here, Emma, so I would say that it's time for me to make the decisions that seem right to me."

Emma frowned as she followed Jeannie outside. "You can't just give up on your marriage, Jeannie."

"Who said anything about giving up? I spent most of last night praying on this, and God seems to be leading me in certain ways." She held out her plain skirt and curtsied. "Got the clothing down," she said, "and I was up most of the night slowly but surely ridding our lives of superfluous stuff." She made the sign of checking something off a list. "Next, we need to get Sadie in the best position possible for her next court appearance, so come on, and let's pray that Rachel Kaufmann has the right plan for accomplishing that."

Chapter 42

Matthew

Unlike his parents and Sadie, Rachel Kaufmann actually seemed to be aware that Matt was in the room. A couple of times she had turned to him and asked him for his ideas or opinion as if it mattered. Not that her noticing him was in any way going to change his plan to run away. After all, he didn't live with Rachel and her son. He lived with his folks and Sadie. But maybe down the road if he needed a place to stay. . .

"Matt? When I spoke with your folks last night, I suggested that everyone write something that Sadie could read today about how that person felt her actions brought them harm and pain. I wonder if you might want to start?"

He had actually been so wrapped up in figuring out how he was going to come up with enough money to repay his gambling debt and still get out of here that he'd forgotten all about the assignment his dad had mentioned after they finished evening prayers. "No ma'am. I mean, I didn't write anything."

"All right, would you be comfortable just telling her now?"

Matt glanced at Sadie. She had that wide-eyed look that she got when she wanted to impress their folks that she was paying close attention. He was not fooled. "How do I know she'll really listen?"

"I'll listen, Matt, and I'm right here. You can say anything that's bothering you."

Matt swallowed a smile. Sadie sounded more like her old self—a little annoyed with him.

"Your parents have chosen to write down their feelings, Matt," Rachel told him. "But there's no one right choice here. Whatever feels most comfortable."

"You can think it over, son," his dad said.

"I'm ready now." And he realized that he was. He realized that he had been ready to tell Sadie how her stupidity had changed his life for some time now. He saw Rachel exchange a look with his parents. His mom looked worried—no surprise. His dad nodded.

"Okay, Matt," Rachel said. "Talk to Sadie."

"And then I get to leave?"

"Well, not exactly. Talking or writing out how Sadie's actions affected you is the first step of a process."

"Then what?"

"Once Sadie hears from those she harmed, then we start the part where we come up with a contract of reconciliation—specific things that Sadie needs to do in order to gain forgiveness—your forgiveness."

Matt sighed and leaned back in his chair. It seemed to him that there was no way this could end anytime soon—not just the VORP thing. The whole thing. He had never been more certain that his plan to leave and get on with his life was a really good idea.

"So, if you still want to say how you feel. . ."

Matt looked over at Sadie on the edge of her chair. Now her eyes were wary. She was nervous. Matt felt a sense of power like he'd never known before. It was both exciting and a little scary. He had the power to make his sister suffer the way he had had to suffer through all these weeks. He glanced toward the window and then back at Sadie.

She was his sister. The older sister who had read to him when he was just a little kid. The sister who had played games with him—and let him win. The sister who had confided in him, trusted him with her hopes and dreams for a future that they both knew their parents would not approve.

He drew in a breath and said, "It's been hard, Sadie."

She nodded.

"At school everybody looks at me different. My friends whisper about you when they think I'm not listening. A few kids have teased me about my sister being in jail."

"What else, Matt?" Rachel said softly.

"Mom and Dad are sad and worried all the time. They don't know how to make this go away and that scares me. People in the store or that we pass on the street don't look at us the same way. Nobody smiles."

"What's the worst thing, Matt?" Rachel coached.

Matt glanced toward his aunt and then bowed his head. "Uncle Geoff believed in me—in what I might be one day. I could talk to him about anything, and everybody knew that. You knew that. But you cared more about your stupid boyfriend than you did any of us. You chose him."

"I didn't—" Sadie protested.

"Let him finish," Rachel said.

Matt stood up, shaking his head from side to side. He wheeled around to face his parents. "You always told us that we have choices and that if it's a hard choice, we need to pray for God's help. Why didn't you pray that morning, Sadie? You knew it was wrong to drive with Dan."

Sadie swiped at a couple of tears falling onto the backs of her fisted hands. "Do you hate me now, Mattie?" she whispered.

He didn't know how to answer that. On the one hand, he was already regretting what he'd said to her. She had hurt him, but that didn't mean that he had to hurt her back.

Turn the other cheek.

Instead of answering, he looked at Rachel, "That's it. That's all I have to say."

"What about Geoff?" Jeannie asked softly.

Matt looked directly at Sadie instead of his aunt when he answered, "He basically hates me now, and it's all because of you."

Chapter 43

Jeannie

Jeannie had to hand it to Sadie—she took the blows that Matt hurled at her without flinching. She never once tried to make excuses for her behavior. And she never once tried to make any of them feel sorry for her by pleading her case. Her niece had grown up a lot in these last several weeks.

In the end, the five of them came up with a plan that Sadie could reasonably fulfill and still one that would remind her almost daily of the ripple effect of her actions. Sadie herself had started things off with two suggestions.

"I could take a job at one of the restaurants or gift shops and give all of my earnings to Aunt Jeannie and Uncle Geoff."

"We don't need your money, Sadie."

Sadie thought a long moment while everyone else in the room glanced around nervously. "Then it can go to a fund to pay the court costs the judge mentioned. And what if I visit Tessa's grave every week and make sure that there are flowers and no weeds and such?"

Emma glanced at Jeannie.

"We could go there together," Jeannie said softly. "Tessa would like that."

"Thank you," Sadie whispered. She bowed her head to hide

the sobs she could no longer hold at bay.

Rachel gave Sadie a moment to compose herself and then kept prodding. "What else?"

"What if Sadie had to do all my chores as well as hers?" Matt suggested.

"And how would you then practice responsibility?" Lars asked his son, but Jeannie could see that there was a hint of amusement in the way he asked the question.

"Just a thought," Matt grumbled and folded his arms tightly across his chest.

Emma was right, Jeannie thought. Matt was not himself. He'd always been such a cheerful boy, always concerned for others, always eager to help. In the past, that exchange with Lars would have ended with a sheepish smile from Matt and possibly a murmured, "Worth a shot." But now he had the sullen stare of the teenagers she had often seen when she attended functions at the school with Geoff. Young people making it perfectly clear that they would rather be anywhere but with their parents and teachers. Tessa had never been one of them. Nor had Sadie, and certainly Matt had never been that way—until now.

She continued to study Matt's reactions as Rachel led them through the rest of the process. She was barely listening to the terms and conditions that Sadie had agreed to follow—even if the judge sent her away. Geoff would know what to do about Matt's change of behavior, so as soon as they were finished here, she intended to find her husband and ask for his help.

"I want to add one more condition," Sadie said when it seemed that they had formed the required contract.

"Be very careful, Sadie," Rachel warned. "You have agreed to quite a list of things here. You have to keep in mind that right now you want very much to do everything you can to repair and heal what happened as a result of your decision to drive that day, but this contract is a long-term agreement. It will take years for you to fulfill all of the pieces—in some cases, like caring for Tessa's grave, you are agreeing to continue this for the rest of your life."

"I know, but Uncle Geoff isn't here to. . . I haven't heard from him about all the horrible ways I've hurt him, and well, if he can't ever forgive me, then what's the point?"

"We're forgiving you, Sadie," Emma said.

"You love me," Sadie shot back.

Jeannie was stunned. "Geoff loves you, Sadie."

If doubt had a face, Jeannie knew that she was looking at it when Sadie glanced up at her and then back at Rachel. "I just need to leave a place for Uncle Geoff to be able to have his say," she said.

"That could take a long time," Rachel warned. "And it might come at a time when you are finally beginning to feel as if you've achieved reconciliation."

"I don't care. I don't even understand how Aunt Jeannie can be in the same room with me." She turned to face Jeannie. "I killed Tessa," she whispered.

Without a second's hesitation, Jeannie opened her arms to this girl whom she had loved as her own. "Come here," she said, relieved when Sadie willingly came to her, laying her head on Jeannie's shoulder as the two of them stood rocking gently from side to side. "You didn't kill anyone, Sadie. Your reckless behavior caused an accident—a horrific accident that none of us ever could have imagined. And yet it did. We can all find some blame in others—and in our own actions—but none of that will change what happened. We can only move forward, sweetie."

"But Uncle Geoff. . ."

"Shhh, he'll come around." As she looked over Sadie's shoulder, she saw Matt watching her closely. And she realized how very much he wanted to believe what she was saying. But then in an instant, his young hopeful face changed to that of a boy who had seen his world turned inside out by something he had no part in and could not have prevented even if he'd known.

Gently she pushed Sadie back toward Emma. "I have an errand," she said as she turned to Rachel. "Can we get back to this maybe tomorrow? There's something I really need to do."

"Ja. Danke, Jeannie. I am so very aware of the courage it took for you to come here today."

Jeannie stared at her new friend for a moment, thinking about all that Rachel had had to endure over these last months since her husband's sudden death. "I may need to lean on you from time to time, Rachel. You're a lot further down this dark road than I am, than Geoff is."

"I'm here," Rachel promised.

"Me, too," Emma assured Jeannie. Lars nodded.

Jeannie looked at Matt, but the boy just looked down at his shoes and said nothing.

Outside, she mounted Tessa's bike and headed for Geoff's school. She had gotten too used to driving wherever she needed to go and had forgotten the feeling of freedom that came with riding a bike. The ties on her prayer covering playfully tickled her cheeks as she rode, and inside she felt the stirrings of the kind of lightheartedness that had always been her trademark. She knew she had a long and difficult journey ahead of her. She could summon the pain of Tessa's death by simply remembering that moment when she had sat with Geoff on the driveway in the rain holding their child as her very life seeped out of her. But for the first time since that morning, she understood that somehow she would go on.

Geoff was running the football team through a scrimmage when she braked the bike, jumped off, and leaned it against the new storage shed. She couldn't resist fingering the shiny lock—the one they had been searching for keys for that morning. What if they had not found the keys? What if instead of being in the driveway waiting for Sadie and Dan, Tessa had just that moment run to their garden shed to get the keys that Jeannie had hidden there?

And what then? Would the car have struck Geoff? And would her loss have been any less?

She heard Geoff call out a play and knew that whatever happened between them, she loved this man. He was a gifted teacher, a good coach, a loving father, and a tender and devoted husband. Watching him now as he ran onto the field when one of his players went down hard, she understood for the very first time the source of Geoff's anger. He had not been able to save Tessa—he had tried and failed. And just as he took very seriously the fact that the parents of every player on his team had trusted their child to his care, how much more seriously would a man like Geoff take the responsibility of fatherhood?

As the hurt player limped off the field with the help of a manager and another player, Geoff dismissed the team for the day. He checked on the injured boy and was apparently assured by the team doctor—a parent of one of his players who had volunteered to be present whenever possible—that the kid would be okay. Indeed, the boy was almost walking normally by the time he headed for the locker room. Jeannie heard Geoff tease him about faking an injury so they could go home early.

The boy laughed.

And so did Geoff.

She stood on the sideline, savoring the sound of his laughter and relishing the way he took off his battered baseball cap and brushed back his hair.

Then he looked up and spotted her. At first he looked confused. He actually nodded politely and then started across the field, following the others. But suddenly he stopped and turned back, and this time he stared open-mouthed.

Jeannie waved and walked toward him. "It's me," she said, self-consciously fingering the ties on her prayer covering.

He met her halfway, his eyebrows raised in question.

She had come to plead with him to reconsider being a part of the program to reconcile with Sadie. She had come to plead with him to go and find Matt, have a long talk with the boy, and take him for ice cream. She had come hoping that he might see her and beg her to take him back.

But that was before she had seen him run onto the field to tend the injured player. That was before God had shown her what Geoff must have felt when all she could manage to consider was her own pain.

"Why are you. . .is something wrong. . .has something. . ."

She shushed him with a finger to his lips. "I just came to tell you that I'm sorry. Through all of this, I have thought only of my pain, my needs."

He started to protest, but she again silenced him, this time with words.

"Oh, I convinced myself that I was taking care of you, defending you and your pain to those who didn't understand. But the truth is that I didn't understand—not until today. When that boy went down, I saw such fear in your face."

"Can I talk now?" he asked, his voice the husky whisper of a man fighting to keep his emotions in check.

Jeannie nodded.

"What was different about today?"

"I told you—when I saw you with that boy," she said and then shrugged. "Oh Geoff, maybe it wasn't just today. I've had a lot of time to think and pray."

He glanced at the white prayer covering. "You're going back to your family's church?"

"I don't know, maybe. Clothes are just clothes, aren't they? But right now dressing this way reminds me of how I was raised, what I believe, what we taught Tessa to believe. And I just began to think that the best way for me to honor who she was would be to find my way to forgiveness and to accept the kindness of others."

Geoff frowned. "You mean the money for the bills?"

"That and other things. Think of it, Geoff. If this had happened to someone else we know—even if it had happened to a family you knew only because their child was in your class, we would be there. We would make food and take care of chores, and yes, we would give money if that was what was needed. Why? Because that's what we do—that's who we are—that's who we taught Tessa to be."

Geoff looked out toward the setting sun for a minute, his eyes damp. "I miss her so much."

"Me, too." She took his hand and brought it to her lips. "I love you, Geoff, and I'm so very sorry for—"

This time he quieted her. He pulled her into his arms. "Let's go home, Jeannie."

Jeannie had prayed to hear those words, and here they were. She looked up at him, her smile feeling as if it must rival the sun. She wrapped her arms around her husband's neck and kissed him.

"Hey, Coach," one of his players shouted amid a background of whistles and cheers, "get a room."

Chapter 44

Sadie

It's over, Sadie. You're free."

That's what her father had murmured after the judge accepted the recommendation of the probation team for sentencing.

Earlier that morning, Joseph had explained the procedure. "The probation team has interviewed people and studied the trial transcript. It's up to them to give the judge their recommendation. The judge really has to accept this unless he can make a good argument for doing something else. There's still the matter of him passing sentence, but given this report, that's most likely to be probation and community service."

But Sadie no longer trusted in such promises. So in spite of the relief that she could see on the faces of her parents—both looking suddenly younger and more themselves—and the twinge of relief she felt as well, she knew deep down that for her it would never truly be over. Tessa was dead, and however anybody explained it, the fact was that she was dead because Sadie had thought only in the moment and only of herself—her needs, her desire to impress Dan Kline, her certainty that nothing bad could possibly happen. It never had before, and she'd foolishly assumed that because they were all good people, nothing like this would ever happen to them. How wrong she had been.

She accepted the embrace of her parents and people from the community who were in the courtroom to support her. She looked around for her aunt Jeannie, but she had slipped out of the courtroom as soon as the judge adjourned the case.

"You're free to go, Sadie," Joseph Cotter told her. "Time to start living your life, building your future."

And fulfilling the conditions of the contract I made with my folks, Matt, Aunt Jeannie—and hopefully one day, Uncle Geoff.

"Sadie?" Joseph was looking at her with a worried frown. The lawyer had become a good friend, someone she knew she could rely on to be there if she needed to talk.

"Thank you," she said. "I don't know how to thank. . ."

Joseph waved off her gratitude with an embarrassed but pleased smile. "Just doing my job."

Rachel Kaufmann was waiting at the back of the courtroom, and when Sadie saw her, Rachel gave her a wave. "Let's go," her mother said. "Matt will be home from school soon, and the four of us can have a nice supper and then maybe just. . ." Tears of relief leaked from the corners of her eyes as she stroked Sadie's cheek. "It's over," she whispered.

But Sadie knew that it wasn't over for her mom either. While Jeannie had willingly agreed to participate in the process to craft a reconciliation contract, the fact was that Uncle Geoff had moved back home. No one could say for sure how that would affect things. Once again Jeannie's loyalties had to be split, and that meant that the truce between Jeannie and Sadie's mom was not exactly solid.

Somehow Sadie understood that her aunt still blamed herself. How could that be? It wasn't her fault. Sadie promised herself that now that she could come and go freely, she would go over to Jeannie's house—when Uncle Geoff was at school or football practice, of course—and spend time with Jeannie talking about Tessa, remembering Tessa. Rachel had told her that it was important to remember.

But first she wanted to sit down with Matt. Her brother had remained indifferent to the process, commenting to her the night before that some stupid contract wasn't going to fix anything. She was only now beginning to appreciate how much she had hurt him, how much he had had to pay for her actions by living day in and night out with their parents always worrying about her. He was the one who had seen his life put on hold, who must have sat at many meals where the silence of their parents' worry and fear had made normal conversation impossible. And then when she learned that Uncle Geoff had basically abandoned Matt—all because of her. . .

"Matt, we're home," her mother called out as soon as they were inside the house. "Matt?"

By the time they had finally finished up at the courthouse, it was past time for Matt to be home from school. But the house was the kind of quiet that said nobody was home.

"He must be out in the workshop sweeping up," her dad said and headed for the back door. "Matt?" he called, but Sadie could see that the workshop door was closed, the padlock undisturbed.

A now all too familiar sense of panic gripped her. Something was wrong—terribly wrong. Her dad stepped outside and walked around the yard. "His bike isn't here," he said when he came back inside.

Sadie ran down the hall to Matt's room. She opened his closet and checked on the top shelf. Matt had a special T-shirt that he wore only when he attended one of Uncle Geoff's games.

It was gone. And she knew that there was no game scheduled for that night.

"Mom?"

"What is it?"

"I think Matt's run away."

"No. I'm sure not. Why would he do such a thing? Today of all days?"

Sadie showed her the box that Matt always hid the shirt in. It was the box of an old board game they had played when they were younger.

"Lars," her mom called out. Then she took the box and headed back toward the kitchen. "He's gone," Sadie heard her say.

Her brother had run away, and it was all her fault. Sadie sat down on the side of Matt's bed and wondered if the ripples of her foolish action would ever stop coming.

She heard the muffled sounds of her parents discussing what to do. But she was the one who needed to fix this. She glanced around Matt's room, unsure of what she was looking for but certain that there must be something that would give her a clue. Neither of them was known for neatness, but there was a pattern to the way Matt stored his things. It might look haphazard to their parents. That was the whole idea. But to Matt—and hopefully to Sadie—the placement of his belongings made perfect sense.

Knowing that her brother did nothing without first making detailed plans, she began going through the papers on his small desk. She was mystified when she found several printed sheets from a computer about playing poker. The other side of the paper had material that showed it to have come from the Sarasota library. When had he gone to the library downtown, and how had he gotten this paper? He must be doing a report on the evils of gambling, she decided and put his schoolwork, including the notes on poker, back where she'd found them.

Next, she dumped out his wastebasket and started smoothing out the crumpled papers. On the third paper, she found a rough sketch that looked like a map.

"Dad?" she called out.

Both parents came at once. "What is it? A note?" her father asked hopefully.

"Better," Sadie said. "It's a map."

The three of them gathered around as Sadie spread the wrinkled paper on the desktop then turned it sideways to see if that made more sense.

"It's Payne Park," her dad said. By the way he looked at Sadie's mom, she knew there had to be a connection.

"What?" she asked.

Her mom told her about the night that Matt had gotten lost and had been brought home by the police officers. "We didn't want to worry you."

Sadie glanced at the paper again, realizing it was drawn on the back of a page from the day calendar that Uncle Geoff had given Matt. She read the date aloud.

"It's the same date," her father said, taking the paper from her and studying the map more closely. "He must have sketched this out that night, and the only reason to do that would be so that he could find his way back there again."

When her parents headed for the door, Sadie started to follow them and accidentally knocked Matt's schoolwork to the floor. The papers about poker spilled out from his notebook. Sadie had an idea. "Dad? There was this kid in my class who got in trouble last summer for playing cards. . .for money. He was slipping out to meet some boys from town." She picked up the papers and handed them to her father. "You said something about Matt going out to meet friends after supper, and I found these inside Matt's school folder."

Her father's already ruddy cheeks turned even redder. He passed the papers to her mother and headed down the hall still clutching the map that Matt had drawn.

"Let me go with you, Dad," she pleaded, and to her surprise, he gave her a curt nod.

"Emma, stay here in case the boy comes to his senses and comes home."

Sadie knew that there was not even a question of alerting others and certainly not the authorities in Sarasota. This was a private matter that her parents would try to handle alone. If the time came when they needed help, they would turn first to other family—usually Jeannie and Geoff—and then to Pastor Detlef and other leaders of the congregation. Calling the police would be an absolute last resort.

When Sadie got in on the passenger side, the map was lying on the seat. She picked it up and prepared to navigate for her father. "It looks like you turn left at the corner," she said.

"I know the way, Sadie," her father said, and then he softened his rebuke by patting her hand. "Sorry. I'm just worried."

They rode in silence with Sadie scanning the side streets hoping for a glimpse of Matt or his bike. When they reached the park, her father stopped the car and got out. "Let's see if there's any sign of him or if there's anyone around who might have seen him," her dad said.

"I can search that area," Sadie volunteered as she started off across toward the tennis courts.

"Nein! No Sadie, I nearly lost you once, and now your brother is missing. I need to know where you are. We'll do this together."

It amazed Sadie how these simple words touched her. A knot she'd carried in the center of her chest for weeks—a knot of her own making because she was so sure that no one in her family would ever be able to love her again the way they had before. She slipped her hand into her father's and walked with him.

After they'd searched for several minutes without seeing anyone, Sadie caught a flash of color. "Dad, over there?" she whispered excitedly.

Her father followed her pointing finger then started striding quickly toward the lone figure bent over a picnic table, his back to them. Sadie had to practically run to keep up with him.

"Hello," Lars called out.

The boy turned and quickly gathered whatever had been on the table and stuffed it into his pockets. Then he leaned back against the edge of the table nonchalantly and watched them come. "I'm not doing anything wrong, mister," he said with a sullen frown when they were close enough to see his features.

"I did not accuse you," Sadie's dad replied. "I am looking for my son, and I have reason to believe that he might have come here to this park. Have you been here for some time?"

The boy cocked an eyebrow as he studied their plain dress. "This kid—he's one of your kind?"

"He's my son," her dad repeated. "Have you seen him?"

"Maybe." The boy took a sudden interest in a tree branch hanging over the table. "What's in it for me?"

To Sadie's surprise, her father actually smiled.

"Are you asking to be paid for information that you may or may not have?"

The boy shrugged. "Kid's about my height but younger? He's got hair like yours only not as white but still cut in that dorky way? Rides a bike that's like a bazillion years old? That kid?"

Sadie felt her heart begin to hammer. "Yes," she said, "that kid." Her father squeezed her hand, silencing her.

"All right," her father said, keeping his voice calm as if he and the boy were negotiating a price for a piece of his furniture. "It appears that you know my son. Did you also know that he is missing?"

"He's not missing. I just saw him."

"Ah. So he was here."

The boy let out a sigh of pure exasperation. "Didn't I just say that?"

"Where is he? Where did he go?" Sadie demanded, unable to keep still a minute longer. It pleased her to see the boy sit up a little straighter.

"I don't know to both questions. He owed me some money. He paid up and then took off." He stood up. "I gotta go. I got business."

"Which way was he headed?" Sadie asked and noticed that her father seemed to have accepted that the boy was more likely to answer her questions.

The boy pointed toward the tennis courts.

"How long ago?"

"Do I look like I own a watch?"

"Thank you for your help," Sadie's dad said and then steered her in the direction the boy had indicated. When she glanced back over her shoulder, the boy was gone.

The tennis courts were deserted as was the area around the community auditorium. Her dad checked every nook and cranny of their surroundings. She also noticed how with every passing minute he seemed to lose hope.

"We'll find him, Dad," she said and prayed that she was right.

Chapter 45

Geoff

It was good to be home. Even though he hadn't been moved out for more than one night and the day that followed, it felt like weeks. Of course, he and Jeannie had been heading in different directions ever since Tessa's funeral. But now this house seemed more like the home they had established when he and Jeannie had first married. In his short absence, Jeannie had gone through the house packing up a lot of the things that served only to remind him of all their debt. She continued to dress in the plain clothes of her youth, and he found that somehow comforting.

He was even beginning to consider the wisdom of accepting the money members of their church—and Emma's—had raised to help pay off the hospital bill. Jeannie had made a good argument for that. How many times over the years they'd been married had they done the same for those in need and never once thought about it?

Pride goeth before a fall, he thought. He had allowed his pride to keep him from accepting the kindness of his neighbors and friends. He fingered the large brown envelope where Jeannie had placed all of the cash and checks people had left for them. "I'm going to stop by the hospital and set up a plan for paying that bill off," he called up the stairs where he could hear Jeannie doing more cleaning.

She ran to the head of the stairs and looked down at him. He was still not yet used to seeing her face cleansed of makeup, but he liked it. She looked younger, more like the girl he'd fallen in love with sixteen years earlier. Somehow it made him think that it might actually be possible for them to start over.

He smiled up at her. "Love you," he said, and she grinned.

"Me, too."

When they'd been courting, he had teased her about that answer. "I know you love you, too," he'd said, "but what about loving me?"

She had always thrown her arms around his neck and kissed him. He actually considered giving her their trademark banter now, but he wouldn't have her run all the way down the stairs just to kiss him. "How about we go out for supper?" he said.

"We haven't done that since. . ."

"I know. It'll do us both good."

"Okay." She lingered at the top of the stairs. "See you," she said.

"Love you," he replied as he picked up his keys.

By four he had finished his meeting with the billing person at the hospital, turning over the funds to her and setting up a payment plan for the rest. As he drove home, he tried without success to suppress the lingering remnants of his anger at Sadie, the urge to force her to earn the money they owed. From everything that Jeannie had told him, Sadie was going to get off pretty easy, and this whole contract business did not begin to make up for all the harm done by Sadie's reckless behavior.

"You have to know that coming home doesn't mean that I can forgive and forget," he'd warned Jeannie the night before as they lay together.

"I know." She waited a beat and then added, "And you have to understand that they are my family, Geoff, and I can no more turn my back on them than I could on you."

He had been surprised at that. In the past, Jeannie had always been so eager to please him and everyone around her.

Suddenly she was thinking of her needs, and he found that he liked that even if meeting her needs meant going against him.

"So, that's the contract between you and me?"

"No, Geoff, that's us accepting that we have to do some of this alone even as we get through most of it together."

"Sounds like a plan," he'd murmured as he pulled her closer. "And who knows. . .in time. . ." It was, he realized, the first time that he had allowed himself even to consider the idea that there might come a day when he could forgive Sadie.

And then there she was—Sadie. She was standing at the kitchen door, gesturing wildly as she talked to Jeannie. He got out of the car prepared to defend his wife from whatever tirade Sadie was having.

"It's Matt," Jeannie said as soon as she saw him. "He's run away."

Before he knew what hit him, Sadie had rushed forward and was clinging to his arm. "Please, Uncle Geoff," she sobbed. "I know you hate me, and you have every reason to, but this is Mattie—please. . . ."

"How long's he been gone?" Geoff asked Jeannie.

"When they got home from court yesterday afternoon, he was gone. Lars and Sadie talked to a boy in Payne Park who knows him and had seen him, but there was no sign of him."

"Payne Park?"

Sadie was still clutching his sleeve. It seemed the most natural thing in the world to put his hand on hers.

"We think he's been going there to meet some kids from town to play cards," Sadie told him. She talked about papers she'd found about playing poker and then a map they had used to try to find him.

"Why didn't Emma call yesterday?" Jeannie asked. She sounded a little hurt.

"You know Dad. He wanted to try to find him—just us—but now he's been gone all night and all day and there's no sign of him anywhere. It's like he's just disappeared, and it's all my fault."

"Stop that right now," Geoff ordered. "We have to think. Where are your folks?"

"Dad and Pastor Detlef and some men from the church have been out all day searching. Mom's been waiting by the phone in case he calls or something."

Jeannie looked at Geoff. "Maybe Zeke could help. He knows people who hang around that park."

Geoff nodded. "Sadie, I want you and Jeannie to go back to your house and stay with your mom. She needs you both right now. I'll go find Zeke and see if he has any ideas."

"Please find him, Uncle Geoff," Sadie pleaded.

He hesitated, seeing in her uplifted face the child who had been like a sister to Tessa, the child who along with her brother had been in his house almost as much as Tessa had, the child who had in one flash of irresponsibility so typical of young people her age changed all their lives forever.

"Geoff?" Jeannie was next to him, her hand on his shoulder, her face close to his. A worried frown creased her forehead.

He patted Sadie's hand and spoke directly to her, "I'll do my best. You go on home now. Your folks need you."

On the strength of the radiant smile that Jeannie had given him as he got back in his car and drove to the marina, Geoff rid himself of the last of his fury at everything and everyone surrounding Tessa's death. It felt good to focus on someone else's need besides his own for a change.

He found Zeke exactly where he thought he might find him, downtown near the marina talking to friends.

"Alone in a park overnight?" one of Zeke's friends said shaking his head. "Must be one scared boy by now."

"Lars and Sadie searched the park yesterday and talked to a kid that said he'd seen Matt, but then that kid disappeared. They didn't get a name."

"Come on," Zeke said, and when Geoff followed him without question, he noticed that the group of other homeless people were also coming with them. It struck Geoff that they must have made an odd picture walking up Main Street together—Geoff still in the business clothes he'd worn to make a good impression on the hospital billing clerk, and the rest in the scruffy clothing that probably constituted their entire wardrobes.

They reached the library and went inside. There the others spread out, some heading upstairs while others canvassed street people who spent their days there reading. He followed Zeke and was surprised when his friend left by the second doorway and walked quickly across town until he reached the park.

"I like to travel light. The others mean well, but too many people will scare the kid off."

"You know where Matt is?" Geoff couldn't believe that Zeke might actually have an idea where to find his nephew.

"The other kid. His name's Duke—or that's his street name. Hangs out here with a couple of other boys. My guess is that if Matt got caught up in playing cards, these were the guys he was playing with. It's a place to start."

Geoff nodded. "So, what now?"

"We wait," Zeke said as he slid to a sitting position against the side of a building.

The sun was setting when Zeke nudged Geoff and nodded toward a figure sauntering toward them. "Duke," he called out, getting to his feet. "What's happening?"

The kid couldn't be more than thirteen. He was thin and skittish.

"Hey, Zeke," he said even as he eyed Geoff suspiciously.

"I understand you've found a new player."

The kid shrugged. "Found and lost."

"Meaning?"

"He played most every night for a couple of weeks, lost some money and won some, and then yesterday he finds me here and gives me all of it—the whole enchilada—three times what he owed me." Duke shook his head. "I don't get that."

I just bet you don't, Geoff thought and shoved his hands in his pockets to keep from yelling at the kid to tell them where Matt was.

"You see this guy around?" Zeke asked, looking off toward the park entrance as if it didn't matter to him one way or another.

"I told you. He was here yesterday. Oh yeah, and then this man and a girl came looking for him. After they searched everywhere except the right place, I told him he'd best get home."

Geoff thought he might have to beg God's forgiveness for strangling the boy.

"But that didn't happen," Zeke said, still in a tone he'd use to discuss the weather forecast.

"Yeah, I know. He hung around last night with us. Wouldn't get in the game though. Said he was done with card playing. Too bad. He was good."

"And then?" Geoff could no longer hold his tongue.

Duke glanced at him. "He went off with Tony."

"Tony who?"

Duke glanced at Zeke. "You know, the black kid. Tony."

Zeke nodded. "Thanks, little dude." He fumbled in the pocket of his too-small cargo pants and tossed the kid a coin. "All I can spare."

Duke grinned as he took off. "No worries, man. It'll grow."

To Geoff's surprise, Zeke sat back down.

"You know this boy, Tony?"

"Yeah."

"Well? Shouldn't we do something about finding him?"

"We are. We wait right here, and he'll find us."

Sure enough, shortly after the park streetlamps came on, Geoff saw a small African-American boy coming toward them. And with him was Matt. The two of them were deep in conversation and didn't seem to see Zeke or Geoff. Geoff was on his feet at once, but Zeke held him back. "Don't startle him," he warned. "Just let them settle in."

He's not a wild horse, Geoff thought, annoyed with any further delay in getting Matt safely home. But he did as Zeke coached.

Moments later, three other boys appeared, including Duke who glanced their way but said nothing as all the boys took places around a picnic table, some straddling the bench seats, others kneeling on them. Geoff saw that Matt stood quietly at one end of the table, watching the card game intently.

"Now," Zeke whispered. "Follow my lead or you're gonna blow this thing."

"Yeah, like I don't know how to deal with a bunch of junior high. . ."

Zeke ignored him and started across the park.

"Matt Keller, is that you?" Zeke asked, his voice friendly in a surprised-but-glad-to-see-you way.

Matt looked up but didn't take off.

"Hi, Mr. Shepherd," he muttered.

"Mr. Shepherd?" Duke crowed. "I didn't even know you had a last name."

"Just like you, Dwight Buginski."

The other boys howled with laughter and started in on Duke, teasing him about his name. At the same time, Zeke motioned for Geoff to move closer to one side of Matt while he did the same on the other, just in case Matt decided to run.

Geoff placed a gentle hand on Matt's shoulder. "Hello, Matt," he said and felt Matt jerk, so he held on tighter. "How about you and me go get some pizza and talk? It's been awhile—too long."

He watched as Matt struggled with wanting desperately to go with him and at the same time being afraid to be hurt again. "It's over, Matt. If you're willing to forgive me, I'd like to make things right with you."

Matt picked up his backpack and shouldered it the way Tessa had that morning. "I'd like that," he said warily. "You mean it?"

"I mean it." Geoff nodded to Zeke, who took a place at the picnic table with the rest of the boys and dealt the cards. The other boys didn't seem to notice when Matt and Geoff walked away. But then Duke was there. "Here," he said, handing Matt a couple of crumpled dollar bills. "You paid too much."

"I don't want it." Matt pushed the money back at him.

"Too bad, dude. Take it or leave it. I really don't care." He turned his back on Matt and headed back to the game.

Matt stared at the money.

"Hard to know what to do with that, huh?" Geoff said.

"I won it playing cards," Matt told him. "Gambling is a sin. What should I do?"

"Maybe give it to charity?"

"I could do that."

Geoff wrapped his arm around Matt's shoulders. "First, we need to call your folks and let them know you're with me. Then,

I am seriously starving, and I need to run an idea for a new play by you to see if you get it."

Matt walked with renewed confidence. "I'll get it. Question is will the rest of the players get it?"

Geoff laughed and again realized that the weight of all those hours of anger and self-pity had suddenly evaporated. It felt good to laugh again, to be with Matt again, to be living again. It occurred to him that Tessa would be pleased, and that made him realize that he'd spent so much of these last weeks thinking about his feelings, his needs, his pain that he had barely thought about how Tessa might see all of this.

"Seriously, Matt, you need to think about being there for Sadie now. I mean, think about it. She still has to face going back to school, and she's going to need somebody who understands how tough it can be facing those other kids."

"Maybe," Matt said. "Yeah, I guess that's true." The thought clearly lifted his spirits. "But first could we go for that pizza? I am. . ."

". . .seriously starving," Geoff said in unison with him.

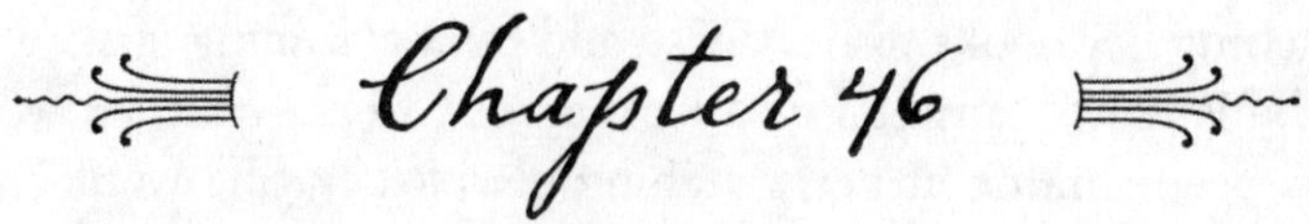

Chapter 46

Sadie

Sadie was nervous about actually going back to school. In the weeks that she was home while the judge decided her fate, her parents and teachers had agreed that homeschooling by Matt's teacher was best. Now that she was free, it was time to start getting back into the life she had known before that terrible rainy morning.

But how would everyone react to her being back? How would her teachers treat her? Would her friends still walk with her between classes and want to sit with her and share the news of the day? Most of all, what was it going to be like to see Dan again?

She didn't have to wait long for her answers. As she turned a corner to go to her math class, there he was.

He was not as tall as she had remembered him all those days she'd spent in detention—nor nearly as broad-shouldered. Compared to the huge guards—male and female—at the detention center, he was actually kind of small.

He saw her at the same moment she first spotted him. She looked away. But not before she saw his cheeks glow an embarrassed pink. His discomfort gave her courage.

"Hello, Dan," she said as she eased past him and into her classroom. "Nice to see you."

"Yeah," he muttered as he hurried past her. "You, too."

He was waiting for her when school let out.

"What was that?" he asked, his voice now filled with irritation. "Hello, Dan," he mocked in a high falsetto. "Nice to see you."

"I believe it was a socially acceptable greeting," Sadie replied, fighting her own irritation. "How are you?"

"Fine—better."

"Matt tells me you're back playing football."

They were standing on the steps outside the school. She was clutching her books to her chest, and he was leaning against the wall, his hands jammed into his pockets. In the past, he would have been smiling at her, watching her closely. She would have been looking down but smiling as well, unable to believe that this guy was even talking to her. What a baby she'd been.

"You lied in court," she said. "I forgive you."

He let out a snort of laughter. "Are you for real? I didn't lie, Sadie, and I don't need or want your forgiveness."

"You're not angry with me," she continued, realizing that he was nervous and that being with her made him uncomfortable. Yet he had waited for her. "You're upset with yourself, and you'd really just like for everything to go back to the way things were for you before."

"And you know this because?"

"It's something I've learned over the last several weeks. I've had a lot of time to work through some stuff—and a lot of help doing it. I wish you had someone you could talk to about what happened. Keeping it all bottled up is not good, Dan."

"You sound like my pastor."

Sadie shrugged. "So maybe you should listen to what he has to say."

Dan pushed himself away from the wall. "You've changed," he said, making eye contact with her for the first time.

"We both have."

He ground a toe of his shoe into the concrete. "Do you think about it like all the time?"

"Pretty much."

"Me, too." He drew in a long breath and let it out slowly.

"Coach is devastated, and yet he's never—not once—said anything to me. Do you think he'll ever forgive me?"

"I think he probably already has, but you should talk to him, Dan. It would do you both good."

He went back to staring off into space, lost in thought, and Sadie turned to go. "I'll see you around, okay?"

"Hey," he called when she reached the bottom of the stairs, "how about I walk you home?"

"I'm not sure that's a good idea, but if you want to take a walk around here and talk some, that would be okay."

Dan grinned at her, and a little of his usual self-confidence radiated from that handsome smile. "Good idea. How about down to the creek?"

They had shared their first kiss while walking along the banks of Phillipi Creek, and she understood all too well that need to latch onto something from the past that might just give them the feeling that nothing had changed.

But everything had changed.

"How about to the park? We can sit on the benches in the shade there and watch the play on the shuffleboard courts."

"Gee, why didn't I think of that?" Dan shoved his hands deeper into his pockets and scowled at something in the distance. He wasn't used to not getting his way. He was used to charming others into giving him what he wanted, and right now he apparently wanted to pretend that everything was the same between them.

"We aren't the same people we were before the accident, Dan," Sadie said. "I want to be your friend, and I want you to be mine, but beyond that?" She touched his hand to draw his attention. "You and I both know we can never go back. There's been too much. . ." She was surprised that her eyes had filled suddenly with tears and that her mind had brought forth an image of Tessa. "I miss her so much," she whispered.

"She was a good kid," he agreed. "Smart, funny in that quirky way she had. She always seemed older than she was."

Sadie smiled. "I used to tease her about being an old lady before her time. Of course, to me then an old lady was like my mom—or her mom."

Dan fell into step beside her, and he reached to take her books from her. "Have they forgiven us? Her mom and yours?"

"Us?" She glanced at him.

"Yeah, us," he said biting the words off. "Look, I'm not proud of how I handled myself in court that day. I was scared. And my folks. . ."

Sadie didn't want to hear excuses, so she took his hand. "Come on, I want to go by the cemetery, and it's getting late. My folks get nervous if I'm not home ten minutes before they start to worry, which is about five minutes after they know school is out."

They walked along in silence for a few blocks.

"You said you've forgiven me. I don't get that. I ruined your life."

"It's just the way we do things," she said. "I have to tell you that while I was locked up, I wasn't feeling very forgiving toward you at all."

They had reached the cemetery. Sadie led the way to Tessa's grave. She put her books on the ground and then knelt to clear away some dead leaves and other debris. Dan remained standing.

"How was that? I mean, being locked up." He actually shuddered.

"It was an experience I never want to repeat, and at the same time, I'm beginning to see that it was something that made a big difference in how I am, how I look at my future."

"And your family?"

"My mom and Tessa's mom have always been so close, and when I think about how close they came to never being able to know that closeness again, well, it was scary for me. But they were raised like they raised me—and Tessa and Matt—and that's just who we are. We forgive."

"And forget?"

"I can't imagine ever forgetting Tessa, or that horrible day, Dan."

"Because there were times when Coach—"

"Uncle Geoff has had a really tough time. I never realized this, but he blamed himself because he didn't save Tessa. He thought that his job as her father was to protect her, and when he couldn't, it must have been so awful."

"He told you that?"

"He wrote it." She explained about the VORP program and the contract, telling him about how everyone affected by Tessa's death had taken part in making her see the ripple effects of her careless behavior. "And selfish," she added. "I was so very selfish."

"But he's coming around? Coach, I mean?"

Sadie nodded and continued to pick dried flowers and leaves off her cousin's grave. "Oh, he still looks at me like the very sight of me is a physical wound for him, but Mom tells me that in time. . . The most important thing is that he and Matt have become close again."

Dan smiled and bent to help her. "Yeah, it's good to see the kid back on the sidelines. You know, sometimes he can explain Coach's crazy plays better than Coach can."

"Get me some water, will you?" She nodded toward a spigot, coiled hose, and bucket.

"I'd like to do something," he said when he returned. "Will you ask that lady who did this VORP thing with you if I could meet with her?"

"Sure."

"I've been thinking about asking if I could speak about all this at the next school assembly."

"That's a wonderful idea, Dan."

Her uncle Geoff thought it was a good idea as well, and two weeks later at their weekly assembly where Dan usually presided as president of the student council, he walked to the microphone and cleared his throat. Sadie sat in the front row with Geoff. They both looked up at Dan and nodded.

"I want to talk to you this morning, not as the president of this student body. Not as the quarterback of your football team. I want to talk to you as someone who knowingly broke the rules—rules that seemed pretty dumb to me as rules often do when you're our age. I thought I was above those rules. I thought that those rules did not apply to me because I was too smart, too cool to need them."

Sadie felt as if she could hear people breathing throughout the packed auditorium—it was that quiet.

"Here's the list of all the rules I violated in just one morning—in less than an hour," Dan continued as he unfurled a scroll-like paper filled with printing. "I was running late but allowed no time for that. It was raining—pouring. I knew the defroster in my car wasn't working properly. I. . ."

He continued reading, cataloging each item on the list, and when he finished, he looked out over the upturned faces and said, "Any one of those things was reason enough not to get behind the wheel of my car that morning, but I'm Dan Kline—senior, co-captain, council president, honor student. I was way too cool to admit that there was anything I couldn't handle. And so I made one more mistake—I encouraged, no, I practically dared Sadie Keller to drive from her house to Coach Messner's house so we could pick up her cousin Tessa, even though I was legally too young to ride with her."

He looked directly at Sadie then.

"And I did that knowing that she would do almost anything I asked of her."

Sadie realized that she was nodding, and she forced herself to be still.

"Then I made another mistake. Instead of coaching Sadie on how to drive, I took out this. . ." He produced his cell phone and held it up for all to see. "And I started texting my friends, making fun of Sadie's driving and laughing at their replies—laughing at her, never for one minute realizing how every snicker only added to her stress."

It was too much. She was as much to blame as he was. He was taking it all on himself. Sadie sat forward, but Dan stopped her with a look and a slight shake of his head.

"And when Sadie pulled into that driveway that rainy morning, she saw her cousin Tessa waiting, and you know who I saw? I saw Coach. I saw the man who has been my inspiration. The man who has spent hours shaping me and many of you as athletes and solid citizens. I saw a man that I love like I love my own father, and we were headed right for him. So I made my final mistake—I tried to make up for all the mistakes I had made that morning by grabbing the wheel away from Sadie."

He paused for a moment, and Sadie heard a couple of girls sniffling behind her. "Only God knows what might have happened if I hadn't done that, if I hadn't done any of this." He shook the long list and then dropped it to the floor. "Maybe Sadie would have swerved the other way. Maybe Coach would have jumped out of the way. Maybe. Maybe. Maybe. But you all know what happened next. A girl who was to start her first day of classes here with us that morning died that day. A girl who a couple of years from now might have been standing where I'm standing now leading this student body died that day. A girl who was everything to Sadie and Coach and their families died that day."

Sadie had thought she could not possibly have any more tears to shed, but she'd been wrong. Tears were leaking down her cheeks unabated. She felt a nudge next to her, and when she looked at her uncle, he was holding out his handkerchief to her.

Chapter 47

Jeannie and Emma

The sisters worked in tandem, going room by room as they cleaned Jeannie's house. She had removed all of the extraneous clothing, furnishings, and—as she called it—just plain stuff. Much of it she had taken to resale shops around town. The profits from her sales were beginning to come in.

"I was in the consignment shop where I took most of my clothes the other day, and the owner told me they were selling like hotcakes," Jeannie told Emma as they scrubbed down walls and washed floors side by side. "We'll have our bills paid off in no time."

"Das ist gut, Jeannie." Emma stood up and stretched her back. "Ready for Tessa's room?" she asked. It was the one room in the house that had remained untouched.

Jeannie looked away toward sunlight streaming through the upstairs hall window. "Yeah. It hasn't had a good cleaning since. . ."

"We don't have to take anything out or pack anything away if you're not ready, Jeannie."

"I know, but we should really move everything so that we can get behind the furniture and into the corners and all. Then we'll put it all back, right?"

"Exactly as it is," Emma assured her.

They worked together, each clearing off the various surfaces in the room—Tessa's dresser, her desk, her bookcase. Emma stripped the bedding and carried it downstairs to put it in the washer. When she came back, Jeannie had moved all of Tessa's clothes into the guest room. Together they rolled up the area rug and slid all of the furniture to one side of the room. Emma started sweeping the hardwood floor.

"Jeannie, when I went down to put the laundry in, I couldn't help noticing that Tessa's backpack is still there by the back door. Do you want me to go through it and have Sadie return any library books?"

"No, I'll do it."

Emma stopped sweeping when she noticed how reluctantly Jeannie moved toward the stairway. "Bring it up here. We'll do it together," she said.

By the time Jeannie returned with the backpack, Emma had finished sweeping one side of the room and was brushing the collected dust into a dustpan.

"So heavy," Jeannie noted, "She was so thin. How did she haul this around?"

Emma leaned the broom against the wall and sat on the side of Tessa's bed. She patted the spot next to her. "Come sit a minute. You know, this could wait."

"No. Geoff and I talked last night about how Tessa would want us to move forward. She would absolutely hate the idea of some sort of shrine, and having the backpack there by the door day after day has been a little like that, I suppose."

Emma resisted the urge to remind her sister that keeping Tessa's room as it was might also be considered a kind of shrine. *One step at a time*, she thought and watched Jeannie unfasten the clasps on the backpack.

There were numerous compartments—pockets on the outside that held pencils and pens and markers, a hairbrush and a tube of pink lip gloss that made Jeannie smile. "I suggested that she might want to carry this with her. She, of course, rolled her eyes as if that was the dumbest idea she'd ever heard. But here it is."

In another zippered compartment they found untouched notebooks and a daily calendar, and from inside the main compartment they removed a heavy dictionary, a thesaurus, Tessa's Bible, and four library books.

"That's it," Jeannie said as she ran her finger down the spines of the stack of books.

"Not quite," Emma replied, lifting the backpack. "There's something in this compartment here inside the main part." She pulled the zipper and took out a handmade journal with a fountain pen clipped to its cover.

"You found them!" Jeannie exclaimed happily as she reached for the book and pen. "Oh Em, I've turned this room upside down half a dozen times looking for this, and all the time it was right there on the chair by the kitchen door." She fingered the leather ties on the journal.

"Are you going to read it?"

"I don't even know if she wrote in it. We only gave it to her that night after the picnic."

"One way to find out," Emma said as she scooted back on the bed and leaned against the pillows stacked against the wall.

Jeannie smiled and loosened the thin, knotted ties. She turned the first page where Jeannie had written, "To Tessa, Love, Mom and Dad," with the date underneath. The next page was filled with Tessa's unique printing.

"Let's read it together," Jeannie said as she pushed herself back on the bed so that she and Emma were side by side.

"Don't you want to wait for Geoff?"

Jeannie took a minute to consider this and then said, "The way I see it is that it was no mistake that we found this together—you were the one who suggested I go through the backpack. I don't think that was an accident. I think we're being led to do this together the way we've always done everything together throughout our lives."

"Maybe we should. . ." Emma was still doubtful.

"Em, it's a prayer answered."

"It is that. Your prayer that you would find this precious link to your daughter and my prayer that you would find it in your heart to forgive mine."

The two sisters looked at each other for a long moment, and then Jeannie moved the journal halfway onto Emma's lap as the sisters bent their heads toward each other and read Tessa's journal.

Epilogue

Tessa

Mom and Dad have always given me a small gift to start the school year, but this is so special. Look how beautifully Grandpa's pen writes—so much better than any roller ball or gel pen. I love it—and the journal. I think Mom made this for me. She's been fooling around lately with some art projects, and I thought I saw the paper on the cover of the journal lying in the guest room a few weeks ago.

But it's getting late and tomorrow is a big day—I've tried hard to be cool about it, but the truth is that I'm excited to be finally starting my years at the academy. Sadie has been there a whole year already, and the way she talks about it. . .well, I can't wait. But I am making a promise to myself right now that every single night I will write in my new journal—filling it with all the things that happen over the coming year.

Where to begin?

I have no idea, and I so don't want to look back on this and find it filled with silliness. I know! I'll take a Bible passage, the one from church that Sunday and write about that and how it fits what's happening in my life all that week.

Last week the pastor preached about the Sermon on the Mount—a favorite of mine. I just love the way the words flow, like they have comfort and the promise of better days ahead just pouring out of every syllable.

"Blessed are the poor in spirit: for theirs is the kingdom of heaven." I guess that "poor in spirit" means when someone is sad.

"Blessed are they that mourn: for they shall be comforted." Pastor says that we can mourn many things—not just the death of a loved one but any kind of loss—the loss of a friend or a favorite book or an opportunity to do good.

"Blessed are the meek: for they shall inherit the earth." Well, not really sure I want this earth, but I am meek, so maybe it's all part of God's plan for me.

"Blessed are they which do hunger and thirst after righteousness: for they shall be filled." That's more me, I think—and our good friend Hester and her husband, John—those two are always hungering after some new way to make things right for others.

"Blessed are the merciful: for they shall obtain mercy." Is mercy the same as forgiveness? I'll have to ask about that. It seems like that might be right—like tonight when I could see that Aunt Emma was really upset with Mom for taking Sadie to get her permit, and yet she forgave her. Was that mercy?

"Blessed are the pure in heart: for they shall see God." That's my all-time favorite!

"Blessed are the peacemakers: for they shall be called the children of God." Close second!

"Blessed are they which are persecuted for righteousness' sake: for theirs is the kingdom of heaven." I really hope that one day I'll be brave enough to stand up for others—or for my beliefs—purely because that is the right thing to do.

"Blessed are ye, when men shall revile you, and persecute you, and shall say all manner of evil against you falsely, for my sake. Rejoice, and be exceeding glad: for great is your reward in heaven: for so persecuted they the prophets which were before you."

I think this is maybe the biggest reason that I'm glad we're Mennonite. Pretty much everybody in our faith stays away from the blame shame game. We take care of each other like a ginormous family, and even when we get mad at each other, we always find our way back—like sheep coming into the fold in the darkness.

And speaking of darkness, it is so late and I am so tired and tomorrow is going to be so special. It's starting to rain—good sleeping weather, my dad always says.

Discussion Questions

1. How does Emma's forgiveness of Jeannie for her impulsive act in the beginning of the book set things in motion?

2. How many instances where characters sought forgiveness throughout the story can you name, and in how many instances was forgiveness granted?

3. How did Geoff's past influence his ability to forgive Sadie?

4. How did the fact that Jeannie and Geoff were already having some problems in their marriage before the accident influence how they handled their grief?

5. What role did blame play in the story?

6. What role did trust—or lack of trust—play?

7. Given the title of the book, in what ways did Emma forgive Jeannie? And vice versa?

8. The story is told from all major characters' points of view—take them one by one and discuss how each was impacted by Tessa's death and how each of them changed.

9. The Mennonite faith is rooted in the teachings of the New Testament. What lessons did Jesus teach his followers about love, forgiveness, and reconciliation?

10. How did the characters in this story apply those teachings (or not)?

11. In your own life (or the lives of those close to you) has there ever been something that threatened to tear your family apart? If so, how was that resolved? If not, how do you think you and your family might weather a situation such as the one the characters in this book had to face?

12. Think about all the ways characters in this story sought comfort. Talk about those that worked—and those that did not.

13. In her journal, Tessa wonders if mercy is the same as forgiveness. What do you think?

Anna Schmidt is the author of more than twenty works of fiction. Among her many honors, Anna is the recipient of the *Romantic Times*' Reviewer's Choice Award and a finalist for the RITA award for romantic fiction. She enjoys gardening and collecting seashells at her winter home in Florida. To contact Anna, visit her website at www.booksbyanna.com.

Come back to Pinecraft in November 2012

for the conclusion of

The Women of Pinecraft

and Rachel's story of

A Mother's Promise